Turn u[nable] Terry Spear's

O9-ABG-022

3 9223 037792614

"A delightful and tant[izing]... spirited and realistic…"

—*Thoughts in Progress* for *USA Today*
bestseller *A SEAL in Wolf's Clothing*

"A sultry nail-biter… The suspense will keep readers flipping the pages feverishly."

—*RT Book Reviews* for *SEAL Wolf Hunting*

"Dark, sultry, and primal romance… The chemistry is blazing hot and will leave readers breathless."

—*Fresh Fiction* for *Savage Hunger*

"In[...] y and [...] r [...]f

"Crackles with mystery, adventure, violence, and passion."
—*Library Journal* for *Seduced by the Wolf*

"A sizzling page-turner. Terry Spear is wickedly talented."
—*Night Owl Reviews* for
Savage Hunger, Reviewer Top Pick

"The vulpine couple's chemistry crackles off the page."
—*Publishers Weekly* for *Heart of the Wolf*

"Sensual, passionate, and well-written… Terry Spear's writing is pure entertainment."
—*Long and Short Reviews* for *Wolf Fever*

Billionaire IN WOLF'S CLOTHING

TERRY SPEAR

sourcebooks
casablanca

Sourcebooks and the colophon are registered trademarks of Sourcebooks, Inc.

Published by Sourcebooks Casablanca, an imprint of Sourcebooks, Inc.
P.O. Box 4410, Naperville, Illinois 60567-4410
(630) 961-3900
Fax: (630) 961-2168
www.sourcebooks.com

Printed and bound in Canada.
MBP 10 9 8 7 6 5 4 3 2 1

To Christy White-Smith, who was our social coordinator at the library, making sure that everyone had birthday or other well-wishes for every occasion. Giving you well-wishes back in your place of rest, Christy. You and your family are in my thoughts.

Chapter 1

JADE ASHTON HAD MADE A LOT OF MISTAKES IN HER LIFE, BUT returning to her brother's pack topped the list. She should have known the pack members wouldn't accept her son, the product of a love affair with a human, despite pretending they were fine with it. She glanced at her three-year-old son, napping on the daybed in her office in her brother's home where she alternated between sketching new designs for intimate apparel and for a new baby and toddler wear line she had developed when her son was born.

Toby had just fallen asleep, looking angelic with his blond curls resting on his cheek, his dark brown eyes closed as he licked his lips. No way would she ever give him up, despite how everyone in her pack viewed him as a grievous error in judgment.

She felt a little dizzy, probably because she'd been so busy that she hadn't had anything to drink in hours. She got up from her chair and headed out the door, practically running into her twin brother moving silently down the hall like a wolf. She fell back and gasped softly when he grabbed her arm to steady her.

"We need to talk." Kenneth started to guide her to the den, his blond hair much darker than hers, his amber eyes focused on her in a way that said he had serious business to discuss.

Did he know she intended to leave the pack, again?

Or did he want to tell her he didn't think her being here was working out? "I need to get some water. And we can't talk long because Toby will be waking in a half hour or so."

"This will just take a minute."

It had better, because she wasn't going to be drawn into any long-winded discussions with her brother. She hadn't told him she was leaving first thing in the morning. She wasn't sure how he'd take it. She had to admit she was afraid he'd try to talk her out of it. But she was determined.

Every time he and the others had looked at her son in judgment, she'd been annoyed. Not only that, but she'd caught Kenneth and the others having secret conversations and then abruptly stopping whenever they saw her approaching. The pack members pretended to tolerate her son, but she saw through the facade. They didn't like her having a human son who couldn't shift. They believed he could be a danger to the pack.

Which was one of the reasons she had left just after her son was born. She had also wanted to save his human father from her brother's wrath. But raising Toby on her own had been tough. When her brother had promised that the pack members wanted her to live with them and have the backup they could provide, she had agreed. She and her son had left southern Texas far behind, so she figured she'd never run into Toby's father again. And Kenneth had sounded sincere in wanting to ensure her protection—just like a pack leader should. She wanted to be part of a family again. She didn't have a lone wolf personality.

She didn't believe Toby would be welcome in any other pack either.

Clearly, the members had changed their minds about having her and her son there. Unless they had never wanted her back and it was all her brother's idea. He was the pack leader, so ultimately, it was his decision—one he was apparently coming to regret. He was just being stubborn, didn't want to admit he'd made a mistake, and didn't want to have to tell her to leave.

Then again, maybe he realized she was planning to leave. Being twins, they sometimes sensed things like that before they really shared with each other. She hadn't packed anything yet. She planned to tell him in the morning, before he left for work at his auto body shop. She thought it would be easier on all of them that way. She'd call him when she got settled and let him know where she was staying. It was for the best—for her son, for her, and for Kenneth and the pack.

Having detoured from the direction of the den to go to the kitchen so she could get something to drink, Kenneth leaned against the granite counter, his focus on her, his expression still ultraserious. "I have a job for you."

She raised her brows, then grabbed a glass from the kitchen cabinet. Between raising Toby and running her own businesses, she didn't have time for a whole lot else. But if this was something quick that she could do this afternoon, she would, to thank Kenneth for taking her in—and then she was through with the pack.

"It's simple. And hell, you might get real lucky."

She snorted, pouring water into the glass and adding crushed ice. "Lucky?" She drank several sips of the water.

The front door shut, and she figured Kenneth's girlfriend, Lizzie, was running out for something. She was a wolf too, which meant they were sleeping together, but he hadn't decided to mate her yet so they hadn't gone all the way. If they did, he'd be stuck with her as his mate for life. Jade didn't know why the she-wolf put up with her brother. If Jade was in a situation like Lizzie's, she'd tell the wolf that either they mated or she'd look elsewhere. But Jade supposed Lizzie wanted to be a pack leader's mate and was sticking around in case Kenneth decided she was it. Total beta wolf.

"You're living off me so you can put more money into your apparel business that isn't making enough to really sustain you and your son. So, I need you to do this job and—"

"Like hell my business isn't making enough money." She was extremely tight with her money. No fancy food for either of them. No special entertainment. No expensive clothes. Since *lupus garous* lived so long, she had worked other jobs to help pad her bank account before Toby was born. She wasn't wealthy, but she got by just fine. As long as she was frugal. "That's okay. Being here with the pack isn't working out for Toby and me anyway."

Kenneth's eyes widened. "You're not leaving."

"Listen, Kenneth, you know no one wants my son here. And they barely tolerate me. You make Lizzie babysit Toby sometimes when I really need someone to watch him so I can work, but it's not fair to her. The rest of the pack worries about him. I appreciate all you've done for me. I really do." She shrugged. "But…I know this is the right thing for me to do. And for you and the pack too. I'm leaving tomorrow, and we can get together from time to time…later." She really didn't believe that would happen, but she'd make the gesture anyway.

"Like I said, I have a job for you."

What part of she was leaving did her brother not get? He was so stubborn! Or did he feel it was his place as pack leader to decide if she was leaving? He hadn't decided things for her since before she left the pack nearly four years earlier, and she wasn't going to allow him to start now.

Even so, she'd humor him because she *was* leaving tomorrow, with or without his consent. "What's the job?"

"Do you remember when that doctor was taking blood samples from us last week?"

"Yeah, Dr. Aidan Denali. He wanted to take some of Toby's, and I said no. What of it? He's not asking to take blood samples from Toby again, is he?"

"No, but here's the thing. I looked into his background, and his brother is Rafe Denali."

"So?" She'd never heard of the guy. Not that she'd heard of Aidan Denali either before she'd met him at Kenneth's house. Since Toby wasn't a shifter, there was no reason for Aidan to take blood from him. Though she hadn't given the doctor that reason since he hadn't needed to know.

"Rafe Denali's a billionaire. Real estate mogul."

"So?" Her brother was usually much better at getting to the point.

"The good doctor told me he's close to finding a cure for our longevity issues."

"Okay. What has this got to do with me? Or *you*, for that matter?"

"I need you to find out where he's living. Where he does his research."

"What?" She narrowed her eyes. "Why?" She was getting really bad vibes about this.

"His brother is ruthless. Hell, he's the reason our grandparents lost their manufacturing business."

She closed her gaping mouth. She had never known anything about her grandparents. Since her brother had taken over the pack when their parents died, he'd been the one interested in all things family. She'd been rather a wild card growing up. She'd always known she would never run the pack, so she'd done her own thing. After her son was born, she'd thrown herself into her work and raising him. No room for getting into any further trouble. She was faced with enough already.

"Okay, so I don't get the connection between what happened with our grandparents and what you want me to do. Or why you want to know where the doctor lives."

"Rafe is well-known—"

She opened her mouth again to tell Kenneth she had never heard of Rafe, so he couldn't be that well-known.

"—in financial circles. The kind that you don't belong to. I know where he lives. He and his brother are close, but Aidan lives somewhere else. I want you to befriend Rafe and learn where Aidan lives."

"Why would you want to know that? Besides, I don't run in billionaires' circles. You already said so yourself."

"He's a bachelor wolf. He's not dating any she-wolves. I've checked. If he sees you, and you intrigue him, you can cozy up to him and learn where his brother lives."

"I'm not interested. Besides, didn't the doctor give you his business card and tell you to contact him if you have any concerns?"

"It has his phone number. That's it."

"Why do you want to know this anyway?"

"I told you. Rafe is ruthless. When he gets hold of a cure for our condition, he'll sell it to only those who can afford it. What if *lupus garous* begin to age even more rapidly than we are now? What if we don't just end up with a human's life span, but our bodies begin to age rapidly to match all the years we've already lived? Hell, your boy would lose you, and he'd have no one to raise him. Think about it."

She *had* thought about it. But she wasn't one to live with a fatalist viewpoint on life. She hadn't thought her brother was either. Until now.

"If you really want this information, ask Rafe yourself. Or call his brother. You have his phone number."

"As if either would tell me."

"Send Lizzie." Jade turned to leave, and her brother seized her arm. She rounded on him, yanking her arm away from him, and said, "We're family, Kenneth, but that doesn't give you the right to make me do things that go against what I believe in. If the worst-case scenario ever comes to pass, I'm sure wolves can unite and make the brothers see the right in this."

Kenneth folded his arms. "Lizzie isn't right for the part. She's not as classy as you."

"Oh, wow, give me a break. I hope you didn't tell *her* that." Jade started heading back to her office, but she hadn't taken more than a few steps when her brother cleared his throat.

"I need you to do this. Whatever it takes. After that, you and your son can be on your way. You really don't have a choice."

"Nothing would make lying to the Denalis worthwhile, no matter why you want this information. Toby and I will be leaving tonight." Sooner—once she could get her car packed and Toby ready for the journey. She'd have to plot a course too. Had her brother known about the wolf geneticist *before* he'd asked her to return to the pack? She whipped around. "How long have you known about Aidan? Is this why you asked me to return to the pack? So I could be your spy?"

When Kenneth didn't deny it, she swore under her breath. "I thought you were concerned about me and my son. Or at least me. Thanks for letting me in on the truth." Furious with her brother, she stalked off toward the office and had nearly reached the doorway when Kenneth let his breath out in a huff.

"You will do this for me, and *then* you can have your son back."

His words made her stomach fall and her head spin as she rushed into the room.

Toby and his soft leopard blanket were gone. All that was left on the daybed was his blue rainbow-colored teddy bear.

Lizzie! She must have taken him when Jade heard the front door open. Lizzie was the only one who was close enough to Toby that if she woke him while taking him from his bed, he wouldn't cry out. He'd settle in her arms and go back to sleep. Kenneth had stalled Jade long enough for Lizzie to gather up Toby and leave.

Shocked at what he had done and angrier than she ever thought she could be, Jade hurried out of the room, ready to kill her brother—but only after he told her where her son was. "Where is he, Kenneth? I swear I'll—"

"You'll do this one thing for me, and he's yours. And

then you can damn well leave the pack. But if you ever cause any trouble for our kind, I'll kill both of you."

So furious she couldn't think straight, she beat on her brother's chest with her fists, cursing at him until he grabbed her wrists and slammed her against the wall. "I'm serious about this, Jade. Do what I say, and your son won't meet his father's fate."

"What?" Tears filled her eyes, but she tried to get a grip on her emotions so he wouldn't see her as weak. Kenneth had promised he would leave Stewart alone if she left the area before he even knew she was pregnant, and she never had anything more to do with him.

She felt sucker punched. "Why? You said..." It didn't matter now. All that mattered was Toby's safety. "Damn you, Kenneth."

She kneed her brother in the crotch with one good shove as a final comment on how she felt about him taking her son hostage. Kenneth collapsed to his knees, swearing that he'd make her pay if she didn't do what he said.

Maynard Myer—one of the men who worked in Kenneth's body shop—interrupted them, red-faced. He was a redheaded bulldog of a man who had brazenly shown his contempt for her and Toby when he dropped by the house. She suspected Maynard didn't want to intrude on this scene, but the news had to be serious enough for him to do so.

"What?" Kenneth growled at him, still on his knees on the floor and holding his crotch.

"Grayton wants his money now. You've got two weeks to pay up or..." Maynard glanced in Jade's direction.

She didn't know who Grayton was, although the

name sounded like he might be a wolf. If he had loaned
Kenneth money, and now her brother was in arrears...

"What are you involved in, Kenneth?" she asked.
"Gambling? The horse races? I've got money—"

"Get out of here, Jade. You want to see your son in
one piece, leave and do what I told you to do."

No matter how angry she was, she knew she didn't
have a choice. She had to get her son back before her
brother killed him. She grabbed Toby's rainbow bear
and hurried into her room to pack, praying she could pull
this off without getting her son killed. If Grayton was
threatening her brother, what if he took out Kenneth's
debt on his closest relations? Her and her son?

What would the Denalis do if they learned what she
was up to?

Jade had driven by Rafe Denali's house numerous times,
watching for Rafe to leave so she could run into him wherever he ended up going. Accidentally. The palatial mansion was set back off the road, a long circular drive visible
beyond the gates and providing a glimpse of the white
stucco house with its ocean view, but not much more.

This was the first time she'd seen him leaving the
estate. He was alone, driving a bright-blue Maserati with
the top down, and she followed him to a farmers market
and parked several cars away.

Wearing a pair of blue shorts, sandals, a pale-blue
T-shirt, and mirrored sunglasses, he climbed out of his
car. He didn't look like he was a billionaire, except he
had a hot car, but otherwise, he just blended in with the
rest of the shoppers.

She hurried to catch up to him. She couldn't imagine what he'd be buying. Wouldn't he have someone else buy his groceries? If she were shopping, she'd get fresh corn and tomatoes.

He stopped at a colorful booth filled with flowers, a bright-red canopy shielding the bouquets and shoppers from the afternoon sun.

In all of the research she had done on Rafe, she hadn't seen one thing that indicated he had a girlfriend. She let out her breath. Just her luck.

She hesitated, feeling jittery and uptight, but she had to run into him, making it look real and not faked, and then apologize. He'd smell she was a wolf and maybe get interested. God, how she hated this. But she had to do it for her son.

She drew closer, the crowd of shoppers helping to conceal her as she focused on the flowers as if they were her goal and not the hot wolf.

Just as she was getting closer to him, a fair-haired man wearing jeans, sandals, and a black muscle shirt approached Rafe. "Hey, getting something for Consuela?"

"Yeah, Derek. Not sure what else to get her. But I thought she'd like these." He paid for the bouquet of red and pink roses, and the two men walked off.

Damn. If the breeze had been blowing in her favor, he would have smelled her, turned, and checked her out, at the very least.

She wasn't going to get anywhere with this while he was with a friend—or whoever Derek was. But since it was the first time she'd seen Rafe leave his place, she decided to wait in her car for him to leave and see where he went next. Or maybe try running into him when Derek left.

She climbed into her car and rolled down the windows, then Googled Rafe on her cell phone. The site that mentioned him the most was written by a photojournalist named LK Marks. He seemed to be obsessed with Rafe's lifestyle—how Rafe hosted charity events but seemed reclusive otherwise. A number of times, LK Marks mentioned that Rafe was one of California's most eligible bachelors.

The last posting anyone had made concerning the billionaire was a week ago. So maybe the paparazzi were off chasing someone else for a change and Rafe was old news. Which was good news for her.

An hour passed. The breeze helped keep her cool, but she was annoyed that Rafe was taking so long to return to his car.

Then two hours passed. She left her vehicle and was searching for him when she spied him sitting on the veranda of a Mexican café, burritos on his plate and a glass of iced tea beside it. He was talking with Derek, a couple of packages on the table next to the bouquet of roses. So they must have gone shopping. She let her breath out in an irritated huff. She wasn't cut out for spy work.

Now what? She needed to get Rafe alone. Unless she could take a seat near him and he caught her wolf scent and piqued his interest, but all the tables out on the veranda were full. She asked the hostess how long it would take to get a veranda seat. Approximately an hour. Across the street, there was a sandwich shop. She headed to it, figuring she could get a view of the Mexican café from there and watch until he left.

Twenty-minute wait there. Trying not to look obvious

that she was watching Rafe, she quickly glanced over the menu and decided on a chicken and provolone sandwich. She was called to her table, and when she walked with the hostess through the restaurant to the outdoor seating, she saw where the woman was leading her. Perfect. Flowers obscured the men's view of her, but she could peek through to watch them. She took her seat and thanked the hostess, then looked over at the men—but they were gone.

—⁓—

Early in the morning, Rafe Denali perched above the rest of the world, reclining on his poolside lounger and eyeing the aqua-colored Pacific Ocean, the foamy, white waves crashing against the beach with their usual unpredictable rhythm. A rainbow-colored hot-air balloon and a bank of puffy clouds drifted across the bright-blue sky, pushed by the ever-present salty sea breeze. Seagulls called out as they soared high above, and long-legged sandpipers ran across the wet beach as the water began to recede, looking for a meal. A few beachgoers had erected colorful umbrellas in blues and yellows and pinks, along with chaise longues or chairs, and were sunbathing or reading. A few were walking the beach. Life couldn't be better. Rafe had needed a break after making another thirty-million-dollar sale, and what better way to do that than by sipping a mixed-fruit smoothie while visiting with his best friend, Derek Spencer—also one of the filthy rich and, like him, a wolf.

But he couldn't relax completely. Rafe was certain that different men had been following him for the past week or so, watching his every move. He'd had one of his private investigators trying to learn what was up, but without success.

He knew those following him hadn't been paparazzi looking to capture shots of him to show to the world, or sexy women looking to catch his attention—he was used to that. After all, he was an extremely eligible bachelor, at least as far as the unknowing public thought. He was certain that if human women knew he was also a wolf, his single, male billionaire status wouldn't have as much appeal.

The problem was that the men following him were wolves—just as wary and capable of concealment and evasion in their human form as in their wolf coats. What had tipped him off was that the men *hadn't* been carrying cameras when following him as humans. And when he'd caught them watching him at various restaurants or stores, they'd quickly looked away. But when he'd tried to track them, they'd always given him the slip. Sometimes, they left a bit of a telltale wolf scent behind, as if they'd used hunter's spray for concealment but hadn't quite masked their own unique scent.

Rafe took another sip of his smoothie. This was so different from when he'd lived with the pack of his birth. He had moved on, left that life behind, wanting something more. The power to make things happen in the human world, not just with a pack.

"Has your brother learned anything from the research he's been conducting?" Derek asked.

"When he's running his experiments, he doesn't like to discuss the results—or, I should say, details—with anyone. Certainly not with me, since that's not my field of expertise. Just like I don't discuss the details of my real estate ventures with him."

"I heard he was off to check some other leads besides testing *lupus garou* blood samples."

"Yeah. He's let me in on his other research so I'll know where he is at all times. He's studied children with progeria, a premature aging syndrome. He also investigated an eight-year-old girl who still had the physical maturity of an infant, having barely aged in all that time. Another case was that of a forty-year-old man who looked like a ten-year-old boy. A couple others: a twenty-nine-year-old man who appeared to be ten, and a woman who was thirty-four but looked like she was two years old. So the rate of aging was significantly different for each of them.

"Aidan had wondered if any of them were wolves, which was one of the primary reasons he checked into their cases, but he learned none were. Since *lupus garous* age at the same rate humans do until they are young adults, he really hadn't believed they were our kind, but he still wanted to determine if any of their conditions were similar to ours."

Derek finished his smoothie and set the glass on the table. "With all the research he's doing, I think he needs a bodyguard. Knowing how to return us to our original wolf life spans could be dangerous in the wrong hands."

"Agreed. I have a man watching his back, even though Aidan wouldn't approve if he knew. So I haven't mentioned it to anyone. Aidan doesn't believe he's close to learning anything." Rafe studied a couple of bikini-clad babes running along the beach below his estate. He swore the women were plants, seeking to catch his attention. Most of the wealthy landowners up here were older. Truth be told, he was much older than them. But in human years, he appeared to be thirty. He was also looking for anyone who seemed to be watching him, but he didn't see anyone like that here today.

What really caught his eye was a woman wearing a pair of white short shorts with what looked like a one-piece bathing suit underneath, though the back plunged so low that all he could see were the royal blue straps. What piqued his curiosity even more was how low the front of the swimsuit was cut. It was funny how sometimes a one-piece and a pair of shorts could be more enticing than a tiny bikini.

When she began wading up to her thighs in the surf, watching the sea, her golden hair whipping about her shoulders in the warm summer breeze, he sighed, reminding himself he couldn't be interested in a human woman for any kind of permanent relationship.

"Enticed yet?" Derek asked, smiling, his attention focused on the scantily clad bathing beauties jogging along the beach.

Rafe finished his smoothie. "Are they different ones, or the same two who were out here yesterday?"

"Hard to tell. They have all the right curves, the tanned bodies, the skimpy bikinis. I think one was a redhead yesterday though. So you think it's a ploy to see if one of them would appeal more to you?" Before Rafe could reply, Derek tacked on, "Given a choice, which would?"

"None of them."

"Not even if she was a wolf?"

Rafe glanced at his lifelong friend. Tall, tanned,

and muscular like him, Derek was much fairer, his hair blonder and his eyes amber. They didn't exactly appear like the billionaire type. Not to mention they had a wolfish wild side to them. Both were wearing board shorts—his green with a blue ocean wave, Derek's an orange-and-white floral—and they looked more like surfer dudes, except neither of them surfed. As a wolf, Rafe preferred swimming, hiking, running, boating, or climbing—freestyle.

In a gesture of feigned exasperation, Derek threw up his hands. "Okay, so most are interested in our money more than anything. Sometimes it's important to just have fun."

Rafe checked out the woman walking deeper into the water. He grew worried when he saw the telltale signs of danger. The surf was flatter there, looking like a road heading out to sea. The color was lighter than the surrounding water, the foam on the surface moving out to sea, instead of being drawn into the shore like the regular breakers. A rip current. Which could imperil the woman.

Instantly, Rafe bolted from his lounger and raced to his private stairs to the beach, wishing like hell he'd noticed the water before. His attention had been solely on the woman the last time he looked.

"Hey, where you going?" Derek asked, jumping up from his lounger and hurrying to catch up as Rafe ran down the stairs.

"To rescue the third woman this month who's headed for trouble in the surf." Rafe reached the electronically locked gate, threw it open, then sprinted across the sun-warmed sand.

A summer of storms and hurricanes had altered the landscape of the ocean floor along the Pacific coast, creating more rip currents, which had resulted in more lifeguard rescues in the area. Except they didn't have any lifeguards here. That meant whenever Rafe took a breather from work and relaxed poolside, he watched the situation in front of his estate as if he were the local lifeguard. He couldn't help it. If he saw someone in danger, he was compelled to lend a hand.

Rip currents typically flowed faster than any human could swim. If the woman he saw walking into the rip current was caught up in it, she could be pulled out to sea as much as half a mile or more before it ended. It wouldn't pull its victim under; usually, those who drowned had attempted to swim against the flow, panicking in an effort to return to the shore through the path of the rip current, tiring them to the point of exhaustion. If she was a good swimmer and knew how to navigate horizontally to the beach, or remained calm and treaded water until the rip lost its drive, she should make it just fine. But he didn't want to risk her safety.

He raced around the beachgoers soaking up the sun. No one seemed to notice the possible danger.

Rafe reached the incoming waves, bolted through the water, and heard his friend splashing behind him. The woman was up to her shoulders in the surf, and Rafe dove for her just as the current swept her off her feet and pulled them both out to sea.

Chapter 2

"JUST REMAIN CALM," RAFE SAID, HIS ARM WRAPPED AROUND the woman's curvy body, hugging her close. Her breasts pressed against his chest as he let the rip carry them out. He had to remind himself he was just on a rescue mission, but that changed when he smelled her delectable wolf scent. Her soft, huggable body made his react instantly to the intimacy.

Her blond hair was wet and looked darker, cascading over her shoulders and sweeping up against him in the flow of the water, her dark-brown eyes taking him in, her pink lips parted in surprise. But no more surprised than he was. He suspected she was just as shocked that he was a wolf as that he had come to rescue her.

"Are you from around here?" Lots of people who went to the beach regularly died from rip currents. They didn't realize the danger until it was too late.

"No, I'm from Amarillo."

That explained her lack of knowledge about the currents. "On vacation?" At this point, he could have swum out of the rip current with her and then let go of her. He probably didn't even need to swim out with her. But this was just too damn nice, so he kept holding her close and treading water as the rip continued to pull them out.

"Uh, yeah."

"Alone?" he asked, sounding a tad too hopeful. Hell, women were always after him because of his wealth, so he was always putting on the brakes. With her? This was a completely different story. Mainly because she was a wolf. And intriguing. Well, and for an instant, she had needed his rescue. At least as far as he believed. He liked feeling needed—and not just for his money.

"Yeah." She seemed so hesitant that he thought she might be concerned about his intentions.

He couldn't blame her one bit. Even though he'd like to think his intentions were perfectly honorable, his wolfish half was enjoying the intimacy between them a whole hell of a lot more than he should have been.

Still, she wasn't trying to get away from him, and she fit so nicely against him that he wanted to take advantage of the moment. He wondered why she would take a vacation here all alone though, his cagey wolf side instantly coming to bear. What if she was involved with the male wolves who were spying on him? Maybe she'd been sent to do a different mission up close and personal—not just watch from afar.

"My name is Rafe." He didn't want to give his last name in case she'd heard of his wealth. But if she was with the men who had him under surveillance, she already knew who he was. If she wasn't part of that group, he didn't want his wealth to influence her. It had a way of instantly changing the dynamics. Not only that, but no one except for his friend, his brother, and a few other wolves he did business with knew they all were wolves. He liked to keep it that way. Otherwise, he could see single she-wolves stalking him next.

"I'm Jade. Thanks for your help. Do you think we're safe now?" The twinkle in her dark eyes and the soft smile on her shimmering pink lips said she knew he was holding her close for reasons other than her safety now.

"Almost."

That earned him a bigger smile.

He smiled back. Well, hell, even if this whole thing was a setup, he had to admit he was enjoying the connection between them too damn much to care.

"So…do you do this often?" She had a sweetly alluring voice that he enjoyed hearing over the gulls and breakers closer to shore.

"Rescue ladies in distress? You bet. But never one *quite* like you."

"A wolf, you mean."

"From Amarillo." His body was reacting way too much to hers. He hoped she wouldn't notice, though he suspected she was noticing everything about his body as much as he could feel her nipples pebbling against his chest. Not that she seemed like the kind of woman who scared off easily.

"I think the current's strength is dwindling," she said, but she still didn't make a move to pull away.

"You might be right. Are you doing anything for lunch?"

Her brows lifted marginally. "I have a date with the Crab Shack."

"Alone?"

She chuckled. "Yeah."

"Mind if I join you?"

"What if someone else needs you to rescue him or her? I'd hate for you not to be here when disaster struck."

"I've done my rescuing for the day." He motioned to Derek, who was standing on the shore, arms folded across his chest, and smiling at them. "It's Derek's turn next."

"Friend of yours, I take it?"

"Best."

"Part of a pack?"

"Nah. Just my brother, Derek, and me. But we're not a pack. You?"

"Yeah, but they're back in Amarillo."

"They're not worried about you being out here all alone, getting into trouble in the ocean?"

"I'm sure they'd think I'd be just as safe playing in the water as I thought I'd be."

"I take it you don't have a mate. If you were mine, I'd damn well be out here with you."

She laughed.

He waited for her to confirm she didn't have one. He wasn't getting mixed up with a mated wolf no matter how much he enjoyed being with her like this.

She was still smiling when she shook her head. But he swore her smile was a little pinched this time. He'd lived too many years not to be able to read people, though he couldn't read her well enough to know why the mention of a mate bothered her.

He couldn't believe someone as delectable as she was didn't have a mate already. Unless she had lost him and the mention was troubling her. "Ready to have lunch? I think I can get us back in safely now."

She laughed. "I just bet you can."

He smiled at her.

"What about you? Have a mate?"

Her expression had turned impish. But he wondered—did she already know who he was? He would love to say something about being one of the most eligible bachelors around, just to judge her reaction, but he curbed the inclination.

He shook his head.

As soon as they moved out of what was left of the rip current and into the breakers, a wave hit them. Before they could react, the briny sea carried them both under. He instantly lost hold of her and panicked but broke to the surface to search for her just as she tumbled into him. Again, he grabbed hold of her, telling himself she needed his support or at least a way to stop them from banging into each other, even though it was more than that. As a wolf, she was damned intriguing, and he was determined to know her whole story. Was this a chance encounter or something more?

"You do know how to swim, don't you?" Wolves normally did.

"Yes." She paused in the surf and sneezed. "Sorry, some of the water went up my nose."

"A hazard of playing in the surf."

"But a fun hazard."

He got the impression she meant because of his rescue. If she was perfectly innocent of any deviousness, he hoped he could get to know her better.

Letting go of her, he swam with her toward the shore. As soon as he reached shallower water where he could stand on the sandy bottom, he felt something slice into his foot, pain erupting immediately. *Hell*.

He dove and felt around on the ocean floor until he found a broken seashell half buried in the sand. He dug it out, came up out of the surf, and threw the shell out to sea as far as possible so no one else could cut themselves

on it. He was instantly annoyed with himself for getting
injured—not that he could have seen the shell or avoided
it in the stirred-up water. Still, he was glad Jade hadn't
been the one to step on it instead. Lifting his foot to
head in, he saw a wave headed their way and quickly
grabbed Jade to rescue her. It pulled them both under,
and they were washed ashore. Her soft, wet body was
planted against his. His body was as hard as it could get.

For a moment, she just looked at him, and then she
leaned in and kissed him softly on the lips. "Thanks for
the rescue. Again."

Hot damn! He would suffer any indignity for another
kiss like that.

She seemed to be going for just a short, sweet kiss
on the lips, but he slipped his arms around her shoulders
and pulled her down for something hotter, more wolfish,
more of a thank-you.

For a second, she hesitated to respond.

"I've been injured," he said, hoping for sympathy.

To his delight, she pressed her lips full on his mouth
and their hot, wet bodies melded together, their pheromones spiking. The kiss was better than any he'd ever
had. He hoped she was going to be here for a long time,
because he definitely wanted to get to know the she-
wolf better.

―――

This was so wrong, and Jade hated the deception. She
hadn't planned to get herself sucked out to sea, and it
would have been frightening if the hot wolf hadn't rescued her. *Rafe Denali*. After missing her chance yesterday to run into him at the farmers market, she had been

trying the beach again. She'd been here a number of times already, walking the shore in front of his palatial mansion on the cliffs and trying not to look as though she was checking out his place, but he'd never been out while she was here. She'd begun to think he never sat on his patio.

She'd tried to learn where he went during the day and at night so she could bump into him, but he must have done a lot of business at home, because she didn't see him leave much.

This time, she'd spied two men lounging poolside, the water reflecting off the patio roof, and hoped one was Rafe. From the beach, she hadn't been able to tell. She knew she had to do something, though she'd never intended to drown herself. Not when she had a young son who needed her.

She'd thought she'd play in the water so she could stay near Rafe's house and maybe catch his eye. She'd considered leaving the water wet, her clothes clinging to her and showing off her curves a little—something she never would have done to catch a man's eye if she hadn't felt the desperate need to do so. With all her heart, she'd wished Toby was here—seeing the ocean for the first time, chasing the hermit crabs, wiggling his toes in the wet sand, and feeding the gulls.

She admired Rafe for coming out to rescue her and couldn't help but be amused at the way he had continued to hold on to her.

But she reminded herself that nothing else mattered except fulfilling her mission so she could get her son back. She really hadn't planned to kiss the wolf like that, not when her brother said Rafe devoured his competition whole. Her research had shown that Rafe *had* taken over a number of real estate ventures, including their grand-parents' business, a couple of decades ago, proving her brother's claims were right. So what would Rafe's brother do if he could wield the power over their longevity? And if not him, then how ruthless could Rafe be with that knowledge?

It wasn't important. Getting her son back safely was all that mattered.

Chapter 3

JADE HAD TO ADMIT SHE'D ENJOYED KISSING RAFE WAY TOO much, considering where her priorities had to remain. But he was so wolfish and tan, and smelled enticingly of coconut oil, the salty water, and sea breeze. His skin was soft, but everything else was hard—his muscles, his arousal, his chiseled, gorgeous face—all except the cute little dimples that hinted at whimsical amusement. She shouldn't have been enjoying any of it, but she couldn't help it since *she* was a wolf too. His board shorts were a pretty design—a green wave over dark blue—and so molded to his package that she tried not to notice.

As soon as the waves pulled back out to sea, she moved off him. She couldn't believe it when she saw his foot bleeding all over the wet, golden sand. She thought he'd been kidding about being injured.

"Ohmigod, Rafe." She noticed his friend had left the beach, probably figuring Rafe needed some alone time with her. She could have used the friend's help now. "You cut yourself."

"On a broken seashell." He was frowning as he sat up, propped his foot up on his other thigh, and examined the cut.

They had wolf healing genetics, which would make the cut heal faster, but not instantaneously. Instead of offering to take him up to his house—she didn't want him to know she knew he lived there—she said, "I've got a car parked in the public parking lot, though it's a hefty hike across the sand. We need to bandage your foot before you walk anywhere."

The way he had come to her rescue, he was definitely an alpha male, so when he hesitated to say he lived up at the big house, she assumed he wasn't sure he wanted her to know. She supposed women who knew how rich he was would throw themselves at him, trying to win him over or at least enjoy some perks until he tired of them. She had no intention of throwing herself at him. Well, any more than she had already. That certainly wasn't her mission. And she'd never planned to go this far with him. It just…happened.

For now, she quickly came up with another solution. "I'll run back to my car. I have a first aid kit in it. You just wait here, and I'll be back as quick as I can."

"No need," Rafe said, catching her hand before she moved away from him. "I live in the house up on the hill."

She was glad he'd told her the truth. Pretending she didn't know anything about him was hard enough. She glanced up at the home on the cliffs. The stucco wall had a wrought iron railing and flowers in profusion. Loungers and colorful umbrella-topped tables covered the patio.

"You live there? Who with?" She hoped his brother lived there too. But Kenneth had said Dr. Aidan Denali lived and worked elsewhere. Some of their pack members had been watching Rafe since Aidan had taken their blood samples, and not once had Aidan been to the house. His mail wasn't going there either. Rafe seemed to be the only one who lived there. Probably a staff person too, but her brother didn't know. All he'd cared about was where Aidan lived.

"I'm the only one who lives here. Unless Derek is still up there," Rafe said. "But he just visits. And my personal assistant, but he's busy with other things at the moment. He has his own guesthouse connected to the main house."

"Wow." At least she wasn't lying when she acted impressed. She hadn't known he had a guesthouse up there too. She frowned as she helped Rafe to stand. "They better not be up there watching and not coming down to help."

"They wouldn't be. Unless they thought I wanted to be alone with you."

She sighed. "No offense, but I'm way out of your league."

He was smiling down at her as if he didn't believe she meant it. Which she didn't, but she didn't want him to think his wealth intimidated her. Which it didn't.

She slipped her arm around his waist, glad he wasn't trying to be all macho and do this on his own. He was limping on the heel of his foot, attempting to keep the sole from touching the sand, which was impossible.

He was trying to pretend it didn't hurt, but his wincing told her the truth.

"I have an outdoor shower up there for rinsing off, but just a spigot down here for washing feet to keep the sand off the stairs."

They cleaned their feet, and then he punched in a security code to open the gate.

Climbing the stairs took forever. She wasn't sure if that was because he wanted the closeness to last longer or if he really was hurting that much.

"No live-in doctor to take care of your injury?" She could have kicked herself for saying so afterward. She hadn't been thinking of his doctor brother, just that Rafe was wealthy enough to have a complement of staff. Maybe he couldn't find staff who were wolves.

"No. Just by myself unless…"

"Derek is still there. Or Sebastian was there."

"Which I doubt. They would have seen the trouble and come to my aid."

"I wish I could have carried you up the stairs."

Rafe laughed. "If you'd stepped on a shell and I carried you, that would be heroic. You carrying me?" He laughed again.

She smiled, thinking just how funny that would look.

When they reached the patio and she saw the aqua-blue pool, she wished Toby could be here. The two of them would jump right in. It looked so inviting. How could anyone live like this all by himself? A huge pack could live here and enjoy the place.

Maybe he was a growly, disagreeable wolf and no one was interested in him. Then again, probably no one knew he was a wolf.

"Why don't you sit on the bench and I'll wash you off, and then, well…" She really didn't want to run into his house to find a first aid kit when she didn't know him or where he kept anything. And she was just as sandy and wet as him. Not to mention that washing him off would be a lot more intimate than she wanted to get.

"We can rinse off, then we can go in, and I'll get the first aid kit. You can find something for us to dry off with in that chest over there."

Aside from towels, she also discovered a stack of

towel robes. She grabbed a couple of each and carried them over to where the shower spray was running all over his glorious body. She couldn't help but watch with fascination—the sight was just too mesmerizing not to enjoy.

"So what made you come here on vacation?" he asked.

She slid her gaze from his glistening torso. "I did an Internet search and found a bed-and-breakfast near here. I was dying to spend some time at the beach."

"What do you think of the area so far?" He carefully stepped out of the open-air shower, which featured a privacy glass-block wall on the beach side. He grabbed a towel off the bench and dried off. Then he pulled on a robe and drew it around himself, cinching the belt before he sat down to wait for her.

"I love the beach. I just didn't realize how easy it was to drown yourself. I'm used to lakes." She pulled off her shorts. The one-piece bathing suit she was wearing was one of her creations, though she wasn't sure she would offer a swimsuit line. But she loved the suit. Even though it was a one-piece, the front had a lot of see-through crocheted netting; the top and bottom were bikini-like; and the thong backside was cut high on the cheeks to add to the sex appeal. She'd been wearing shorts so she wasn't as exposed to the crowd. As she showered, she felt sexy and self-conscious at the same time, mainly because of her wolfish audience and the way his tongue was dragging on the patio.

She wished she could strip off her bathing suit and rinse the inside because she still felt sandy.

"I think you would have been okay if you had just

relaxed and didn't try to swim in against the current.
If I had known you were a wolf, I would have thought
you were strong enough to make the swim on your own.
Believing you were human, I couldn't take the chance."

Yet when he'd learned she was a wolf, he still hadn't
let go. "Thanks, Rafe, for saving me out there."

"Hey, you saved me too, remember." He held up
his foot.

She sighed. "Yeah, but that wouldn't have happened
if you hadn't come to my rescue. Let's get this taken
care of before you need hospitalization."

He just laughed.

Rafe didn't believe Jade's story. Not exactly. He wanted
to. He was tired of being wary of people's motives
related to his wealth and power. Just once he'd like to
meet a she-wolf like her who wasn't looking for a sugar
daddy or a glamorous lifestyle. But it was too much of
a coincidence that she'd happened to catch his interest
when male *lupus garous* had been following him around.

He didn't think she'd acted shocked enough that
he owned the beach house, as he called it. He didn't
believe anyone as pretty as she was, and a wolf, would
be here on vacation without having a pack member with
her. And he didn't think she would have picked this
particular spot to vacation. Why not somewhere closer
to where she lived? Maybe South Padre Island on the
Gulf of Mexico, or Galveston. Why come all the way
to California?

Why come to where a billionaire wolf happened to
live and potentially drown herself in the ocean right in

front of his house? He hated that he couldn't believe she was here by coincidence.

He would continue to talk to her, to learn more about her. If she hadn't been so intriguing, he would have sent her on her way. He really was curious to see if she had some devious plan in mind. In the meantime, he'd have one of his men learn all he could about her.

If he hadn't been so interested in her, Rafe would have left her on the beach and taken care of his injury on his own. But he enjoyed seeing her so concerned and willing to take care of him. He hadn't had anyone do that for him since he was a boy.

Unless someone wanted money for the service.

The first aid kit was in his master bath. He led her into the bedroom, then motioned to the seating area. "I'll be right back." Instead, she walked over to the french doors to observe the view from the veranda.

"Be right back." He was still annoyed about cutting his foot. He'd wanted to walk with her down the beach to the Crab Shack, even though it was two miles south of where he lived.

He heard the french doors open, and when he returned to the bedroom with kit in hand, he saw her standing at the railing, looking out to sea, the wind sweeping her damp hair around. In that instant, as he walked out to join her, he really hoped she was there without any ulterior motives.

"About lunch…" he said, taking a seat and putting the first aid kit on the table.

"Here, let me do that." She hurried over to sit opposite him and lifted his foot onto her lap. She retrieved supplies from the kit and cleaned the wound with care, then dried it and bandaged it, the intimate gesture filling him with a strange longing.

"So about lunch… I had thought we'd walk along the beach," he said.

"You can't until your foot heals up." She tucked the rest of the supplies away and set the kit aside, his foot still on her lap.

"I can drive us there."

She sighed. "The reason I wanted to go there was that I'd be sandy and wet and…" She shrugged. "They have a patio for the bathing suit crowd, but I don't want to mess up your car."

"I can change into something dry. I'll throw on some sandals and a T-shirt. And we can take a couple of towels for you to sit on in the car. We could drop by your bed-and-breakfast, and you could get a change of clothes. Or just go as is. It's up to you."

"'As is' is fine with me. I'll just sit by the pool until you're ready to go."

"Okay. Be ready in a jiff." He had a meeting this evening with an interior decorator about one of the homes he wanted staged before he put it on the market, but he wasn't letting this opportunity go if he had a chance to spend more time with Jade. He'd ask his personal assistant to take care of the meeting.

As soon as Jade returned to the pool still wearing one of his towel robes, Rafe texted Edward Manning, an ex-Navy SEAL who served as a bodyguard and as whatever else Rafe needed that required muscle, intelligence, and finesse.

Rafe texted: Got a job for you.

Edward texted back: Yeah, Boss?

Need you to check out a woman for me. All I have is her first name, Jade. She's here now. I just want you to learn all you can about her.

No response.

Edward?

Yeah, sure, I'm on it.

We're going to the Crab Shack in just a few. Then I'll drop her off at her car sitting in the public parking area. You can take it from there.

Will do.

Rafe had never had Edward check out a woman for him. He could just imagine what the lone wolf was thinking about that.

———— ❦ ————

Jade was dying to take off her salty, sandy bathing suit. She was used to swimming in lakes, and this wasn't the same. Her skin would be chafed and miserable if she didn't rinse off more. She knew Rafe would take some time getting dressed, so she practically sprinted for the patio, then spied a table with a piece of junk mail addressed to the current resident. She sailed past the table and outside, yanking off the robe and tossing it on the bench. When she reached the outdoor shower, she stripped off her shorts and bathing suit and quickly washed herself all over again.

Thinking back to the piece of mail sitting on Rafe's side table, Jade realized she probably couldn't find any snail mail that would tell her where Aidan lived. He probably got in touch with Rafe through emails, text messages, or phone calls. Even if she could get ahold of Rafe's phone, it was no doubt password protected, and she wouldn't be able to access his contacts. Aidan's address might not even be listed in Rafe's phone book. She only had phone numbers in hers.

Rushing to rinse off, she thought that while she might not be here for a perfectly innocent reason, enticing the wolf into a mating wasn't in the plans. She was certain he would have offered her the use of his shower, or some other in the house, but she hadn't wanted to ask or impose. Out here, she could rinse off the salt and sand and not leave a big mess. Though she supposed that was silly, because his maid service would clean it up. But she was a wolf too, and she didn't feel the need to be pampered or to impose on him any more than she had to. She liked her low-key lifestyle.

She rinsed out her bathing suit and wrung it out. Slipping back into a wet bathing suit was a lot harder to do, and she hoped Rafe was moving really slowly.

Wolves shifted naked in front of each other when they were with their pack and used to one another. This wasn't the same. She didn't want him to get the idea she was doing this to try to snag his attention.

She rinsed out her shorts and was tugging them over her bathing suit when he opened the patio door.

"Are you sure you don't want to drop by your place and get a change of clothes?"

Not expecting Rafe's sudden appearance, she jumped a little, hating that she looked so guilty.

"Listen, I'm probably too wet to ride in your car." As much as she hated to delay this, she didn't want him to think she was too eager and make him suspicious of her motives. She couldn't chance it. "Maybe we can make it some other time. Tomorrow, if you're free."

She really felt uncomfortable about this. She'd been trying to tell herself that although he seemed nice, he wouldn't be Mr. Nice and Agreeable if she had business dealings with him. All she wanted was her son back. Dealing in deception? This was *so* not her.

"Nonsense. My car will survive. Let's go." Rafe sounded like he was afraid he was going to lose his lunch companion, but she knew that, before long, he'd wish he'd never rescued her in the surf.

Chapter 4

RAFE HAD LET HIS PERSONAL ASSISTANT, SEBASTIAN, KNOW where he was going before he took off, having caught a glimpse of Jade gloriously naked as she'd rushed to remove her bathing suit and rinse off in the outdoor shower. He wished she'd felt comfortable just using a guest bathroom. He hadn't wanted to catch her nude, or her to catch him seeing her like that. He knew by the way she was rushing that she wasn't trying to get caught, but he took advantage of the moment to snap a close-up of her face so he could send it to Edward so he could use it to investigate her. Her face had been tilted up to the showerhead, her eyes closed, her hands on her wet hair, and her lips parted, kissed by the spray of warm water. She was busty and had nice childbearing hips and long legs—that he was trying not to look at too much. He had to admit she was beautiful.

After he'd quickly moved away from the glass door, he'd finished his conversation with Sebastian. He'd rushed, worried he was moving too slowly because of the soreness of his foot, and she would be tired of waiting for him. Though once he'd seen her naked, he wasn't sure if his conversation with Sebastian had made any sense.

Now that they were on the road, Rafe didn't see any sign of Edward, but Rafe knew he would be watching for him as he drove his Ferrari convertible to the Crab

Shack. Other than his wolf friends and brother, no one Rafe knew hung out here. Not those who had money. He loved to meet Derek and his brother here from time to time just to go slumming.

Rafe might have a nice car, but he was wearing cutoffs, sandals, and a well-worn T-shirt like he usually did when he ate at the Crab Shack. He would have dressed up for Jade, but since she was wearing just her bathing suit and shorts, he didn't want her to feel underdressed.

As they drove with the top down, the wind whipped Jade's wet curls about. She was smiling as they tore off down the road, and he wanted to go a lot farther than the two miles to the restaurant. Maybe she'd agree to a longer drive just for the hell of it. He realized then he hadn't asked for her full name, because at the time, he hadn't intended to share his. Now he wanted to know it. Edward could learn who she was as soon as he ran her license plate. But then Rafe had another thought. Maybe he could take her out on the yacht, the *Lo-Lee*. He knew he shouldn't plan for anything long term. But damn if he didn't want to throw caution to the wind and enjoy the ride while he spent time with her. That was his wilder wolf half talking.

When Rafe escorted her into the Crab Shack, the hostess seated them on the deck, the fragrance of the salty sea air and seafood dishes wafting around them. Seagulls called out overhead, and people played and laughed on the beach as the waves crashed on the shore. It was a beautiful day to be here, and he had to admit that being with Jade made it even more special—if he didn't overanalyze *why* she was here.

They ordered the king crab feasts, and Jade made her

selection so quickly that he wondered if she had been in the area for a while.

"So how many days are you going to be here?" he asked, settling back in his chair.

"Another week."

"Have to use up some leave time at work?" He shouldn't have asked, but he really was curious why she was here by herself.

"I needed a break. A way to clear my head so I could get creative again."

"What do you create?" He was thinking of art, sculptures, maybe writing.

"Lingerie fashions. I sell them to upper-end stores all over the States."

"Lingerie." He smiled a little. Now *this* was totally unexpected. "Like Victoria's Secret?"

"What would you know about Victoria's Secret?" Jade was smiling.

"Not a whole lot, really. But secrets always sound intriguing."

She smiled. "True. So, what do you do that you make enough money to afford the shack on the beach?"

"I dabble in real estate."

"Dabble."

"I've made some good investments and consequently some good sales. I just have an eye for what might do well."

"Your house is incredible."

"Thanks. I'm rather fond of it. I've lived in the city, but I like living on the beach best."

"Do you take trips to the woods?"

"To run? Sure. To be myself—to let the other side

of me out. I have a jet on standby for anytime I want to get away from all of this. I love running on the beach at night as well."

"A jet, wow. So you really do love to still be wild?"

"Hell yeah. No pressing business, no modern tech stuff, just being one with nature—that's what it's really all about. What about you? You don't have any woods to run in around Amarillo, do you?"

"No, but we have a lot of wide-open spaces out there, so I run at night."

"Do you want to run with me tonight?"

Their crab baskets were served, and after making sure they had bibs and everything else they needed, their server headed for another table.

"I'd like that. Thanks." Jade tied on her bib.

He smiled at the saying on it: *The Best Kind of Crabs to Have!*

Rafe sure as hell hoped Edward wouldn't find anything discouraging about Jade that would ruin what until now had been the nicest dating experience he'd ever had. Not that bad news would change his mind about seeing her, at least until he learned the truth directly from her—and then?

His thoughts drifted to seeing her naked in the shower. Ah, hell, he was aroused all over again. No matter what she was up to, he knew reining in his wolf needs was going to be easier said than done.

Of course Jade said yes. If she wanted to earn his confidence, she had to accept his invitation to run. But this whole charade was going to be a nightmare to keep up with. Yes, she created lingerie, and yes, she sold to upper-end stores, but she didn't sell to that many. She certainly wasn't wealthy by any means, but even so, she didn't feel he was too rich for her blood, and she appreciated him for making her feel that way. Maybe it was because he was a wolf too.

She could see the wolf in him even now—with the cutoffs and the T-shirt washed a million times, the old sandals that looked like they'd seen thousands of miles, and the stubble just appearing on his jaw. He leaned back in his chair, his relaxed posture indicating he was comfortable with who he was and content being with her.

For the last two weeks, Jade had been so uneasy around her brother's pack that she wished she could feel more at ease around Rafe. Unfortunately, her reason for being here kept her from enjoying herself. She couldn't quit thinking about Toby, yet she had to be on guard so she didn't slip up and mention him. The jig would be up then. But keeping her son out of her thoughts was impossible. Everything reminded her of him: kids building sand castles or playing at the edge of the surf, squeals of childish delight, even a family sitting nearby. The child was in a booster seat, fisting a fat french fry while Dad handed him a sippy cup.

Jade started cracking open a crab leg, then looked up at Rafe. He was concentrating on one too. "Do you come here often?"

"As often as I can with Derek. Sometimes with my brother."

"So both of them live in the area?" This was the first

opening she'd had to ask casually about his brother, but she was afraid her accelerated heartbeat was going to give her away.

"Derek does. Aidan doesn't."

"Are you close to your brother?"

Rafe dug out some of the meat from his crab leg and dipped it in warm butter. "I am. But we don't get to see much of each other because of the work we do."

"So, he's not a real estate mogul too?"

"Hardly. He's more the scientist in the family."

"What about Derek?"

"He plays the market. Some years are good and some years not so good. But he's had a lot of years to invest, and like me, he's got a knack for seeing the trends and picking the winners. What about yourself? Family?"

This was a hazard of asking Rafe about his brother and friend; Jade would have to share about herself if he asked. She wanted to stick as close to the truth as she could. But she couldn't mention her son. Not when Rafe would want to know why she'd abandoned him to come on a vacation alone. Wolves were super protective of their offspring. Her story wouldn't ring true. Or he'd think she was a bad mother.

"I have a brother. We were close at one time. When he took over the pack…" Crap, what did she say now without spilling the whole story? She pulled out a piece of crabmeat. "Things are strained between us."

"But you stay with the pack?"

Jade looked up at Rafe. He was watching her, trying to read what was wrong between her and her brother and why she would stay—trying to learn what was going on behind the scenes in her head. Wolves were intuitive creatures, and she feared she was failing miserably at keeping up the charade.

"Not for long," she said, probably a little too angrily as she stabbed her fork into a green bean. Before she'd fallen head over heels with Stewart, she'd been happy with the pack. Relationships between *lupus garous* and humans rarely produced children. So she had been just as shocked as everyone else. But that had changed everything for her. Not only were her brother and the pack furious, but raising a human child with the pack could spell disaster for all of them.

Jade had tried to convince Kenneth she wouldn't have anything more to do with Stewart and that she'd move away so he wouldn't learn about the child, but Kenneth didn't believe she'd give her human boyfriend up. Kenneth had been certain there was only one way to deal with the possible threat of Stewart's learning what they were. Killing him.

Kenneth's concern wasn't just a vague one. Stewart had wanted to marry her. And he had wanted kids. But changing him could have been a disaster. And Kenneth wouldn't have it. Besides, convincing Stewart to leave his mom, stepdad, brother, and half sister behind wouldn't have worked. He had been devoted to them, which she'd liked. Family had been so important. Her brother had said that if she left the area, he'd leave Stewart alone. But damn Kenneth. He'd lied and never told her until it was convenient to threaten her own son.

"So how did you get the idea to start a women's lingerie business?" Rafe asked.

She pulled her attention from her morose thoughts and stopped digging at a crab leg to look up at Rafe.

She wondered if he had been studying her the whole time, waiting for her to elaborate about her brother and changing the subject when she didn't.

"I was looking to create something that was easier for women to remove in a hurry—for our kind, you know. That meant a lot less material, and my creations turned out to be pretty sexy."

He smiled.

"But it was hard selling them to anyone but our kind for eons until a big change in women's fashions caught on."

"I always thought less was better."

Jade laughed. "So did she-wolves. Then I started a specialty baby and toddlers' line, Tykes and Tiaras, high-end infant and toddlers' apparel." She had no intention of telling him what had inspired her to create that line of fashion.

"Sounds good."

Rafe didn't seem as interested in that line as he did in the intimate apparel one. Which was totally understandable.

"What about you? What made you get into the real estate business?" she asked, then sucked out another piece of sweet meat.

He watched her, smiling a little. "First property I bought as an investment was a block of old buildings—boarded up, a hazard to the community, and no one wanted to do anything with it. I had all the buildings torn down, except for a corner service station. I expanded it and turned it into a 1950s ice-cream shop and the rest of the block into a park. The ice-cream shop does a phenomenal business, plus locals work there and the residents love the park."

Jade hadn't expected that. Had he changed over the years as he'd built up his wealth? "You can't have made a lot of money off that when you turned most of it into a park."

"You're right. But it made me see how a rundown area could be revitalized and made it better for the locals, when they really needed that. It's not all about making money. I've done that with other ventures. I love to turn areas that once thrived but have been abandoned into green-space parks, walking and biking paths, places where people can enjoy the area."

"So your wolf still longs for nature."

Rafe finished another crab leg. "Yeah. Just as yours wanted to create something that made it easier for women to be wolves."

Someone standing on the beach and looking in their direction caught her eye. Worried that one of her brother's men was spying on them, Jade turned to see who it was. The man wearing jeans, a T-shirt, and sneakers wasn't from her pack, but he was getting ready to take a picture of them. Rafe might not be a movie star celebrity, but his wealth still made him a powerful man.

"There's a guy taking a picture of us. Why in the world would he do that?" She feigned ignorance that Rafe had the kind of wealth and power that would entice the paparazzo to take shots of him. Well, of them.

"The photojournalist taking a picture of the two of us sharing lunch? I make enough money that some people are interested in what I do with my social life. It comes with the territory. Most of the time, I don't even notice photographers unless they get in my way. Do you mind?"

Yeah, she did, because she didn't want people to believe she was dating him when she wasn't, not that she could do anything about it. "I guess not. I just never expected anything like that to happen." Jade wasn't used to mixing with celebrities or billionaires, and she really hadn't thought she'd be caught up in this too. The pictures she'd seen of Rafe all had to do with parties, either that he put on or that he attended, not having lunch at a seafood shack on the beach with a friend.

"Because I'm not a movie star?" He smiled.

She thought he would make one great-looking movie star.

"A confirmed billionaire bachelor raises lots of speculation."

Jade choked on her water. "I…guess he would." She coughed a little bit and tried to catch her breath. She hadn't expected him to tell her the truth.

"Are you okay?"

"Yeah. Thanks. I've never been interested in the lifestyles of the rich and famous. I've never met one in the flesh before. You look pretty ordinary to me."

Rafe smiled.

Her face burned. No way did he look ordinary, but he fit in with the general beach crowd. "I mean, you don't stand out."

His eyes twinkling with mirth, Rafe chuckled and saluted her with his glass of water. "It's been one hell of a way to live."

Now Jade worried that if the photojournalist thought the two of them were an item, he would look into her background and learn who she was. Even if she and Rafe weren't dating, she imagined stories could be made up.

She'd never considered that kind of trouble. One good thing, if he did learn Kenneth was her brother, Kenneth wouldn't screw up this deal by mentioning Toby was her son.

Taking a breath to calm her raw nerves, Jade dove back into the conversation as if she hadn't been concerned about anything. "Do you ever worry about losing it all?"

"Nah. I can live with a lot less and be perfectly happy." Rafe wiped his hands off on a wet towel. "So what is the name of your intimate apparel company?"

She *knew* the lingerie line had really snagged his attention.

"The press will be checking it out and linking the two of us before long, now that a paparazzo has caught us together. A picture of a beautiful woman dining with me won't be enough."

Jade smiled. "Thanks for the compliment." But that's just what she'd been worried about. She cleaned her hands with the warm, soapy cloth and removed her bib. "Sweet and Sassy Secrets. Maybe they'll think you're looking to invest in my silky intimates." She meant her lingerie company, but the roguish gleam in his eye and his wolfish smile said he was thinking of something a lot hotter than that. She felt her whole body flush.

"Most likely," Rafe said, still grinning.

If he didn't hook up with women much—that the press caught sight of, anyway—she figured they'd really be interested in who she was. She thought back to what she and Rafe had been doing earlier. What if a paparazzo, this one possibly, had photographed them kissing on the beach? She'd been too busy worrying about Rafe's cut foot and the lie she was living to think of anything else or notice anyone on the beach.

"When we were on the beach, do you think a paparazzo was taking any shots?"

"Maybe. Sometimes one captures shots of starlets who come to the beach. If one had, what a story that would be. Me rescuing a beautiful woman and...*the rest*."

Jade groaned out loud. *The rest* was what she was worried about. "My reputation is ruined."

He laughed.

"Thanks so much for lunch, Rafe. I...need to head back to my place and get cleaned up." She was still feeling salty and sandy and needed to wash the sea out of her hair and off her skin.

"Want to do something tonight? Besides the run? A movie? Dinner? I mean, if you're alone and want to do something else." He looked so hopeful, and she felt like such a heel.

Jade thought about it and decided seeing too much of him would not be a good idea. The more she was with him, the more she was afraid she'd be caught up in her lies and give away her secrets, including the one she had to keep at all costs. Why she was truly here. At the same time, she needed to continue to see him, but not to the extent that he got the wrong notion.

She didn't want to hurt Rafe. Before he'd rescued her, he was just a billionaire in a bunch of news stories she'd looked up. No one real. But he'd treated her so nicely that she was having an even harder time with this than she'd thought she would.

If she weren't in her current predicament, she would have eagerly taken him up on the offer of spending more time together. He was gallant and generous, fun to be with, and she wanted nothing more than to see him again. But only if she'd had a clear conscience.

"The run will be fine."

Rafe paid the bill. "I'll take you to my favorite place to run."

"That works for me." He'd know the safest places, and she hadn't gone for a run since she got here, so she was itching to stretch her legs as a wolf.

"I'll pick you up at eight."

"Okay." Jade thanked him for lunch.

Before she could suggest meeting him later at his place, he drove into the public-beach parking lot and asked which car was hers. She pointed out her classic 2002 Firebird convertible in canary yellow.

Rafe eyed it appreciably. "I love your car."

She got out of his Ferrari before he could open the door for her and patted the frame. "I have to say the same about yours."

Looking pleased, he smiled. "Seven then?"

"What happened to eight?" She thought he had mistaken the time, but the sparkle in his eyes and the smile on his lips said otherwise. He was cute, she had to admit.

"I can't wait that long."

Jade laughed. "All right. Seven then." She climbed into her car, waved good-bye, and drove off, hating the deception all over again and wishing that this could have been a real date with someone like Rafe. But she couldn't stop thinking about Toby. She was afraid he'd fuss because he wasn't with her, and she hoped Lizzie wouldn't become exasperated and treat Toby poorly.

With her heart in knots, Jade pulled into the parking lot of the Lace & Lavender Bed & Breakfast, a two-story colonial with a wraparound porch surrounded by lavender gardens that had a view of the beach. Her brother was paying for the expensive room so she could stay near Rafe's home. She was planning to get cleaned up, take a nap to make up for the restless sleep she'd had last night, and go on another walk. She couldn't do anything about anything right now, and exercising helped to calm her nerves.

As she parked, the man who had photographed her and Rafe at the Crab Shack jumped out of a Jeep and ran to join her, startling her. She was instantly wary.

"Hi, I'm LK Marks, a photojournalist, and I wanted to get your name for the article I'm writing for *Gossip Galore*."

She hadn't recognized him on the beach because his photo on his website showed a younger man by about twenty years. He was forty-five instead of twenty-five, with a receding hairline, a few wrinkles beneath his eyes, a smattering of gray hairs mixed in with the black, and about twenty or so pounds heavier. "About?" As if she didn't know.

"Rafe Denali. This is the first time I've ever captured him on a date. So if you don't mind, I'd like to get the real story."

"I do mind. But thanks for asking." Jade said it in a really sweet way—smiling and meaning it, not wanting to antagonize the man—and headed inside.

To her annoyance, Marks followed her. She raised a brow, surprised at his boldness, even though she knew she shouldn't have been. That was his job. He wouldn't get anything noteworthy if he was shy and went along with what she was willing to tell him.

"I think we both know your little swim in the Pacific Ocean was a means to get Mr. Denali's attention."

So he had witnessed everything. Had he been stationed near Rafe's house, watching to see if the billionaire took a spin with the woman he'd taken up to his place? Jade wanted to groan.

"And then having lunch with him? Is that why you stayed here? Near where he lives? So you could just *happen* to catch his eye and then risk your neck to get *more* than that?"

Again, she smiled amiably. "What would the odds be of that?"

"Yeah. You'd have to keep walking up the beach for days to catch his eye. Check around to see where he frequented in case you could run into him."

Her heart was beating harder. She was glad he wasn't a wolf and couldn't hear it. She hoped Marks hadn't been spying on her all along.

"I wouldn't have thought the one-piece and short shorts would have caught his attention. Me? I like the skimpy bikinis."

"Then maybe you should return to the beach to catch what you're really after. Good day, Mr. Marks."

"I like your wheels. You're a classy dame. And you've been nice and respectful to me. I'll be nice too." He tipped his head to her and left the bed-and-breakfast.

Jade wondered if he meant he was going to be nice in his version of their story or if he meant something else. She didn't need this right now and hoped her brother didn't learn of it.

Dressed in a bright-yellow-and-orange sundress, Fiona Miller, the bed-and-breakfast owner, was standing behind the check-in counter, a cell phone in her hand. "I was going to call the police if he continued to hassle you." Then she frowned. "You had trouble on the beach?"

"You know I'm from the Texas Panhandle. No rip currents there." Jade shrugged and was about to turn to head to her room when Fiona commented again.

"Rafe Denali, one of California's most confirmed billionaire bachelors, *really* rescued you?"

"Yeah. Who would have guessed?"

"Wow. I wish it had been me. Not that I want to drown or anything, but…wow. I don't know how many times I've walked up that beach, looked up at his house, and wished he was watching *me*."

"I wasn't expecting needing to be rescued, and especially not by someone like him." Jade didn't want anyone to believe she'd pulled a stupid stunt in the hopes that Rafe would come down and rescue her.

Fiona smiled, but she looked like she didn't believe her.

"So," Fiona said, leaning against the counter. "Did he invite you to the social he's hosting? I've heard it's this Friday, and as usual, he doesn't have a date. Since you already had lunch with him…"

Jade wished she'd arranged to drive to Rafe's house instead of having him pick her up. She suspected Mr. Marks was going to watch her every move. And Fiona would speculate even more about what was going on between Jade and Rafe.

Jade shook her head. "Wouldn't have a thing to wear.

Thanks. I'm off to get cleaned up. I'm still covered in salt and sand. Talk later." She hurried off to the stairs. Fiona was nice, but she hadn't been that chatty before. Jade figured she was thrilled to have someone staying at her place who had hooked the billionaire for a date. And who knew what else.

"Later," Fiona called after her in a singsong fashion.

Jade was trying to think of another way to get Aidan's address. What if Rafe had it on a computer? But he would undoubtedly have it password protected. Getting to it without Rafe being right there with her would be a problem too. Unless she was invited to the ball; she could check out the computer while everyone was busy socializing. Still, she didn't have any hacking skills. And what if he didn't have a contact list on his computer anyway?

But as soon as Jade opened the door to her room, she saw her back patio doors were wide open. The ocean breeze was blowing into the room, and she smelled the scent of her brother.

Chapter 5

RAFE MET WITH SEBASTIAN AND DEREK IN HIS PRIVATE GYM to tell them Edward was checking into Jade and her pack's background in Amarillo. He loved this house. He had everything he could want—the pool, the beach, even a small ballroom where he could have his charity balls.

Though Derek had his own personal gym, he liked dropping by to spar with Rafe and Sebastian. Edward too, when he wasn't on a job for Rafe. Or some of the other men who served in various capacities, all trained as bodyguards in case Rafe needed more than one.

"I understand there's a close-up shot of her face while she was taking a shower and no body to go with it," Derek said, punching a bag while Sebastian and Rafe did martial arts training.

Rafe smiled. "Edward tell you?"

"Hell yeah. I knew Edward was looking into the mermaid wolf, and I knew he'd need a picture of her before he could do a thorough search. I just never thought the picture would be of her taking a shower. 'Course, I asked how the hell he got a photo like that, and he assured me you took the shot."

Rafe laughed. "You already saw her."

"Not enough of her!"

"I haven't seen the picture," Sebastian said.

Rafe stopped, moved off the mat to get his phone, then

showed Sebastian the shot of Jade, thinking he needed to get another one that wasn't so hot. Though he couldn't imagine taking any of her that wouldn't look just as sexy.

"Hell, Boss, where's the rest of her?" Sebastian asked.

Rafe shook his head.

"So what do you want me to do about the little lady?" Sebastian asked, much too interested.

"I just need you to know that there's a game afoot. I'm disappointed, of course, that we didn't meet under different circumstances."

Frowning, Sebastian studied the picture further. "Where did you take this? Poolside?"

"Of course."

The shower in Rafe's bathroom had the same glass privacy wall as the pool shower, so the guys couldn't tell which shower Jade had been using.

"I'll have to check your surveillance camera footage and see what you left out."

Rafe laughed. Sebastian wouldn't be able to see what Rafe had because the cameras were only positioned to catch anyone climbing the gates or walls. Rafe wanted his privacy. What if someone broke into his home and stole his surveillance tapes? And saw him shifting as a wolf? And shared that with the world? So there were no security cameras on the inside or around the pool shower, just on the walls and entryways.

"So what do you want me to do?" Sebastian asked.

"Just act your usual charming self."

"Ha!"

Rafe raised a brow as they got back to their training.

"Around *her*? You want me to act my usual charming self? I can see me losing my job in a heartbeat."

Rafe let out his breath. "Nothing can come between us if she's here for nefarious reasons."

"So it's okay if I see her socially afterward? Once the truth is out in the open? If she's not really up to something too bad? Just something small?"

A slow smile appeared on Sebastian's face, and Rafe realized he was giving his personal assistant *the* look that said he was ready for a wolf fight—and not in play.

Sebastian continued to smile. "That's what I figured. The lady is *all* yours."

Derek had stopped punching the bag, waiting to see how this all played out. Then he swore under his breath and started hitting the bag again. "Hell, here I thought I had a shot at her."

———

"What are you doing here?" she growled when she saw her brother sitting on her patio watching the view. He was trying to appear relaxed, but he was drumming his fingers impatiently on the table, his body tense.

Jade didn't want her brother to hear her sprinting heart, the fear racing through her blood. She had never expected Kenneth to sneak into her room. Was he here to threaten Toby further?

"I paid for the place. Seems only fair that I can drop in when I feel the need."

To watch her? Make sure she was doing what he wanted her to?

"You've got a good start. Eating with him. What's next?"

"We're running tonight." She hated having to tell

Kenneth anything, afraid he'd think she wasn't doing enough, fast enough.

"How's that going to help you learn where Rafe's brother is?"

"Kenneth, if you have a problem with gambling debts, I told you I've got money saved. You can have it. Just give me Toby back."

Her brother was out of his chair in an instant with his hand at her throat, pinning her to the wall. He didn't squeeze her throat, just locked on it, his eyes narrowed in anger. "You don't know anything about it. It's none of your affair. Just do this and you're free."

Her blood had turned to ice. She'd never seen her brother in such a rage. "Toby—"

"Yeah, and the damn brat."

"He's your nephew, your flesh and blood," she said, tears in her eyes. She hated showing how emotional this made her when all she wanted to do was hurt him, like he was hurting her.

"He's no kin of mine." Kenneth released her. "I'm watching you. So just keep that in mind. And get the job done."

Then he left.

Wiping the tears off her cheeks, Jade tried to compose herself. She couldn't look like she'd been crying when Rafe saw her next. She checked her neck, but Kenneth had been careful not to bruise her.

How much did her brother owe Grayton? If Kenneth wasn't accepting her savings in payment, he probably owed way more than she could afford.

But she still couldn't understand what Rafe's brother had to do with any of this.

Her room phone rang, and she jumped a little. She grabbed it up, answered, and Fiona said, "I just wanted to check to see if everything is all right. A man just walked through the lobby, and when I asked if I could help him, he said he was your brother and was just dropping by to check on you. I hadn't seen him come in earlier, must have been in the little girl's room for a sec. I know a Kenneth Ashton paid for your room. Was that your brother?"

"Yes, thank you. He said he'd be checking in every once in a while."

"Okay, good. Had me worried for a moment."

Jade couldn't believe her brother had dropped in on her. If only she could get ahold of Lizzie and offer to pay her the savings to turn Toby over to her. But Jade knew Lizzie had every intention of being the coleader of the pack, and freeing Toby was not the way to earn Kenneth's affections. Damn him.

Around six, Jade got a call from Rafe, saying he was downstairs. She was surprised he had arrived so early. She couldn't help worrying that her brother was somewhere just out of sight, watching their every move. She suspected some of his men might be, but the fact that Kenneth was here meant this had to be really serious business. Not that taking her son hostage wasn't serious enough.

As soon as she met Rafe in the lobby, Jade saw Fiona smiling, her cheeks flushed as she talked to him.

Rafe was smiling, congenial, but as soon as he saw Jade coming down the stairs, he said, "Got to go." He slipped his arm around Jade's shoulders, which she really hadn't expected, and headed for the door.

"Have a nice night," Fiona called out.

"Thanks," they both said.

As soon as they were outside, Jade whispered a warning to Rafe. "That photojournalist who took a picture of us at the restaurant? His name was Mr. Marks, and he met me here and asked all kinds of questions. He's probably watching us now." She didn't want to pull away from Rafe, but she didn't want to give Marks the impression something really *was* going on between them. She didn't want to give Rafe that notion either.

Rafe led her to his Ferrari, and when she got in, he shut the door for her and stalked to the driver's side. Once he was seated and took off for his place, he said, "No problem. As long as it doesn't bother you, I don't have any trouble with it."

"I don't, but I didn't want you to have any." She sat back against the seat. "You didn't wait until seven."

"I came early, just in case you wanted to get some dinner," Rafe said. This time he was dressed in jeans, sneakers, and a black T-shirt.

"Someplace casual." She was wearing a pair of pale-blue jeans, tennis shoes, and a floral blouse, but she had a hoodie too, because she figured she'd need it for the cooler ocean breeze later that night. She hadn't planned on dinner, and her stomach was fluttery from apprehension. How long could she play her role without being caught? "How's your foot?" She was afraid he might still have difficulty running on it.

"Much better."

"So you can run all right as a wolf?"

"Yeah, it's healing just fine."

She'd expected him to drive her to his house so they could run along the beach.

When he drove away from the coast, she felt a bit panicky, her skin prickling with unease. "Where are we going?"

"Someplace where I love to get away and run."

"Far from here?"

"A ways out."

When he pulled up to a small airport, she stared in shock. "We're *flying* somewhere? You don't mean to run at the airfield, I take it."

"We're flying to Big Bear Lake."

"Ohmigod, this is…" Jade couldn't even finish what she was going to say. He was already leading her to the hangar, but she didn't see a pilot waiting for them.

"Going to be fun," Rafe finished for her. "You probably haven't been there, have you?"

She shook her head as she climbed into the jet and saw seating for about seven, with room for skis, golf clubs, whatever a jet-setter would need. This was amazing. She'd never expected anything like this. When he moved into the cockpit, she was even more surprised. "*You're* flying?"

"Been flying since they invented airplanes, practically. Air Force fighter pilot. Flew in two wars. Not that anyone would ever know. I used a couple of other identities back then." He motioned to an icebox. "There are drinks in here, if you'd like something before dinner."

"Where are we eating?"

"At the best little bar and grill in California."

"That sounds good." She pulled out bottles of water

and sat in the copilot's seat. Rafe talked about the places they were flying over while she watched the scenery pass beneath her.

She was feeling a little better about Toby because Lizzie had shared a video of them earlier this evening on her cell phone. They were playing hide-and-seek, and Toby appeared really happy. The video had been taken indoors, and Jade didn't recognize the sparsely furnished place. She imagined her brother had assumed she'd be too distracted from her mission if she was worried about her son and so had had someone take the videos. Unfortunately, they had disabled the geotagging feature so she couldn't get a location on it.

"Does your brother take jets around like this too?"

"Yes, but he has a pilot fly him wherever he needs to go."

Jade bit her lip, realizing this was the perfect opportunity to broach the subject of his whereabouts and said, "So he has a long way to come to get to your place?"

"A fair way."

"From where?" she asked, hating this.

"All over." Rafe gave her a charming smile, but she swore something about his response said he didn't trust her. Was she just being paranoid now?

And how could she ask again without it sounding odd?

When they landed at another small airport, she kept thinking how this was the experience of a lifetime. She hated the deception but didn't know what else she could do to rescue her son from her brother.

After she and Rafe left the plane, he escorted her to the parking lot, where he unlocked a black Yukon Denali.

"It has your name on it," she said. He didn't own a car company too, did he?

"That's why I bought it. It's the perfect four-wheel drive SUV for trips to the lake. But it isn't named after our family. I thought it was a nice touch."

"How many cars *do* you have?" she asked.

"I have several in various locations so that when I arrive, I'm all set to go. Cars are kind of a passion of mine. I have a dozen scattered around."

He drove her to the Bear Paw Bar and Grille, where two carved wooden bears stood out front on a wooden porch. The overhang on the porch shaded guests sitting on benches, waiting to be called when their tables were ready.

A garden surrounded the sides and back, and Jade and Rafe walked around so she could see the garden seating, fountains, and flowers. Bronze statues of bears were on display: one on its back with a cub climbing onto its belly, another fishing for koi in a pond at the edge of the gardens, another taking a sip of water out of a fountain. Stained glass hangings of bears were situated all over the gardens, catching the sunlight and looking fairylike. Wondrously whimsical. Jade loved it and would have loved showing it to Toby.

When they walked inside, she figured Rafe would give his name to the hostess and they'd have a long wait out on the porch like the others—maybe about twenty in all—but he didn't even have to give the hostess his name. She smiled at Rafe as if he were her best friend and said, "Right this way, Mr. Denali."

Jade had never been with anyone who had that kind of influence. She closed her gaping mouth as several

people waiting for tables glanced at them, probably
wondering why they got immediate seating. She touched
Rafe's arm and whispered, "We shouldn't cut—"

Then a woman waiting with a family asked the hostess, "We can't make reservations, but they just arrive
and get seated?"

"He's the owner," the hostess said, smiling.

All gazes instantly switched to him.

Someone whispered, "He's the billionaire."

"He owns the place?" someone else asked.

Jade looked up at Rafe. He shrugged and said for her
hearing only, "The owner doesn't need to have a reservation. He just has his personal assistant call ahead, and
he always gets the best seat in the house."

Jade laughed and slipped her arm through his, rethink-
ing their preferential treatment as the hostess escorted
them to a table with a view overlooking the gardens.
"Okay, I agree with you there. It would be strange if
you had to wait to be seated at your own restaurant. This
is truly the best experience I've ever had. I can't thank
you enough for saving me in the ocean and making my
vacation the grandest one ever."

"I'm glad you're enjoying this. Just think of it as a
Californian's welcome to the great grizzly bear state."
He slipped his arm around her shoulders and gave her a
squeeze. Something had changed between them, though
she wasn't sure what. He was still friendly and interested, but she sensed a subtle change in him. He was
more reserved, she thought. She worried again that he
knew she was a fraud.

He pulled her chair out for her, and once they were
seated, they looked over the menus and ordered their meals.

"Do you look a lot like your brother?" Jade asked, trying to figure out something to say to lead him into revealing something of his brother's whereabouts.

"A fair amount."

Their salads, rolls, and drinks arrived, and while they ate their salads, Jade said, "I had a friend whose twin sister looked just like her, and they pulled all kinds of pranks on boyfriends. Have you ever used your similar looks to pretend you are your brother or vice versa?"

Rafe smiled a little. "A time or two. We couldn't do it with our kind. Our scents would give us away. But if we weren't together, we could pass ourselves off in each other's place."

"When you were young? Or do you still do it today?"

"When we were young, we did it on purpose. Today, it's a case of mistaken identity. Aidan doesn't live where I do, but if he visits the places I frequent without me, or with one of our mutual friends, they've thought Aidan was me."

"Does he tell them he isn't?"

"No. They call him Mr. Denali, and since he is also named Denali, he just leaves it at that. Technically, his title is doctor, but rather than confuse the clerk or waiter, he doesn't correct him or her. Now, if the person has a business relationship with me and needs to speak to me about it, he'll explain he's my brother and tell the person to call me."

Their filet mignons and baked potatoes were served, and Jade took in the delightful aroma of the beef. "So your brother visits you often?" she asked, slicing into her tender steak.

"Not very. I'm sure if he did more frequently and people saw us together at the same spots, they wouldn't be as apt to make the mistake."

"Are you close?"

"We are."

"But you don't see each other that much."

"We're both busy with our own endeavors."

She didn't know what else she could say to get him to reveal where his brother was.

After the meal, Rafe drove Jade to a lodge he owned. The walls and high-vaulted ceilings were covered in cedar paneling. Everything from lamps to paintings featured grizzly bears, except for an intricately detailed yacht model in a glass case hanging on one wall.

"Beautiful yacht. You didn't put it together, did you?" she teased. It would have taken days to do it, and she couldn't imagine him taking the time to work on all the painstaking details when he was probably too busy making his millions.

"Yep."

"Do you do a lot of them?" she asked, impressed. She walked over to the model and studied the fine work. "It's beautiful."

"No, just that one."

"The *Lo-Lee*," she read on the side of the yacht, just in front of the stern.

"That's her name. My mother's, Lois, and my father's, Lee."

"Oh, how nice."

"I could have taken you out for a spin on the yacht."

"You mean this is a model of a real yacht?" she asked, shocked.

"Yeah, at the marina. We could go tomorrow, maybe? If you'd like? I haven't been out on it in ages."

"Wow. I don't know. I could get seasick." Heaving her guts out over the bow would be just delightful.

"We'll do it."

She noticed he was a take-charge kind of wolf. She didn't mind because if she really didn't want to do something, she would say no. "Okay, as long as nothing else comes up by then." Just in case. She glanced around at the rest of the room, surprised that it was decorated in a bear motif. "I would think you'd have everything decorated in wolves rather than bears here."

"I would have, but this is Big Bear Lake, and it goes with the territory. It would seem a bit odd to have all wolves. Though I had considered it. Let's have some wine on the porch, and we can enjoy the sunset."

He brought out a bottle of Cabernet, sharp cheddar cheese, and salty crackers, setting everything out on the patio table, then they sat on the porch waiting for the sun to set.

"Are you enjoying yourself so far?" he asked.

"I am."

"Enough to help inspire your work on your creations?"

She nodded, smiling when the bands of orange and purple streaked across the sky and reflected off the glassy lake. "Just beautiful."

"I love it here, as much as seeing the sun set poolside at the house. Are you ready to run?"

"I am."

He showed her a guest room where she could strip and shift, and then he left her alone. She was afraid he might try to come on to her while they were here, especially since she'd already kissed him earlier on the beach.

The problem was that she would have a hard time keeping *her* distance. She needed to keep this as a friendship with absolutely no benefits whatsoever.

She felt his interest—the lingering gazes, the focus on her mouth or curves—and yes, the wolfish awareness was still there. But he didn't seem to be acting on instinct. Maybe he wanted to show her he could be a friend first and build a relationship more slowly. But she couldn't really see him doing anything slowly. Not the way he kept asking her out and then even coming early tonight to get to spend more time with her.

She let out her breath, telling herself to chill and to quit trying to analyze this so much.

When she joined him as a wolf, she thought he was beautiful, his coat mostly gray and black, his face tan, and his eyes big, brown, and discerning. When he saw the way she looked as a wolf, he smiled a little, showing off his canines, showing he admired her wolf appearance.

Appreciating his attention, she smiled back, and then he led the way through a wolf door in the den that opened up to the deck. He ran through the woods surrounding Big Bear Lake. She soaked up the smells and the sights and sounds, loving the chance to run with a wolf like Rafe. But she knew it would be short-lived.

She saw a whip-poor-will, a couple of mockingbirds, a nighthawk, and a hoot owl. A bunny scampered out of her sight, and two squirrels stopped playing to see the wolves, then raced up the tree and out of danger.

Rafe led her to a sandy shore where an interesting

rock formation sat in the lake. He began to swim out to it. No rip currents here. This was more like home, except that the water was cooler than in Texas. When they reached the rock formation, they climbed all over it and then sat and rested at the top near a pine tree while she looked out on the lake, the San Bernardino Mountains, and the pine forest. She wished *this* was her life. She could really see living at this lodge with Toby and doing all her design work here.

Running in the forests at night, being part of the natural order of things, teaching her son about their other halves. She'd love it all. And she knew her little boy would too.

After a half hour or so, Rafe licked her cheek and headed down the rock formation into the water again. They swam together to shore. On the return trip, Jade smelled raccoons, coyotes, foxes, and bobcats in the areas they traversed. Even deer and a black bear, but she didn't see any of them. She smelled the fragrance of wild roses and the scent of pine. Though she was loving everything about this excursion, she started worrying about her son again. Did Kenneth intend to take Dr. Aidan Denali hostage until he had the cure for their aging process?

She hadn't thought so at first, but the more she thought about it, the more likely it was that Kenneth planned something violent. She couldn't trade her son for the doctor's life. She couldn't let Aidan be taken hostage either.

If she told Rafe, she was afraid he would dump her back at her bed-and-breakfast and tell her to deal with it after she'd deceived him. He might not even care

about a child she'd had by a human, just like her own
pack didn't.

When Jade and Rafe returned to the cottage, she
was still feeling anxious about her mission. She didn't
believe she had much of a choice but to do as her brother
told her to do, up to a point. Then? She wasn't sure what
she would do, but she wasn't going to risk Aidan's life
if Kenneth had anything like that in mind.

What if she could hire someone to search for her
brother and rescue her son? But what if Kenneth learned
of her deception?

She feared that would be the end of her son.

Rafe noticed the constant changes in Jade's emotions.
He assumed she was enjoying being with him but
was afraid he'd learn the truth about her shenanigans
before long. What was driving her to be here? She
seemed so genuinely happy at times, like when she
was eating with him or running through the woods
with him as a wolf, yet when she took a breather
atop the rocks, looking out at the vista, she seemed
to no longer be in quiet awe but again troubled. He
swore he saw a tear roll down her cheek, but then
he figured it was just a drop of water from the swim
across the lake.

Still, he could tell she wasn't always "with" him.

He couldn't stand not knowing the truth. He was
used to getting at the root of things, not patiently waiting them out like he was trying to do with Jade. He kept
thinking back to things she'd said. How she and her
brother were not getting along, yet she'd stayed with

the pack. Coercion? Desperation? Fear of leaving and being on her own?

If he took things further with her, would she come clean and finally tell him she was currently mated? Or something else just as bad?

Maybe she needed money to be able to leave the pack since she wasn't getting along with her brother. Rafe would give her the money if it meant she could be happy. The more he thought about it, the more he wanted to do it. From what Edward had learned, she had a moderate income from her apparel business, but any specialty business could have real losses during downswings in the economy.

Rafe could give her a low-interest loan, if that would make her feel better about accepting money from him. Then she could go wherever she wanted to live and create her apparel lines to her heart's content. Hell, he could even invest in her business and help her make it a success, like the self-made billionaires did on the *Shark Tank* TV show. Rafe could be considered a wolf version of the "sharks."

He could really get into that. He always loved having a goal in mind. Especially in this situation when he couldn't make himself see Jade in a bad light, no matter how much he told himself he'd better be prepared for the worst. In any event, he needed to talk with Sebastian and Aidan before he decided to make any kind of financial offer to Jade. Hell, several times he'd wanted to ask her what was going on. But he really wanted her to tell him the truth on her own.

—᷍᷍᷍—

Jade shifted and dressed in the guest room. The double bed was covered in a patchwork quilt featuring all kinds of different bears, and a large faux polar bear rug covered the floor in front of a fireplace. She'd loved the run, but when she had sat atop the rocks, she'd felt saddened that Rafe had treated her so wonderfully, and she was here under false pretenses.

When she returned to the living room, she found Rafe locking up the cottage.

"Ready to return to your place?" he asked, his gaze catching hers, making her feel deceitful all over again.

"Oh, yes, absolutely. I had a wonderful time."

Then they were off, his smile in place, but he seemed distant, which made her worry. "Is anything wrong?"

"Real estate deal," he said. He shrugged and drove her to the airport. They were soon airborne and were quiet as they flew across the state.

"It didn't work out?" she finally asked, not knowing enough about real estate investments to ask much. And she didn't want to sound like she was prying into his business, not when she needed to focus on his brother.

"Some investors are sharks. Win some, lose some. No big deal."

Okay, so it had nothing to do with her, and she felt a bit of relief over that.

When he dropped her off at her room in the bed-and-breakfast, he seemed reluctant to leave without kissing her, but a stone wall seemed to have been erected between them. She was glad she couldn't date him. She wouldn't care for the ups and downs in their relationship just because of a sour investment, and she wondered if he was showing his true personality. Yet deep down, she didn't think so.

"Thank you, again," she said. "I don't know when I've ever had more fun."

"Me too." He leaned over and kissed her cheek, that one little kiss making her feel he wanted more but saying he needed to cool it and couldn't get involved.

Which was for the best. So why did it bother her so much?

She smiled. "Night." She opened her door, walked in and locked it, then sank to the floor, hating what she had become.

Chapter 6

WHILE SITTING ON HIS PATIO TALKING WITH EDWARD over the phone that night about all he'd figured out concerning Jade, Rafe learned she did have a small lingerie company and a separate children's clothing line. She was from Amarillo, and she was a member of a pack there led by her brother, Kenneth Ashton.

As far as Edward could determine, she'd had no run-ins with anyone, was a model citizen, and wasn't mated.

"Hey, Boss, it's a hell of a far-out notion, but what if this has something to do with your brother?" Edward said.

"Aidan?" As if Rafe had any other.

"Yeah. I tried getting ahold of him, but you know how he is. If he's busy conducting research, he won't answer calls from anyone but you, in case it's an emergency. What if this pertains to his research? Could you check with him and see if he took blood samples from their pack?"

"Yeah, I sure will. Get back with you in a bit."

That was one thing Rafe had never considered. But if Jade and her pack were up to no good concerning his brother…? He growled, rose from his lounger, and gave his brother a call.

"Yeah, what's up, Rafe?" Aidan asked. "Must be important if you're calling."

"Did you have any dealings with a pack in Amarillo? By the name of Ashton? Kenneth Ashton, the pack leader?"

"*Yeah*," Aidan said, elongating the word as if he was expecting bad news.

"Okay, you've only taken blood samples from about ten wolf packs, since *lupus garous* aren't listed as such in any directory, right? So your sample size isn't all that big."

"No, but I keep finding new packs to test. What's this all about?"

Was it mere coincidence that Aidan had taken blood from Jade's pack, and then she just happened to be vacationing on this beach down the road from his estate?

Rafe didn't think so.

So why was she here? Nearly drowning herself in front of his home? She had to have seen him and Derek lounging poolside. Had she taken the chance to catch his eye? It was a long shot but still possible. He ran his hand through his hair and paced across his patio. Hell, he really liked her too.

"Okay, listen. I don't know what's going on exactly, and I know you hate these charity functions—worse, I might be setting you up for trouble—but I need to make sure you're coming to the charity ball I'm having on Friday night."

"About that… I'm in the middle of research and was going to bow out this time—"

"It's important. I think someone wants to learn what your research is all about, and they're using a she-wolf to do it."

"Wait. A she-wolf?" Aidan sounded intrigued.

"Yeah. Hell, I keep hoping there's nothing to it. That she's just the dream she appears to be." Rafe explained to his brother about rescuing her. "She seems so sweet and innocent."

"Sounds like she's a siren of the sea and she's pulled you right in. And that never happens, as wary as you are."

"That's what concerns me. Since you took blood from their pack, I just find her appearance suspicious."

"Statistically speaking, I'd have to agree with you. Do you have a picture of her?"

"Yeah, hold on." Rafe uploaded the outdoor shower photo of her, figuring his brother would react as everyone else had. He really should have taken another picture of her.

"Hot damn, when the hell did you take *that* shot?"

"She was rinsing off in the outdoor shower after being dunked in the ocean."

"Where's the rest of her?"

Rafe chuckled. "Come to the function and you can see the rest of her. Clothed." He wanted to be the only one seeing her completely naked. "I'll have plenty of protection there for you. I want you to come early and meet her."

"Play cat-and-mouse games?"

"Yeah, like old times." Rafe hated to do that when he really liked Jade. But he couldn't risk his brother's safety. If he and Aidan could deal with this at the ball, learn what was truly going on, so much the better.

"She's beautiful," Aidan said. "Though I'm curious if you took more of a shot of her and you're just not sharing."

"Of course she's beautiful. What better way to capture my attention? And no, I only captured her face surreptitiously. She was naked."

"On purpose? I mean, trying to catch your attention?"

"No, she was in a rush to get back into her swimsuit. You know what it's like to wear one that's still covered with salt and sand."

"Yeah, irritating. What's her name? I'll look her up in my database and see if I have any notes that'll help jog my memory."

"Jade Ashton."

"Take a sec." The tapping of keys sounded in the background.

Hell, Rafe hated that he was sweating, hoping beyond hope that Jade being there was perfectly innocent. But knowing that wasn't the case, no matter how much he tried to delude himself.

"Okay, how much do you like kids?"

"What?" Rafe was getting a really bad feeling about this. Had she lost her mate and she was raising kids on her own? Sure wolves loved pups—in their wolf pack. Sometimes lone wolves would mate with a wolf that had lost her mate and help raise the pups. And certainly a single *lupus garou* could fall in love with a she-wolf and raise her kids as his own. Rafe didn't see himself in that category though. He wasn't a playboy in that he couldn't settle down with one woman—but she had to be a she-wolf. He hadn't met any in his circle of friends.

Yet, he couldn't see himself raising someone else's kid. He'd have to deal with being a father from the ground up and get used to the idea while the baby was growing in his mate's belly. Then he would have plenty of time to prepare himself mentally.

"I remember her because she had a son—about three years old, light-blond hair, long curls, dark-brown eyes, shy and clingy. He stuck to his mother, holding on to her leg or hand the whole time. Three other she-wolves were in the pack, but the boy wouldn't go to anyone else when I had to draw blood from Jade."

"Her mate?"

"No male came forward to take care of the boy either. Toby was his name. I wanted to test him too, but Jade wouldn't let me, which was another reason I remember her so well. In fact, everyone looked horrified. I thought it was odd. When I explained he wouldn't be hurt in any way, except for feeling the prick of the needle, she just shook her head. Before I could say anything further, the pack leader said, 'Next?' And then Jade and her son disappeared from the family room. I was busy with the rest of the pack members after that, and then I was ushered out. She must have had an important role in the pack, because the pack leader had her go after he gave blood."

"His sister."

"Okay, makes sense. So…how do you feel about kids?"

Rafe snorted. "I'm not mating the wolf. I just want to know what she and her pack are up to."

"All right, I'll come. But not early. I've got to let these cultures work their magic, so I'll fly in that afternoon."

"Okay, good show."

"What are you going to do about the lady?"

"Continue to treat her like a woman after my own heart." Which was what made this whole situation so disagreeable. Rafe really did feel like he could fall for her. But now with this new wrinkle of having a kid?

Edward arrived at the house, found Rafe on the patio, and handed him a catalog of Jade's women's apparel — sexy, yet tasteful. Jade hadn't acted as though she was trying to impress Rafe or come on to him, not like some women who hoped the confirmed bachelor would finally settle down.

She acted like she was interested in him—a wolf's interest couldn't be hidden from another, not with their enhanced ability to identify scents—but she'd said no to dinner and a movie and had only wanted to run, until he changed her mind. Maybe it was because she was hurrying home soon—to a son—and she didn't think Rafe would be interested in helping to raise him. Maybe she'd had a bad experience with losing a mate? He didn't think so, or she wouldn't have kissed him like she did.

But she couldn't know for certain that he'd object to her son. What woman would want to leave all this behind when she had a shot at becoming his mate?

A woman who was trouble.

—⁂—

Jade called her brother to let him know her progress and asked to speak with her son. It was killing her to be apart from Toby for this long, and she hoped the people taking care of him wouldn't treat him meanly when they weren't videotaping him playing with Lizzie. She didn't really trust any of them. Not after they'd taken him from her.

"He's sound asleep. Hell, it's two in the morning. Did you find out where Aidan is?" Kenneth asked, getting to the business at hand.

"No. I don't want Rafe to suspect I'm trying to learn where his brother is because of the research he does. There's no sign of any mail he keeps around the house. I'm certain he has an office, but he's always with me and his computer would be password protected anyway. Same with his phone. It's always on him, but even if I managed to grab it, I'm certain it would have a password. Not to mention he would smell my scent on his stuff if I tried to sneak a peek when he wasn't around. I keep asking in subtle ways, but Rafe hasn't said."

"Need I remind you that the doctor will turn his research into a moneymaking proposition? If a wolf wants to live longer, he'll have to pay the price. If he wants to survive—should our longevity shorten more quickly—well, the power to decide who lives and who dies shouldn't be in the hands of one man. Or, I should say, Aidan and his brother. I truly believe Rafe will be the one to set the price on wolves' lives, since he's the ruthless businessman in the family."

Holding Toby's rainbow bear close to her heart and wishing she was holding Toby in her arms instead, Jade looked out her window at the ocean. She wished Rafe was far away from her. What would he think of her having a human son? Would he be just as condemning as her people were? Even so, she didn't want to hurt him. Or his brother either.

"Kenneth, I want to know what this is all about. What do you plan to do if you find out where Aidan lives?"

Silence. She would kill her brother. She knew now that he planned to do more than just talk to Aidan.

"If you're thinking of telling Rafe what this is all about—"

"No. I just…I just thought if I had a good enough reason to approach him—"

"I don't give a damn how you find out as long as Rafe doesn't suspect anything." Then Kenneth gentled his tone, though it sounded like it was killing him to try to convince her he was in the right. "Listen, from what the good doctor told me, he's close to making a breakthrough. He said a cure will cost almost prohibitive amounts because development would cost him so much. So anyone who wants the cure will have to be ready to pay," Kenneth said.

For all the research Aidan was most likely conducting, Jade understood.

"None of our pack members will be able to afford the price Aidan intends to charge. You and I agreed that the cure should be available to everyone."

She did agree…to an extent. If they were suddenly going to turn to dust—yes. Her son would lose her, and there was no one else to raise him. She couldn't bear the thought. But if the drug just returned them to their previous longevity, which wasn't vital for survival? No.

"Why not just let Aidan work on a cure, or something that will reverse the condition, until he actually has the product? When he begins charging exorbitant amounts for it, wolf packs can unite and help pay his costs and a salary, and then force him to make the cure available to all wolves."

"By then, he and his brother will have a real force in place to ensure they're well protected. You know how it is with wealthy men."

She also knew her brother well enough to suspect that when he had learned a geneticist was working on this, he'd wanted a piece of the pie—a way to sell the fountain of youth to *lupus garous* all over—so that *he'd* be making a lot of the money, not giving the cure away to wolves at a reasonable price. She wished Aidan had never found their pack. Then her brother would never have learned about the doctor's work.

"I thought your business was doing great," she said.

"Jade, damn it, Rafe Denali took over our grand-parents' company and forced them to lose everything they'd worked so hard to build. Do you want the power over how long we live in the hands of someone so cold-blooded?" Kenneth ignored her mention of his business, and now she suspected he was in serious trouble.

She kept reminding herself that her son was the pawn in this whole matter, and little Toby would be expend-able if she didn't do what her brother demanded of her.

When she didn't say anything, Kenneth said, "Just remember where your loyalty lies."

She was careful not to respond. She knew just where her loyalty remained—not with him or with the pack, but with her son.

"Call me tomorrow to let me know your progress." Then he hung up on her.

She ground her teeth and threw the phone at the bed. She would kill her brother if he harmed her son in any way.

―――⁂―――

That night, when Rafe went to bed, he couldn't sleep. He kept thinking about Jade and her dark, chocolate-brown eyes and how her hair had caressed him in the ocean as they'd held on to each other and treaded water. Or how her curls had tickled his shoulders when she'd been lying on top of him, kissing him on the shore. He couldn't quit thinking about the way she'd rested against his groin with her sweet body, her tongue tangling with his. Or how she'd held his foot in her lap, treating his injury so gently.

Or run with him as a wolf through the woods, genuinely enjoying the area. It certainly wouldn't have been the same if he had taken a human woman to the grill. For one thing, the women he knew were all wealthy in their own right. They wouldn't be awed by taking a spur-of-the-moment private jet trip to have dinner somewhere. That was just something they did if the mood dictated. He had enjoyed seeing the joy the trip had brought Jade, even though he could tell she'd been trying hard not to appear overjoyed like a kid at Christmas. Even that had endeared her to him. But he didn't like how troubled she seemed sometimes, as if her reason for being here was not something she was happy to do.

He tossed onto his side. He shouldn't have wanted more time with her. But he couldn't help wanting to learn more about her—about her mate and her son. He told himself he only cared as far as it pertained to his brother and his work. But he couldn't fool himself. She was like a breath of fresh sea air, both luring and intriguing.

But family and friends meant everything to him. If someone came into his life with a sinister plan to use his brother for his or her own greed or some other despicable purpose, Rafe couldn't forgive that.

The notion that Jade had a son? That was another story. Just the fact she had left him behind to come here on vacation said something about her parenting skills. She wanted to protect him from giving blood samples, but was willing to abandon him for over a week to take a break so she could come up with more designs for her company?

He raked his fingers through his hair. That didn't make any sense.

From what his brother had said, the boy was completely attached to his mother and no one else in the pack, which was unusual, but it also meant that leaving him behind was cruel.

Hell, no matter what, Rafe couldn't get the she-wolf out of his thoughts so he could get any sleep. Throwing off his covers, he headed outside. He ran down the steps and pushed the gate aside, closing it and shifting in the dark. Then he ran as a wolf, straight to the bed-and-breakfast where Jade was staying.

He wanted to growl and howl at the moon as he stood beneath her balcony, desiring her with a wolf's craving, hating how hung up he was on the she-wolf, and swearing he would learn the truth one way or another. He ran for ten miles that night, not caring if anyone saw the "loose" dog running along the beach, but when he returned home, he still couldn't quit thinking of the woman.

And he was back to Plan A: question her in a subtle way and try to get her to tell him the truth on her own. He couldn't help it. He already cared too much about her to do it any other way.

⁓

Early the next morning, Jade jogged down the beach as others ran or walked on the firmly packed wet sand. This time she was headed away from Rafe's home. She no longer needed to catch his attention. She'd gotten it. Every time she talked to her brother, she wanted to strangle him, and jogging helped her to focus. She was beyond furious that Kenneth hadn't let her speak to her son this morning either. Yes, Toby might have been asleep, but her brother's refusal made her worry that he was trying to prove *he* was in charge of her and her son because she was asking too many questions.

She returned to the bed-and-breakfast and was taking a shower when she heard her cell phone ring. Turning off the water, she grabbed a towel and hurried to get the phone, fearing it was her brother, intending to dictate further rules or threaten her son's life again. As soon as he had taken her son hostage, she knew she'd have to take drastic measures of her own. Not against Rafe or his brother, but against *her* brother.

After this call, she was contacting a PI. Then she took a deep breath. Hell, she didn't know any. And she didn't want to risk contacting one who wasn't a wolf.

Jade grabbed her phone and saw the caller was Rafe. After she said hello, she practically held her breath.

"Do you want to go for a run?"

She sagged with profound relief, glad he hadn't discovered the reason she was here. "Sorry, I jogged down the beach and just had my shower."

"But no breakfast?"

"You'll miss your jog. You'd get all out of shape, and I couldn't allow that to happen."

He laughed. "Then come with me."

"Once per morning is enough for me. We can run again tonight if you'd like and don't have any other plans."

"All right. I can go for a swim and you could join me. What time do you want to come over for breakfast?"

She let out her breath, wishing that she could see him for different reasons. Although she could imagine

Toby being a major turnoff for Rafe if he had been here with her. She couldn't do this anymore. She'd tossed and turned all night, running different scenarios through her mind. Rafe would probably know a wolf who was a certified PI. But could she ask without him learning why she needed one? She had to risk it.

She swallowed hard. "Rafe…I-I need to ask you something."

He didn't say anything, and she was afraid the line had gone dead.

She gritted her teeth. She couldn't let him know she was about to break down over this. "Are you still there?" she asked, her voice softer than she wanted it to be. She almost wished the connection had been lost. If her brother knew what she was going to do…

"Yeah." Rafe's voice was dark, gruff.

She took a deep, steadying breath. She truly was risking everything by doing this, but she didn't trust her brother. She was scared for Toby. She was worried about the doctor. She needed to try to resolve this herself. "I have…kind of a problem."

Again, complete silence. Did he know?

Her heart in her throat, Jade paced across the floor. "I need…I need to hire a private investigator. But I don't know any. Not who are wolves. I hoped you might know of one." She was trying so hard not to sound like she was falling apart, but the tears were already welling up in her eyes, and despite how hard she was trying to keep them at bay, they began spilling down her cheeks. She didn't want him to know how upset she was. Or how grave a situation her son could be in.

"What's this all about, Jade?"

"It's…it's personal. I just…"

"I'm coming over to get you."

"No, I just…" She should have known Rafe would want to take charge, when she couldn't have him involved. She had to do this on her own. Make it look from all outward appearances like she was doing what Kenneth had told her to do. She was afraid Rafe would act differently around her, like he knew what was going on. Only, her PI would be searching for Toby to rescue him, and then she would vanish with her son like she had done before.

"I'm coming over," Rafe said again. "I'll be there in a minute."

"No. I'll… I'll…" She broke down and sobbed. Damn it.

Not in a million years had Rafe expected this. Not that he knew what "this" was, but he was damn well going to learn the truth. Why the hell did Jade need a PI, and why was she sobbing her heart out, unable to say anything more?

Damn it to hell. He was rushing out of the kitchen, phone to his ear, when he saw Edward coming from the front of the house.

"Hold on," Rafe said to Jade. He covered the mouthpiece. "Edward, I'm headed over to the bed-and-breakfast. Jade needs a PI, and she's sobbing her heart out."

"She's in some kind of trouble then."

"Or it's all a ploy to catch my interest by pretending something terrible is happening and then reeling me right in," Rafe said, heading out to the garage.

"Okay, Boss. You just let me know how you want me to handle this."

"For now, just keep out of sight. I think she'll feel freer to talk to me if we're alone. I'll call you as soon as I know what's going on."

"You got it. Do you want me to tell Sebastian too?"

"Yeah, let him know I need privacy for a while."

"Gotcha."

Rafe got in his car and peeled out of the garage and down the driveway. "Jade, listen. Whatever it is, we'll work it out. I'm on my way. Talk to me."

The phone clicked dead in his ear.

Shit.

He sped down the road, frantic to reach her, hoping this really wasn't some part of a game plan. He'd sworn he'd never again be taken in by a crying woman after he'd had the misfortune to date one who cried at whim. But Jade's sobs wrenched at his gut. What would cause that kind of heartbreak?

He'd bet his first million bucks that her little boy, Toby, was at the root of the heartbreak. And that it was very real. Not part of *her* game plan at all. And it was scaring Jade to pieces.

As soon as he pulled into the parking lot at the bed-and-breakfast, he saw Jade's car. Relieved that she hadn't taken off, he stalked into the inn and tried to mask his growly wolf side when he saw Fiona at the check-in counter. She smiled sweetly, but hell, he couldn't manage anything more than a growled "Morning."

Then he tore up the stairs to Jade's room.

He was trying damn hard to rein in his temper, and he didn't have time for niceties. He just hoped Fiona wasn't ready to call the police, saying some enraged billionaire was about to terrorize one of her guests.

He banged on the door before he thought better of hitting it so hard. "Jade, it's me. Let me in."

He wanted to take her to his place. He was worried that the bed-and-breakfast's walls were too thin for the discussion that was about to take place.

She didn't answer the door.

"Damn it, Jade," he said, growling, but his voice was much softer in volume now, hopefully low enough that Fiona couldn't hear him. "Open up. I'm not leaving until you do."

He heard footfalls on the stairs and turned his glower in that direction.

Fiona.

He had to give her credit for looking worried about her guest and brave enough to approach him.

"Is there something wrong, Mr. Denali?" Fiona asked, her words soft and polite.

"Nah. We can't agree on what to eat for breakfast." He gave Fiona a small smile.

She looked worriedly at the door.

"The door's unlocked, Rafe," Jade said, sounding like she was calling from the bathroom.

"The door's unlocked," he told Fiona, as if she hadn't heard Jade say it already, to remind the manager that he was there by invitation, not in coercion.

"She likes fruit…for breakfast," Fiona said. "When she eats here. If either of you need anything…"

"Nah, we're fine. The door's unlocked. Sorry for all the racket." He waited for her to leave.

Fiona hesitated and nodded, then slowly descended the stairs, clearly reluctant to leave.

Rafe let himself in, locking the door behind him. He

instantly smelled a male wolf's scent in the room. Was it her brother, or one of the men of his pack?

Rafe found her sitting on the porch, overlooking the gardens and the beach.

"I'd prefer to discuss this at my place. Less of a chance for anyone to overhear what's going on," he said, standing behind her, trying not to intrude in her space.

She was dabbing her eyes and cheeks, and blowing her nose, just staring out at the vista.

He had to remind himself she could still be one hell of an actress, but he really didn't believe it. He took in a deep breath and pulled her from the chair and into his arms. "Jade," he said softly.

And she sobbed all over his bare chest. Hell, in his rush, he'd left the house wearing only his board shorts.

—∿∿—

Rafe spent an hour trying to calm Jade down enough that he could take her back to his place. She'd even wanted to walk down the beach to avoid Fiona, but Rafe wouldn't hear of it.

"Everyone has meltdowns like this from time to time," he reassured her.

She looked up at him with red, teary eyes.

"Well, when I do it, I do more ranting and raving than sobbing."

That earned him a little smile. He was dying to learn what the matter was.

"Whatever this is all about, we'll deal with it, all right?"

"Breakfast," Jade said, giving a cute little snort as she remembered what he'd told Fiona to explain the difficulty between them.

"Hell, I'm not really good at coming up with a story when a woman I care about is sobbing her heart out behind a locked door."

"It wasn't locked."

Rafe smiled. "I didn't know that at first." For an hour, he'd held her on his lap, just comforting her, watching the seagulls, listening to her heart beating, feeling the heat of her body pressed against him in the warm summer breeze. He hoped to hell they could work it all out. Whatever it was.

"We can stay here until nightfall, if you'd like, but I'd really like to get you to my place and take care of this as quickly as possible."

She began to move off his lap, and Rafe realized he should have said that earlier. Then again, she hadn't seemed to hear much of anything he was saying before.

He was on his feet right away, following her into the room, and then locking the door to the balcony. He stopped her before they got very far. "Why don't we grab a bag of your things?"

She glanced up at him, seemingly confused.

"I think you should stay the night at my place." He didn't want to push any further than that. "If you decide you don't want to, no problem. But if you decide you'd rather not be alone, then you'll be all set."

Jade nodded and began to pack a bag. As soon as she pulled out some of her intimate apparel, two thoughts came to his mind: Did she design them? And wouldn't she look great modeling them.

He couldn't help himself. He wanted her, and there was no fighting the attraction.

As soon as she was packed, Rafe took her bag and her arm. "If you want, I'll do all the talking."

He was afraid Jade might dissolve into tears again if she had to say anything to Fiona. He assumed Jade would fall apart when she finally told him what this was about. He just didn't want her to feel any more embarrassed when she left the inn than he knew she already was.

He walked her down the stairs, and Jade actually managed a smile for Fiona. "See you later," she said, her voice sounding like she'd been crying for some time.

Fiona looked sympathetic but unsure of what to say. "Hope you get to feeling better." She turned her gaze on Rafe, giving him a look that said he'd better not be the one who had upset Jade.

He smiled, kind of. "She'll feel better in the morning."

Fiona raised her brows.

Aww, hell. He realized now that she thought he was planning to make love to Jade. While he'd like that, it would mean a mating, and he wasn't going there.

After that, he loaded Jade and her bag into the car—no sign of the paparazzi, thankfully—and zipped down the road for home. He had the top up, in case Jade wanted to talk, but she looked exhausted and just stared out the window. He knew whatever it was weighed heavily on her mind. And he was certain it had to do with her son.

When they got home, he carried her bag and led her into the house, her hand in his, and set her bag in the guest room. He had no intention of her going back to the bed-and-breakfast tonight.

"Do you want to eat breakfast or an early brunch?"

She shook her head.

"Tea? Coffee?"

"Water?" she asked.

He got her a bottle of water and a box of tissues, which made her smile. Then he took her to sit in the den where she could see the beach.

He settled next to her. "Okay, tell me why you need a PI."

Chapter 7

When Rafe had arrived at her room at the inn, he'd been wearing blue board shorts and nothing else. Which had surprised Jade. And, she suspected, Fiona too. Jade guessed he'd been getting ready to go swimming. He must have been so concerned about her that he just dropped everything and came to her aid. She had to appreciate him for that.

She hadn't expected him to nearly break down the door of the room, when she'd already unlocked it for him. She hated how she had fallen to pieces. Even now with him sitting next to her on the sofa in the den, rubbing her arm consolingly, she wasn't sure if she'd made a mistake in asking him for the name of a PI. She hadn't planned to tell him what was going on. She didn't want to get him involved. Didn't want her brother to get wind of it. Hated what Rafe would think if he knew the reason she was here.

"Can you give me a name and not ask what this is all about?" Jade asked, wiping her eyes.

Frowning, Rafe looked down at her. "I can give you half a dozen names, all damn good PIs and all wolves, but, Jade, whatever is going on with you, I'm serious about wanting to help. I have no intention of stepping back and letting you run this show on your own if you're in trouble."

She clammed up.

"Okay, let's just talk. Have you been seeing a wolf?" Rafe's dark brows rose in question.

Did he think she was mated? Great. "No. As soon as a wolf knows I design intimate wear for women, he wants me to model them for him. And he wants to know my finances."

Rafe smiled a little, then frowned. "Kind of like women with me—as far as the finances go. Not about modeling intimate wear."

She loved that he could cheer her up a bit.

"Except that the women I've dated, mostly for charity functions, are human. I haven't run into any she-wolves in my line of business."

She let out her breath. "Other than my brother's pack, I haven't really met any other wolves."

Rafe didn't say anything, and she imagined he was trying to figure out the puzzle of her life. Then finally he said, "My brother, Aidan, is looking for wolf packs that he can take blood samples from so he can try to unlock the clues to why our aging process has sped up so much. If he hasn't located your wolf pack yet, I'm certain he would like to talk to the leader to see if the members would consent to having their blood tested."

Her heart rate increased. She knew Rafe heard it accelerate. "Dr. Aidan Denali?" She realized then that she wouldn't be able to pretend she didn't know him if she met him at the ball. He probably wouldn't remember her, but she couldn't risk it. All Rafe would have to say to his brother was "Did you take samples from Jade's pack?" And when Aidan answered in the affirmative, her wolf would be cooked.

"Yes, he came to our pack in Amarillo and took samples from us," she said honestly.

Rafe nodded. She thought he looked sterner again.

"You asked if he was in the same business as me yesterday." Rafe sounded suspicious.

She wasn't meant for spy missions. "A doctor can be an investor too. They usually have income to invest, and what better way to do so than with someone you trust? You, his brother, would know all the ins and outs."

"True." But Rafe didn't look any less tense or harsh. "I wanted to ask if you could come to a charity ball I'm having here a few days from now. The place will be packed, but you've already met my brother, and you know me, so that will be two people you know, at least. Derek can visit with you too to help keep you company. Wolves need to stick together."

She couldn't look at him. She was going to leave all of this behind once the PI found her son. No way would Rafe want to deal with a kid who was human, no matter how much he might think he liked *her*.

"About the PI?" Maybe if she kept pressing, he wouldn't insist on the details.

But Rafe asked, "So what do you think about our aging process speeding up?"

Jade was studying him, trying to get a feeling for what he was thinking. Did he already know why she was here? Why else would he bring that up? "I try to enjoy every day to the fullest and not worry about what may come." She wiped her eyes again. She was being completely truthful.

"I think that too many of us were so used to having so many years to live that we squandered our lives away and didn't appreciate our time here. We're still aging more slowly than humans, about five years to their one year. But having fewer years to live forces us to take chances that we might not otherwise."

"Like courting a wolf you might not have?"

"Maybe."

"So you're all right with the notion we're not going to have the wolf fountain of youth any longer?" Rafe asked, still looking like he wasn't sure he believed her.

"Yes, I am." If he knew why she was here, did he think she wanted this?

"And your brother?"

She looked down at the bottle of water in her hands. "He's like others who would like to live forever."

"If Aidan found a formula to allow us to have our longevity back, would you be happy with that?"

"I believe our kind was fortunate to have the longevity when we needed it. In other words, we needed time to increase our numbers, ensuring our species survived. Now that there are more of us, we don't need to live as long as before. I really am fine with it the way it is. I think it was hardest as young adults because we were like twenty for decades. And we had to change our identities or move because we weren't aging as fast as humans."

He let out his breath. "Same here."

"What about you? Do you want Aidan to change us back the way we were?" she asked, curious.

"I'm like you. I'm perfectly fine with the way things are. Keeping up the charade can be really complicated, though I have to admit I learned and did a lot of things I wouldn't have been able to, had our longevity been much shorter." He took hold of her hand, cold from the bottle of water. "You do know that Aidan isn't trying to find a way to restore our longevity, right?"

"No. I thought he was." Now that really surprised her. Her brother wouldn't like to hear that.

"He's not. He was just concerned that the aging process could continue to speed up and all of us of a certain *lupus garou* age would suddenly turn to dust, like vampires that had lived for centuries being exposed to the sun."

Her jaw dropping slightly, she couldn't contain her surprise. Had her brother lied to her? As if he hadn't already! What if he knew Aidan wasn't looking for a way to return to their previous longevity? What if he planned to force the doctor to do that research instead?

"He hasn't found any evidence that it will happen, but he's trying to learn what changes our bodies have gone through. Right now, as you say, we still seem to be aging less slowly. But will that change in a few years? That's what he's trying to determine."

Jade swallowed the lump in her throat. "Is he making any progress?"

"No." Again, Rafe was watching for her reaction. "It could take decades for him to learn anything, and he might never know more."

"Oh." She felt her heart sink. She wasn't the least bit sad about the news, but that she didn't think her brother would believe it. Then again, what if Rafe was lying?

"You look disappointed."

"I think my brother believes Aidan might be close to having a breakthrough in his research."

"Well, he isn't." This time Rafe sounded annoyed— not with his brother, but with her.

She hated giving him any reason to hate her. But she needed to know that Rafe and Aidan would remain safe if she was able to grab her son and run. "Does your brother have a bodyguard?"

Rafe tightened his hold on her hand. "Why?"

"Some people might think they could profit from his work and want to take advantage of him. Well, what about you, even?"

"What about me?"

"You said you're worth a lot. You should have a bodyguard."

"Too bad that isn't the line of work you're in. I'd hire you in a heartbeat."

She rolled her eyes. "Be serious."

He reached for her and pulled her onto his lap. Her heart beat unevenly. He was looking down at her, his expression dead serious. "I *am* serious."

Jade wished they could do something about the heat that was escalating between them, knowing that as soon as he realized why she was truly here, he'd be furious with her and want her gone. Which would put her son at risk. She had to somehow pretend to her brother that everything was fine. She just hoped Rafe's recommended PI would get the job done without her brother knowing. She had to be gone before he could retaliate.

She wasn't sure why she brought the next point up. Maybe she wanted to clear the air between them before she had to leave Rafe for good. "You took over my grandparents' shoe manufacturing business and left them penniless."

"Your grandparents?" Rafe shook his head.

"Yes. Scott and Martha Manning. My mother's family. They lost everything they had when you took their business from them."

—◌◌◌—

"*Wait* just a minute." Rafe couldn't believe what Jade was saying, nor did he recall any dealings with wolves where he had given them a raw deal. Were she and her brother going after Aidan because of some notion that Rafe had made their grandparents destitute?

He pulled out his phone and did some checking. He couldn't believe Jade was here because of this. Or that's why she was so upset. He knew it wasn't the whole story. But she seemed to want to talk about everything other than the core of the problem.

As soon as she said he and his brother needed bodyguards, Rafe was certain she wasn't there of her own free will.

"Okay, I bought out the Manning Shoe Manufacturing twenty-two years ago. The building was on prime real estate overlooking a river. Scott and Martha Manning contacted me with a proposition to sell the land and building, to turn it into something that would allow more people to enjoy the surroundings. They were in the red, ready to foreclose, and risked losing everything because your grandfather said he had a problem with gambling and had taken out two mortgages on the place to pay off his debt."

"Ohmigod, and my brother has issues with gambling."

"Gambling? This is what it's all about? Your brother owes a loan shark?"

Tears filled Jade's eyes. "I think so. To a man named Grayton. So you didn't just take the business away from my grandparents?"

"No, Jade. They knew I had the means, and they'd

seen what I had done with other such projects, so they thought we could come to an arrangement. I paid them a generous amount so they and the long-term employees who had worked for them for decades could all retire in comfort. But if your grandfather couldn't get his addiction under control, he might have lost it all, and your brother thought I had taken him for everything I could get out of the deal and left them destitute.

"The building was torn down, and trees were planted, walking and running paths added, and jobs created. We made a community gathering spot, and I've been able to extend the greening to other areas, with paths from one to the other. I don't know what your grandparents might have said that was negative about the process, but when we signed the deal, they were relieved to be out from under the stress and strain of a business going under. There's even a memorial in their name dedicating the site to them."

Tears filled Jade's beautiful eyes, and when they spilled down her cheeks, she quickly looked back out the windows and brushed the tears away. "My brother lied about it. He told me my mother said…" She shook her head. "My brother lied."

Rafe held her close again. "*What* is this all about?"

"He…Kenneth, my brother…he said Aidan was nearly at a breakthrough in his research. He said Aidan told him this."

"He isn't, believe me. I'd be the first to know."

"Kenneth wants to know where Aidan is doing his research, where he's living."

"Okay, why?"

"He says you… Oh, Rafe, he says you and your

brother are going to control the cure for our longevity issues, and you're going to keep the price so high that most of us could never afford it."

"Which isn't true. My brother is doing the research to aid our kind. Besides, he's kind of obsessed that way. This is the first time I've seen him so caught up in his research—concerned about how our aging process could spiral out of control and finding a way to stop it. But he wouldn't deny anyone the cure."

"But the cost of research…"

"I handle it."

She chewed on her bottom lip.

"Tell me everything, Jade. I'm not the ogre your brother has made me out to be."

She let out her breath. "How do you feel about a child that is the result of the union between a human and one of our kind?"

"It doesn't happen. Or so rarely that it's not something I've ever given any thought to. I would think if the woman is human, the wolf would leave her because the child couldn't be a shifter unless the wolf turned both of them. I'm not sure how that would work. Would the child then shift only when the mom did? Probably not, because the mom didn't give the baby the shifter genes.

"If the mother was a *lupus garou* and had a child with a human, she'd be better off giving it up for adoption. If she was with a pack, pack members would be taking a big risk with shifting in front of the child; the same if the mother did. A child wouldn't understand that he couldn't tell others his mother could turn into a wolf. Not until he was older. Even then, he wouldn't see it the same way that a child who shifts when his mother does. It could be a real mess."

Seeing Jade's hurt expression, Rafe frowned at her. "Don't tell me you have a human child." Aww, shit. No way had he ever, would he ever have considered the boy could be human. No wonder she didn't want Aidan testing his blood. Not that their blood would show anything but being human, but her son wouldn't have their longevity either, so no sense in testing for it.

"Yes, and no way in hell would I put my child up for adoption. He's as much a part of me as I am of him," she growled at Rafe, immediately trying to leave his lap.

As much as he wanted to hold her, he let her go. He was torn about this new revelation. He'd never known any *lupus garou* who had a child with a human. He'd thought it was an urban legend. He couldn't even imagine the ramifications of a human child in a wolf pack. "Aidan said a little boy was clinging to you when he took blood samples."

"My son, Toby."

"He's with your brother now?" Rafe really didn't believe Jade would have left her son behind and come here unless she was coerced, but what did he know? She could be playing the innocent in all this.

"My brother has taken him hostage." Her eyes filled with tears, but she didn't look away. She was gritting her teeth, trying to keep her composure again.

Hating her brother already, Rafe clenched his jaw, trying to get his temper under control, and left the couch to join her. He pulled her gently into his arms and rubbed her back. "Any wolf that mistreats women and children, whether they are *lupus garous* or human, is worse than despicable and doesn't deserve to live. Hell, Jade."

"He's using me to…to learn where your brother is. Once he finds Aidan, Kenneth will release my son to me and I'll leave the pack. He's threatened to kill my son because of what he is. My brother believes he's a liability to the pack. Just as *you* believe."

Not about to comment on that issue, though Rafe did feel his thoughts on the subject had merit, he asked, "What about Toby's father?"

"Kenneth killed him. I didn't know until Kenneth took my son and forced me to come here. Kenneth promised if I left Stewart, he would spare his life. He lied."

Beyond concerned for her safety and her child's, Rafe rubbed his chin, thinking of a way to get her son out of the predicament without him being injured. "Hell, Jade. Why didn't you tell me this from the beginning?"

"You were supposed to be ruthless."

"I am. When it comes to matters like this."

She pulled away from him.

"Toward rogue wolves, which is what your brother is."

"I just need to get my son back and take him far away from my pack. I don't want any harm to come to you or your brother either."

"How do you propose to go about getting your son back? Besides getting a PI." He thought it was important to find out if she had any ideas, since she knew her brother and their pack better than Rafe did.

"Do you know anyone that specifically can handle a job like that? I guess not just a PI who could locate him, but someone who could safely extract him?"

"Yeah, I do. But we'll need more time to locate him.

When did your brother think you could discover Aidan's place of residence?"

"During the ball. Kenneth said your brother usually attends your charity functions."

"Not always, but this time he is. Okay, we have a few days until then. We'll pretend we're just getting to know each other. In the meantime, I'll have several men looking into it. They're from the various branches of the military, one a former SWAT officer. All wolves. I'm sorry to hear about your human lover. Had you planned to turn him?"

Rafe didn't like that Jade had had a child by a human, or the notion she might have intended to turn her lover. And having a child who didn't understand wolves like they did? Wasn't one when his mother was? Couldn't play with other wolves to learn how to socialize? He could imagine that would be a real nightmare both for her and her pack.

"No. I really liked Stewart. But I had no plans to turn him. He cared too much for his family. I never thought I could have a child by him. We don't. Or so rarely that, like you, I'd never known any she-wolf who had. I left the pack for nearly four years, and then my brother finally located me. He said he'd give us a chance, but I learned afterward that he'd already heard from your brother, who wanted to take blood samples from our pack. I think my brother wanted me for this role and nothing else. Taking my son hostage would force me to see you. I only agreed to return to the pack because it's hard being a single mother—a wolf with a human child. I thought he really wanted me home. Now I'm ready to kill my brother."

Rafe let out his breath, feeling protective of the she-wolf and her offspring, even if the child was human. He was still a child, solely dependent on his mother. "Will you turn your son?"

"I want to. He needs to learn to be a pup around others. But…I've been afraid to. What if I changed him, and he shifted at any time? He probably would. He wouldn't have any control over it. I wouldn't have any control over it. I could envision being in the grocery store, my three-year-old in the cart, and suddenly he's a wolf pup wearing a T-shirt, coveralls, and cowboy boots."

"Cowboy boots? Texas, gotcha." But that scenario was exactly why Rafe seriously believed a human should be raised by humans. "All right, how is your brother keeping track of you?"

"Through texts."

"No tracking devices?"

"No. Well, if he thought to put some on my clothes, he's out of luck. I bought new clothes on the trip here. He might have put one on my car though." She let out her breath. "My phone maybe."

Rafe was glad to hear she'd been wary enough to think of her clothes. He'd have Edward check everything over. "Has anyone been following you?"

"I don't think so, but now that I'm here, he may have someone following me to make sure I'm doing what he believes I should be. And he did sneak into the bed-and-breakfast somehow."

"So that's who I smelled in your room. Had he threatened you?"

She nodded.

"Damn him to hell and back, Jade." Then Rafe

frowned. What of the men who had been following him? Rafe bet they were with her pack. "To keep your son safe, I understand your need to keep your brother apprised of where you'll be. So if you're going to be seeing me—with the notion of trying to locate my brother—we might as well make it look like we've really got a thing going for each other."

She parted her lips to speak.

He pulled her close again and rubbed her back, his mouth brushing her forehead. "Just for show. Just in case he does have someone watching us. I'll contact my sources to search for your son. Do you have a picture of him?"

"Lots. I have them on my phone. And, Rafe, thanks for being so nice about all this. I was afraid you'd throw me out of here and..." She swallowed hard and looked down at his chest, trying to hide fresh tears.

"When your son's life is at risk?"

She looked back up at him. "He's human."

"He's a child. Even if he were grown, if a wolf took him hostage, he'd deserve to be rescued." He rubbed her arms, and she tucked her head against his chest and wrapped her arms around him. "Is there anything you had your heart set on doing before Friday night's ball? Something that you would like to do if you were truly on a vacation here?" he asked. "To make this look good? Like I'm just courting you and nothing else is going on?"

When she didn't respond, he pulled away and led her to the kitchen to fix her some brunch. "Seriously. Nothing is out of the realm of possibility." Before he asked her what she'd like to eat, he got on his phone and said, "Sebastian, I know why Jade is here now. I need you to make some emergency calls, pronto. And tell Edward he needs to check over Jade's car and other items to see if her things are bugged."

"They sent a video of Toby playing. I didn't recognize the house, and it wasn't geotagged," she said before Rafe ended his call.

"I'm sending you a video of Toby. Have one of our men look into it, see if he can ID a location, Sebastian."

"Will do."

"We'll find your son, Jade," Rafe said, trying to reassure her and hating that she looked so anxious. Maybe the video would give them the break they needed.

Chapter 8

RAFE HAD TALKED JADE INTO VISITING THE REDWOOD National Park today to get her mind off her son and to show they were courting for Kenneth's benefit. Though Rafe wasn't doing it all as a ploy.

He'd been watching to see if anyone was following them and had alerted Edward to be on the lookout too. His personal assistant had also sent a team of ten private investigators in search of Toby Ashton, with orders to be discreet so as not to alert Kenneth Ashton and risk the boy's life. Rafe had to admit that Jade's little boy was cute. Blond ringlets, dark-brown eyes, his mother's smile complete with dimples. Even Edward had said he was a cute kid when Rafe shared the pictures with the PI team.

Edward was following Rafe and Jade today to watch over them. He was a Navy SEAL, a bodyguard, and a certified PI, so he would ensure they both remained safe if Kenneth tried to force the issue.

Rafe had seen a bit of apprehension in Jade's expression when he told her she might need an overnight bag. He had no intention of seducing her. If he made love to her all the way, she'd be his mate for life. Though he had to admit the idea was appealing, despite the situation and her human son.

Jade was fun to be with, and he hadn't realized how much he'd missed by not having a she-wolf in his life.

He couldn't imagine going to any of these places with Derek. The redwoods, sure, but they'd done it years ago, and it wasn't the same as going with a she-wolf. *This* she-wolf.

And Aidan? All he ever thought of was his research.

"Are we going to hike?" she asked as she took the copilot's seat.

"Anything you'd love to do, I'm sure I'd love too."

She was busy with her phone this time as he flew north. Rafe hoped she wasn't already bored with his jetting her around and was just letting her brother know where she was headed.

"It says we can hike on eighty trails and see all kinds of wildlife, like bobcats, deer, raccoons—"

He was glad Jade was focusing on their excursion. She seemed more at ease now that she had told him why she was really here, and he had men searching for her son. "All of which will stay out of our path as we run through the woods as wolves."

"Oh, good. I thought we'd just walk on the trails."

"We could spend a week there having a blast."

She sighed. "No dogs allowed on the trails."

"Good. They bark and make a mess. Besides, we'll be running through the wilderness as wolves. Less of a chance for anyone to see us."

"I can't quit thinking about my son. Kenneth won't even let me talk to him until I have news of where Aidan is living."

"*Bastard*. If he's harmed one curly lock on your son's head, he'll pay for it." Rafe glanced at her. "But worrying about him when you can't do anything about it won't help. Just relax. I've got men on it."

Jade took a deep breath and looked back at her phone. "The site says the temperature ranges from seventy-five to ninety-five degrees, but it's in the forties and fifties at night. I don't have anything warm enough for that. Not with me."

"We can stop at a gift shop and pick you up a sweatshirt."

"Okay. They have ancient redwoods, mixed conifers, oaks, chaparrals, and waterfalls. It can take half a day to hike on the trails. And parking will be pretty full if we don't get there early enough. How long before we get there?"

Rafe laughed.

She smiled. "Okay, I'm sitting back and enjoying the view."

"Good." He was glad to see her watching out the windows, appearing just as interested in the view as she had when he took her to the lake yesterday. "Have you been inspired with any new designs for your intimate wear?"

Jade shook her head.

Not with worrying about Toby, Rafe belatedly realized. "Do you have anything to wear to the ball?" He imagined that bringing an evening gown would have looked too suspicious when she didn't have any plans except to enjoy the beach.

She chewed on her bottom lip as she looked up at the clouds. "I have a sundress. Will that do?"

"Would you mind if I picked up a gown for you?" Rafe was glad she wasn't prepared to attend the ball and that he could help out.

"A sundress wouldn't do? It's a long dress, not short."

Rafe smiled. "On you, it would be beautiful. But everyone will be dressed up a lot more."

She looked back out the window.

"No strings. I can afford to be extravagant at times. I enjoy it."

"I wouldn't ever wear it again, most likely."

"You can sell it at a resale shop afterward."

"I don't ever buy anything I don't intend to get a lot of use out of."

"Just let down your hair. Do what you normally would never do."

"All right. Thanks, but just something that will get me by. Nothing too expensive."

"Not to worry."

"I mean it."

"Right." The best money could buy. Was he crazy? He wanted her to feel comfortable at the social event. "So what's there to do in Amarillo?"

Jade told him about the outdoor theater in Palo Duro Canyon featuring the musical *Texas* and the steak house that had the biggest steaks in Texas.

"Sounds like a wolf's kind of meal."

"It is, but you have to eat the rest of the meal too, all within an hour, and then it's free."

"I'd rather pay for the meal and enjoy it."

"Me too." She let out her breath. "Will they find him? Safe?"

"They'll find him. And they'll be cautious. He'll be in good hands." At least Rafe prayed his men would find the boy soon.

Once they got to the airport, Rafe had another car waiting.

They stopped at a gift shop so Jade could pick up a sweatshirt. Now this wasn't something he did either—shopping with a woman, and a she-wolf at that. He didn't care about clothes himself, just bought them when he had to. So he really didn't think he'd be interested in what Jade picked out. But as soon as she began displaying the various sweatshirt colors—from soft blue to dark purple—against her chest, he couldn't help but offer his opinion on what *he* liked best.

"The aqua one," he said.

She was still eyeing a lilac one.

"That one too."

"But you like the aqua one best."

"We'll get both. You'll have plenty of time to wear them while you're here. I'll get them."

"But you said you were going to get me the gown."

"My treat. They're a souvenir of your trip to California." But he couldn't help hoping she'd make California her home.

"Thanks, Rafe. I can't thank you enough. For everything."

Before long, they were headed down a winding, tree-lined road toward the park station. "What will we do about shifting?" she asked.

"We'll take a backpack, go off trail, tuck our clothes in it, shift, and run."

After the forested drive, they arrived at the parking lot, left their car, and headed down the trail.

When Rafe found the spot he had visited some years earlier with Derek, he guided them off the path when no one was around. "Here we leave the trail and head into the redwoods."

They'd traveled about an eighth of mile into the woods when he said, "This looks as good a place as any other."

They quickly stripped out of their clothes. He wasn't sure how Jade would feel about stripping next to him, so he was trying to be the perfect gentleman and not look while she got naked. Just as he pulled off his boxers, she nudged his naked hip with her cool, wet nose. He smiled down at her and was struck again by her wolf beauty. They really were two separate beasts—human and wolf. Her facial mask was blond, the fur framing her face reddish brown, and her belly was blond. A darker saddle covered her back. Her ears were framed in black, and the tip of her tail also sported black guard hairs. He had no doubt if the American Kennel Club had a wolf class, she'd be Best in Show. He realized *she* had been watching him strip, even if he hadn't been observing her.

Rafe smiled down at her, really wishing this whole situation was what it seemed when he first met her—just a chance meeting.

She began panting, and he laughed. "Hot, huh?"

Jade closed her mouth, then woofed at him softly, in case anyone thought to send in a ranger patrol to find the hiker who was walking off the trail with a dog.

He tucked their clothes in the backpack and stuck it under some ferns, then called on the urge to shift, his bones and muscles stretching, making his whole body heat. Then he dropped to all fours and panted too. Right before she licked him full on the mouth.

He licked her right back. He realized he could get used to this, being with her… Yet, she had a son who, no matter how cute he was, could be a real problem.

Rafe wasn't even sure he could handle a child who was a shifter. He had zero experience, and he really didn't know if he was suited to the role of papa wolf. But the boy would really need a father growing up.

Rafe and Jade raced through the trees, playing. He leaped over fallen trunks; she followed with powerful leaps, sometimes over the tree trunks, sometimes on top and then down the other side. He dove into ferns and waited for her to catch up, then tackled her. The first time, she looked surprised, jumping back, then ready for revenge, but before she could lunge to tackle him in play, he'd taken off again. They moved so much faster than humans would on trails, especially visitors to the park who were taking pictures.

He thought about that and realized Jade might like to take some pictures to remember her trip here. The notion she would be leaving, that she wasn't staying in the area permanently, bothered him. He wanted to get to know her better. To know she was close by. To know she was safe and her son was protected from tyrants like her brother. Would she ever be able to find a mate when she had a human son to raise? He figured that could be a real issue.

But he also knew she had to find a new home. Not his home, but her own place safe from worries.

He led her to a creek, where they drank the cool, refreshing water. Normally, humans would have to filter the water if they wanted to drink it. As wolves, they didn't need to.

She kept stopping to poke her nose at bright-yellow banana slugs, looking amused. He was used to seeing them, and he loved witnessing what seemed to tickle her. She scared a rabbit out of a hole, but just watched as it bounded away, not giving in to the natural wolf tendency to take chase when the bunny was already scared enough.

He led her to the first waterfall in the area, the water splashing over the top of the cliff. He breathed in the sweet, earthy fragrance of redwoods and the fresh, clean scent of natural running water. He loved it, and especially loved being here with the she-wolf. It was a nice wolfish way to take a break from the wheeling and dealing of his work. Despite the drought affecting the state, the falls were beautiful: the water cascaded over the rock walls, surrounded by the green moss and ferns, and shade from the giant trees made the setting look like a fairy forest. They waited in the woods, watching, not wanting anyone to see them while walking on the path to the falls and stopping to take pictures.

They didn't hear the sound of humans in the area. Humans were always so noisy and never thought to be quiet so as not to intrude on the wildlife around them, which made it easier for Rafe and Jade to stay away from them.

Rafe moved closer to the waterfall, his paw pads able to cling to the slippery rocks. Jade followed him, sniffing the air and watching for signs of anyone. Then the tension in her body alerted him that she was lunging into the waterfall. Amused, he dove after her, their outer guard hairs repelling much of the water. They raced through to the other side, and then they were off again. He was eager to show her the next waterfall.

They ran through the mix of Douglas firs, maples, oaks, ferns, and ancient redwoods. The sun was shining, but the trees were so tall that the rays only poked through like small sunbursts, and most of the time they ran in shade. They paused on top of a redwood that had toppled. Around the circumference of the tree trunk, sprouts had taken root—able to reach the amazing height of eight feet in a growing season—and had produced a ring of trees known as a fairy ring. He would have to tell Jade what it was called later in case she didn't know. But first, he went around, pointing out the trees that were nearly as tall as they could grow in a single growing season, and then they went on their way.

After spending a wild time exploring, playing, and having fun "hunting" humans, they headed back to where they'd left their backpack. He'd had a blast and he hoped she had too, despite how much she must be worrying about her son.

When they shifted, they were both muddy. "Ugh," she said. "Is there a place we can get cleaned up?"

"I've got wet wipes in the backpack, but if you're game, I do have a cabin near here."

"Naturally."

He pulled out the package of wet wipes and handed her a couple. "We could go there, take showers, have lunch out, then have s'mores by moonlight."

"All right. Will we return to your place tonight?" she asked, hurrying to wipe mud splatter off her legs and feet.

She was beautiful, he thought. Tan, shapely. Beautiful. "It's completely up to you." He was starting to wipe the mud off his legs when his phone vibrated. He pulled it out of the pack and saw that it was Edward. "Any word?"

"Hell, yeah. There's a guy who shifted in the forest and was tracking you while I was tracking him. When he returns to his clothes, he'll find a nasty surprise."

"Oh yeah?" That's one thing Rafe valued about Edward. He didn't need to be told how to proceed if there was a problem. He just took care of it. Rafe watched as Jade pulled her shirt over her head, her expression worried. "Not about your son," he said softly to her. "Just a tail."

"Yeah, somehow the oily sap of poison oak got into his briefs while he was out running as a wolf. It'll bother him for a few hours if he doesn't catch the slightly sweet fragrance—or doesn't recognize what it is," Edward said. "Teach him to tail you."

"Hopefully he won't discover the surprise until it's too late. Good job. Now I know why I pay you the big bucks."

"Right, Boss. Are you going home now?"

"I'll text you the schedule. Not sure after that. We'll just wing it."

"All right. Got to go before he's on the move."

Jade leaned down to tie on her hiking boots. "So what's going on?"

"I'll tell you in private later. Did you want to get some photos of the redwoods before we leave?"

She pulled out her phone. "I sure do."

They headed back to the trail, and just like an excited tourist, she took tons of pictures of the redwoods, banana slugs, ferns, moss, birds, and the sun's rays filtering through the trees. He loved seeing nature up close, but he really enjoyed seeing how much she wanted to capture it. "To show Toby when he's with me," she said softly.

Rafe rubbed her back and kissed her cheek. "He will be."

When they were finished, he took her to his cabin, almost feeling guilty because it was so lavish. Everything he owned was rather extravagant, and he assumed she'd been living modestly. After they took showers in separate rooms, she said, "Okay, so what happened?"

"We had a tail. Edward, my PI, followed him." Rafe proceeded to give her the rest of the details.

Her face turned from shocked to amused. "Don't ever let me get on your bad side."

Rafe smiled. "Yeah, well, he shouldn't have been tailing you. Not when you're keeping your brother posted on your whereabouts."

"He's controlling that way."

"I can tell."

Afterward, Rafe drove her to a small town that featured several restaurants—from Mexican food to a chicken-wing place. They decided on the wings, a wolf's favorite, and shared parmesan-crusted chicken and mild, spicy wings. He was curious if the guy following them would give up on tailing her, or if her brother would send someone else.

He hoped his and Jade's plan wouldn't backfire and hurt her or her son. Then he got a call from Sebastian. "Yeah, any news?"

"When our tech enhanced and isolated the sounds in the background on the video of Toby playing, he heard a cow mooing, so a country location. There was a church bell ringing. Someone in the background mentioned a street. Pine Grove? But he couldn't identify anything other than that."

"Okay, hold on." Rafe asked Jade if she knew of Pine Grove, where the video might have been taken.

Jade's face brightened, her eyes widening. "It's a ranching community. My grandmother lived there years ago." She gave him the location south of Amarillo.

Rafe told Sebastian, "Have our men check it out, but carefully, in case it's a wild-goose chase and Kenneth has men watching to see if anyone investigates it."

"Okay, will do. Our tech says that if he hadn't used his equipment to analyze the video, no one would have heard the street name mentioned in the background."

"Okay, good. Well, make sure the men are super careful."

Chapter 9

Jade prayed Rafe's men would locate her son at the old farmhouse, that it wasn't a hoax and that Kenneth's men weren't waiting to see if she had betrayed him. She was worried sick but hopeful too.

She was just about to take a bite of her chicken when she got a text. She wiped off her shaky hands and pulled out her phone, figuring it was her brother.

And it was. Dread pooled in her belly as she worried he'd learned she'd double-crossed him.

Kenneth texted: I don't know how the hell you did it, or this Rafe did, but no more tricks.

Her heart did a flip. She texted back: I don't have any idea what you're talking about. Let me speak with my son.

Rafe asked, "Is it from your brother?"

"Yeah."

Rafe moved to sit beside her so he could read the texts.

Kenneth: You can't if you're with Rafe. Unless you've told him what's going on. You haven't, have you?

Rafe rubbed her back.

Her heart beating triple time, thinking her brother could know, Jade texted: How could I? He'd feel the same way you do about Toby. Besides that, don't you think he'd just kick me out and that would be the end of this? You think he'd just ignore the sneaky way I wormed my way into his life?

Kenneth: My man says you're awfully cozy with him. I told you to do whatever it takes, except tell him what's going on. If I learn you've told Rafe what's up, your son is dead.

Her stomach taking a dive, Jade texted back: I want to talk to my son as soon as I'm free to. If you harm him in any way, you're dead.

She fumbled to tuck her phone back in her pocket, her hands trembling.

"That sonofabitch," Rafe said.

"I think he believes we had something to do with the tail. He keeps threatening to kill Toby if I let you know what's going on or don't learn your brother's location."

"Damn him. Your brother is living on borrowed time. You know that, don't you?"

She nodded. She never would have thought she'd want him dead. But how could he want her little boy dead? She understood the problem with the boy's father, if he had learned she was pregnant. He'd have wanted to marry her. Then she would have had to turn him, which could have been a real mistake. The whole situation could have turned into a real nightmare. That's why she had left the state—to prevent any of that from happening.

Stewart hadn't needed to die. He didn't know she was a *lupus garou*, and she'd ended it between them and left. She would never forgive her brother for killing him.

Rafe reached over and took hold of her cold hand. "We'll find him, Jade. We'll bring him home."

She nodded, knowing his men would be doing everything they could to secure Toby safely, but until he truly was safe with her, she couldn't stop stressing over it.

"Let's return to the cabin. I have a bunch of games there we could play, then we can have s'mores by the light of the full moon, though we might not see much of it. The fire pit should give us plenty of light."

"All right." Though her heart wasn't in playing games. She managed to finish her wings and then they took off for the cabin. She wondered if the guy who was tailing them was still doing so, or taking care of his poison oak rash. She hoped he wouldn't try to retaliate.

Rafe took her for a drive through the redwoods and then to the cabin. "Did you know that the shorter trees encircling a fallen tree are called a fairy ring?"

"No. That's really cool."

"Are you okay, Jade?"

"Not until Toby is safe. I've been trying not to think of it, to pretend everything is all right, so you wouldn't become suspicious. But now…I'm so scared that one of your men will tip Kenneth off. What are you going to do at the ball if you haven't found Toby by then?"

"The men aren't only looking for Toby; they're also searching for your brother. I think he's realized how this could backfire if I learn he's after Aidan. The best way to eliminate the threat is to eliminate him."

"You checked his house?"

Rafe parked at the cabin. "He's vanished, along with the rest of the pack. I assume he wouldn't go anyplace you'd know, just in case you're telling me all about this situation. But we're checking out the farmhouse, in the event that Toby's there."

"What…what if whoever's tailing us attached a bug to the car? To the cabin?"

"I have men watching out for us and the places we're

staying, the vehicle, the plane—both for safety and for privacy. We have detectors that can reveal electronic testing or tracking devices."

"Our backpack? Our clothes? If he followed us, he could have bugged our clothes or backpack before he shifted and took off after us."

"Edward was watching him. He's an excellent tracker."

They snagged their bags and moved into the cabin.

"Do you want to play Monopoly? I promise I'll go easy on you."

Jade took him up on it.

After an hour of playing, Rafe sat back in his chair, observed all her monopolies, and shook his head. "I should have asked you to go easy on *me*."

She laughed. "I'm only ruthless in a game."

"I'll have to remember that."

His phone rang, and he checked the ID. Barely breathing, she hoped he'd have good news this time, but he looked up at her and rose from his chair suddenly. "All right. I'm on it."

"What's going on?" Jade asked anxiously, leaving her chair with the same abruptness.

"My brother showed up early at my place. We've got to return there now."

"Then your brother is at risk."

"He's got two bodyguards, and I have a couple of men watching the place while we're gone, so he should be all right, but we need to talk to him. He wasn't supposed to arrive until the afternoon of the ball." Rafe grabbed their bags, then locked up the cabin. "We'll have to come back here another time."

As soon as she had her son in her arms, she was

gone. Even if Rafe thought he might be able to build something with her, she was certain he had changed his mind when he learned about Toby, and he would be glad to be rid of her. Toby wouldn't fit in with the billionaire wolf's lifestyle. Even if Toby had been a *lupus garou* too.

Rafe immediately got on the phone in the car and called his brother, but there was no answer. Jade had a bad feeling about all this. Then he called Edward. "Hey, we're headed back home. Why don't you come with us this time? Aidan's home, and I can't get ahold of him."

"I'll meet you at the airport."

Rafe then got hold of Hugh Holloway, the man in charge of Aidan's bodyguard detail and said, "Hey, where's Aidan?"

"Swimming, Boss. You know how he hates to fly, so he said he wanted to swim as soon as he got here."

"Pool?"

"Yeah. We're covering him."

"Did he say why he came early?"

"Said he was needed."

"All right. I'm on my way there."

When they arrived at the airport, Jade hesitated to text her brother. "Should I tell Kenneth I'm on my way back to your place?"

"Yeah. And that you're moving in with me."

Surprised, she gaped at Rafe for a moment. "I don't think that's…"

"Necessary? A good idea? It sure as hell is. What if your brother thinks to threaten you next? Send one of your pack members to lean on you further? I'm not using you as bait for anything. You'll stay with me until this is all cleared up. I've got plenty of guest rooms. I just want to make sure you stay safe."

"What if he believes I've made a bargain with you to help free my son?"

"He might, but you can't help your son if you're also a target." And Rafe wasn't going to risk her safety on a gamble.

—◦◦◦—

At Rafe's place, Jade met Hugh Holloway and Sebastian, Rafe's personal assistant. Edward had ridden in the plane with them, but now that they were at Rafe's home, she felt a little intimidated. All the men were tall like Rafe, but Edward's stern look indicated he meant business. He clearly didn't trust her: his whiskers roughened, his hard jaw remained firm, and his blue-gray eyes studying her intently. Like the other men, he was in great shape. He was dressed in black jeans, a dark-olive-drab shirt that suited his darker look, and Timberland hiking boots as if he was planning to go on a journey or to kick some ass.

Sebastian was just as hard around the edges, but he smiled warmly at her. He looked more like a charmer to her, his light-brown hair streaked by the sun and his light-brown eyes smiling back at her. He was clean-shaven and wearing jeans, a blue denim shirt, and docksiders—casual, but dressier than sandals or sneakers. Aidan's bodyguard was dressed in jeans and a buttoned shirt and sneakers, looking casual but, like Edward, all business.

Hugh excused himself to check on the grounds out front.

Jade gave Sebastian the key to her room at the bed-and-breakfast so he could grab her things and pay the bill, and the key to her car so either Edward or Sebastian could drive it here.

"I'll call over there to let Fiona know this is legit." Jade hoped this wasn't a bad idea. She figured Fiona would be rampantly speculating once she learned Jade was leaving early, but that Rafe's staff was picking everything up would say a whole lot more. Jade hoped the paparazzi wouldn't be around watching the whole thing. When she got ahold of Fiona, she said, "I'm moving out, but I'm fine with the charges."

"Is everything all right?" Fiona asked, sounding concerned, probably even more so after Rafe had picked Jade up at the inn when she had been so upset.

"Yes, thanks. Sebastian and Edward, who work for Mr. Denali, will be picking up my car and my things."

"You're…you're not leaving the area?" Fiona's voice was definitely surprised.

"No. Thanks for everything. Your place is lovely. I'm just going to be staying…somewhere else." As if Fiona couldn't guess where.

"Wow. Congratulations and good luck." Fiona sounded bubbly.

"For…?"

"I take it you have new accommodations, and that would mean a fantastic upgrade."

Jade chuckled. "Thanks. And yes." Then they ended the call. "Okay, she's good with it. My brother is footing the bill, so no problem with that."

"I'll take care of it. I don't want you having to owe him anything," Rafe said, his expression stormy.

"Won't he be suspicious that you're taking me into your home and paying for the room?"

"He'll know you're moving out and coming over here, if he's got anyone watching you. And yeah, he might be suspicious. Anyone who commits crimes usually is. But if we play our cards right, we'll be fine. He might not have figured I'd fall head over heels for you—"

She rolled her eyes.

He smiled. "But he'll believe so now. And if he imagines you've got me bamboozled, so much the better."

She didn't think her brother would believe that. But sometimes he surprised her—like when it suited him.

She saw Aidan coming from the back patio, a towel around his waist, his hair dripping wet, a T-shirt in his hands that he began to pull over his head as soon as he saw them. He was a little shorter than Rafe, his hair darker and his eyes also, but he looked too much like him not to be his twin brother. His charcoal-gray T-shirt caught her attention next: *Real men eat cupcakes*.

She smiled. She hadn't expected the geneticist to wear anything like that. Just like she hadn't expected Rafe to dress so casually. Or even his staff.

"My twin brother, Aidan Denali," Rafe said. "And this is Jade Ashton."

Aidan looked her over and said, "I remember the lady well. Let me get dressed, and I'll join you and we can talk."

She thought he looked a little wary of her too. Not that she blamed him.

Rafe led her into the den, and she loved the fantastic view of the pool and beach. She hadn't really noticed the last time she was here. This time, she saw a large photograph on one wall of his yacht, the *Lo-Lee*. On the deck, Aidan, Rafe, and Edward stood grinning as they showed off their catches. She wasn't into fishing, but it sure looked like it would be fun.

The couches in the den were all navy-blue leather; a huge screen television covered one wall; and the floor was terra-cotta-colored tile, with the rest of the theme nautical. Before she could choose a chair, Aidan rejoined them.

"So tell me what's going on," he said, eyeing both of them.

After Jade took a seat on a couch, Aidan sat on a nearby chair, and Rafe took the chair opposite. Then she explained the whole situation.

"They can't force me to learn anything quickly about the changes our kind are experiencing," Aidan said. "It could take decades for a breakthrough, and I might never get anywhere."

"Right. Well, my brother thinks that, based on something you said, you have nearly uncovered the key," Jade warned.

"He misunderstood what I was saying. I'm nowhere near discovering anything except to make correlations between our current longevity and human longevity." Aidan turned to Rafe. "So what are we going to do about her son?"

"I've got men looking for him and her brother. Jade will stay here because her brother is threatening her at the bed-and-breakfast. Now that you're here, I'm planning to take your place in case they try to grab you. As much as I hate to do it, from now on, I'll wear the glasses you normally wear when you're out in public."

"Gave them up. Everyone still thinks I'm you, with all the publicity you get, so no sense in wearing fake glasses." Aidan shook his head. "I'm the one who reached out to Jade's pack, creating this trouble in the first place."

"And I'm the one who has the training to take these people down."

"My brother expects me to tell him where you live," Jade said.

"For now, I'm here. Just where the two of us can deal with this. What does he think? He can learn where my research is and try to move it? Take me hostage?" Aidan asked, sounding perturbed.

"He doesn't know I've told Rafe why I'm here. And he believes you're about to make a breakthrough. He wouldn't believe me if I told him it wasn't true," she warned.

"If I gave him a serum, just a placebo, he wouldn't have any idea if it would increase longevity beyond what it is now," Aidan said. "It would take more than five years to learn if our cells were aging faster or slower like they used to. It's not something that can be rushed. Also, two wolves can age at different rates. Biological and chronological aging are two different theories. Even humans are researching whether the biological process of aging can be slowed down, stopped, or reversed. So I'm not the only one who is testing theories on the subject. Maybe even other wolves are testing our own species. I don't know."

"The problem is that my brother is holding my son hostage. Not only that, but he's in hiding, apparently. Which worries me even more. Does he think I've told Rafe that he's holding my son?"

"Or he's worried you're going to send a hit team to take him out," Aidan said.

"As if I knew where to find one. In the intimate apparel business, that's not really something I would know about."

Aidan glanced at Rafe.

"That's my business."

Aidan smiled, then cleared his throat. "So what do we do next?"

"I was going to take Jade yachting tomorrow to pretend to court her. Then we'd be at the ball in four more days. But now that you're here, that changes things."

"Why?"

"They've been following us. She's been telling her brother our whereabouts so he doesn't harm her son, but in the event he does know you're here, she'll need to tell him. Otherwise, if he knows you're here and she hasn't told him, he'll suspect we know what's going on. And if we're running around having a good time, he'll wonder why she's not trying to learn something from you."

"I agree."

"I'll text him." She pulled out her phone, then hesitated. "If he wasn't paranoid and had GPS detector tracking devices, you could have tried to track his calls."

"Sounds to me like he has something to hide," Rafe said. "What does he do for a living?"

"He has a paint and body shop, restores old cars, and resells them. He makes a bundle flipping them."

Rafe and his brother exchanged looks. "All legitimate?"

"I don't know. I...never gave it any thought. I don't know anything about cars."

"And the Firebird convertible you own?" Rafe asked.

Jade ground her teeth. "I bought it from him years ago. I love it. If it was stolen…"

"Most likely not, because if you ever got into trouble for it, you'd know exactly where to lay the blame. We'll have Edward check it over as soon as he gets back with your luggage. He's a jack-of-all-trades," Rafe said.

"Hey, someone mention my name?" Edward asked, joining them in the den. "Took care of the bed-and-breakfast. Pesky photojournalist LK Marks was there asking why I was driving the lady's car. But he gave me the article he wrote about you and Jade. I thought you might want to see it." He handed the paper to Jade first. "We normally don't read the tabloids, but you're new to the game," he said to Jade, "and I made sure it sounded okay."

She barely breathed as she began reading the article. Her jaw dropped. "Well, he said I was a real beauty that Rafe Denali rescued from the sea. Not only that, but that I owned two clothing lines and that it was refreshing to meet a real woman, not a Hollywood version of one." She took a breath. "At least that's good."

"I'll say," Edward said.

Rafe nodded. "If you would, check and see if Jade's car is legal."

"Sure thing." Edward stalked out of the room.

She got goose bumps at the thought that she might have been driving a stolen car all these years. She wondered what would happen now with the paparazzi learning she had moved out.

Rafe went to the bar. "Jade, would you like a drink?"

"I need to do a small load of wash. My jeans got a little muddy when we dressed out in the park."

"Why don't you have a drink first, and then I'll show you the laundry room."

"All right. Do you have the fixings for a margarita?"

"Sure do. On the rocks or frozen?"

"On the rocks, no salt, please."

"Okay. Aidan, your usual?"

"Yeah, you know me."

"James Bond wannabe."

Aidan laughed.

Rafe handed Jade's giant glass to her, decorated with a tiny, bright-pink parasol and a slice of lime and a cherry. Then he fixed Aidan a martini and a drink for himself.

"What are you having?" Jade asked.

"Hotel California: champagne, gold tequila, pineapple, and mandarin orange juice."

"I might have to try that some time."

Edward walked back to the patio room. "Your car looks legit. Checked the VIN against what the car should list as, and it all matched up. No sign that it had been tampered with or changed out."

She was so relieved; she hadn't realized how tense she'd been.

"Want a beer or mixed drink?" Rafe asked Edward and Sebastian.

"I'll take a beer," Edward replied.

"Beer," Sebastian said.

She was surprised Edward and Sebastian would be drinking with them when they were supposed to be working for Rafe.

They all moved out to sit by the pool. Jade drank most of her margarita, but she was worried about not texting her brother. "Where's your laundry room, Rafe?

I'm going to start my wash and text my brother about Aidan being here. And hope he isn't suspicious about me staying at your place."

"Sure thing," Rafe said.

She was trying not to feel nervous about it, but she couldn't think of anything but reporting in.

Rafe took her to the laundry room and showed her where everything was. Then he put his hands on her shoulders and looked down at her. "We'll get Toby back, and we'll take care of your brother."

She nodded, but she was scared that Kenneth would do something drastic if he thought they were out to get him.

"Do you want me to stay with you while you text him?"

"No, thanks, Rafe. I can manage. I'll join you in a bit. Did you want me to wash your muddy jeans too?"

"I have… Sure, that would be great."

A maid, she thought he was going to say, which she always forgot about. He most likely had everything done for him, except he liked to cook.

"Be right back," he said.

She was throwing in other clothes when he walked back in with his.

"Thanks. If you need me, just holler."

"I'll join you in just a few minutes. And thanks again, for everything."

He rested his hands on her shoulders again and kissed her, hard and long, possessively and passionately. Why couldn't she have had someone like this in her life without all the horrible complications she was facing now?

"Don't be long." Then Rafe kissed her on the cheek and left her to do the laundry.

Unsettled about the whole business with her brother, she started the wash, then texted him, praying that he hadn't guessed what was really going on.

As soon as she texted Kenneth, he texted right back: What the hell is going on?

Chapter 10

RAFE HOPED KENNETH ASHTON DIDN'T CAUSE JADE ANY more grief, but he suspected her brother would. He hoped she'd share what her brother said to her verbatim so Rafe knew just how to deal with the bastard.

He and Aidan were seated poolside while Edward was standing at the railing with Sebastian, both looking at the beach, but Rafe knew they weren't just doing it for fun. They were looking for anyone from Jade's pack who might be spying on them.

"I was surprised you arrived earlier than planned," Rafe told his brother.

"When I learned you were getting yourself in deep with some femme fatale she-wolf, I knew my place was here."

Rafe realized his brother must have really been worried about him this time, because Aidan's experiments always took priority. "She's not like that."

"She lured you right in, played on your sympathies, and despite that she was here on dishonest business, you completely trust her?"

"Yeah. You said yourself she had a son who was clinging to her when you took her blood to test it. I don't believe she'd be here enjoying the beach without her son if she wasn't being forced to do it. She had hundreds of photos of him on her phone. She loves him, and I believe her son's life is hanging in the balance."

"What happened to her mate?"

"He was human, and her brother killed him."

Aidan's eyes widened. "She had a son by a human?"

"Yeah. I know, it rarely happens."

"Does the boy shift? The only other cases I've heard of, the offspring can't shift."

"Same here."

"What are you going to do after you rescue him?" Now his brother looked sympathetic. For Jade or for him?

Hell, Rafe didn't know what he was going to do about this. "Keep them here for now. For their protection."

Aidan smiled a little.

"What?"

"You don't know the first thing about raising a kid."

"I'm not raising him. She is."

"Right."

As soon as Jade told Kenneth she'd moved in with Rafe and that she had moved into the guest room and was unpacking her bags, he called her on the phone and started threatening her. "If you've told the Denalis what this is all about…"

"Rafe has taken a real interest in me. Wasn't that your plan? The good news is that his brother arrived before we returned. I'm taking a minute to get settled while the brothers are visiting on the patio so I could tell you what is going on."

The room was decorated as if fit for nobility—a high-rise bed, a royal-blue satin comforter, and curtains around the bed, along with a private deck with a view of the beach. The room was beautiful. It even had a private bath, which she really appreciated because she didn't want to be running into anyone at night when she needed to use the bathroom.

"Who are the other men?" Kenneth asked.

So he *was* having someone watch Rafe and the others on the patio. "His personal assistant and a bodyguard for his protection." She wasn't going to pretend Edward was a friend. Her brother had to know that Rafe, and probably his brother, would have a couple guards. "He treats them like they're family, from what I've seen." She only mentioned it because the two men were having drinks on the patio, and her brother might not believe Rafe would share drinks with his hired help.

"Where is he from?"

"Aidan?"

"Who else?"

"I hope to learn that before the ball, now that he's here. I'll let you know as soon as I do. But Rafe said Aidan wasn't even close to any kind of a breakthrough."

"You *asked* him?" Kenneth sounded suspicious.

"No. Rafe asked about taking blood samples from our pack. What could I say? Pretend he hadn't? And then if Aidan recognized me? Then what?"

"I want something soon, Jade. Now that Aidan's actually there, I want results."

"I'm trying, but unless you want me to just come straight out and ask—and tell him why I need to know this…"

"Don't get smart with me."

"If you want me to be careful, I've got to do this right."

"Don't fail me. Or you'll fail your son."

Before she could tell her brother to let her speak with

Toby, Kenneth hung up on her. She prayed Rafe's men would find her son and end her brother's tyrannical quest soon.

She left the guest room and saw Edward on his phone near the living room. He glanced over at her, and she hoped he had some good news about her son.

"All right." Edward pocketed his phone and said to Jade, "No luck yet. Does your brother suspect anything?"

"I'm sure he does. Even if he thinks I might be telling the truth, he's wary."

"That's because he's a liar and a thief. One of the men discovered a number of stolen vehicles in his body shop. No one's there right now. We suspect he's hiding out with your son in the place he hopes to take Aidan."

She was furious with her brother because of his additional involvement in illegal activities. "What are you going to do about it?" She knew that no *lupus garou* involved in criminal activities could be incarcerated—too risky.

"We'll be taking everyone in who's involved in the operation. You can help identify anyone who had no knowledge, or who didn't help with the theft, money laundering, and selling of the stolen goods. You never worked there?"

"Ha! No. I never speed, never run a red light or stop sign, never do anything above the law. I imagine my brother knew I'd never have gone along with what he was doing. None of the women were involved, and only five men, my brother included, worked in the shop."

"We'll pick up who we can if we can locate any of them. Do you have any idea where your brother and his girlfriend might have gone?"

"No. I'm sure they wouldn't go to any place I might think of, in case you figured out what I was really doing here and made me tell you."

"All right. We'll find them and your son."

Hoping he was right, Jade rejoined the men out by the pool, but she couldn't concentrate on the conversations. She vaguely heard Rafe talking to Aidan about the charity function and heightened security. The other men were quiet, watchful as they surveyed the surroundings.

Jade heard the wash finish and excused herself to put the wet clothes in the dryer. As soon as she pulled them out, she saw white spots all over their blue jeans. She stared at them in disbelief, then looked at the bottle of detergent she had used. Crap! She had used one with bleach in it!

Tears filled her eyes. Not just because of the ruined jeans, but because of Toby. Even if they got him back safely, Kenneth would continue to be a threat.

She heard someone coming and turned to see Rafe stalking into the room.

"When I didn't hear the dryer running, I was afraid you had another text from your brother… Jade? What's wrong, honey?" he asked, pulling her into his arms.

She still had the wet jeans in her hands, but she wrapped her arms around Rafe and sobbed.

Rafe didn't know what to do about Jade, except the only thing he could do: hold her tight, give her solace, and show her he cared. He realized then how much she must have been holding back, trying to hide how she felt about her son from him and from herself, afraid to let go, afraid to reveal the truth of Toby's existence while playing this role her brother had forced on her.

Telling her they'd get Toby back safe and sound didn't mean they really would, and she knew that. Rafe wished he could do more, and though he wanted to say the spotted jeans didn't matter, he knew that wasn't what had upset her. Her son was at more risk with them searching for him, and the jeans were the last thread holding her emotions together.

"Sorry," she said, sniffling, still holding on to him like she needed this, needed him, someone to comfort her when she was all alone in the world. Until now, she'd had no one she could tell without fear of her brother taking it out on her son. Rafe couldn't imagine how difficult it had been to be all alone with no one to confide in, worrying about her son, and then about him and his brother.

"No problem," he said, kissing the top of her head, holding her close again, letting her lean on him for moral support. He wanted to say more, to reassure her more, but he knew she didn't need that. She just needed this.

When she seemed to gain control of her emotions, she let out her breath. "I'm sorry about our jeans."

He smiled down at her. "We can be a matched pair. Why don't we throw them in the dryer and—"

"Thanks, Rafe. For...everything." Then she moved away from him, tossed the jeans in the dryer, and started it. "I'm tired."

"Why don't you go to bed then. I'll finish this and see you in the morning."

"Thanks." She kissed him on the cheek before she left him in the laundry room.

He would kill Kenneth for putting Jade through this nightmare.

Rafe headed for the patio as she slipped down the hallway to her bedroom.

"Everything all right?" Aidan asked immediately.

Rafe had thought his brother would be sitting still, but he'd been pacing across the patio until he saw Rafe, his look worried. The other men were doing their duty, watching the beach, but both turned to see what had happened.

"Yeah. She's just exhausted over everything and concerned about her son. She's been through a hell of an ordeal, and hiding the strain is draining." Rafe sat down as his brother also took a seat.

"Did she go to bed?" Aidan asked.

"Yeah."

"Hell, we've got to find the bastard," Aidan said.

"I agree."

"And the boy." Aidan looked back at the doors to the house. "So what are you going to do when we rescue Toby?"

That was the question of the century. All Rafe could think about was how smiley the kid was. Cute. But since when did he begin to think a kid, any kid, was cute? When he wore Jade's smile.

The next morning, Rafe took Jade out on the yacht. She appreciated his concern for her, and he hoped to get her mind off the search for Toby. They'd had six leads, but every one of them fell through. Kenneth Ashton hadn't been taking chances and had left a trail of red herrings, then nothing again.

Sebastian had contacted Rafe's part-time crew to man the yacht so they could go out for the morning. Edward was captaining the yacht for the time being.

"Jack-of-all-trades," Jade said, as she leaned against the railing, watching Edward take them out.

"Yeah, though I have a captain for the job, Edward loves to take her out when he can. When we have the time, we go diving, and he'll give the controls up to my captain."

Jade smiled and looked back out to the ocean, the wind whipping her hair around as she felt the sun and the salt spray on her skin. The yacht was big, but the ocean was so much bigger as the boat rose on the swells and crashed into the troughs. She couldn't imagine being out here during a bad storm.

What would it be like to sail a ship across the vast blue-green oceans in search of a new continent? The pale-blue horizon stretched forever, and the ocean looked like it dropped off the end of the world. She decided that though she loved being out here with Rafe, she wouldn't want to be out on the ocean for months on end, even if she knew land would be in sight at some point.

"Penny for your thoughts," Rafe said as one of his staff brought them fresh orange juice.

"Thanks." Jade took a sip and looked back out at the wind-swept ocean. "I was thinking what it must have been like to sail far away from home in search of a new world to find riches and treasures there."

"Aidan, Derek, Edward, and I took off for a month once and were caught in a couple of storms we thought we might not make it through. Derek broke his leg during the second one, and we had to put in to port. It was an adventure we never regretted, but storms can turn deadly in a matter of minutes. Still, we cherished the time we spent at sea."

"Incredible. I can't imagine being out to sea for that long. What about running as wolves?"

"We hit a couple of deserted islands along the way. Some boats occasionally anchor there, but when we were there, the islands were deserted and we ran around to our heart's content. Come on. Let me show you the rest of the craft and the cabins, in case you need to use one of the bathrooms."

They walked to the bow of the main deck so he could show her the most impressive cabin first. "This is the main quarters, the master suite. Because of its location, it has quick access to anywhere on the yacht."

"The captain's quarters," Jade said.

"Yeah. But it sure could use a captain's mate."

She smiled at him, not believing he could be seriously considering her for a mate.

There were no stairs to climb to reach the main quarters, which she thought was really neat. The room took up the whole bow, the full width of the yacht, with portal windows across the room on either side. It was furnished with a king-size bed. A spacious lounge area had a love seat for watching videos on a HD flat-panel TV with a Blu-ray DVD player, music, and a desk for working on a laptop. Unbelievable. She was expecting a tiny cabin.

"Each of the guest rooms has a bathroom en suite. Everyone has unlimited hot and cold water and air-conditioning with individual controls."

Then Rafe showed her the next two cabins located forward of the main salon, which was the common room on the ship. Each of them featured a spacious floor plan with queen-size beds and a separate daybed, as well as portholes for letting in light.

"Drawers are under the beds to store clothes and the like. Glassed-in showers and the rest in here," Rafe said, pointing to the cabin's bathroom. Then he took her to another cabin in the stern and showed her the interior. "This one has two beds and a small love seat for seating." He showed Jade the bathroom, then led her to the last cabin and said, "For those who want to spend more time on deck, this one has two single beds and built-in storage on the starboard side. Bathroom in there. So room enough for several guests."

The smaller cabins were still spacious enough to move around, but closer to what she had expected. "Wow, just beautiful."

He guided her to the covered aft deck, where chairs were placed for a lovely view of the ocean, and the covered fore deck where bench seating was available. Then Rafe showed Jade the main salon for indoor dining and relaxing.

"It's all beautiful."

"I love it out here but I don't go out as much as I'd like. Ready for some breakfast?" he asked.

She was expecting Rafe to fix breakfast since he liked to cook for himself, but he had a chef for the cruise, a white-haired wolf with twinkling amber eyes and a ready smile. Jade thanked him after he served them fruit, omelets, hash browns, and ham in the main salon.

"You keep her, no?" Chef Pierre Fontaine asked.

Rafe only smiled, and she swore the unspoken message was that he had every intention of doing that.

She was enjoying herself so much. They ended up spending the whole day out at sea, having lunch and dinner out there. Afterward, they were standing on the deck, looking toward land, but the wind began to whip about, and she could smell rain coming as they headed home.

"Storm's coming." The ocean swells grew higher, and Rafe took Jade inside. The yacht rose and fell, and she lost her balance, realizing she'd have to be on the water for a lot longer than just a day to earn her sea legs.

Rafe caught her before she fell, held her tight, and kissed her. He knew that everything could change between them once they located Jade's son, but he loved being with her. If they hadn't had another care in the world, he would have already swept her off her feet and made her his mate.

He loved his yacht and had hoped she'd love the sea as much as he did. And she seemed to, lost in the moment while thinking about the explorers of old, just as he had done countless times.

She was good with his staff, so polite and respectful, not like some of his wealthy human guests who had seen them as hired help and not worthy of their time. Jade always thanked them like she really appreciated anything they did for her. It was refreshing and made him care for her even more.

And there was this, the kissing that made him want to go further than was prudent. Right now, with her arms wrapped around his neck and her tongue in his mouth, sliding over his, her hot little body pressed against his, he wanted to take this to the next level and not be cautious about what would happen when she was reunited with her son. He wanted to carry her to the master suite, undress her, and make hot and passionate love to her, turning this trip into the most memorable experience he'd ever have. It was killing him to kiss her like this and always have to let go.

He brushed the wind-tossed strands of golden hair from her face and kissed her cheeks and nose and mouth. She was mouthwateringly sexy in a halter top and short shorts, and he wanted nothing more than to pull them off and kiss her satiny skin all over.

Her breathing was fast-paced and erratic as she held on to him, partly for balance as the waves built and the craft rocked up and down.

"Are you all right?" he asked, kissing her ear and nibbling on the lobe.

"No," she said so breathlessly that he looked at her expression, her eyes closed, her luscious lips parted.

Her comment worried him and he frowned down at her. "Seasick?"

Her eyes opened and she smiled at him so vixen-like that he knew his smile was hotly wolfish in return before he claimed her mouth. The yacht was bouncing too much for this. He moved her to one of the cushioned bench seats and laid her down. Then he was partly on top of her, untying her halter top, and baring her breasts to him. No one would intrude on him while he was with the she-wolf, but he wasn't sure she'd be okay with this development.

She seemed to be because she pulled at his T-shirt. He quickly discarded it and began kissing her beautiful breasts. The rosy nipples peaked, begging him to taste and tease. He swirled his tongue around one and made her arch her back. She was so responsive, and he knew from the smell of her that she was already wet for him.

He slid his hand down her shorts, expecting panties, but she wore none. A smile curved her lips again, probably because he looked a little surprised at first. He smiled right back. A she-wolf after his own heart.

He inserted his finger into her slick, wet heat and pulled it out to rub her sensitive bud. Then he began kissing her again—bolder, more insistent, keeping up the strokes—as she gripped his bare shoulders, her touch fanning the fire burning in him. She arched against him while the yacht rose and fell beneath them.

He felt her nearing completion as she barely breathed, and he licked her neck and her throat, keeping up the pressure, the strokes, until she cried out. He covered her mouth with his and kissed her deeply again, his hand caressing her breast, the need to plunge his cock into her so great that he had to bite back the inclination.

He finally pulled away, tied her halter top, and brought her up to a sitting position so he could just hold her, get through the bumpy ride, and try to put his own desire out of his thoughts.

"Did you…"

"No," he said quickly and kissed her cheek, having to be satisfied for now.

She sighed and clung to him. "Thank you for…taking my mind off the storm."

"If it would help, I could take you to the master suite."

She smiled. "I think…this is safer."

"For now." He had to agree. But he also didn't believe this would end here.

———∿∿∿∿———

Jade had loved the cruise, and though she knew damn well she shouldn't have gone as far with Rafe as she had, it just felt so right, so perfect. When they arrived back at his place, he checked with his men about Toby, but still no word. Jade thanked him for the grand day, and she swore he wished she'd retire to bed with him, as if he was really considering mating her. But he couldn't. Not unless he could love her son as much as he could care for her.

Then Rafe got a call, and she waited anxiously, hoping he'd finally have word about the men checking out the farmhouse.

"Okay, thanks." Rafe pulled her into his arms and hugged her. "The farmhouse is vacant and furnished, but had a For Sale sign out front. One of my men checked with the real estate office that had listed it, though the listing agent already had an offer on the house. The agent took my man out there to show him the place in case the deal fell through. He smelled wolves, but they hadn't been there for a couple of days. Looks like they used it for a brief time and then left. He checked the fridge and kitchen cabinets as if he were looking to buy, but he found no food at the house. If the contract on the house went through, the new owners would want to move in right away, so the wolves couldn't have stayed there much longer anyway. I'm so sorry, Jade."

Her stomach tightened with distress, but she was glad she had Rafe and his men trying to locate her son.

With a lingering kiss good night, she left him alone to speak with Sebastian about his real estate business.

That night, she had another horribly restless night, dreaming of the beautiful cruise and having full-out sex with that hot wolf, but then the dream turned into a nightmare as she saw her son whisked away from her, and she couldn't reach him before he vanished. She was still struggling to find him when she heard a strange sound in the distance, bringing her to full awareness.

It was morning and someone had sent her a text message.

She grabbed her phone, expecting it to be from Kenneth.

When Jade found a text from Lizzie, it took her a moment to comprehend that it wasn't from Kenneth. Her heart began racing, and she quickly read the text. Not believing what she was reading, she read it again.

Your brother isn't going to mate me, and he's shown interest in a new she-wolf who isn't a member of the pack. Do you believe it?

Like Jade cared. But yeah, she believed it. She didn't know why Lizzie thought Kenneth wanted her. But all that was important to Jade was her son and his safety. If Lizzie felt betrayed and was ready for revenge, Jade hoped to use this change of events to her advantage.

Jade quickly texted her back. Do you have Toby?

I could kill Kenneth, you know?

I don't blame you. He's used you all along. Where is Toby? Is he with you?

Yes, but Kenneth plans to sell him to a human family desperate for a toddler as soon as he figures out how to grab the doctor. He says you'll appreciate that he's doing this. Thank him even. That Toby will be where he belongs.

Ohmigod, no. Had Kenneth never intended to return her son to her? Jade's stomach was twisting into knots. She was already out of bed, fumbling to get dressed and praying Lizzie wasn't trying to deceive her. Once Jade was dressed, she was heading toward Rafe's bedroom when she heard the men out on the back patio talking. She rushed to go there instead, praying that the texts weren't really from her brother, using Lizzie's phone.

You know he flipped the wrong car and he owes money to Grayton, don't you? Grayton lends money to poor fools who get themselves into gambling debt. But it was one of Grayton's cars that Kenneth's men stole and sold. Grayton found out who had it stolen.

Where is Toby?

With me. But I have to run if I'm going to keep Kenneth from selling Toby. I'll need money.

Jade bit her lip. Hell, the woman had been in on the

whole thing until she thought she was about to lose out. And now she wanted money?

Jade threw one of the patio doors open, startling the men. Rafe jumped out of his seat and joined her. She showed him Lizzie's texts, then texted, How much?

A million bucks.

Edward was on his phone immediately. Aidan joined them to see what was being said. Sebastian was standing, tense, waiting to get word of what he needed to do next.

Rafe glanced back at Edward and said, "It's Lizzie, texting about handing Toby over for money."

Jade wanted to tell her no way could she get that much money together in a hurry, but she figured Rafe might be able to. She didn't want to risk telling Lizzie no and then having her sell Toby to someone else who had the money. Not that she thought anyone would pay *that* much for a young boy.

Tell us where you are, and we'll pick you and Toby up. Then you'll be paid and you can disappear.

No. There's no guarantee you'll pay me. You could just...make me disappear.

I want my son back, unharmed. You know I'll do anything.

Jade paced across the patio, waiting for a response and staring at the phone. "Come on. Come on."

Jade texted her again. Lizzie? We have to bring you both under Rafe's protection.

What if Rafe wants to kill me? Kenneth says he thinks you might have made a deal with Rafe, and Rafe's got men trying to find us as we speak.

This was so not good. Jade texted her again. Under Kenneth's coercion, you took my son away from the house. Kenneth needed you to do it, right? Jade felt Lizzie *hadn't* taken her son under any kind of coercion—she did it because she thought she'd be on Kenneth's good side. But Jade was trying to coax Lizzie into believing she didn't think ill of her.

Yes.

All right. And you've been taking good care of Toby, correct?

Yes.

Jade prayed Lizzie was telling the truth. Okay, then we'll help you get away from Kenneth, while protecting both you and Toby. All right?

He's coming.

Wait! Where are you?

Jade stared at her phone, hating that she hadn't

learned a location, hoping Kenneth wasn't behind the request for money instead.

Jade was certain that no human family would be willing to pay a million dollars for a three-year-old boy. But Lizzie might try to sell him on her own, if she thought that would be safer than dealing with Rafe and trying to get his money.

Since no messages were forthcoming, Jade stopped pacing and looked up at Rafe. "Lizzie said he was coming. I hope she didn't get caught." She ground her teeth, and he wrapped his arm around her.

"What did we get, Edward?" he asked him.

"We've got a location on the phone Lizzie was using," Edward said. "Only a half hour from here."

Ohmigod, Jade couldn't believe it. She'd thought everyone was waiting for her to get the location from Lizzie.

"I've called it in. A couple of other guys are meeting us there," Edward said as they all moved back into the house.

"I can't believe they're that close," Jade said, completely shocked. She figured they'd be far away.

She stalked toward the garage.

"We didn't think they would be either. Most of my men have been looking for Lizzie and Kenneth's men in and around Texas since they know the place better," Rafe said. "And our kind are territorial. I didn't believe Kenneth would be foolish enough to be right here in the neighborhood, so to speak. I thought he'd made sure we couldn't track Lizzie and Toby."

"Maybe Lizzie's phone wasn't being protected. I don't know."

"Shouldn't you stay here?" Aidan asked, as she hurried to leave.

Jade *wasn't* staying put. "I know Lizzie. I can convince her to give me my son." Not that this was open to discussion.

"I don't like it, but we'll do it your way," Rafe said, rushing along with everyone else out to the car.

On edge and terrified they'd reach Lizzie's location too late or that the text had really been from Kenneth, Jade frowned at Aidan. "Shouldn't you stay at Rafe's place?"

"Are you kidding? The only reason I'd stay would be to watch over you."

"You're the one my brother wants for his own nefarious reasons," she reminded him as they climbed into a Hummer limo. For a minute, she just stared at all the features it had: a refrigerator, glasses for drinks, and tiny white lights for illumination. It looked like a party-mobile.

"Bulletproof windows, bulletproof armor and tires," Edward explained when he saw her jaw drop.

"And the drinks?" Jade asked, moving into the back with Rafe. Aidan sat up front, while Edward drove.

"For thirsty guests." Rafe pulled her into his arms on the bench seat, and she leaned against him, though she couldn't relax.

What if Kenneth killed her son as revenge because she'd gotten Rafe and his people involved? And killed Lizzie for betraying him?

Rafe rubbed her arm with a soothing caress. "We need to be prepared in case this is a setup."

"Which is why I thought Aidan should be left behind," Jade said.

"And you." Aidan glanced over the seat at her. "Now

that Kenneth most likely believes you're courting Rafe, he could easily think that if he took you hostage, Rafe would want to pay to get you back."

"Don't be ridiculous. That would be such a long shot. My brother wouldn't take the risk. Let's say somehow he did get ahold of me. Then he'd have me and my son. Period. He could still try to sell Toby. Me? All I could do is cause trouble for him."

Rafe kissed her on the top of her head. Jade knew her son could be a real problem for him and his friends. Even though she and Rafe had some real chemistry between them, the issue of Toby couldn't easily be settled.

"Would he kill you if he asked for ransom and Rafe didn't pay it?" Aidan asked.

She let out her breath in exasperation. "A few days ago, I would have said no. But he took my son to force me to learn where you were, and then I find out he's been dealing in stolen cars, has an out-of-control gambling addiction, and plans to sell my son instead of returning him to me. I can't be certain."

"Aidan's got a point. No way could I let him get ahold of you, but if something did happen like that, I'd sure as hell pay the ransom. The problem is that your brother is way too unpredictable. Who knows what else he's been doing or plans to do," Rafe said, rubbing her arm consolingly.

"What about your other men? Are they still looking elsewhere for Kenneth, or is everyone going to converge on the same place?" Jade asked.

Rafe shook his head. "We've told a couple more of my men to join us in case we need their help, but the rest are still searching for anyone in your pack, including Kenneth, in case he's not with Lizzie, or in case they've already left the area by the time we get there."

"Where are they exactly?" she asked. The homes in the area they were driving through were smaller, with smaller yards.

"Looks like the location is near a small shopping plaza," Aidan said.

Jade was staring out the windows, trying to see if she could recognize any pack cars. Then she saw Lizzie's red Camaro. "There! That's her car!"

"I heart Lizzie?" Rafe asked, when he saw the license plate.

"Yeah. That's it. That's her! In the pink blouse and flowery pants."

She was getting out of the car to meet with a middle-aged blond-haired couple who were leaving a blue Ford sedan.

Lizzie quickly greeted them, so eager to do her business that she didn't see Edward pulling up behind her car, blocking her in. There was no sign of Toby, and Jade prayed he was in the backseat.

The man offered his hand to Lizzie.

Jade was out of the car before Edward had even come to a full stop, and Rafe bolted after her. She practically flew to the other side of the car as Lizzie screamed in shock to see her.

Lizzie attempted to bolt while Jade tried the door handle, but the car was locked. Thank God Toby was sound asleep in his car seat.

Aidan chased Lizzie down in the parking lot.

"You can't take me in. I was babysitting him. Her

brother made me," Lizzie blurted out, struggling to get free of Aidan's iron grip on her arms.

"Did he make arrangements with these people and then you took advantage of the situation because you knew it was in the works, or did he intend to sell Toby to someone else?" Aidan asked, tying her hands behind her back with a plastic tie.

"These people."

"Where are the keys to your car?" Jade asked, ready to punch her.

"In my pocket," Lizzie said quickly.

Jade dug out the keys and ran back to where Rafe was still safeguarding the car and Toby. Her hand was shaking so hard that Rafe offered to unlock the car for her. Tears spilled down her cheeks, and she was mad at herself for being so emotional. She didn't want Toby to see her so upset and be worried.

Rafe unlocked the door and moved back so Jade could reach inside and unbuckle Toby. He woke as she was struggling with the harness, frustrated that she couldn't unfasten it because she was rushing. She took a calming breath, and Toby suddenly said, "Mommy," his voice groggy.

Edward motioned with a badge to the couple and started questioning them about buying a toddler from the woman who had stolen him from his mother. They were stammering and stuttering about it being legitimate.

Jade got her son out of his car seat, grabbed his leopard blanket, and headed for the safety of Rafe's car while Rafe unfastened the car seat.

"Mommy, where were you?"

Someday, when he was older, she could explain what

had happened. Right now, she only wanted to hold him tight, shower him with kisses, and fight the tears that kept threatening to spill.

"And you'd pay for the boy in a public parking lot and make the transfer here?" Edward asked the couple, sounding like he didn't believe them one bit.

"We…we thought it was a good idea at the time," the man said.

Another car pulled up, and two men got out. Both were wearing black suits. Rafe nodded to them.

"We'll let you off with a warning," Rafe said to the couple as he removed the child's seat to put it in his vehicle. "But," he continued, carrying Toby's seat to his car, "we'll get your information first. We're on a special task force to take down people like this woman and her partners. If we learn you've tried to buy another child through irregular means, you'll be going to prison for a very long time."

Jade wanted them all to go to prison. But she knew that since Rafe and his men were *lupus garous*, they couldn't be involved with the police.

The men in suits started to take down information from the couple, and once they were released, they didn't hesitate to leave.

Toby hugged Jade and she kissed him all over the face. "Toby, are you okay?"

He nodded and hugged her tight. She scooted into the backseat of Rafe's car, worried her brother might show up when he discovered Lizzie was gone. Jade imagined Lizzie wasn't supposed to be out with Toby, but in the text, Lizzie had warned that Kenneth was coming. Was that a lie? Just a way to stop the texting and do what she planned to do? Sell Toby on her own once she learned Kenneth was interested in another woman?

"Drive Lizzie to the safe house. One of you take her car," Rafe said to the other men. "Learn where Kenneth Ashton is. We'll take the boy and his mother from here." He didn't say back to his home, but Jade suspected that's what he meant.

She couldn't have been happier to have her son safe in her arms. But she feared that if she left to go somewhere else, Kenneth would hunt her down.

Edward stayed with them as their bodyguard and driver, and Aidan returned to the passenger seat of the car. Then Rafe climbed in with Jade and Toby, wrapping his arm around her shoulders and holding her close, as if she wasn't now holding her little boy in her lap.

She leaned against him as Toby told her the stuff he'd eaten, how Uncle Ken was mean to him, and how Lizzie was nice and played with him lots. She said they were going on an adventure. "Where were you, Mommy?"

"I—"

Toby frowned at her.

"I'm here now, and I'm not leaving you again like that."

He snuggled his head against her chest, but then he lifted his chin and studied Rafe, who was looking down at him. "Daddy?"

"I'm Rafe," he said, smiling a little. "A friend of your mom's." Rafe glanced at Jade, but she was too busy cuddling her son to notice. Had the boy's father looked like him? No, the boy had never met his dad.

"Lizzie said Daddy was coming to take me home."

Toby folded his arms across his stomach and gave Rafe a mutinous look.

Rafe noticed Edward glancing at the rearview mirror and his brother peering over the front seat at him, smiling. Toby reminded Rafe of himself at that age. Only he'd been a cantankerous wolf.

"Rafe is a friend. You can call him Rafe," Jade said, finally helping him out, though she'd watched him squirm a bit before she said anything.

He wasn't used to kids. Sure, he'd been one once, but what did he remember about it?

Then Toby began to talk nonstop again. "We played hide-and-seek and chase, and I got to color. I got hot dogs whenever I wanted. With cheese on top. And ice-cream cones. And pizza. But Lizzie made me take naps. I don't take naps. I told Lizzie I'm too old for naps."

Jade smiled at him. "Even adults take naps when we're tired."

"I wasn't tired."

Rafe had no plans to let Jade go anywhere until Kenneth had been dealt with. She would be perfectly safe at his place, but he wondered just how childproof he needed to make the house. What he would need to make the boy comfortable. Did he sleep in a bed? Need diapers? A special potty? *Hell*.

"Okay, I need you to make me a list of everything you need for Toby while the two of you live with me," Rafe said.

"Shoot, all I'd thought about was getting Toby back. I didn't think about clothes or anything else." She said to Edward, "Can you take us to a children's clothing store and a grocery store?"

Aidan checked his phone for the location of a children's clothing store, then set the GPS to take them there.

"Nothing fancy," she said.

"Whatever's convenient," Rafe said. "None of us like to shop. I'd say it's our least favorite duty in life."

When they pulled into a parking lot, she stared at the fancy summer dresses and little boys' suits displayed in the windows of the shop Aidan had directed them to.

"Can we go to another store? Just something cheap?"

"No, let's go in. I'd rather just shop here, and then we can go to the grocery store after that and get you both back to my house," Rafe said.

"Okay." Jade started to leave the car, but so did all the guys. She realized it was hot out and they probably couldn't have stayed in the car for too long without overheating. Or maybe they were worried that her brother might suddenly show up and grab her and Toby. But she didn't imagine he'd try it in a children's clothing store. With Toby in hand, she headed for the shop while Rafe held the door for her. Everyone waited until Rafe followed her inside.

She didn't want to take too long, but she needed to make sure she got enough clothes to last about a week and ensure they weren't too expensive. Which is why she'd wanted to go to a discount children's shop. She didn't need fancy; she just needed wearable.

Jade walked straight to the sales racks, not expecting Rafe to follow her. But he did, closely, and said, "Get what you need. I'll put it on my card. Don't worry about the cost."

She wondered if he was afraid of how it would look to anyone who saw him with her son wearing normal, everyday clothes, but she quickly discounted that notion as she considered Rafe's jeans, T-shirt, and boots, which made him look like an undercover police officer, not a real estate mogul.

She thanked him, but she continued to look through the sales clothes.

Toby began to run his hands through soft sweaters and picked one up to hold against his chest like she did when she was measuring him for size. "This one, Mommy."

It was a purple sweater for a little girl.

"How about you look at these sweaters." Jade motioned to another table and folded the purple sweater back onto its stack. "They're for boys."

Toby eyed the purple sweater, then nodded and headed for the other table. He picked out a bright-orange one, and she thought he'd look like a pumpkin. "This one, Mommy."

She hated to look at the price tag. The fall clothes didn't have any sales.

"Looks good," Rafe said, smiling, his hands folded across his chest. "Just the one I would have picked."

Toby grabbed another and offered it to him. "Here's 'nother."

"Little too small. But next time I'm in a men's shop, I'll see if I can find one."

"Okay. We can match."

Edward and Aidan were standing near the door in the little girls' section, looking highly amused. Jade imagined that all three men were totally out of their element here. Toby handed the sweater to Jade and then glanced at Rafe's stance and copied it, arms folded over his small chest, watching Jade.

When she pulled out a brown gingham shorts set with a train appliquéd on the T-shirt, Toby frowned at it, then looked to see if Rafe liked it. He raised his brows. Toby shook his head. Rafe shook his head.

"Oh, for heaven's sake, you two." Jade kept pulling out different shorts sets that met with negative responses until she found a blue T-shirt set with a brontosaurus appliquéd on it that she knew Toby would love. He loved all things dinosaur. Wolves too, but finding them in toddler's clothes was nearly impossible. She had to order those online.

Toby immediately smiled.

But then he looked at Rafe to see his take on it, and Jade gave Rafe a warning look that he'd better like it. Although he wasn't paying any attention to her, Rafe gave Toby a smile and a thumbs-up.

"I like it, Mommy."

She sighed and found one with baseball bats, another with a puppy dog, and a few others she got *both* to agree on. After trying a jacket on him, making sure it was a little bigger so Toby could wear it longer, she picked up everything else she needed, including jeans, sandals, another pair of sneakers, and underwear.

Rafe carried her merchandise to the counter. Rafe pulled out his credit card and handed it to the clerk. "Maybe the owner or manager would be interested in *your* children's specialty designs," Rafe said.

"Janine Pragley is in her office. I'll call back there, if you'd like to talk to her," the store clerk said.

"But…" Jade looked down at Toby, worried about having him with her while she tried to talk to the manager.

"Toby and I will just wait for you with the others. Right, Toby?"

"Right," he said, nodding vigorously.

"She said she'd see you," the clerk said when she returned. "Just go into the office through that door." She continued to ring up the items and fold them neatly on the counter.

"Thanks." Jade looked up at Rafe. "Are you sure you're all right with this?"

"Absolutely." Rafe smiled back at her, but she wasn't sure if he could handle Toby.

"All right. Behave yourself with Rafe, Toby."

Chapter 11

WHAT COULD GO WRONG WITH WATCHING A THREE-YEAR-old? Rafe didn't believe he'd run into any trouble.

"So what do you like to do?" Rafe asked Toby as Jade rushed off to speak with the manager.

"Play ball. Do you?"

"Volleyball. In the pool." Rafe and his brother had been into long-distance running—in competition against each other either as wolves or humans. They'd also done the usual outdoor sports for wolves—climbing, hiking, running, bicycling, swimming. Playing group sports like baseball, basketball, or football meant mixing it up with humans, and they didn't care much for that, except when it came to business and they had to. Even the human social gatherings that Rafe still had were all to do with business.

He and Aidan hadn't gone to human schools, so they hadn't done a lot of things that Toby would probably do when he was a little older.

"You got a pool? I need a bathing suit. Mommy didn't get me one."

"Got to remedy that. One swimsuit coming right up." The clerk smiled.

"Be right back." Rafe walked back to a table with swimsuits and began digging through them, looking for the same size as Jade had picked out. Toby was like a little puppy dog, brushing up against his side as if he didn't want to lose him.

Toby began pulling out the swimsuits and discarding them quickly, just like Rafe, but Rafe was doing it because the swimsuits weren't the right size. He pulled out a pair of board shorts covered in blue fish. "What about this one?"

They ended up getting that one, plus Mickey Mouse shorts, a sun-protective rash-guard swimsuit featuring palm trees, and a bright-neon rash-guard swim set with sharks.

"No wolves." Toby's dark-brown eyes widened. "Oh, oh, oh, gotta have pj's. Mommy forgot."

That meant a trip to a table stacked with pj's, where they ended up with Ninja Turtles, Superman, Spider-Man, Captain America, and a couple of different kinds of dinosaurs.

"Anything else?" Rafe asked.

Toby looked thoughtfully around the room. "Floaties?"

"We'll go to the toy store for those."

"Yes!"

Rafe took the clothes to the counter, and the clerk began ringing up the rest of the items just as Jade came out of the manager's office, smiling.

Then she frowned at the new pile of clothes.

"He reminded me he needed pj's and swimsuits for the pool."

Toby grinned. "And we're going to get toys."

She groaned. "Don't you talk him into buying the whole store out. Just a couple of things."

When the cashier had finished ringing up their purchases, Rafe took the sacks of clothing but gave the smallest bag to Toby. "Gotta help your mom carry the bags."

Toby seized the bag with his arms and crushed it against his body. "*Mommy's* not carrying any."

"That's because we're being extra nice and carrying them all for her."

Jade slipped her hand around Toby's arm. "Can you manage okay?"

"I can carry it."

"Good. That will give you big muscles like me," Rafe said, showing off his bicep.

Toby looked like he was getting ready to drop the sack, but when Jade offered to carry it for him, he shook his head. "I got it."

When they left the store, Rafe asked, "Good news?"

"Yes, I have until the end of the year to get an order ready for the store for spring."

"Good deal."

"Thanks for buying everything, Rafe."

"No problem."

"You didn't have to buy that many swim trunks."

"Yes he did. I wanted them," Toby explained.

She just shook her head. "You are such a pushover, Rafe. Who would have ever thought?"

Aidan laughed and Edward was grinning as they approached the door.

When they arrived at the toy store, Rafe couldn't believe all the fun things kids had to play with. Jade was right. He wanted to buy a little of everything.

Aidan said Toby had to have a bike, and he helped him pick out the right size and the color—a bright-red one. "I've wanted this my whole life," Toby said.

Edward tracked down floaties and enough swimming toys to practically fill the swimming pool. Rafe hadn't expected Edward to get into this, but he wasn't surprised that Aidan would head for the bicycles first.

Rafe helped Toby pick out a fleet of toy trucks and cars to play with. Jade picked up a bunch of books, a couple of coloring books, crayons, and a big, snuggly green-and-blue dinosaur.

"Need a toy chest, Boss?" Edward asked, his arms full of packages of inflatable pool toys, including a smiling, colorful gecko float, an octopus ring toss, and a basketball hoop for kids.

"Yeah, let's get one." Rafe figured even when Jade left, he could help her get settled into a place of her own close by, and she could take all this stuff with her. He hoped she would agree to stay here in California. He'd already decided he didn't want her returning to Texas. Too far away and too close to her pack.

He eyed the bicycle in the box resting at Aidan's feet. "Sure you can put it together by yourself?"

"Edward said he can do it. I'll help," Aidan said.

Rafe had never been to a toy store. Neither had his brother or bodyguard. He and the others had been children way before toy stores were around.

As they loaded the trunk with the booty, Rafe said, "I was thinking we could take Toby to Disneyland. And the San Diego Zoo."

"Pleeease, Mommy?" Toby asked, holding her hand and giving her a wide-eyed look that was sure to convince her to go along with the plan.

"What about Kenneth and his pack?" she asked Rafe.

"We'll take Edward and Aidan with us. No one will hassle us," Rafe said.

Looking for his consensus, Jade glanced at Aidan.

He shrugged. "Never been to either. First time for everything. I have nothing better to do until the charity ball."

Edward said, "I do whatever you tell me to, Boss."

"See? It's all settled." Rafe opened the back door.

"See, Mommy? It's okay."

Rafe chuckled. He liked the kid, though he thought the tyke would mess up his organized way of living. He had to admit it remained to be seen how this would all play out while they stayed with him. For instance, would the toys stay in their appropriate places, or would they be scattered all over the house? Granted, it was a large house, but Rafe liked it neat and orderly.

Would the boy sleep in, or would he be up at all hours?

Rafe knew he shouldn't take on any role other than protector for both Jade and her son, but he couldn't help wanting to spend quality time with her. Alone. He could just imagine snuggling with her on the couch and Toby wanting to curl up on her lap. Or kissing her and getting caught. Or wanting to watch a movie with her that might be unsuitable for youngsters when Toby wanted to watch an animated feature…with them. At least Toby wasn't as clingy with her around Rafe as he had been when Aidan took blood from her in Texas. Toby had stayed with Rafe without objecting one bit when Jade talked to the clothing store manager. Maybe Toby had just been uncomfortable around Kenneth and his pack.

As soon as they got home, Toby wanted to play in the pool. He was like a kid at Christmas, and Rafe swore Edward was too as he carried the pool toys outside and began to blow them up.

Aidan, Rafe, and Jade helped carry the rest of the

packages in—groceries, toys, and Toby's clothes. Toby carried the stuffed dinosaur himself, though he stumbled a bit because it was so big.

"Want to trade this package for the dinosaur?" Rafe asked. The package had Toby's swimsuits in it and was much lighter and more manageable.

"No, thanks. But you can play with Dino later."

"Thanks. I'll do that," Rafe said.

Jade started to carry Toby's clothes into her room, but Rafe stopped her. "Did you want one of the other spare rooms for Toby?"

"No. I'm sure he'll want to sleep with me for now. When I leave here, he'll have his own room again."

Even though Rafe knew where this was headed, he didn't like that she planned to leave.

"Hey!" Aidan called out from the kitchen, and Rafe and Jade went to see where Toby had gone.

"He just raced across the patio in his birthday suit," Aidan said.

Jade laughed. "All little boys do that. You probably did too, even if you don't remember."

"Hey!" Edward called out to Toby. "Where are your swim trunks, buddy?"

"My name is Toby," he said, eyeing the octopus Edward had been blowing up. "Are you going swimming?"

"Maybe you ought to ask your mommy. She'll probably go swimming with you. But you should have some suntan lotion on and a pair of swim trunks."

"Toby, why don't you pick out a bathing suit you want to wear? They're lying on my bed. Come on. And Edward is right. I need to put some suntan lotion on you so you don't burn."

Toby followed his mom inside and said to Rafe, "Will you go swimming with us?"

"Maybe later. I need to make a couple of phone calls."

"Will you?" Toby asked Aidan.

"I'm putting away the groceries, Toby. Maybe later."

"Aww, everyone says that." Toby ran for the bedroom that he must have seen Jade entering, but she stopped him.

"Toby, this isn't our house, so you can't leave your clothes lying all over the place. Pick them up and take them into the room. Then we can get dressed and go swimming."

He made a big deal of raising his shoulders and dropping them as he reluctantly picked up his clothes.

Rafe couldn't help smiling. Somehow that jogged some memories. He might like things neat now, but he wasn't always that tidy. "Were you like that?" Rafe asked Jade as Toby ran into the bedroom carrying everything but a sock he'd missed.

"Yeah. You?"

"I guess most kids are."

"Are you sure none of you guys want to swim?"

"Later. I've got to make some business calls." Rafe also had to check what was going on with Lizzie and give his men direction.

"Okay, sounds good." Jade slipped into the bedroom. "Oh, you want to put on the shark one. I really like that one. I'm going into the bathroom to change. Be out in a second."

Rafe thought about how Jade had slipped out of her swimsuit under his poolside shower and how that would never happen again. A child changed the dynamics to such a degree. Well, a human child. Wolf children were used to stripping and shifting with siblings, parents, and the pack. It was natural and necessary. But Rafe understood that when Toby started school, he couldn't mention something like that to his teachers. Everyone in a pack with him would have to act as though they were human.

He could see why Jade wouldn't want to give up her son, who ran past him for the patio and pool while Rafe called one of his men for an update on Lizzie and locating Kenneth.

"Wait, Toby. You need to wait for your mom," Rafe said.

But Toby was already out the door and headed for the pool.

"Whoa, no getting in until your mom's out here," Edward said.

"But you're out here."

"And not dressed to go swimming. Do you know how to swim?" Edward asked.

"Sure. See?" Toby jumped in and so did Edward, just as Rafe ran onto the patio. Toby came up and dog-paddled toward the shallow end.

Fully dressed, Edward swore under his breath as he swam toward the edge of the pool.

Rafe laughed.

"You owe me a new watch and a phone, Boss." Edward pulled off his watch and set it on the patio. He slipped his phone out of its pouch and set it next to his watch, then swam to the shallow end.

"Toby!" Jade scolded as she ran out to see what had happened. "What have I said about getting in the water at a pool or lake?"

"Not to go in unless I have superbision."

"Supervision."

"Yeah." Toby pointed a finger at Edward. "He's swimming with me."

"He wasn't dressed to go swimming with you. You probably scared him to pieces," Jade said.

"He did." Edward climbed up the pool steps, sopping wet. He began pulling off his shirt.

"Are you going to be all right for the moment, Jade?" Rafe asked.

She was wearing a shimmering blue bathing suit, cut low on the bust and with a plunging back, but it was a lot more suitable for a mom who was going to play with her son in the pool than the one he'd seen her in before. Still, she looked just as hot in that swimsuit as she had in the other.

"Yes, we're fine. Go do your business." Jade turned to Edward. "I'm so sorry."

"No problem. Working for Rafe can be…different. I never know what to expect." Edward winked at her, and he only seemed darkly amused, not angry or annoyed.

Rafe was glad Edward wasn't mad. After what had happened to Jade and her son with her pack, she needed to feel safe and welcome.

Jade dove into the pool and swam after Toby. She tackled him in the water, and he squealed. Rafe wished she had done that to him.

Rafe moved back into the house and headed for the quiet of his office, talking to Hugh. "Okay, sorry about that. Did Lizzie tell you where Kenneth is?"

"She says she's innocent. That Kenneth made her do it."

"What did he have on her that would give him leverage to use against her?"

"Nothing she could tell us. Just that he'd kill her if she didn't do it. We don't believe her. She wanted to mate Kenneth, and when he got involved with another she-wolf, Lizzie realized she was going to lose out on everything. She felt used—her words—and thought she could get the money out of Jade, but then was afraid you'd kill her rather than pay for Toby's release and let her go. So she figured she was better off selling the boy to the couple that Kenneth had contacted and then taking off with the money."

"If she was innocent, why didn't she just contact us and turn the boy over?"

"That's what I asked her. She said she didn't have a job, and if she had to flee Kenneth's wrath, which she'd have to do, she'd have to have getaway money. She had Kenneth's new number, but it's been disconnected."

"Great. Where's Kenneth?"

"She took us to the furnished rental unit, but it's been vacated. She said she thought he got spooked when she slipped out with the boy. Maybe he saw the whole scene play out in the parking lot, so he took off to cut his losses."

"Did Lizzie know what Kenneth wanted Aidan for?" Rafe asked.

"To get back their longevity. We know your brother is just trying to find a way to stop us from aging even faster than humans, if that comes to pass. But Kenneth wants to live forever. And he thought Aidan was about to find the cure, make a ton of money on it, and manage the cure. Kenneth thought this cure was a fast way to make a load of money without having to do anything for it."

"Ironic, isn't it? He won't get my brother or his research, but his life expectancy will be cut shorter than he ever imagined."

"Agreed. What do we do with Lizzie? Kill her? Let her go? Hold on to her?"

"We've got to catch Kenneth. I don't trust that Jade is safe on her own. He might want Lizzie dead for betraying him. So she can be bait. If he comes for her, you can grab him. I'll deal with him after that."

"If we have no choice but to kill him?"

"It's your call. But let me know if you get any leads."

"Will do."

After they ended the call, Rafe got ahold of Sebastian. "Hey, listen. We got Jade's little boy back, and for the next few days, I'd like to hang with Jade and Toby in case Kenneth makes the fatal mistake of trying to grab either one of them. We'll be going to Disneyland for the day tomorrow and to the San Diego Zoo the next day. If you need me for anything, just call or text."

"Gotcha. If you need me for anything else, just let me know."

"I need you managing the business right now. So, thanks for the great job as usual."

"Are we still on for the charity ball?"

"Yeah." Which reminded Rafe that he needed to take Jade shopping for an evening gown.

Though the house was well insulated, he could hear Toby's childlike laughter poolside and realized how foreign that sounded. Adult conversation and laughter, yes, but no one played in the pool except for when he, Aidan,

Derek, or Sebastian swam laps. Sometimes they played volleyball. But a child's laughter seemed so out of place.

"Sounds like someone's having fun," Sebastian said, his enhanced wolf hearing picking up sounds humans couldn't hear.

"Yeah, Toby and his mom are swimming."

"And Aidan. Edward is catching the ball when it goes out of bounds…when it's out of the water. How come his pants are soaking wet? He's gotten rid of his shirt too."

"Long story." Rafe assumed Sebastian was at his separate guest house grabbing lunch and was watching all the activity from his kitchen windows.

"Okay, Boss, good show. I'll take care of it."

"Thanks. Out here." Rafe should have been looking for his next big real-estate deal, but he knew Sebastian would be taking up the slack for him. All he wanted to do was see what was going on at the pool. Well, more than that. He wanted to join in on the fun.

He realized he was usually more serious, more business-oriented, definitely more used to adult kinds of pursuits. He stripped out of his clothes and pulled on a pair of board shorts, then headed out his patio door to the pool.

Sure enough, Sebastian was right. Edward was shoeless and shirtless, his hair and skin wet, his pants still soaking from the earlier swim.

Aidan was now shooting baskets with Toby, giving the tyke a boost so he could reach the basket. Rafe paused to watch as Jade sat in the water on the stairs observing her son and Aidan. Edward pulled off his sopping-wet jeans and hung them over the wall, then spotted Rafe.

In his boxers, Edward grinned at him.

Amused at his bodyguard, Rafe smiled a little and shook his head. Then he walked over and dove into the deep end. If Aidan didn't mind, Rafe would leave him and another bodyguard here to watch over Toby while Rafe and Edward took Jade to shop for a dress. Rafe wasn't used to always having a bodyguard with him. He'd enjoyed his free time with Jade before this, but with Kenneth still on the loose, he planned to take every precaution.

Jade was smiling at him as Aidan continued to play basketball with Toby. The boy seemed tireless and unaware Rafe had joined the pool party. Jade swam out to Rafe, and he was glad she did. Not that he wanted an audience, but as soon as she got close, he pulled her into his arms and paddled to keep afloat with her.

"I didn't know my brother would be good with kids."

She smiled up at Rafe. "You too. That's the first time Toby has stayed with an adult male without fussing to go with me."

Rafe shrugged. "I was a kid once. Though it was a very long time ago. Listen, we still need to go shopping for you to buy an evening gown."

"I really don't need to go now. I'll need to keep Toby under wraps. I'll just stay with him in the bedroom. You have a large-screen TV there, and he'll love it. You practically bought out the entire collection of toys at the store, and we can play to our hearts' content."

"Absolutely not. We can have him at the party for a while, and then someone else can sit with him in the den, play, read him stories, and watch TV with him."

"Rafe—"

"We'll make sure he has fun. And if you feel uncomfortable with the crowd, you can slip away. But I want to warn you, I've contacted a few specialty children's clothing shop owners in LA, and they're excited to meet you."

"Ohmigod, Rafe, you couldn't have."

"Yep."

"You bribed them?" Jade looked so incredulous that he smiled.

"Not exactly. The notion they could hobnob with the upper echelon and get on my good side?" He shrugged. "Believe me, they were thrilled to be asked, and just as excited to meet with you. I told them you had a toddler of your own, and several said they were shooting new ads for fall and spring and would love to have your son model for them. I sent them the photo you shared with me."

She laughed. "Wow."

"I want you to live nearby where I can watch out for you and provide resources so your son can be taken care of when you need to work."

Jade had tears in her eyes, and he hoped they were happy ones. "No strings attached?" she asked.

"Hell no. There *are* strings attached. Unless you find some other wolf you fall head over heels for, I want to take you places—Toby too. I want to take you on dates. And that's why I want someone we both trust to take care of him. I don't want you leaving my home until we've resolved the issue with your brother and your pack though." Rafe let out his breath, afraid he was rushing through all of what he wanted to say but wanting to get it out while Aidan kept Toby preoccupied. "I don't want you to feel I'm taking over your life, but I want to be there to support and protect you when you need a friend or help." He sighed. "How do you feel about this?"

"Rafe…I-I don't want to be an imposition. I can just hear your hired help complaining to one another about having babysitting duty. Or poor Aidan will never visit you because he's afraid he'll be stuck watching Toby."

"Are you kidding? He'll probably get him a junior science kit and start teaching him all about science stuff. And I heard him say he's going to take Toby bike riding out front later today."

"Still, Aidan doesn't have to see Toby full time because he'll be leaving after the ball. Whereas you will when you're not working while we're staying here."

"Let's just see how it goes," Rafe said, wishing to take this a hell of a lot further with the hot she-wolf who turned his thermostat up to sizzling. But he wasn't sure he could deal with the issue of Toby being human. "As for my bodyguards?" He just chuckled. "I've never seen Edward so desperate to rescue someone, much less to get in on the act and play with Toby and Aidan while they're in the water. Don't worry about it. This has been a nice diversion for them. If they've got a beef with me, they'll let me know about it. They wouldn't talk behind my back. They know I'm perfectly up-front with them, as they are with me."

"Hey," Aidan called to them. "Toby's hungry, and we've decided to have a couple of man-size pizzas. Edward, you want to join us?"

"What about Mommy? And Rafe?" Toby asked, finally realizing they were at the far end of the pool.

"They have some boring things to talk about. We're going to have fun and see if we can find those Ninja Turtles on TV and have a pizza," Aidan said.

"We'll be in later," Jade said to Toby.

"See you soon," Rafe added.

Edward was already opening the door, towel wrapped around his waist.

As soon as Aidan got a couple of towels and wrapped Toby in one, he headed inside, carrying the boy over his shoulder.

And Rafe cupped Jade's cheeks, lifting her face to his, and kissed her.

Chapter 12

THE KISS WAS DIFFERENT BETWEEN JADE AND RAFE THIS TIME as they floated in the pool together. Their first kiss on the beach had been hot, but then he'd put on the brakes. In the laundry room, that was another story.

Now, there was quiet desperation. Of wanting to get to know each other better, and yet being unsure about how Rafe felt about her son. She understood that, knew she'd have to deal with Rafe's feelings toward Toby. She didn't want to regret having Toby, but she couldn't deny she loved how Rafe made her feel—loved, desirable, sexy, and needed in his life. She thought the world of Toby and had believed he would be enough to make her whole. She'd thought they didn't need the rest of the world, and living with her brother and his pack had solidified that notion.

Until she'd met Rafe. She was falling hard for the wolf, and she realized she needed that adult part of her life too.

She kissed him now as if there was no tomorrow, because there very well might not be. Not if Rafe couldn't deal with a ready-made family, and one that could really cause problems for him. It would be years before Toby was on his own, making a life for himself.

She understood all of that. The perfect life with someone like Rafe was most likely well out of her reach, and she'd best remember that. So why was she kissing him and holding him tight, showing him she needed his kisses and his touch just as much as he seemed to crave having hers?

His eyes were smoky with desire, his kisses full of want. This wasn't just a need for sex. Though *lupus garous* definitely had those needs, there was also a type of bonding that showed they wanted to go beyond a courtship. Wolves who accepted each other like this became mates.

She wrapped her legs around his waist and tongued his mouth, knowing she should give it up, but not wanting to. Jade had always had a rebellious streak, and hers was coming straight to the forefront now—when she knew darn well she should rein it in.

Rafe took advantage of the closeness, kissing her as if he had no regrets, but she knew this dream couldn't last. That reality would come crashing down, and she would be back where she'd been for the last three years. She had no intention of disrupting Rafe's life, and she knew in the end it would be just her and Toby against the world.

Rafe groaned as he hugged her tight against his chest. "I know," he said, his voice deep with desire. "I said if you fell head over heels for someone, I'd butt out, but hell, Jade, you can't do this to me and not expect me to want more."

She smiled up at him, loving how no matter what, he had a sense of humor. Then she lost the smile and said honestly, "There is the hurdle of what to do about Toby."

"You know what I think? We need to just take this one day at a time. Not that being with you like this

makes that easy." He kissed her forehead. "Do you want
to go in, have some pizza, and then we can go shopping
for that dress?"

"Sure." What she really, really wanted was more
of this.

As soon as they left the pool, they threw on robes and
walked into the house.

"I'll have to get a couple of pint-size terry cloth robes
for Toby," Rafe said, and she smiled up at him, thankful
he wanted to make sure her son was taken care of. It
wasn't the same as saying he wanted Toby in his life,
but she appreciated anyone who treated Toby as though
he were important and not a horrible mistake.

The smell of pepperoni pizzas cooking made her
mouth water. In the kitchen, Edward, Aidan, and Toby
were all topping another couple of pizzas. Edward was
cutting up the mushrooms and shredding the cheese,
and Aidan and Toby were sprinkling them on the pizza.
She wished she'd had her phone on her to capture the
moment. They were all so cute. Toby was concentrating
hard to do everything just like Aidan, getting cheese on
the floor, on the counter, and on his shirt as he stood on
a stool to reach the pizza.

"Next we add the pepperoni, just like you wanted,"
Aidan said, and he showed Toby how to space the slices
on the pizza.

Jade smiled, loving Aidan for being so good with
Toby. "We're going to get dressed and join you. Then
Rafe wants to take me shopping for a dress."

"I wanna go," Toby said, looking up from his work.

"You don't want to watch the Turtles with me?"
Aidan asked, feigning hurt.

She couldn't imagine him *really* wanting to watch the animated show with her son.

Toby looked torn — be with Mommy or stay to watch the Turtles.

"We'll have ice cream too," Aidan said, attempting to tilt the scale in his favor.

"Okay." Then Toby went back to helping with the pizzas, won over by an ice-cream cone.

Rafe led Jade away from the kitchen. "What did I tell you? My brother is a natural, and Edward looks to be doing well himself."

"All right." She wasn't certain the fun would last. "But I'll give them my number, and if Toby starts fussing, we can head back here. Not that he should be allowed to always get his way, but I don't want Aidan and Edward to have to put up with it if he doesn't and complains."

"They'll be fine."

She sure hoped so. A three-year-old could change from an angel into a tyrant in the blink of an eye.

Sebastian stayed outside the formal-wear dress shop to guard the entrance, while Jade and Rafe walked inside. She eyed the beautiful gowns, the whole place screaming, "Too rich for my blood."

"Maybe we could go to another place that has more of a selection."

"Let's look here first," Rafe said.

"How did you know about this place?" She wondered if he'd bought gowns here for women before. Why else would he know?

"Sebastian looked it up for us."

"Sebastian. He sure comes in handy."

"You don't know the half of it."

"What color do the women wear to these functions?" Jade asked as she began sifting through the gowns.

"Whatever color they like best."

She glanced up at him. "You don't know."

"I only know what I'll like," he said, pulling out a clingy, red silk gown.

She laughed. "Why is it that men love red dresses?"

"They're hot. I like this one."

"I'll have to try it on to see if it even fits."

A woman took the selection Jade had picked out as well as Rafe's red gown and set them up in a large, posh dressing room, complete with a fancy wrought iron bench with a tapestry seat cushion, paintings of Paris on the walls, and a large floor-to-ceiling mirror on one wall. So this was how the other half lived.

Jade hadn't wanted to look for price tags when she was on the floor, so she looked for them now in the privacy of the dressing room. And couldn't find one price tag. Why? If you had to ask, you couldn't afford it? Ugh.

Before she could even remove her clothes, Rafe said, "Be sure to model them for me."

She smiled. She figured she'd model the red dress last because, otherwise, he might buy it without even bothering to look at the others.

When she modeled a royal-blue one, he said, "Hell, Jade, you're going to look so good in all of them that I won't be able to choose just one."

She laughed, loving how sweet he was. "But I only need one."

"What about for the next event?"

She lifted a brow.

"Just saying."

"Be right back." She wasn't going to get more than one gown. Still annoyed that they didn't have prices listed on the dresses, she wanted to say to the saleswoman that if they didn't have a price tag, they were free, right?

She tried on four more gowns, but when she modeled the red one, Rafe said, "Sold."

She laughed. "You'd think I was at auction."

"Speaking of auctions, I need to buy you a necklace."

No way. Wolves rarely wore jewelry, and she wasn't going to start now. Then she realized everyone would probably be decked out in diamonds. *Sigh.* Well, he could get her a cubic zirconia and she would wear it just to this event.

When they went to check out, he wanted the royal blue gown too, overruling her objections.

He handed his credit card to the clerk, who looked at it and said, "We haven't seen you in here before, Mr. Denali. Would you like to open an account with us?"

"Later."

The woman smiled at both of them.

Jade frowned a little, hoping the woman didn't think she was Rafe's mistress, but the clerk didn't appear to know who he was.

They finished the transaction, and Rafe carried Jade's gowns out in the special dress bag.

"Thanks, Rafe."

"What about shoes?"

"I've got some that will work."

They climbed into the car and Rafe said, "Take us to the nearest fine jewelry store."

Sebastian's lips curved just a hint.

"For a faux diamond necklace," Jade said, not wanting Sebastian to get the idea Rafe was getting her an engagement ring, though she'd never known a wolf to wear an engagement or wedding ring.

"Sure thing, Boss," Sebastian said, still smiling as he did a search for the jewelry store. "Looks like you got what you needed here, so we don't need another dress shop, right?"

"We're good," Jade quickly said before Rafe wanted to take her to another one. On the way to the jewelry store, she asked, "Did you hear anything from your men about Lizzie?"

"Just the location where Kenneth and his men had been holed up—a furnished unit that can be rented by the day, week, or month. But they'd already packed up and left."

"Great. He could be anywhere then. Maybe he's given up on this whole charade."

"He's about thirty in human years like the rest of us, right? We still age more slowly than humans. Why is he in such a panic about this?" Rafe asked.

"No mate? As far as I know, he hasn't been interested enough in any she-wolf to make the commitment. I caught him yanking out a couple of gray hairs on the top of his head the other day when he was looking in the mirror in the living room—he didn't see me. Dad prematurely grayed. Mom didn't. I think Kenneth is starting to feel the age issue closing in on him."

"Well, if I get ahold of him, it will be closing in a lot

faster than he'd ever imagined. He won't have to worry about any more gray hairs," Rafe said.

"But I think it's mostly about him getting the money from the venture, as if there is going to be any." She had mixed feelings about her brother's impending disposition. She wouldn't feel she and Toby were completely safe unless Kenneth was eliminated, but the notion still weighed heavily on her. He *was* her twin brother. But Toby's health and welfare remained her focus.

"Are you okay?" Rafe asked her as he slipped his arm around her shoulders and pulled her close.

"Yeah," she said, leaning against him. "Sorry. I know Kenneth could continue to be trouble for Toby and me. It's just that…" She let out her breath.

"He's your brother."

"Yes."

"Which is damn well why he should be protective of you, not using you or your son, not threatening to kill Toby and not planning to sell him."

"Agreed."

"Here we are, folks," Sebastian said, pulling into a jewelry-store parking lot.

They headed inside, only this time Sebastian came in with them. Jade wondered if he wanted to see what she was getting.

She noticed right away that there was no faux jewelry of any kind. Everything glittered under the bright lights. She started to turn to tell Rafe that she wanted to go to a different store, but a salesperson started talking to him and then brought out a necklace Rafe had pointed to in the case.

The design was beautiful, like an Indian princess

would wear—rubies and diamonds all along the gold chain, with four large ruby teardrops surrounded by diamonds hanging off each side, all leading the eye downward to a larger ruby surrounded by a double row of diamonds. Stunning. It also had a matching set of ruby and diamond earrings.

Before she could say it was too much—glitter-wise, cost-wise, and every other kind of wise—Rafe was placing it around her neck, and she looked at it in the mirror.

If Jade were a little girl playing dress up with a faux necklace, it was perfect. But she wasn't.

She took a deep breath and exhaled before opening her mouth to say they'd look further. Maybe she could pick out a nice ruby pendant. The smallest one they had.

"We'll take it," Rafe said. "And the earrings. The clip-on variety."

"Rafe…" Jade started to object.

"What do you think, Sebastian?" Rafe asked.

"It's perfect. Great for Christmas too. Valentine's. Fourth of July social. Works for me."

"I was thinking—" Less would be better, she wanted to say.

"We'll take it," Rafe said and placed the necklace on the velvet display board.

Then he paid for it and escorted her out to the car. "Anything else?"

"That's way too costly and…"

"If he wants you to have it, it's yours. No talking him out of things when he's made up his mind," Sebastian said. "Of course, when he wants to be extravagant in paying for something for me, I'm all for it."

"Like what?" she asked, thinking that if Rafe

was always generous with his staff and friends, it wouldn't seem so overboard for him to get her a couple of nice things. Except for the cost. But like the dress, the cost was hidden, and Rafe had just paid for it without asking.

"A new car. He wanted me to have a vehicle that was more reliable than the old jalopy I used to drive. He pays good money, mind you, but cars are not a priority to me like they are to him."

Jade smiled, thinking of all the cars Rafe had.

"What if I don't go to anything else where I can wear such an extravagant necklace?" she asked Rafe.

"We'll make sure that you do. And I'll make sure we have different guests so you'll feel comfortable wearing it again at an event."

"Ha! As if I'd change out jewelry for every party. I don't even wear any, like most of us don't."

Rafe rubbed her shoulder. "You might not care, and it wouldn't matter to me because *you* are what is important, but some of the upper echelon—the women—can be terribly catty."

"I'll say," Sebastian remarked.

Jade could put the women in their place, but if she were to do business in the area, she figured she'd have to be nice.

As soon as they arrived home, Toby raced to see her and threw his arms around her as if she'd been gone for days. "I missed you all day."

She laughed. "We were only gone a couple of hours. Did you have fun with Aidan?"

"We're putting the bike together."

"Is it all together now?"

"Edward had to help. Maybe you can do it." He tugged at her hand to take her to the den.

She smiled. "It's getting late. You need to take a bath, and I'll read you a story before you go to bed."

"Aww."

"Remember, we're going to Disneyland tomorrow."

His eyes grew big. "Oh. Yeah."

"Did you eat something yet?"

"Peanut butter and jelly sandwich."

"Okay, good. We need to go to bed so we can go in the morning."

He pulled her hand and led her to the bedroom.

"Wait, say good night to everyone and thank them for your bike and everything else Rafe got you."

Toby ran into the den and said, "Good night and thanks. Gotta go to bed so we can go to Disneyland."

"Okay, buddy," Aidan said. "Good night."

"My name isn't Buddy. It's Toby. Night." Then he grabbed Jade's hand again and dragged her to the bedroom.

"I'll be back in a while," she said to Rafe as he surveyed the sight of the bike in pieces, tools lying out, and Edward on his knees with a wrench in hand while Aidan read the directions out loud.

"We only just started," Edward said, sounding defensive.

Rafe said, "Looks like we'll be at this for a while, so no rush."

"Okay."

After Jade tucked one sleepy little boy into bed, she read him a story as he snuggled with his dinosaur and his bear. She was so glad to hold him close again. Between the two stuffed animals, he was barely visible.

She kissed him good night. "Sleep. I'll be back in a little bit. I'm going to help put your bike together. Love you." She gave him a big hug.

"Love you too." He hugged her tight, then he closed his eyes, rolled over onto his stomach, and yawned.

She left the night-light on in the bathroom, then joined the men in the den. Although Rafe wasn't there.

"Where's Rafe?"

"Grilling shish kebabs," Aidan said. "He gave us the task of finishing this."

They were drinking beers now, and she considered where they'd left off on the bike. She had put Toby's tricycle and a swing set together. She knew she could do this too.

She began to work on it, and once it was standing in one piece, the guys shook their heads. "We should have just waited until you came home," Aidan said.

"I can't thank you all enough for everything," she said.

"No problem," Aidan said. "If you need us for anything, just let us know."

Edward and Sebastian nodded.

Rafe came in and announced, "Food is ready. Want a margarita?" he asked Jade.

"Yeah, sure. Thanks."

At dinner, they talked more about how they were going to handle the situation with Kenneth, how they would take one car to Disneyland, and how Sebastian would stay behind to handle financial matters.

"You're going to miss out," Aidan said to Sebastian. He only smiled.

After they ate, Rafe guided Jade out to the patio while

Aidan went to watch a movie in the living room, where he could see the hallway if Toby should get scared or begin to wander around, looking for his mother. Sebastian said good night, and Edward went to get some shut-eye for the Disneyland adventure tomorrow.

"You know you're going to have to turn Toby," Rafe said, snuggling with Jade on a cushy love seat poolside as the stars filled the night sky and the waves crashed along the beach. He'd been thinking about it a lot, ever since he'd learned about her human son, and he couldn't come up with any other solution. Once he'd been around Toby, he'd seen him as a flesh-and-blood little boy who needed his mother. And she needed him.

Adopting him out no longer was a solution. The question wasn't whether he should be changed, but when he had to be changed. And that time had to be soon. Rafe knew this had to be Jade's decision, but he also knew why she wasn't doing what she had to know in her heart was right. "He needs to learn how to socialize with others in a wolf pack while he's still young enough. His wolf half won't be able to deal successfully with other wolves as he gets older otherwise."

"And how's that going to happen?"

"We'll all help out."

She let out her breath. "I don't expect you to be at my beck and call whenever I need you while Toby's growing up. If he's a wolf, he can change anytime, especially during the full moon. I'll have no control over it. It's risky."

"Then we get him a reliable wolf nanny. We'll make this work, Jade. He can't be human when you need to have time to shift. Even when he gets older, what happens then? He'll learn to control the shift, but he needs to be one of us. My brother just told me that Hunter Greymere, an alpha wolf who led his pack in the California redwoods, had to resettle his pack at his uncle's cabins in Oregon and mated a woman who had a similar history to Toby.

"She photographs wolves. Her brother paints them. They might not have been able to shift before they were turned, but they were just as drawn to wolves as the wolves are drawn to them. They still have some of our genetic wolf roots. And from what I understand, it was from a grandfather, so even more distant *lupus garou* roots than Toby's are."

"You've only been around him for a few hours today. He gets cranky and unreasonable sometimes. Most of the time, he's really good. But he's still learning how to socialize with children. Take your charity ball. What if he was turned, and he suddenly had the urge to shift?"

"At some point in his life, he's going to see you shift, or someone you know shift. It's inevitable. What are you going to do then?"

When she didn't respond, Rafe tightened his hold on her and kissed her cheek. "Listen, I know you can't do this alone. A single mom with shifter children has a difficult enough time, but at least with *her* kids, they only shift when she does until they're old enough to know not to shift unless it's safe. Which is why you will need others to help you with this.

"I spoke to Aidan, and he said Toby wouldn't have to be bitten. Just a transfer in his bloodstream would be enough. Toby doesn't have the advantage of being born as a *lupus garou*. If he had been, he'd be used to shifting already and playing with others in his pack. So we'll all have to work with him to teach him how important it is to keep secrets."

Jade snorted. "Telling Toby to keep secrets is like telling him not to do something. A friend of mine lost her German shepherd to old age, and I got her a puppy. I told Toby to keep it a secret until we picked up the puppy. As soon as Lisette walked in the door to have lunch with us, Toby blurted out, 'We got you a puppy!' I reminded him it was a secret, but he was so excited, and so was Lisette, that the lesson was totally lost on him."

"We'll figure something out, Jade. As he gets older, he'll understand it better, and he'll have more control over the shifting too. Kids pick up things quickly. If we're all saying the same things to him, he'll get it. And it's even possible he'll be able to control his shifting faster than an adult who has been newly turned. He is half-shifter, so not exactly like someone who has no *lupus garou* roots. He's a bright kid. I know we can do this."

"But we'll have to keep him isolated from everyone."

"The new moon is coming up right after the ball. He'll have a whole week of no shifting. We'll spend the time lining up a nanny and whoever else we might need to make this work."

"This is like one of your real estate ventures, isn't it? Where you're taking a hopeless case and turning it into one that has hope for humanity."

"If we do this, it will be the biggest contribution any of us could make for one of our kind. There's nothing more important than this."

"He's not a social experiment."

"No. He's your son. Part of you, heart and soul.

And half of you is wolf. Just like he should be. Think about it." Rafe really believed this was where she was headed, that she knew this was what she needed to do, but she just needed help with it. He let out his breath and squeezed her tight. "Just think about it. I'm just saying if you want to do it, if you truly believe it's the best thing for Toby, we'll be there to back you up. You shouldn't have to deal with this on your own."

"Thanks, Rafe. That means the world to me."

He kissed her, softly, not pushing, but then the passion that always ignited between them escalated. She was the first she-wolf he'd ever met who triggered such a hunger. He realized how much he wanted her already, not just in his bed, but sharing his waking hours. Yet Toby changed the dynamics. He knew the little boy would. Rafe could offer all kinds of aid, money, help to see this through, but could he mate Jade and raise Toby as his own son?

He supposed that was another reason he was thinking of Toby and his need to be turned. If Rafe mated Jade, their own children would be shifters. Toby would have siblings. He would have to learn to play with them. He smiled a little at the thought.

"What?" Jade asked, pulling away from Rafe.

"I love being with you, you know?"

She sighed. "Same here. I love the ocean breeze, the sound of the waves, snuggling with you…"

"Kissing."

She chuckled. "I'd better get to bed. Toby is an early riser, and he'll be awful to live with when he begins to ask hundreds of times when we're going to leave for Disneyland."

"We'll be leaving early. It's a bit of a drive."

"Okay. Sounds good. Night, Rafe, and again…thanks."

She kissed him again, and he led her back into the house.

She said good night to Aidan, who was sitting on the couch watching a sci-fi thriller, entered her bedroom, and shut the door.

Aidan immediately joined Rafe. "Okay, so what gives?"

"What do you mean?"

"Are you mating the she-wolf? What are you going to do about her son? Did she agree to change him?"

"She might not even want to mate me. She may hate my lifestyle and that the paparazzi will be plaguing her and her son even more if it looks like we're getting married."

"Oh yeah, about that…"

"What?"

"That paparazzo that was hassling Jade before? He was up here asking questions about Toby while you and Jade were out shopping. I'm sure he won't learn anything about him, but I just wanted to warn you that it's already started. And tomorrow? Guaranteed some of them will be watching the house when we leave for the theme park in the morning to try to capture as many photos as they can of you and Jade and the boy."

"So let 'em."

"What about turning him?"

"I suggested the week of the new moon, if she wants to do it. I really believe she's been leaning toward doing this but didn't have the resources to help her out. But she wouldn't say one way or another."

"Okay, well, if she's like any of us, we need to sleep on it. See you in the morning."

"You sure you don't mind going with us?"

"Are you kidding? And miss out on all the fun? No way."

Chapter 13

SURE ENOUGH, AS SOON AS THEIR CAR ARRIVED AT THE THEME park the next day, Rafe noticed the paparazzi following them. "We've got company," he warned Jade, his brother, and Edward. "Just so you know. Unless they get too bold and get in our way, just ignore them. And enjoy yourselves."

He knew Edward wouldn't. He'd be on the lookout for Kenneth trouble. Rafe was amused at the way Toby was so excited about everything, especially the gigantic Disney characters he had to have pictures with. But Jade wasn't the only one taking photos of her son. The paparazzi were taking them of Rafe standing with her as she took the pictures and caught a grinning Toby as the different characters posed with him.

"I take it he's your son?" LK Marks asked Jade as Toby ran back to her, grabbed her hand, and pointed to Ariel posing with other children.

Rafe was ready to discourage the paparazzo if he persisted in bothering her, but he let Jade handle it because he wouldn't always be with her.

"Come on, Mommy. Hurry before she gets away," Toby said emphatically.

"Should we go on some rides?" she asked, ignoring Marks.

"Yeah!"

But he first had to have a picture with Ariel. At least Toby wasn't camera shy.

Jade took Toby on the Mad Tea Party spinning cups after that, while Rafe stood with Aidan and watched them ride. He took pictures, aware of Edward standing some distance off watching the crowd. LK Marks was still taking pictures of Jade and her son, and Rafe knew he'd be trying to determine who the father was and why he hadn't been here all this time.

Rafe and his brother did the same routine when Jade took Toby on Peter Pan's Flight and two carousels. But they all rode on the jungle cruise, Heimlich's Chew Chew Train, the it's a small world water ride several times, and on Donald's Boat. When it came to soaring above in Dumbo the Flying Elephant, the men sat that one out. Then they took several other train rides and the monorail and hit more rides like the Buzz Lightyear Astro Blasters.

Afterward, Toby wanted his mother to carry him, but Rafe leaned down and lifted him instead. "Why don't you ride with me? I have more muscles than your mommy." He carried Toby on his shoulders to the next several rides.

Toby might have been too tired to walk, but he wasn't too tired to go on all the rides he could. Rafe hadn't known what to expect exactly, but he knew one thing: if going to places like this with Toby would be part of mated life with Jade, he could handle it. He could even envision himself pushing a stroller built for two—twin babies he imagined having with Jade—as he carried Toby on his shoulders while they enjoyed all kinds of different adventures.

After riding on Davy Crockett's Explorer Canoes, they headed over to Ariel's Grotto, where they had a reservation. Three different paparazzi had arrived at the restaurant and were taking pictures of them sitting down to lunch.

Toby was looking at the kids' menu, which he couldn't read, but he pointed to something on it and said, "Hot dog."

"Hot dog it is," Rafe said.

Edward had joined them and was about to get up to tell the paparazzi to leave them alone, but Rafe told him to ignore them. He was amused to see several people look at their table, probably trying to figure out if someone was a movie star. One of the Disney princesses came over and began talking to Toby and gave him a hug. He immediately began to tell her all the things he'd seen and the rides he'd been on. The princess nodded and smiled encouragingly while Aidan got up and took pictures of Toby and the princess. Rafe wondered if she thought they were celebrities, because she remained at the table for so long. She definitely would be getting her picture in some tabloids too.

As exhausting a day as Toby had had, Rafe envisioned him falling sound asleep in the car on the ride home. After a lobster dinner for the grown-ups and a few more rides on the way out of the park, Toby was yanking at Rafe's hand to give him a lift.

"Here, let me take you, bud…um, Toby," Aidan said.

Rafe wrapped his arm around Jade's shoulders and walked with her back to the trams for the parking lot. "Did you have fun?" he asked Jade.

"Oh yeah. I always wondered what it would be like. I

wasn't disappointed. You? You weren't too bored with all the kiddie rides, were you?"

"I wouldn't have missed it for anything. And truly, I got a kick out of seeing Toby's excitement about all the rides and such. Seeing the pure joy in a child's expression would have been enough. Although I will say I had fun on the rides too."

She laughed. "But you avoided some of the kids' ones. The paparazzi will have a field day with this."

"They will. I'm sure they'll follow us to the zoo tomorrow and be hanging around my estate while the charity ball is going on."

"They're not invited in, are they?"

"Nope. They'll be posted on the road, taking pictures of all the limousines, and then some paparazzi will be on the beach, capturing shots of anyone who is poolside. Anyone who attends will have their own celebrity status, so the press will be all over this. Does it bother you?" Rafe hoped it didn't because it was just a way of life with him.

"No. I just worry about them questioning Toby."

"Out of the mouths of babes," Rafe said.

"Exactly."

By the time they got Toby into the backseat with them and he had one arm wrapped around Buddy and the other securely hugging Dino, he was sound asleep.

"He did great for a little tyke," Rafe said.

"Hell yeah," Aidan agreed. "I would have been worn out way before that."

"He was too excited. He was so fighting it. I was afraid he'd fall asleep in the restaurant," Jade said. "But he was just having too much fun."

"He's a cute kid," Edward said, "and believe me, I don't say that about kids normally."

Everyone laughed.

When they got home, Rafe carried Toby into her bedroom. "Will he sleep the rest of the night?"

"Most likely. I'll get him ready for bed and come join you."

"Aidan will be on the couch watching a movie again and can keep an ear out for Toby. I'll get us a drink if you'd like. Edward's off to get some sleep. I'll talk to Sebastian and you can join me on the patio."

"I'd like that. Be there in a minute," she said, pulling off Toby's sneakers, then his socks.

"He's a cute kid, like Edward said."

"Thanks, Rafe. I know…I know this is all a real challenge, and I want to thank you again for…well, everything."

"I should be thanking you. You've added a real spark to my life," he said, pulling her in for a hug. "And so has your son. You know the old saying 'Money can't buy you everything'? I've found that to be so true since I met you."

"You've spent a ton on us."

"Yeah, but that's nothing compared to how I feel about you." He kissed her forehead. "Before we wake up your son"—he smiled—"I'll go make those drinks."

After she put Toby to bed, Jade studied him, wondering if turning him would work. Would Rafe still enjoy being with them in the long run? Or was he just offering protection as a friend because he cared for her? She could see the value in having wolf friends like him and his brother and the men who worked for him. They were a good male influence on Toby, positive and patient.

She wondered what kind of spin the paparazzi would put on her now that she also had a son. Would they search for his father and learn who he was? Would they question Stewart's family? She groaned. She had never thought that trying to learn about Aidan would put her in the spotlight. And she hadn't thought about how this would affect Toby and her former life either. With any luck, the paparazzi wouldn't learn about her human lover.

For now, her main concern was Toby and making the right decision about him—leaving him as human or turning him into a *lupus garou*?

She had always figured she would turn him. Now that Rafe had said he'd help her, she could do it a little sooner. Without his help, she had been afraid of failure.

She headed down the hall and thanked Aidan.

"No problem. Sometimes kids wake in unfamiliar places and get scared. If he sees me, I'll take care of him and let you know he's up."

"Thanks, Aidan. I really didn't mean for this to be an imposition on you."

"Are you kidding? This is the most fun I've had on a visit to see Rafe. And I'm looking forward to the zoo too. As for the charity function? Hate those things. So as soon as Toby has greeted everyone and we grab a bite to eat, I'll take him to the den to watch some shows. Best excuse I've ever had to leave the social function early."

She laughed. "All right. But I might be joining you."

"I believe if you did, Rafe would end up with us too."

She laughed again. Then she headed outside to spend some time alone with Rafe.

"You're right," she said, sitting next to him on the love seat. She sipped her margarita and put it on the table.

"About?" he asked, setting his beer aside.

"Toby." She let out her breath on a heavy sigh. "I couldn't do it before. Not without some kind of support system in place. But before the first day of the new moon phase, I want Aidan to change Toby—if he doesn't mind hanging around a couple of more days until that happens."

"Good. He said he would. But I want to discuss us. I want to mate you, Jade. I want to have children with you and help raise Toby, the whole nine yards. I don't want either of you to move out. Ever. I know it's a bit soon to mention it. If we believed in engagements, I'd give you an engagement ring right this very minute, get on bended knee or whatever it takes. I want you to have all the time you need to decide if this is something that you want too. But I want you to know that you and Toby are not just some kind of social project to me. If you left tomorrow, I'd be hunting you down and doing my damnedest to convince you to give me a chance."

"Oh, Rafe, I would if… Well, everything is so uncertain with Toby. What if he's too much to handle as a wolf, and you can't live with the change? What if it causes too much trouble for you? Neither of us knows how difficult this will be for him or for us."

Rafe caressed her arm and smiled. "If that's all that's worrying you, I've had a number of life-altering changes over the years. Every time I learn how to take it one day at a time, just as I would with Toby. What's more important is, do you feel you can learn to love me?"

She gave a little laugh and wrapped her arms around him. "You are the most loving, protective, and generous man I've ever met. And hot? Oh yeah. But...no matter what happens with Toby when he's changed, he's my son, and we have a blood bond that will endure for all time. It will see me through anything he has to suffer."

"Like you have with your brother?"

She sighed. "Siblings are different than a mother and her child. At least for me."

"I promise I will love Toby like he was my own son. He's never had a father, and I would be proud to be his daddy. Say you'll consider it, Jade. I hate losing sleep over this."

She laughed. "I'll consider it, but I don't want to make a decision until at least some time after Toby has been turned. That will give you a chance to change your mind if this isn't something you feel you've signed up for."

"I won't change my mind."

"We'll see. We have another issue though. What if now that the paparazzi are taking pictures of Toby, they begin to look for his father? What if they discover who he was and question his family? Stewart's family doesn't know he has a son. What if Toby's grandparents want to see him? That could cause all kinds of new problems."

"I think it's time for a cover story. What if we say he's mine? And I only just learned of it? We had a fling nearly four years ago, hot and heavy. We can pinpoint a time, and as long as you weren't in the eye of the public about that time, and I can create a fictionalized account concerning where we met and such, we can pull it off."

"Then you'd be stuck having to acknowledge him as your son forever, when you might decide that's not what you want."

He shook his head and pulled her from the love seat. "How can I convince you that I love you? That I can love Toby as my own son just as much? I know you haven't been able to trust your own family, and that's made you wary of believing anyone else can help you or care for you the way I do, but one of the things that's made me so successful is being wolfishly determined to accomplish what I set out to do. Seeing a good investment is something I know about. When I commit to something as important as this, it's for life. I'm going to keep trying to convince you until it's a done deal."

He leaned down and kissed her forehead, her cheeks, her mouth, his hands caressing her arms, coaxing her to agree.

She knew in her heart this was right, as long as Rafe really could handle a small boy, newly turned. She loved Rafe. "I love you, Rafe Denali. You for you alone. If we were without money and living in a rundown shack, I would be just as happy. As long as I was with you. Would Aidan truly mind still visiting? Would your friends and those who work for you really mind?"

His eyes were already smoky with desire, his mouth still so serious, his voice dark and deep. "Hell yeah to Aidan's visiting. He's already said he's staying longer to watch Toby after he's turned, if you agreed to it. And my friends and staff? Are you kidding? If I let you leave me, they'll be banging down your door to try to court you next. So since you love me too, I'd say it was time to do something about it."

"You can't change your mind when Toby is turned," she said emphatically. Part of her said they should wait until Toby had been turned, and after a month or two, if Rafe was fine with calling him his son, they would do it. But that reckless wolfish side of her said to hell with it. She trusted Rafe, wanted him with all her heart, and knew, just from the time he'd already spent with Toby, he was the right wolf for both of them.

Rafe shook his head. "Part of dealing with life is dealing with conflict. He needs a father as much as he needs his mother. He needs a family that can help him through this. He's got it. Are you ready for what's next?"

"What if Toby wakes and wants me?"

"We'll tell Aidan he needs to be the best uncle a boy ever had."

She smiled, but her stomach was doing flip-flops. "Poor Aidan." She had suspected it would come to this, but not now, not this moment.

"Why do you think Aidan came here early? Before the charity ball? He knew I had already fallen for the she-wolf and that meant taking in her son too. And my brother wouldn't be doing this if he didn't want to. Believe me. He has a mind of his own."

She smiled, hugging Rafe and kissing him with all her heart.

Rafe scooped Jade up into his arms and carried her inside the house. When they reached the living room, he asked Aidan, "Can you hold down the fort a little while longer?"

Aidan raised his brows, amused.

"I'll return to him in a little while," Jade said, feeling her cheeks heat.

"Take all the time you need. If Toby wakes, I'll read to him or fix him a milk shake or whatever, until you're ready." Then Aidan broadly smiled at both of them. "I guess congratulations are in order. Looks like I'm going to be one proud uncle."

"That you are, Brother." Then Rafe carried Jade back to his bedroom. She remembered being here before when he had injured himself on the seashell. It seemed so long ago. She never would have expected this from their first encounter—a mate for her, and a father for her little boy.

"You know we'll have to get married. Something simple—the wedding gown and a service, but only wolf guests—and that means just the few I know, unless you know any you want to invite."

She shook her head as he set her on the bed. "Well, maybe Fiona."

Rafe looked askance at her.

"I'll need someone to help me dress in the gown. Unless you want your brother to help me dress."

Rafe grunted.

"She was really nice to me at the bed-and-breakfast. I know she's not a wolf, but—"

"It's your wedding, Jade. Anyone you want to invite is fine with me."

"Will you pay for her bridesmaid gown if she wants to come?"

"If you want her to be in the wedding party, I'll pay for the dress. Just let her know what color you'd like her to wear."

"Thanks, Rafe."

He pulled Jade's shirt over her head. "We'll need to be married quickly. That will end all the speculation about us."

"And whether you're still one of those super-hot, very eligible bachelors."

He smiled and began to remove her sandals. "I never was very eligible. There was a little issue of needing a wolf mate. Once I found her, that was all that mattered."

She ran her hand over his jean-covered thigh. "You're sure about this?"

"I am, Jade. More than anything I've ever invested in during my life."

She rose from the bed and began kissing him and tearing off his clothes, yanking off his shirt and then tugging at his belt. One problem with having a three-year-old? Adult time was at a premium.

Rafe didn't seem to mind that she was in a rush to strip off his clothes, and he was eager to help her out of hers too.

Their mouths fused as they fumbled with buttons and zippers. And then his hard, naked body was pressed against her in a loving embrace, and she was rubbing against him to show ownership. No regrets for her, no going back for either of them. Not once they were mated.

She loved him as he plundered her mouth, holding her head still as he stroked her tongue with his. He was such a wolf, hot, eager, hard, and hungry. This kiss was reminiscent of all the others—the rampant need, the longing—yet this time, all that passion would be channeled into a commitment for life between two wolves of the *lupus garou* persuasion.

His hand molded around her breast, massaging, his thumb stroking the nipple, before he moved his hand around to her back and pulled her tighter against his hard body, crushing her against his chest, her nipples brushing his light hair, his arousal spearing her belly.

She adored him and couldn't get enough of him. Already her sex was throbbing for his touch, her breasts swollen and achy.

"So hot," he mouthed against her lips, and then his hands were in her hair, combing through the strands in a tender way. He leaned his forehead against hers for a moment as if trying to slow the pace, to enjoy this first mating and not rush through it like a wild wolf. He lifted her face to his as she stroked his naked back and hard muscles, his skin satiny soft.

He lay siege to her mouth again, diving in, caressing and pulling out, then plunging in again, his tongue a master of eroticism.

She was so wet and ready for him, and she wanted him to know it. She lifted her leg, pressing her inner thigh against his, rubbing, telling him she wanted more.

When she moved her hand between them to stroke his velvety hard erection, he quickly got the message. He swept her up and set her on the bed. Then he joined her, only this time, his mouth did wicked things to her breasts—his tongue teasing each nipple in turn, then his talented mouth suckling on one breast and finally the other.

He rubbed his erection against her clit, so masculine, so virile. Their hearts were beating in a rush, out of sync, their breathing ragged.

His gaze was intense when he began to stroke her.

She felt the need to meld with the wolf, to feel him join her, consummating the mating. All thoughts faded away as his fingers rubbed her bud, pushing her to that ultimate plane of exquisite existence where heaven and earth collided. Before she could cry out in exaltation, he covered her mouth with his and kissed her deep and long. Then he pushed his erection between her legs slowly, allowing her time to expand, then deeply, and deeper still.

He was thrusting inside her, kissing her, nuzzling her face as she skimmed her hands over every perfect part of him.

He suddenly held himself still, then moved in and out at a slower pace, then thrust hard again, as if he couldn't wait. She lifted her hips for maximum penetration before he groaned out his release.

"I love you," she murmured into his hair as he buried his head against her neck.

"You are perfect for me," he said. "I will love you always."

She meant to relieve Aidan of taking care of Toby after a minute, although hating to leave Rafe for even a second after mating him. An hour later, she woke and realized she'd fallen asleep in Rafe's warm embrace—her lover, her mate, and Toby's new father.

Chapter 14

"I'VE GOT TO GO BACK TO TOBY," JADE SAID, WISHING SHE could stay with Rafe the rest of the night, but she didn't want Toby to wake and be scared.

"Hmmm, we need to turn one of the bedrooms into a boy's room. His room. Whatever he wants on the walls, the bedding, the works. Once he makes it his own, that will help him feel more at home."

"Thanks, Rafe. That would be great. He'll love helping to decorate it. We've never done that before. I decorated his old room before he was born, and then when we moved in with Kenneth, we shared a room. So he'll love that."

"Good show. Every little boy and girl should have his or her own room. About getting married…"

"Yes, yes, that works for me."

"We should have the wedding before we turn him. The day after the ball? He wouldn't be able to shift during the new moon phase anyway, but I want to get this done right away."

"Because of your position," she said, understanding his concern.

"Because of yours and Toby's. Normally as wolves, we keep a low profile around humans, but in my position, it's hard to do that."

"I understand. I better go."

He groaned and gave her a big hug. "We'll shop for Toby's room the day of the charity function. I want to do this right away."

"He may still join us sometimes if he gets scared or needy," Jade warned, climbing out of bed.

Rafe rose from the bed and helped her dress, kissing her all over as he helped. "And that's fine. No problem. I remember a time or two when Aidan and I ended up in bed with my parents."

She kissed him and laughed. "I can't imagine you ever being afraid of anything."

"Of losing you and Toby, yes." He groaned again and said, "Okay, I never thought I'd take a mate and have to sleep alone after that."

She smiled. "We'll work it out somehow."

Then she left him, passed Aidan on the couch, and said, "Night, Aidan. Thanks so much."

"Thank you. You've made my brother happier than anything or anyone else could have. You and Toby have brightened all of our lives. Just let me know if you need me for anything."

"Thanks. Rafe wants to marry me after the ball."

"Low key, right?"

"Dress up, but low key, yes."

Aidan got off the couch and gave her a hug. "Welcome to the family, Jade."

"Thanks, Aidan. Thanks for everything."

She returned to her guest room, not believing that she was a mated wolf, never having imagined she might be. Not with a son like Toby. She showered, put on pj's, and joined him in bed. He didn't stir, but bright and early, he was bouncing around the bed while she was sleeping. "Uncle Aidan and I had chocolate chip waffles. He said to let you sleep."

Jade opened an eye and squinted at her son. "What?"

Toby was wearing a T. rex T-shirt but different shorts, and the shirt was on backward.

"I got up 'cuz you were sleeping and went to see if anyone else was up. Uncle Aidan told me to call him that. He said I should ask you. Is it okay?"

"Yes." She closed her eye.

"He told me about a wolf park. Can we go there? Can we, Mommy?"

"You don't want to go to the zoo?"

"Yeah, the zoo too. But I've never seen a wolf…" He paused, then continued. "I wanna see the wolves. Can we, Mommy?"

That was his wolf genes coming out. Most kids probably wouldn't be into wolves at this age like he was. But Toby had always loved wolves, even though no one had ever shifted in front of him. It was some genetic need to be around wolves.

And yet he wasn't one of them. Because he couldn't shift.

"We'll have to go to the zoo after the charity ball then."

Toby rolled around on the king-size bed. "Rafe said you and he had 'portant news for me. He wouldn't tell me the secret. He said you would."

She groaned. "He's up too?"

"Yeah. Everyone but *you*."

"We're going to fix up your own room like you had before, only it will be here, and we'll decorate it just like you want it."

"With wolf cubs?"

"Yes." She reached over and pulled Toby into a hug. "You have your shirt on backward."

"No. It's the right way. The T. rex is watching my back."

She laughed. "But who's going to watch your front?"

"I am."

"Did…did Rafe tell you he's your daddy?"

"He is? Really?" Toby stared at her for a moment, then jumped off the bed. "He doesn't know. I'm gonna tell him." Then he raced out the door.

She laughed. She hoped Rafe was still okay with Toby being his son, because he didn't have a choice any longer.

A few minutes later, Toby jumped on the bed again and she groaned. "*Toby*."

"He said he was. And I can call him Daddy. But he said to ask you if that's okay. Is it, Mommy?"

"Yes. Go talk to your daddy, and I'll get dressed and join you. Then we can go to the wolf park. Did you tell them you wanted to go there first?"

"Yes. They said *awesome*!"

She laughed. "Okay, go join them."

He bounced off the bed and she heard him say, "She's getting up. *Finally*."

The men laughed.

She was glad he was keeping them entertained.

When Jade emerged from the bedroom, she looked like a breath of sunshine. Rafe was afraid she'd be dragging, tired the rest of the day. Forget Toby falling asleep in the car. Jade would.

"Is everything all right?" she asked, then ate some fruit and a cheese omelet.

"Yeah," Rafe said. "We're getting along great. Toby picked out the bedroom he wanted off the Internet. And we'll go shopping this afternoon after the wolf reserve. If we'd gone to the zoo, we wouldn't have had time for shopping."

"Sounds good to me."

"He says he's never seen wolves before."

"No. But that will change soon," she said.

"We'll start working on the bedroom this afternoon. One nice thing about money is that we don't have to wait for the furniture company to deliver on their schedule. They'll deliver right away. We were looking at pictures and found the perfect one. A tree-house bed."

"I've got to see this." Jade read the description for the bed out loud. "Rustic tree house fort, windows, ladder... Uh, wait. Says not recommended for children under six."

"I'm almost six," Toby said.

Rafe frowned and looked at the ad. "We'll put the bed on the floor, and when he's older, we can move it into the fort. How about that, Toby?"

"Aww."

"You can go up there to play," Rafe said.

Jade smiled. "He walked at nine months like I did. He's a little mountain goat like I was. Climbed out of his crib for the first time when he was a year old, and I got him a daybed, but he climbed out of that and couldn't make it up the steps to get back into bed. So he slept on the carpeted floor next to his bed."

The guys laughed.

"Sounds like you, Rafe," Aidan said.

"Ha! You were the one that..." Rafe paused.

"What?" Toby asked, interested.

Jade quickly put her dishes in the dishwasher. "Ready to go?"

"What?" Toby asked Rafe again.

"I'll tell you when you're older. Don't want to give you any ideas."

"Aww."

They were off to the California Wolf Center after that, and Rafe noticed right away that LK Marks was on their tail.

"Want me to lose that pesky paparazzo, Boss?" Edward asked.

"Nah. He'll lose interest after a while." To Jade, Rafe said, "We need to get Toby a tux for the charity ball."

"I hadn't thought of that. Maybe while we're out shopping for Toby's bedroom furniture."

"Sounds good."

When they arrived at the California Wolf Center, they were able to see several Mexican gray wolves. Jade pointed out one and said to Toby, "That wolf was born in the wild. She's had all kinds of puppies. That's the daddy. He was born in a wolf management facility in New Mexico. They help to provide more puppies and make sure the Mexican gray wolves don't become extinct."

"Like dinosaurs?" Toby asked.

"Yes. Exactly. And over here are several Rocky Mountain gray wolves—from blond to gray to a dark, rusty color."

Best of all, the mated Mexican gray wolves had four pups and Toby was so excited. "They smell like you and Daddy, Mommy! And Uncle Aidan and Uncle Edward."

Rafe frowned at him. "You can smell wolves? A wolf smell?"

Toby shrugged. "Just smell like you. Different. You know."

"I never thought about it, but he's never seen real wolves, so he wouldn't know…" Jade quit speaking.

Rafe nodded. It had to be Toby's diluted *lupus garou* genetics. He hadn't ever known anyone personally who had them. Did they also have the wolf's enhanced senses? Given that Toby could smell the wolves from beyond the fence, most likely.

Both Edward and Aidan were watching Toby curiously now.

One of the wolves lifted his head and sniffed at the breeze, smelling the wolves standing before him, even though Rafe and the others didn't look like wolves. Still, the scent of other wolves would give these wolves pause. Enemies in their territory?

"Can we pet the wolves? I wanna go in there and pet the puppies," Toby said.

Aidan took Toby's hand and said, "We can't go in the pen. Let's go see some other wolves, okay?"

"Yeah!"

"Does he hear better than the average human?" Rafe asked Jade quietly, slipping his arm around her shoulders.

"I never gave it any thought since he's only around me and then the pack, and we all have better hearing than humans."

"And sense of smell."

"Yes."

"Seeing at night?"

"Again, I never really thought of it. I've always been able to. He can too. Makes sense. The genes had to come out in some way, and if he can't shift, getting our abilities is the only other way."

"That's good if he has these abilities already. He's been used to them from birth so they won't scare him. He'll just have to get used to shifting and work on getting it under control. Kids learn things faster, and he's really bright." Sure, all kinds of things could go wrong, but Rafe knew they could deal with it no matter what happened. "Is it okay that he calls Edward his uncle too?"

She laughed and hugged Rafe back. "I don't think I've seen Edward more pleased than when Toby called him that. So yes. I suspect when we see Sebastian, he'll be an uncle too."

Rafe smiled. "I told you that this would all work out."

The wolf center wasn't very big, and after they'd visited the shop and bought Toby a hat and a wolf T-shirt, a sweatshirt, a plush wolf, a howling wolf puzzle, and a wolf flipbook, Toby got excited about getting his new bedroom set. They hadn't seen the paparazzo until they left the wolf center, and Rafe figured it wouldn't have the readership appeal that the theme park had.

They went on a whirlwind tour of furniture stores and bedding shops until they found what they wanted.

"This will do for now," Jade said. "We can do more later. But we've got the toy chest, the bed, a dresser, a bookshelf, the wolf bed linens, and curtains, and that's enough for now."

They went to a formal wear shop and bought Toby a four-piece black tuxedo—single breasted with a black vest so he'd look just like Rafe and the others for the charity ball—and then they went home.

"I think we all need to take a nap," Rafe said, wanting to spend some time alone with Jade. He'd never imagined having to wait this long to make love to his mate again when they were so newly mated.

She smiled at him and squeezed his hand.

Toby frowned. "I'm not tired."

"I'll take him for a swim," Aidan said. "You two can take a nap."

"I owe you," Rafe said.

Aidan smiled. "Yeah, you do. I'll get payment later."

"We need to find a nanny for Toby," Rafe said.

"How can you trust a woman to take care of him when he'll need a bodyguard?" Edward asked, sounding disgruntled.

"Are you asking for the job?" Rafe asked.

"Hell yeah. He's a billionaire's kid now. He needs someone to safeguard him twenty-four seven."

Rafe couldn't believe him. "Are you serious? You want the job?"

"Hell yeah. He's my nephew too, you know."

The men all laughed. Jade smiled and cuddled with Rafe and Toby.

"Okay, you got the job."

"Might need a raise," Edward said.

"You already get—"

"He's right," Jade said. "Toby's going to be a real handful. Edward deserves a raise."

Rafe ruffled Toby's hair. "Did you enjoy the wolves?"

"They were so cool." Toby yawned, put his head in his mother's lap, and fell asleep cuddling Buddy and Dino.

"No nap, eh?" Rafe asked.

"No. I never use the 'nap' word around him. That's a surefire way to get him wound up. I just tell him we're going to rest for a little bit, close our eyes, and that does it," Jade said.

"Are you taking notes, Edward?" Rafe asked, still amused his bodyguard wanted the role of nanny.

"Got it, Boss. Only you and your mate take naps."

Jade laughed.

When they got home, Toby woke.

"I'll take care of lunch for him," Aidan said. "And I'll take him swimming. The furniture should be arriving in an hour or so, and we'll be in charge of that. Won't we, Toby?"

"Yes!"

"Mind Uncle Aidan and Uncle Edward. We'll be out in a bit."

"Okay, Mommy." Toby took Aidan's hand. "Can we have a hot dog?"

"Have you heard anything about Kenneth?" Jade asked as she and Rafe retired to the master bedroom.

"Nothing. I called this morning while you were still sleeping, or trying to sleep. They're still looking for him. They're trying to use Lizzie as bait."

"That could be dangerous for her."

"After what she pulled? Hell, she doesn't deserve a second chance. Not only was she going along with kidnapping Toby, but then she tried to sell him on her own."

"I agree. But she didn't want him dead. It was my brother who kept threatening to kill him."

"We'll safeguard her, but we need to take him down.

You and Toby won't be safe until we do. My brother either, if Kenneth still has this harebrained notion of taking him into custody." Rafe shut the door and led her to the bed. "We need to move your things in here too."

"I'll do that after we rest a bit."

Just then, Rafe got a call, and he yanked his phone out of his pocket. *Not now, Sebastian.* "Yeah, what is it?"

"I found a place for Jade and her son that's close by, just half a mile down the road. If you want me to, I'll put down a deposit on it, as it's likely to go fast."

"Change of plans," Rafe was delighted to say, pulling Jade into his arms and kissing her on the mouth. "They're staying here permanently. I need you to make arrangements for a quick wedding for next week. No invitations. Just our small group—those who work for me, my brother, and Derek."

"Hot damn. I'll get back with you on dates as soon as I've got some. Are you turning the boy?"

"Yeah, after the wedding and at the beginning of the new moon. Aidan will handle it."

"Okay. Let me know if you need anything else. And congratulations."

"One other thing. I want you to find a wolf judge who can sign a marriage certificate that states we were married before Toby was born. We'll make up some story about falling in love and getting married, and then we need to make up a story of why we were separated after that."

"Any ideas?"

"Working on it. Thanks. Talk to you later." Then he set the phone aside and said to Jade, "Now, about that nap…"

—✺—

Jade wished she could be on the yacht again, but this time making wild and passionate love to her mate in that king-size bed in the master suite while they rolled with the waves. She certainly had that in mind for a later date.

For now, they were quickly dispensing with their clothes. Half of the joy of making love to her mate was the cuddling after, and she wanted enough time to do that too. She loved how he didn't just have sex and fall asleep. He enjoyed the intimacy between them just as much.

Even so, she tried to slow it down a bit, sliding her hands up his T-shirt and making him suck in his breath as she ran her fingers over his nipples and teased them.

But then he was unbuttoning her blouse and baring her lace-covered breasts, cupping them, rubbing the centers with his thumbs, sensitizing them to the point that she gave up on trying to do this slowly and began jerking off his T-shirt.

He pulled her blouse off her shoulders and dropped it on the floor, then slipped his hands beneath her lace bra. His warm, large hands molded to her breasts as he kissed her mouth. But she wasn't done with his chest. She licked his nipple, making him groan. She loved it when he sounded like he was losing control, the way he stiffened under her touch. She licked the other nipple, her lips gently pulling at that one, her fingers doing the same with the other.

This time he growled, that feral sound his wolf made when he was ready to rip off her clothes and have his way with her. Loving him, she reached down and cupped his crotch and felt his erection straining against his jeans, running her hand down the length of it with a whisper-soft touch.

He quickly unsnapped her bra in front and slid it off her, tossing it aside, then began working on her jeans.

She kicked off her tennis shoes and tugged at his belt, his hands cupping her face again, his mouth devouring hers, his teeth nibbling gently on her lips.

For the moment, she forgot his zipper and wrapped her arms around his neck, pressing her bare breasts against his bare chest, his hair tickling her nipples, and she gave into the kiss. She loved his kisses, the way he took charge. The way he drew her in and wanted more. His hands skimmed down her back, across her ribs, then lower until he had his hands around her jean-covered buttocks, pulling her tighter against his aroused body.

She loved the feel of him like this—so hard and fit and wanting to please. The way his scents teased her senses—smelling of musk and wolf and male. The way his pheromones drove hers insane.

But then he moved his hands down to her jeans again, unzipping them and pulling them down, helping her out of them. She slid her hand over his briefs, molding to his arousal on the slide down, then helped him out of his boots before he yanked off his jeans and pulled her to stand.

Then they were kissing again, rubbing their bodies together, his hands on her shoulders, until he moved one down, slipping it inside her panties and cupping her sex. She copied him, sliding her hand beneath his waistband and cupping him. He smiled a little against her lips, his eyes glazed over with feral passion. Then he began stroking her, and she molded her hand around his erection.

The pleasure wending through her stole her concentration, although she'd thought she was an expert at multitasking. But not when Rafe was tormenting her with his sweet strokes. Something had to give, and she let go of his cock and clung to his shoulders, making him smile against her lips, the rogue.

She felt herself climbing toward that ultimate peak and falling at the same time, her body on fire, her need to find completion driving her insane.

Their breaths uneven, he continued to plunder her mouth, caressing her tongue, stroking her feminine bud until she cried out, digging her fingers into his shoulders and ready to collapse.

He lifted her and she wrapped her legs around his hips. He carried her to the bed and set her down. As soon as she resituated herself, she parted her legs, inviting him in.

His body piping hot, Rafe accepted his mate's open invitation, pushing in between her wet folds and dying to fulfill his own needs. Though watching her come would always give him pleasure.

Now, she wrapped her warm wetness around him like a silky, hot mitt and stroked him right to the top. Breathing in her warm wolfish scent, he surrounded himself with her essence, the heat of her body, the smell of her, the softness that was all Jade's.

He slowed his pace, enjoying the pleasure sliding inside her always gave him, but it was never enough and it couldn't last. Reminding himself this was only the beginning for them, he pushed hard and deep, thrusting until he felt the climax rising. And shattered. When he was completely spent, he finally rolled over onto his back and pulled her into his arms.

She sighed against him; no words were necessary. She was heaven and earth and every place in between. And for now, being with her like this was more than perfect.

Jade had snuggled up against Rafe, still breathing him in after feeling totally satiated and well loved, thinking it couldn't get better, before she and he slept for about an hour. Slowly waking, she knew she had to get up and take care of Toby. She'd never thought she could make love to a mate and, beyond that, never thought to have a ton of built-in nannies to allow it to happen. Then squeals of delight broke out in the living room. "They're here! They're here! Hurry, Uncle Aidan."

Jade smiled and tightened her hold on Rafe, figuring Aidan had this covered and her son wasn't going to miss her anytime soon.

"Sounds like we've got some more time to fool around," Rafe said, kissing the top of her head.

She laughed. And then he made love to her all over again, proving what a dream come true he really was.

In the afterglow, he sighed, cuddling with her and stroking her arm. "Okay, we need to come up with a plausible reason for us separating after we were married four years ago. Not that it would have ever come to pass if we had been married before you had Toby."

"We had a whirlwind romance somewhere on a trip, married, and I began to worry that we had made a mistake."

"Because of—?"

"How about if you were off somewhere and met me.

No one knew about it. But after the quick marriage, I began worrying about fitting into your lifestyle. Where we were staying, you and I were just everyday people, nothing fancy. Not living the life of the rich and famous. No spotlight on us. I was making a moderate income, but not in your league. But it seemed doable because I wasn't being exposed to all of this."

"Okay, and the trigger why you left me?" he asked, frowning down at her as if she truly had left him over this made-up version of their lives.

"Well, you wanted me to give up my intimate apparel wear."

"*No…*way."

She laughed. "Okay, you had a hot deal on a real estate sale. You'd have to make sure you were there to handle the deal. I was to wait at this modest resort for you, but you kept being delayed and delayed and delayed. You finally had Sebastian call and say you'd send me a plane ticket to take me to your place and you'd meet me there in a month. The notion I would be living at some strange place where no one knew who I was… Well, I couldn't do it, and I figured it had all been a mistake. It would have been bad enough if you had called me, but you didn't even do that. You had your hired help do it! And we were newlyweds. What was I to think? Ten years down the line, it would be even worse! So I went home on my own."

"Hell, I swear I've mended my ways. I had to be an idiot."

She chuckled and rubbed his chest with the palm of her hand, loving the feel of him, the scent of him, that he was all hers.

"Why wouldn't I have sent everyone after you to find you? I would have."

"I was good at escape and evasion. In truth, I was hiding out from Toby's father and my brother. Kenneth didn't catch up to me until your brother contacted him about taking blood samples. So I was living under a different identity."

"What about your intimate apparel wear? I would have learned where you were through that."

"I was out of the country for a while."

"When Toby was born?"

"Before. I returned before Toby was born. I was in a little village in Mexico. You would never have found me."

"And you didn't tell me about Toby? He's my son too, you know."

She laughed. "You're too funny, Rafe. That's another reason I love you. Okay, so you had made a passing comment about not wanting children right away. That you and I had to get to know each other better first. And when I learned I was pregnant with Toby, I knew you wouldn't want that kind of a lifestyle change. I had him at home so you wouldn't know about it. Which I really did, but not for that reason."

"But we're getting a birth certificate made up for him."

"Oh. With your name on it?"

"Absolutely. I'm his father."

She smiled, loving him. He was so right for her. "Okay, so I couldn't leave your name off it, because I did love you and you were his father. But I was afraid you wouldn't want to see him or claim him as your own. So I kept working at creating intimate apparel and then started designing specialty clothing for children too, because Toby inspired the new line. And they have done well. But Toby was in a preschool class, and sometimes the daddies would pick up their toddlers. When Father's Day rolled around, the teachers had the kids make up cards for their daddies. Well, of course, Toby came home and asked who his daddy was."

"For real?"

"Yeah, for real."

"Hell. I'm so sorry, Jade." Then he frowned. "Where's my Daddy's Day card?"

She smiled. "In my stuff stored at Kenneth's house. I kept it. If we ever get our things…"

"Something else we need to do." Rafe took a deep breath and rubbed her arm. "So you felt guilty and—"

"I learned where you were living and thought if you saw me, maybe we could talk. I was trying to get up the nerve to see you. But I hadn't expected that I'd nearly risk drowning myself. Then I didn't let you know you had a son right away, afraid you'd be angry with me. Things were progressing with us so hot and heavy, and I took the chance to tell you about him…"

"Hell yeah. And I don't ever want to let my business get in the way of our pleasure. If I ever am gone too long on business, remind me of what made you leave me before."

With tears in her eyes, she kissed him. "I love you, Rafe."

"I love you just as much back, Jade. We'll make this work."

"So what was the story that Aidan referred to about

something you and he did when I was talking about Toby climbing out of his crib so early?"

Rafe chuckled. "Oh, that. Aidan and I loved Mom's apple pie. So one day we were hungry and the pie was sitting on the windowsill cooling while she was outside hanging the laundry to dry. She'd made the pie for us, and we figured it was cool enough already. We stacked pillows and quilts on top of apple crates and everything else we could find, and climbed up on top until we could reach the pie. We knocked it over by mistake, and it went crashing into a jar of honey, a tin of flour, and a bowl of apples.

"We just watched as they all fell to the wooden floor and broke to smithereens. We couldn't have stopped any of it if we had tried. Mom heard the racket and hollered at us. We knew we were in trouble. But it had all been Aidan's idea—that time. She ran into the house to see what had happened and yelled at us to stay away from the mess. That was only one of the times we got into trouble for climbing on things we shouldn't have."

"Boy, I'm glad you didn't tell Toby that story. I could see him trying to copy you and your brother because he copies everything you do already."

Rafe smiled and kissed her cheek. "I'll say."

"Mommy! Mommy! Come see my new tree house!" Toby yelled out.

Jade hugged Rafe. "Guess the nap is over."

He smiled and hugged her back. "Over way too soon."

They got out of bed and dressed, then joined Toby and Aidan to see what the furniture looked like and watched as Toby asked a million questions of the deliverymen who were putting the bed together.

After the men left and Toby was happily setting up

housekeeping, Rafe shared his and Jade's made-up story with his wolf staff, his brother, and Derek so everyone would have the story right.

"I can't believe you kept Jade secret from me all these years," Aidan said. "Your own brother."

Everyone laughed.

Chapter 15

JADE HAD SPENT THE NIGHT HELPING TOBY GET HIS ROOM fixed up. He was excited about being a big boy again and having his own room to sleep and play in. She was glad because that would give her and Rafe the time to be a real mated couple.

Most of all, Toby loved his tree house. He had climbed up and down the ladder numerous times, hauling toys up there.

Edward had moved into the bedroom next door and told Toby to let him know if he needed anything. Jade had moved all her clothes to Rafe's room and felt more settled in.

Rafe had given instructions to a couple of his men to locate Jade's room at her brother's house and remove everything that belonged to her. She had given them directions to find her room and a list of everything that was in it. No one was living there currently, so it wouldn't be a problem. Especially since Jade had a key to the place, surrendering it gladly to Rafe's men.

Sebastian had been busy making wedding arrangements, something he'd never had to do before. He was well on the way to making it a fairy-tale wedding scaled down in size. If the paparazzi got wind of it, they'd be all over it.

But now she had to buy a wedding gown too.

That night when they retired, Jade told Toby she

was sleeping with Rafe, so if he needed them, he could come get them. He was tired after seeing the wolves, "helping" the men put his tree-house bed together, and carrying a ton of his toys up the ladder. But then he realized he needed Dino and Buddy in bed with him. He climbed up the ladder and dropped Buddy to Jade and then the dinosaur. When he was tucked into bed with his bear and Dino, he was asleep before Jade even finished reading a book to him.

Retiring to bed that night with Rafe, she saw the hungry intrigue in his expression. Unless Toby intruded, she was Rafe's the whole night.

Early the next morning, Rafe made love to a sleepy mate and felt happily satiated. Sleeping all night with her, around the bouts of lovemaking, was the best thing ever. Though he wouldn't have minded if Toby had awakened and felt the need to see Jade, he was glad that he hadn't.

Both Jade and Rafe needed this mating time to be together. He kissed her shoulder, and she snuggled against him. "I promised I'd spar with Edward this morning. Aidan and Sebastian might join us. We'll be in the gym downstairs."

She made a pleasant "hmming" sound, and he smiled, gently laid her back down on the bed, and got dressed to work out, figuring she was going to sleep a while longer.

When he headed down the stairs to the gym, he saw Toby dressed in his Captain America pj's, punching away at a junior-size punching bag.

Aidan was running on the treadmill. "Sebastian got

it for Toby so he could exercise like us guys and build lots of muscles."

Rafe laughed. "Good."

Edward arrived and began to spar with Rafe. Sebastian joined them. "Like your punching bag?" he asked Toby.

"Yeah." But his eyes were wide, his jaw hanging as he watched Rafe and Edward trying to get the best of each other in martial arts moves on one of the floor mats.

"Want to learn how to do that?" Sebastian asked.

Toby nodded. He struggled to get his shirt off and Sebastian helped him. Then Sebastian moved him over to another mat and pulled off his own muscle shirt, though he usually wore one for workouts. Rafe was amused that Toby wanted to act as though this was the way to dress for sparring, because Rafe and Edward were shirtless.

Sebastian showed Toby a few moves, but then they heard softer footfalls on the stairs and all looked up to see who was coming down.

Jade. And she was wearing short shorts and a formfitting tank top for exercising. Hell, now Rafe wanted to spar with her. Forget working out with Edward. As if Edward knew what his boss was thinking, he smiled at Rafe. "Want to switch partners?"

"You boys get your sparring in. I'm going to…" She looked around the room and saw three bicycles. "Go bicycling around the world."

"And then we're going to the zoo?" Toby asked.

"Another day," Jade said. "We have the charity ball tonight, so we don't want to be worn-out for that."

Rafe smiled. He should just take her out on the yacht to relax for the day. He figured Toby would love it too, but Jade was right. They'd take him one of these days. They still had the wedding too.

———※———

That evening, Toby was so excited about the charity ball that he had dressed well before anyone else had, his bow tie just right, his hair combed, his tux just perfect.

Edward was in charge of security, but they also had more bodyguards hired for the night's event.

"Ex-marines," Rafe told Jade. She thought they looked like they could dish out punishment if they needed to—big, burly, frowning—until they saw Toby, and one of them gave him a high five and a smile.

The paparazzi had camped out on the beach and out front earlier today, visiting with one another and watching the comings and goings—the florist, the waitstaff in charge of beverages and food, and an official photographer.

Rafe had been busy but dropped by Toby's bedroom because he'd missed his mate most of the day. Toby was lying in bed, still dressed in his suit and bow tie, his shoes on the floor. Rafe raised his brows at Jade as she read Toby a story.

"We're *resting*," she said, "so he's not all worn-out at the ball."

Rafe remembered her comment about not calling it a nap. "Gotcha. Did you want me to read to him while you get dressed?"

"Sure. I'll check on you after I'm ready for the party." She said to Toby, "Remember, it's a grown-up party, and after you meet everyone, Aidan will take you into the den to just have fun."

Toby nodded.

Rafe started to read a page from Toby's book.

"Mommy already read that page."

"I was just seeing if you remembered it." Then Rafe began reading the next page, and Toby's eyes drifted until they snapped shut.

As soon as Rafe stopped talking, Toby opened his eyes again. "Keep reading."

"I thought you were asleep."

"I was just resting my eyes."

"Oh, okay. Rest your eyes and I'll keep reading." When Toby's hand jerked on top of the wolf cub comforter, Rafe stood, waited a minute more, and left the room. He saw Jade headed for him, looking like a million bucks in her red dress and diamond-and-ruby necklace. She'd left her hair down, the way he liked it, and she smiled at him.

"What do you think?"

"If I hadn't already asked you to mate me, I would be on my knees begging you now."

She laughed. "So I take it Toby's asleep."

"Resting his eyes. Does he usually sleep in a suit?"

"No, but I couldn't get him to take it off for anything. He was sure he was going to miss all the fun."

"It'll be boring for him."

"He'll soon find that out."

"Come on. Let's get a drink before everyone gets here."

Before long, the house was filled with guests in all their finery. Jade felt overwhelmed. She and Rafe greeted the guests as if they were a married couple, which for wolves, they were. But Sebastian had also learned there was a wolf judge in Portland, Oregon, and he flew there to authenticate a marriage between Jade and Rafe for the earlier period of time. He also had finagled a birth certificate for Toby from a wolf clinic in Silver Town, Colorado. When wolves needed a favor, they often were helped by their kind, who were happy to do it. Well, Dr. Weber in Silver Town wasn't happy to be awakened in the middle of the night to do it, but he wouldn't have denied Sebastian in any event.

For a time, Toby stood in front of Rafe and Jade, pressing up against both of them, holding her free hand as he smiled at all the compliments everyone was giving him. "Adorable." "Cute." "Darling."

He was, but Jade was amused at how shy he could be when so many people were eager to meet him.

She perked up a bit when Rafe introduced children's specialty clothes shop owners and some intimate apparel store owners too. At least five of the children's store owners wanted to use Toby in their ads—probably to butter Rafe up. It didn't hurt to be friends with a billionaire. Toby had that cuteness built in and he was great around a camera, so it wasn't hard to see why they would be interested in using him to model their clothes. She would have to make sure they scheduled photos during the new moon, or she might have to wait to turn Toby.

The whole time Rafe was introducing Jade and Toby, he said, "And this is my wife, Jade, and our son, Toby."

She wasn't sure if she could get used to this lifestyle. Rafe, his staff, his brother, and Derek—who was eager to meet her and said he couldn't believe Rafe had let her go the first time—all helped to collaborate their story.

"Never again," Rafe said, giving Jade a squeeze.

"Don't blame you, old man. If it had been me, I would have moved heaven and earth to get her back." Derek crouched down to speak to Toby. "Just call me Uncle Derek, Toby. I'm your dad's best friend in the whole wide world."

Toby grinned at him, then looked up at Rafe as if waiting to see if Derek was telling the truth or just teasing him.

Rafe smiled down at Toby. "He is. He tells me that all the time."

Jade thought Derek looked like daddy material as he shook Toby's hand.

Then Derek kissed Jade's cheek. "If Rafe ever gets out of hand, just let me know." He shook Rafe's hand and slapped his shoulder. "Hell of a great family you've got, Rafe."

And she knew he meant it. Rafe couldn't have looked prouder of his ready-made family.

Aidan finally interceded and took Toby's hand and said, "Come on, Toby. Let's get something to eat."

"A hot dog?"

Aidan laughed. "Don't think hot dogs are on the menu. Let's see if there's something else you'd like to eat. And then we can watch some cartoons."

Jade smiled at Aidan. "Thanks."

"My pleasure, truly." And she realized he wanted to get out of the limelight himself for a while.

She was enjoying herself for the time being.

She got so many orders for designer clothes—both for kids and for intimate apparel—that she was stunned. Whoever would have thought that getting to know Rafe would lead to this? She would have to hire someone to help her make the creations. But what was great was she could now afford to do so.

Rafe had finally left her side to let her visit without him hovering over her like a protective wolf, and she was making the rounds, everyone oohing and aahing over her necklace and her gown. And asking her a million questions. Mostly, how did she and Rafe meet?

Thankfully, she and Rafe had decided to stick close to the truth. She'd been swimming, and a wave had carried her crashing into him. It had been love at first sight. Of course, that was supposed to be the first time they had met before Toby came on the scene. And she *had* crashed into him here, so some of it was the truth—just with time and place adjusted a bit.

"Ohmigod," one woman said. With her boobs big and her spandex gown small, she looked squashed into the gown, but not all the way. "How did you ever manage to snag one of our most affluent bachelors, dearest?"

Jade smiled. She'd been a wolf, dearest. "Sometimes it's just fate. Luck. And a whole lot of love."

"No wonder he wouldn't date anyone seriously," another thinner woman said, her hazel eyes considering Jade's gown and necklace again. Jade was glad Rafe had bought them for her now. Not that she had felt the need to show off to other women, but so it looked like he really did love her. "But who would ever have guessed he had a sweet little wife already, and a son too. And that his wife would run out on one of the wealthiest men in the area."

"Well, it doesn't really matter now, does it?" a petite woman said, her mouth smiling, her blue eyes sharing the expression. "You've lost out and will have to go after some other extremely eligible bachelor—like Derek maybe."

"I swear he's cut from the same cloth. If I didn't know it was otherwise, I'd think he was Rafe's brother."

"Close enough," Jade said. She was about to move off to check on her son and Aidan, when Toby raced out of the den and headed into the path of men and women socializing. "Excuse me," she hurriedly said and rushed after Toby.

He'd yanked off his bow tie and was tugging at his suit jacket when Jade caught up to him, scooped him up, and hurried him to the bedroom.

"Hot, Mommy. Hot." Toby was still trying to unbutton his jacket.

Aidan was right behind her. "He started complaining he was hot. He didn't feel feverish to me. Then he tore out of the den before I could get to my feet."

Jade was reminded of when Toby took off all his clothes to run through the house to go swimming. "Let Rafe know I'm taking Toby to his room and getting him into his pj's."

"All right. I'll be right back to check on Toby."

"Okay, thanks, Aidan." As soon as she entered Toby's room, she shut the door behind them.

"Weird. Feel weird. Hot, Mommy."

"What did you eat?" She worried he had eaten something that he was allergic to and he had hives. Strawberries could do that to him. She set him down on the floor and hurried to unbutton his jacket. He was moving around so much that she could barely unbutton it. "Toby, hold still, honey. I'll get it off faster."

"Hot," he whined. He was still trying to move around,

trying to kick off his shoes. One of them came off, and then the other.

She got his jacket off and was trying to get his pants zipper down when Rafe rushed into the room with Aidan.

"Sebastian and Derek are filling in for us. What's wrong?" Rafe asked, crouching down beside Toby and Jade.

"He's hot, he says. But there's no flush to his cheeks and his skin feels normal to the touch," Jade said.

"Something he's eaten?" Rafe looked at Aidan.

"Nothing we haven't usually eaten. And he's been fine before this. I'll get my medical bag. Be right back." Aidan left the room, shutting the door behind him.

"Toby, are you hurting, feeling achy? Do your arms and legs hurt? Your stomach? Are you itchy?" It was so hard to learn what was wrong from a child this young when he didn't know himself.

"Mommy, hurry," he said trying to unbutton his own shirt, but she began working on it while Rafe pulled off his pants and socks.

"No rash, skin appears to be normal color," Rafe said, still sounding worried.

And then Toby's whole body blurred before their eyes.

Rafe and Jade stared in disbelief as Toby shifted into a wolf pup.

Chapter 16

"WHAT THE…" RAFE SAID, THEN CURBED SWEARING IN front of the boy. They hadn't turned him. Not yet. How could he shift like that without having been turned?

Toby's coloration was similar to his mother's, his mask blond, the fur framing his face more brown than red, and his belly just as blond. A lighter brown saddle covered his back, his ears framed in black, and the tip of his tail sported black guard hairs just like his mom's.

Rafe looked at Jade, but she appeared to be in just as much shock. She quickly removed Toby's shirt, and Rafe tugged off his underpants as Aidan came into the room and stopped dead in his tracks, medical bag in hand.

"Close the door," Jade and Rafe said, their voices forceful but hushed.

Shutting the door, Aidan looked as dumbfounded as they did. "What happened?"

"We have no idea," Jade said. "And we won't be able to ask Toby until he shifts back."

Toby was sitting on the floor watching them, panting. Jade tried anyway though. "Did someone bite you?"

Toby barked.

"This won't help," Jade said. "I have to know who did this to him."

"Someone in your pack?" Rafe asked. "The timing would be right for him to turn now if he'd been bitten that long ago. It can take hours, days—just depends on the individual, like with anything."

"Maybe. Not an adult though, because they would know Kenneth was trying to sell Toby to a human family."

"A child then?"

Jade collapsed on the edge of Toby's bed. "It might be a little girl. She's three and a half and spoiled rotten. No one was supposed to have shifted around Toby. But if her mother shifted and Pammie left her sight and ran into Toby, she might have been in wolf form and bitten him. She was always bossing him around, partly because she's older, and partly because she's alpha. But so is Toby, and he wouldn't let her push him around."

That made sense.

"What do we do now?" Aidan asked.

"We can't all stay in here during the function," Rafe said. "Word would get out that Toby's ill, and then tons of questions would be asked."

"I'll stay with him," Jade said, "and I'll talk to him about what he is and what we are. I don't want to shift until later when the guests are gone. But right now I'm sure he's confused and he needs me."

"I'll check in on you in a little bit," Rafe said, pulling Jade into his arms and giving her a kiss.

"I can spell you for a while," Aidan said, "to show it's nothing life-threatening."

She nodded.

"Our cover story?" Rafe asked Jade.

"He just was overwhelmed and needed to go to his room for a while. He's tired. Which he is. Anyone who's raised a child knows this."

"All right." Rafe went over to Toby and lifted him in

his arms and gave him a hug and a kiss on the top of his head. Toby licked his cheek and Rafe smiled. "We're going to have so much fun playing chase later. I'll check on you in a little while." Then he handed Toby to Jade and she took him to his bed.

"So sorry," Jade said to Rafe, settling onto the bed next to Toby. He rested his head on her waist and closed his eyes. She began running her hand over his head.

"We're just having to deal with it a little sooner rather than later. No problem, Jade. I love you both. Be back in a while. The sooner we learn how to live with it and he does, the better," Rafe said.

"We don't need the wedding since we're already married," she said, not wanting him to feel obligated when they could have issues with Toby.

"We're renewing our vows. I'll just tell Sebastian to set it up for the time of the new moon. And we can go shopping for a wedding dress too. After the new moon passes, we're going on an extended honeymoon, away from civilization where Toby can be himself and we can too. Of course, Edward will come along as his nanny and bodyguard."

"I'm coming too," Aidan said.

Rafe glanced back at him.

Aidan shrugged. "You're on a honeymoon. You'll need to do honeymoon-related stuff." He grinned. "Edward and I will keep Junior busy. He won't even miss you. So where are we going?"

"Rampart Mountain, a place smack-dab in the middle of Bob Marshall Wilderness Complex in Montana. It means we'll have about five days of hiking, seeing grizzly bears and mountain goats, and crossing white limestone and red sandstone streams. Great for the lack of people. Toby can shift at will the whole way there. We'll fly in the private jet to Montana, so no problem with him shifting en route."

"Hell, that's only about fifty miles as the crow flies from Flathead Lake, where part of a SEAL wolf team live with their pack. I took blood samples from them," Aidan said.

"Have they got any kids?" Rafe asked.

"A few. Some around Toby's age."

"Okay, good. We can check in with them and see if we can arrange a play date. Toby needs to play with some kids around his age—as a wolf," Rafe said.

"I'm all for it. I'll contact the pack leaders Paul and Lori Cunningham and make the arrangements," Aidan said.

"Sounds good to me." Rafe glanced at Jade. "All right with you, honey?"

"Yeah," she said, worried. She wanted more than anything to stay with her son through this, but she also wanted to keep up the charade that everything was normal.

"I'll watch him in a little while," Aidan said as if he could read her mind. "I'll play with him if he wakes."

An hour later, Aidan was back. Toby was still a wolf and sleeping on his side. "Come on," Aidan said quietly to her. "You go rejoin Rafe for a while. I'll make sure Toby's fine."

"Ohh," Jade said, trying to get off the bed without disturbing Toby. Aidan gave her a hand.

"I hope I don't look wrinkled."

"You look beautiful, Jade. Every bachelor male out there wonders how Rafe got so lucky."

She smiled at Aidan. "Thanks."

"Rafe's on the patio, waiting for you."

"Thanks." She straightened and headed out of the bedroom before she changed her mind. But she knew this was her new life. The social gatherings. Keeping their wolf secrets. Teaching Toby to be one of them.

She had to wade through scores of people, everyone asking her the same question, "Is Toby all right?" And she had to give them all the same answer. "He was overwhelmed with all the people. He's conked out in bed. Aidan's watching him in case he wakes and gets scared."

Then she was in Rafe's arms poolside, listening to the waves crashing onto the shore, the breeze whipping about them, and smelling the fresh sea air. She loved it here. She loved him. Loved the way he'd taken her and her son in, no matter what the consequence. He was dealing with all of this as if he really *was* Toby's father, and he'd always been married to Jade.

Rafe didn't ask her how things were going with Toby because he knew she wouldn't have left the boy if she was having trouble with him shifting. She put on a smile for everyone, but she was afraid they would realize she was still concerned about her son.

"Do you want to dance?" Rafe asked her privately.

She appreciated his sensitivity. "I'd love to."

The "ballroom" was a large tiled room with a bar on one wall, floral arrangements all around the room, some ornate bench seating, and a live band against another wall. The music was playing as they walked in, a few couples dancing, but when Rafe led Jade into the room, the musicians started playing a waltz, and Rafe held her close as he moved her across the floor.

Every experience was new with him—dancing like this, holding him close, loving him, his face turned down to kiss her. It wasn't a show for anyone there, but just a wolfish way to say she and he belonged together, that he loved her and was glad she was now part of his life.

She felt his heat, his arousal, his pheromones wafting to her, enticing her own to join in the medley. She smiled up at him, his eyes already darkened with desire, and she was certain hers were too. "Do you think it would be too unseemly if we slipped away before everyone left for the night?"

"They'll understand that we're newlyweds all over again and we need some time alone."

"Which means they'll leave soon?"

He smiled down at her. "Free food, drinks, and entertainment? Sebastian will clear them out before long. Don't you want to dance? I like the way you're rubbing up against me, stirring up things."

She nuzzled his neck and nipped at his earlobe. "You won't be able to walk to the bedroom."

He nuzzled her cheek and whispered against her ear, "Nothing would stop me from carrying you right to bed and finishing the moves there."

"What about Toby?"

"After we have our time, you can join him in his room, or he can join us in ours."

"You sure you don't mind?"

"No. Packs sleep together. There's nothing unnatural about it. He'll learn to shift and be comfortable with it, but while he's going through this in the beginning, he needs all the loving acceptance he can get."

"Thanks, Rafe. I didn't want to leave you every night."

"Ditto, honey."

When they finished dancing, the guests began to thank them for a lovely time and then departed. When the last one was gone, Sebastian and Edward made sure no one was still there while Rafe and Jade hurried to check on Toby. They smiled when Rafe opened the door and saw Aidan sound asleep on top of the wolf comforter, Toby still in his wolf form, his head resting on Aidan's arm as if it were a pillow.

"Come on, Jade. As long as they're fine, let's get some sleep."

She looked up at him, a slight smile on her lips. He leaned down and kissed her, then left his brother and Toby to sleep, shutting the door. "Among other things," he said.

"Did we pull everything off okay?" she asked. "I was afraid when Toby acted so strangely that they'd be wondering what was going on."

"They understood he's not used to being around big crowds of adults like this, and you weren't with him either. They adored you."

"Except for the women who were upset that you no longer are in the market for a wife."

"As if I was ever in the market for one of them."

"I hate to mention it now, but I got so many orders for both lines of clothing that I'm going to need to hire some help. But only wolves, if you have any idea where to find any."

"That pack that we know of in Montana? They've got a whole lot of pack members. Maybe you could see if any of them sew."

"Okay, I'll do that."

After their wild day and night, they made love, and then they cuddled until Jade fell sound asleep. Rafe had planned to check on Toby, but between the long day of festivities, the quiet of the house, and making love to his sexy mate, he fell asleep with Jade wrapped in his arms.

Until a yipping, barking, growling, and howling made him untangle himself from Jade, jump out of bed, throw on a pair of briefs, and grab his gun. Jade was out of bed in an instant, but she didn't have a gun and shifted into her protective she-wolf.

Rafe headed for the door, wanting her to stay behind until he saw what the matter was, but he couldn't make her stay here, not when her son was having fits about something.

A shot rang out, and then another.

Damn it to hell and back! "Stay back," he warned Jade. If bullets were flying, it was too dangerous for her.

But a wolf could run a lot faster than a man, and she shot off for her son's bedroom before Rafe could catch up. Now he wished he'd just turned wolf.

Edward was pinned down in his bedroom, shooting at his assailant. Jade dove into her son's room, and chaos ruled as a man screamed out in pain.

By the time Rafe reached Toby's room, he found an enraged she-wolf at a dead's man's throat, a gun lying on the floor beside him. Toby was running back and forth, anxious and upset. "Stay here," Rafe said to both Jade and Toby, quickly checking his brother, who was dead to the world but still breathing.

Rafe shut Toby's bedroom door and hurried to Edward's room, but there was no sign of Edward or anyone else.

"Two men managed to escape through the gate to the beach," Edward shouted, hurrying back to see if Toby and Aidan were all right. Thankfully, Edward didn't have a scratch on him.

"Check the rest of the house," Rafe said. "Looks like one of them gave Aidan a knockout drug. Toby's upset. Jade killed the other man."

"Okay. Checking the rest of the house to make sure it's secure," Edward said.

Sebastian joined them, gun in hand. "What the hell happened?"

"Three men must have pretended to be waitstaff when serving the food. Maybe the drinks. The dead one and the others who were in the house left no scent, so we didn't smell them," Edward called out to them as he began searching everywhere, including closets this time. "They're wearing the same tuxes as everyone else who was serving the meals."

"Probably hid in closets while you and Sebastian were checking the house before we went to sleep." Rafe tried to wake his brother, shaking Aidan's shoulder as Jade woofed at her son.

Toby nuzzled her in greeting, his tail wagging slightly, and then she led him out of the room.

Aidan stirred.

"Hey, buddy," Rafe said, "wake up. You've been drugged."

"What the hell," Aidan said. His speech was slurred, and he couldn't seem to focus.

"What can I get you to help you snap out of this?"

"What did they give me?"

"How the hell would I know? You're the doctor."

Aidan smiled weakly.

Rafe felt a bit of relief.

"Kenneth and his men?" Aidan asked.

"I'm sure of it. We won't know until Jade shifts and can tell us. As a wolf, she killed the man in the bedroom. No ID on him."

Aidan groaned. "I suppose you want me to help dispose of the body."

"No. Edward will call it in and have a disposal crew take care of him."

"How's Toby?"

"Not sure. Jade's taking care of him in our bedroom."

"Go be with them. I'm fine."

Rafe wanted to check on them, but he didn't want to leave his brother if he began to take a turn for the worse.

"They just knocked me out, but I'm coming to. Just go. I'm fine. Do what you need to do."

"All right. Holler out if you need anything. I'll have Sebastian sit with you until you're more yourself."

"Okay."

Rafe headed for the door, glanced back at Aidan, and frowned when he saw his brother close his eyes and go back to sleep.

"I got this," Sebastian said, joining Rafe. "Go check on your wife and son."

Even though Rafe had referred to Jade and Toby as such all evening, it hadn't really sunk in until Sebastian said it. "Thanks. If Aidan doesn't wake up in half an hour, wake him."

"Will do, Boss."

"Thanks." Rafe strode toward the other part of the house and saw Edward shake his head.

"No one broke in. The place is all clear. I've called already to get some men out here to do a cleanup. And others are searching the area for any of the men who ran off."

"Okay, good show."

"I'm sorry I didn't get there quicker. They must have known where everyone was for the night, waited until we were asleep, and injected your brother with something to knock him out. Guess they didn't expect Toby to make a racket and wake everyone. Turns out he was the best bodyguard in the house."

Rafe smiled a little. "He's got a good start on being one of us." But he worried how the boy had taken seeing his mother kill the man in her wolf form when he'd never seen her like that before. Then again, Toby could smell her and that would have told him just who she was.

He strode toward the bedroom and found Jade curled up in bed as a wolf with her son. He loved the image and would remember them like this forever. She raised her head and eyed him. He wished they could talk, but Toby was eyeing him too and this seemed to be the beginning of teaching him about how the other half of them lived. Rafe yanked off his clothes and shifted while both his mate and son watched, then he loped over to the bed. Rafe put his big wolf paws on the mattress so he could get closer and let Toby smell him and know it was still just him. Toby stayed with his mom, but he nosed Rafe's muzzle in greeting. That intimacy between a cub and an adult was heartening.

Rafe's next move was to jump on top of the bed without scaring Toby and curl up with them. He was a big wolf, and he was afraid Toby might be frightened.

But Jade wouldn't be, and her reaction should help to convince Toby that Rafe was nobody to fear.

Hoping this wouldn't backfire, because Rafe didn't want to make any mistakes with this, he jumped up on the bed. To Rafe's surprise, Toby stood and greeted him again, his tail wagging, and Rafe's heart lifted with relief. He licked Toby's face, then settled down next to Jade. Toby watched the two of them as Rafe rested his head over her side, and then Toby curled up on the other side of her and placed his head on her side just below Rafe's. Rafe was amused. The gesture was a show of possession, and he agreed. Jade belonged equally to both of them.

Chapter 17

R<small>AFE WAS SNUGGLING WITH</small> J<small>ADE UNDER THE COVERS AS</small> humans when he realized it was getting to be light out and Toby was no longer in bed with them. Rafe threw aside the covers, ready to panic when he heard Toby's high-pitched voice saying, "Yeah, Uncle Aidan, I wanna go swimming."

Rafe relaxed.

"With your swim trunks on this time, and you wait for me to get dressed, or no more swimming for a week."

Rafe smiled. He hadn't expected his brother to play with Toby so much. Maybe Aidan was doing so because he would be returning to his lab work now that the ball was over and he didn't need to wait to turn Toby during the first of the new moon. But with Kenneth's men breaking in—Rafe needed to confirm with Jade that's who had been in the house—he feared that Kenneth would still be after his brother.

"Can I sit by the pool until you're ready?" Toby asked.

"No," Aidan said sternly.

Smiling, Rafe shook his head and said to Jade, "I'm having alarms set on all the doors so if Toby leaves, we'll know it."

"Good." Jade sighed against his chest.

Edward said, "I've got my coffee. I'll take him out."

"I thought Edward was supposed to be the nanny," Jade said, kissing Rafe.

"Sounds like Aidan is enjoying his role as Toby's uncle for the time being."

"I didn't notice when Toby left the room this morning. Did you?"

"No. I guess we were both so tired." Rafe began getting dressed, needing to see if everything was taken care of in Toby's room and the hall where the rounds had struck the walls and doorjamb. "Were the men in the house part of Kenneth's pack? And was he with them?"

"The one I killed wasn't part of Kenneth's pack. I didn't smell his scent or the others', and I didn't see them. I hadn't wanted to kill him in front of Toby, but he was getting ready to shoot him and I had to stop him."

"I understand, Jade. You had to do what you had to do. Toby doesn't seem to be traumatized by it. I suspect Aidan has talked to him some this morning, now that Toby's back to being human."

"I wonder how long that will last."

"New moon is in another day. Then he won't be able to shift and we'll have the wedding and that'll be settled. I'm going to check on everything. I need to sign some papers for a real estate purchase, and I need to check in with the men who have Lizzie."

"I can't believe my brother is still trying to get ahold of Aidan. Don't you think that's what he was doing, drugging him? Except Toby thwarted them?"

"Yeah. They would have drugged Toby if they'd wanted just to grab him. They must have had only enough of a dose to knock Aidan out."

"But why would Kenneth still want him? I know my brother hasn't given up the notion that Aidan's research will be worth a lot of money, but why would he continue to risk grabbing him?"

"Hell, maybe it all has to do with the guy who wants your brother to pay off his gambling debts. Maybe Kenneth promised to turn over Aidan and his research to Grayton. Maybe both men are under the assumption that Aidan is worth more money than what Kenneth owed Grayton. *If* Aidan could come up with a cure. The price of having the same longevity as we had before? Priceless."

"What are we going to do about it?"

"Talk to the kingpin. But I need to take care of some things around here first."

"You're actually going to talk to him?"

"Yeah. Face-to-face, not like your cowardly brother who takes a young boy hostage to tip the scales in his favor. It's not going to be pretty. If Grayton has the notion he can use Aidan for his own designs, I doubt the man will give it up. Even if I explain that Aidan doesn't have the cure and isn't close to making one. Aidan will stay here. And I'll have extra security set up. I'll leave as soon as I can." No way was Rafe going to allow anyone to test his resolve in this matter.

"What if Aidan doesn't figure into this with Grayton? That my brother wasn't intending to hand him over?"

"For one thing, I believe the idea that Aidan would suddenly have the cure and then be selling enough of it to pay off your brother's debt is too far out. I think your brother knew that. I think the only way he could get off the hook with Grayton was to give him something that would pay him off with tons more interest. But, Kenneth had to grab Aidan first. Or I'm sure his life is forfeit. I doubt your brother has the resources to set up Aidan in a lab in secret somewhere so he can continue his research."

She let out her breath and nodded. Rafe knew she worried about him. "I'll be fine. I'll have enough armed men with me to make sure of it."

"I'll be right out. I'm going to take another shower."

"Maybe…I should take one too."

She smiled. "Go. Check on Toby and do the rest of what you need to do. I'll feel better knowing you're checking on him after what happened last night."

Rafe pulled her into his arms and kissed her. "You saying so means the world to me, honey. Thanks."

She wrapped her arms around his neck and pressed her body against his. "How could I have ever have gotten so lucky?"

"Fate."

"My brother," she said and grunted.

"No. Fate brought us together. We were meant to be together." He kissed her and released her.

She smiled and kissed his cheek, then headed for the bathroom. "I want you back safe."

"I intend to be."

After Rafe checked Toby's room and found it cleaned of any evidence of a killing, he noticed that the damage to the walls and Edward's room still needing to be taken care of. Though no spent shell casings were lying about. Rafe found Toby playing basketball in the pool with Aidan, Edward on his cell as he oversaw the two of them.

"Somehow Aidan looks more like Toby's nanny than you do," Rafe said to Edward as he ended his call.

"I'm sure when Aidan leaves, I'll have my hands full. But we'll need another bodyguard up here to safeguard the family. George MacIntosh?"

"Yeah, he'd be good. Not sure how he is with kids, but that'll work. And the work on the place?"

"Have a wolf coming over in half an hour. I made sure he's someone we know," Edward said. "But we did a sweep of the area to see if we could find any sign of the men or Kenneth and found the catering van ditched on the side of the road. The real caterers were bound and gagged, still sleeping off whatever Kenneth's men must have given them. Hugh made sure they got back to their restaurant safely. Some of Kenneth's men must have left after the ball to make it appear as though they were all leaving, and then a few stayed behind."

"Hell."

"Yeah, the security detail I had checking everyone out who came into the house said they all had proper IDs. Kenneth must have planned this from the beginning, as soon as he knew about the charity ball."

"He's good. I'll give him that. I didn't really think he could pull off something that well planned." Rafe told Edward what he wanted to do about Grayton. "Arrange for the men who will accompany us and those who will safeguard my family. We're going on a trip."

Looking concerned, his face dark, brows knitted, Sebastian headed out to the patio. "Unless you give your private number out to someone, no one can contact you," he said to Rafe. "Which means all calls to you come to me."

"Right, and…?"

"I just got off the phone with Kenneth Ashton."

Even the mention of Kenneth's name made Rafe's blood boil in anger.

"He says he wants a million dollars to keep quiet about Toby's real father."

"He can't grab Aidan, so now he has another get-rich scheme. *Bastard.*" But Rafe really hadn't expected this turn of events. "Toby's father is dead. So what's Ashton going to do about it?"

"Go to the parents. If they ask for a paternity test, they may ask for grandparent rights."

"Did you check into our laws?" They'd had no reason to learn anything about grandparent visitation rights before this, so Rafe didn't know what the laws were.

"Yeah, right after I got off the phone with him. I checked and it said they had to have a preexisting relationship with the grandchild."

Rafe heaved a sigh of relief.

"The problem is that if they do this, it will confuse Toby about who his real father is. And it will cause problems for you and Jade. Even if there was no truth to it, some people would decide the grandparents were truly his grandparents, and if you were a decent kind of guy, you'd let them see him since his real father is dead."

"Damn Kenneth. Hell, the only way we're going to deal with this is to get someone to falsify the record on the samples."

"For court-ordered paternity testing, they'll often have two separate labs handle it to ensure there's no tampering going on."

"Do it. We have the resources and the money to make it happen. As for Kenneth, I'll deal with him. But I also want you to check into the grandparents' background. Are they squeaky clean? If not, I want to know it. I won't use any dirt against them unless it comes to that—and only if the paternity testing doesn't work in our favor. But if they wish to pursue a claim to see him, I want to prove they're unfit grandparents."

"Too bad a bite from you to turn Toby wouldn't have done the trick."

"Yeah, wouldn't have worked. In that case, the connection to me would only show up in his wolf DNA, and they'd wonder why they had a sample of wolf DNA instead of human."

"Okay, I'll get right on this. We're all a go on the marriage."

"Sounds good. But one other thing." After Rafe finished speaking with Sebastian about how he planned to pay Grayton a visit, he said good morning to Aidan and Toby.

"Are you coming in?" Toby asked as if he didn't have enough playmates.

"Not right now. I have some business to take care of. But I wanted to ask if a wolf bit you before we took you from Lizzie's car."

Toby scrunched up his face in thought, then shook his head.

"You're not in trouble, Toby," Rafe said, realizing the boy might think he had done something wrong and had provoked the wolf into biting him. He had to have been bitten. There was no other way he could shift otherwise.

"Pammie." Toby squared his shoulders. "She wasn't playing with the toys, and Lizzie said she had to share."

"So they let you see her as a wolf?"

He shrugged.

"Did anyone know about it?"

Toby shook his head.

"You didn't tell anyone?"

He shook his head again.

"Why not, Toby?"

He looked at Aidan as if he'd help him out of this dilemma.

"He's not upset with you, Toby," Aidan said. "He just wants to learn who bit you and why. Did anyone ever turn into a wolf around you?"

"No. I didn't know it was her at first. I'd never seen her as a wolf. But then she turned into herself and her mommy was calling her and Pammie said if I told on her, she'd bite me even harder. She was mean to me. Always took the toys away from me. Even when she wasn't playing with them."

"You said you had never seen real wolves before," Rafe reminded him.

Toby looked down at the water.

"Toby?"

He let out his breath and raised his arms outward and his hands up as if saying, "What could I do about it?" Then he said, "She told me if I told on her…about shifting into a wolf, she'd kill me."

Angry with the mother over it, Rafe nodded. "It's okay, Toby. Thanks for telling me. You're not in any trouble. If they told you that you were allowed to play with the toys, she didn't have any right getting mean with you. And it's okay that you saw that she shifted. You're one of us and can do it too. Now about last night—"

Toby's gaze shot to Aidan.

"It's okay, Toby. You can tell your dad." Aidan looked amused to be calling Rafe that.

Toby took Rafe's hand, and Rafe lifted him up in his arms, carried him to one of the chaise longues, and sat the boy on his lap while they discussed what it meant to be wolves. "Okay, tell me what you saw."

"Mommy bit the man. He knocked out Uncle Aidan and he had a gun and he was aiming at me. I was biting his ankle 'cuz he hurt Uncle Aidan."

"And you did right. You woke up the whole house, and that meant we could come running and take care of the bad men."

Toby nodded.

"How do you feel about Mommy biting the bad man?"

"She pertected me."

"Protected you, yes. That's what the adult wolves do. Protect their wolf cubs. And we protect others in the wolf pack. Uncle Aidan. And the others."

"Uncle Sebastian and Uncle Edward," Toby said, folding his arms. "Are you going to swim now?"

"I'll come in and play with you after I make some calls."

"Yes!" Then Toby climbed off his lap and went back to playing with Aidan.

"But I have to go on a trip after that."

"Can I go?"

Rafe smiled. "Not this time, Toby. Someone needs to take care of your mommy and Uncle Aidan."

Aidan raised his brow in question.

"Talk to you before I go," Rafe told his brother.

—∾∾—

When Rafe told her the wedding was a go and she needed to pick out a gown, Jade was all set to buy it. She couldn't believe all the money Rafe was willing to spend on her.

"I want to go with you," Rafe said, looking down at her with a worried but loving expression.

"It's bad luck if you see me wearing the wedding gown before the wedding."

He smiled. "So you're really taking this to heart."

"Sure am. First time for everything." Even though their kind didn't need to have a traditional wedding to prove they were mated for life, for Toby's sake and because they were going to be in the limelight so much, she had to do it. So if she was going to be a traditional human and do this, she didn't want Rafe to see the wedding gown before she walked down the aisle.

"Okay, but I want George and Edward to go as your bodyguards. I have other men watching out for you. And Sebastian and Derek volunteered to help you decide. Even though I want to be the one to do so," Rafe said.

Jade laughed. "I'm sure you'll love whatever we pick out." And if the guys liked something she didn't, it was going to be her choice, not theirs.

"Aidan will stay at the house with Toby. I don't want both of you out shopping together without me being there in the event your brother learns you're out. I'll have several men staying at the house with Aidan and Toby to protect them."

"All right." Then she gave Rafe a hug and kiss, and also one to Toby, who looked torn between going and staying.

"Uncle Aidan and you are going to have lots more fun than Mommy is," Rafe said.

"I need a new tux," Toby said.

Jade wondered where he had gotten that notion. "You just got a new one."

Toby looked at Rafe.

He tousled Toby's hair. "He's right. He needs a new one because this is for a different function and not a charity ball. He can wear them to the next socials we have. Right, Toby?"

Toby nodded.

"Right, if he doesn't outgrow them in the meantime." Jade loved that Rafe wanted to please her son, but there had to be limits. He didn't know how fast Toby was growing from week to week.

"I'll take him when I get back," Rafe said.

"I could."

"Nah, this is a guy thing. Right, Toby?"

Toby grinned.

"All right, but we're going to have to talk about this…spending issue later."

Rafe just smiled.

She'd never spoiled Toby like this, and she didn't want to start now. He'd have to learn that when he was grown up, he'd have to support himself, and he most likely wouldn't have this kind of money to start with.

When she and her escort arrived at a wedding boutique, she should have felt strange shopping for wedding gowns with four men in tow, but since she'd never thought she'd have a wedding in the first place, she supposed having men along wasn't much different than having women along. Except they weren't her closest and dearest friends, but there to protect her. A dark cloud prevailed over the event as she worried about Rafe and tried to push her concern out of her mind.

All of the men were eager to tell her which wedding gown they thought Rafe would like best. Not which looked the best on her. In truth, they were really telling her what *they* liked best, not what Rafe would prefer.

"I like that one," Sebastian said.

The two bodyguards, Edward and Hugh, nodded.

Derek was still eyeing the cut of another gown on its hanger.

The store clerk's mouth was pursed as she stood by, waiting for *someone* to decide on the right gown. She probably wasn't used to so many men in her shop at once.

Jade wanted to check the prices on the gowns, because it was something she would wear only once, and it wasn't going to be a royal wedding with millions of people watching, just a select few wolves. But Sebastian was in charge of paying this time, so she gave up on trying to save Rafe money.

The guys all seemed to be in mutual agreement that they liked the gowns that were low cut on the bodice and back and clung to her curves, not a flouncy wedding gown with a full slip underneath to make her look like she was a fairy-tale princess. She really needed to pick what she wanted, but she suspected if the guys liked the clinging gowns best, probably Rafe would too. And that's who she really was wearing it for.

It was either the pearl-beaded lace mermaid gown with the gored skirt, which clung to her body all the way to her knees, or a beaded, lace-appliqué column-style gown.

They finally decided on the mermaid gown. She loved it and hoped Rafe would too. Best of all, it fit all her curves just right so no adjustments had to be made.

When they were leaving the store, Mr. Marks approached her, ignoring all her bodyguards. When Aidan went to intercept him, Jade said, "It's all right." At least she hoped it would be. She really believed that if she was nice to him, which he seemed to appreciate, he would print stories that didn't put her and her son in a bad light.

"I see you're getting ready to be married to Mr. Denali again," Marks said skeptically, as though he didn't believe they were already married. "A renewal of vows, a more public way of sharing your commitment—I love the touch. It makes me think back on how you were rescued on the beach. You know, in the rip current. How he kissed you like he really knew you. So I was thinking, if I went along with the story he's telling, about being married before and not knowing about his son, that you were afraid to approach him in a more direct way…"

Everyone with her appeared uncomfortable with what Marks was saying, but Jade knew if she was going to be in the limelight, she had to deal with this in her own way.

"That made me think you were afraid of Mr. Denali's response," Marks went on. "And that's why you didn't have your son with you at the time. Then when things began to heat up between you like in the old days, he moved you right into his place, you picked up your son, and there you all were—one big, happy family. Now, I know Mr. Denali has the money to make things happen.

I like you, and the kid is cute. The two of you deserve the best, so that's the spin I'm putting on it. But I want to warn you—I did look into you dating anyone else before you met up with Mr. Denali. Some guy named Stewart Roth was seeing you pretty hot and heavy. I made a lot of inquiries. In any event, I might have stirred up some real trouble for you. Which is really why I'm here."

Her heart raced at the mention of Stewart's name. She was afraid her and Rafe's fabricated fairy-tale story would crumble before her eyes.

"Anyway, I truly am sorry that I talked with the man."

"Stewart?" Jade asked, feeling unsteady and light-headed. She felt the blood drain from her face.

Sebastian moved in to support her if she passed out. "Yeah, Stewart Roth. I'm afraid he might be getting in touch with you, trying to cash in on your dream. I really am sorry. I just wanted to warn you."

She couldn't believe Stewart could be alive when her brother said he had killed him. And she knew Kenneth wouldn't have lied about that. She was glad Stewart was alive, but then she felt her stomach drop even more. Had Kenneth mistakenly killed Stewart's younger brother? They were only a year apart, and if they weren't together, they looked like each other. Even together, they appeared to be twins.

That meant Stewart still might be able to lay claim to her son. They couldn't allow him to. Not now that her son was a *lupus garou*.

What a nightmare.

Marks tipped his hat to her and smiled. "Sometimes the underdog needs to win. And that guy isn't worthy of you. I'll get the story right." Then he walked off, and she watched him go, unable to move.

Sebastian took hold of her arm and walked her to the car while the others hurried to get her door or start the car.

As soon as they were in the vehicle, Sebastian asked, "Are you going to be all right?"

"No. Kenneth said he killed Toby's father. That means he probably killed Stewart's brother by accident. If Stewart thinks he can get some money out of this deal by claiming he wants part custody, or he wants Rafe to buy him off—"

"We'll take care of it," Edward said.

"I don't want him killed."

"It would be too suspicious if the guy tries to come here to claim kinship and then suddenly dies. Rafe has paid for all the legal certification to prove Toby's his son, you were both married before that, and you're still legally married," Sebastian said. "Do you want me to call Rafe with the news, or do you want to tell him?"

"I will. Thanks, Sebastian."

"I'll get ahold of one of our PIs and have him verify the story. He'll look into Stewart Roth's life with a fine-toothed comb. If the guy is in the least bit shady, we'll have something to use against him if he decides to play hardball."

"I was kind of a wild card back then," Jade admitted. "He was rather a bad boy."

"Then you met Rafe," Sebastian said, smiling.

"How was this Stewart character a bad guy?" Edward asked.

"Ran with a rough crowd. Raced cars where he

shouldn't have been. I don't know that he ever did anything else illegal, but I guess I just liked his wildness."

"Because you were looking for a wolf," Sebastian suggested.

"I guess. Then I learned I was pregnant with Toby, and that changed my life. I was already working hard on trying to support myself with my apparel designs, but I really became better at marketing them when I knew I had to support my child."

"Rafe wants me to meet with you after the wedding so you can tell me everything you need to set up your design studio," Sebastian said. "We can go shopping for all the essentials, and you can hire whoever you need to make your business more viable. You can hire your own personal assistant if you'd like, but in the meantime, I'll help you with getting set up and dealing with the day-to-day business. Like scheduling Toby for photo shoots for the ads for the specialty shops."

"I'd love to hire a couple of seamstresses to make up the designs."

"You've got it. I'll contact a couple of wolf packs and see if any of them have seamstresses in the bunch. We'll take care of relocation expenses. But Rafe didn't want me to bother you with this until after the wedding, so you wouldn't be stressed about your business too."

"Thanks for being my wedding coordinator too, Sebastian. I couldn't have done it without you."

He smiled. "I never know what job I'll get next. It makes it interesting and fun. Though I'm still down about not getting to go to the toy store. I would have picked up a bunch of puzzles for Toby."

She laughed.

After they returned home, Toby ran to give her a hug. "Mommy, Daddy left on his trip. But he said if we were really good, he'd bring us something special."

She drew Toby into a hug and tried not to cry. What if Rafe never came home?

Rafe had flown to Amarillo as soon as he'd learned where Todd Grayton lived and worked. Rafe had men at both locations, waiting for his arrival. They were his own team of hotshot fighters, every one of them eager to take care of the bastard if Rafe believed this man had anything to do with Kenneth's attempts at grabbing Aidan. Some might believe Rafe's men were nothing more than mercenaries, every man for himself if things went south. But these men were the good guys—they'd fought in several wars like Rafe and were well decorated and dedicated to protecting a wolf who might be able to stop their kind from premature extermination. Not to mention, they were all good friends of Rafe's. Sure he paid them well, but they had to earn a living too, and he didn't begrudge them the high wages they earned on any mission he took them on. He knew if he needed their help, they'd have offered it in a heartbeat, without any thought of payment.

They were smart wolves and could think fast on their feet—no need to have a leader to tell them what to do. Even though in a case like this, they waited to see what Rafe wanted of them. But if they got into a mess on their own, they were perfectly capable of handling it.

"Do we know where he is yet?" Rafe asked Edward. He was ready for a fight, to take out Grayton if he was involved in any way with this business with Aidan. But he would have to still eliminate Kenneth. It was the only way. Even if Kenneth suddenly had his debt wiped out, the guy was an addict. And that wouldn't go away. The next time Kenneth was in debt up to his eyeballs, he'd come up with another harebrained plan and possibly hurt Jade, Toby, or Aidan. Only by then, Rafe might have let down his guard.

Edward got off his phone. "He's at an office at the track, but one of our men said he usually leaves for late lunch about this time. He either goes to a sit-down meal at one of the restaurants in Amarillo, or he heads home."

"Let's hope he heads home. I want to get this over with and return home myself so I can take Toby to get his new tux." Rafe wasn't discounting how deadly the situation could be. But he wasn't going to dwell on it. He had more interesting plans he'd rather think about.

The ten men with him were quiet, tense, waiting to learn their role in this.

As soon as they arrived in Amarillo, they climbed into three waiting Suburbans, all black, all looking like they were the FBI in takedown mode.

"He's at his horse ranch out in the country. Just got there. Was late getting out to lunch. Might not return to the office," Edward said.

"If he's not cooperative, I can guarantee he won't be returning to the office today or any other." Three of his men gave Rafe a thumbs-up.

Like him, they'd rather take down a wolf scumbag for good than negotiate. Especially when they knew he would continue to cause problems and put their kind at risk.

Rafe rode in the first car, Edward at the wheel.

"Nothing much out here but prairie grass, a few prairie dogs, mule deer, and a few horse ranches way off the road," Edward said.

"It's all good then. No one but us wolves will know what's going to happen way out here." Rafe thought the scenario couldn't get any better than this.

They saw a wild turkey running through the short grasses, and the wind blew a tumbleweed across the road.

"I feel like I'm back in the Old West," Edward said, "six-shooter ready."

Rafe smiled. And he had to agree. "Only this time the gunmen have something more to back them up, even though it would be better if no one sees any wolf bite marks on the guy. No wolves in Texas any longer."

"Agreed."

The men he had situated at the racetrack remained there in case Grayton called his men to come to his aid. Rafe's men would stop them in a heartbeat.

"So what do you think, Boss? Think Grayton knows about Aidan?"

"Aidan never knew about Grayton's pack—he hadn't taken blood samples from them. Kenneth must have been scheming this from the beginning. So yeah, I think Kenneth didn't tell Aidan about Grayton's wolf pack and had already decided to use this scheme to get himself out of hot water."

"Think Grayton might know we're coming?"

"He might. But the men we have situated around his land said nothing has changed. They did recon there already, so they know the layout of the place. He's got five men there, so I suspect our visit will be a surprise.

With the kind of business he's in, I imagine he always has protection. But if he knew we were coming, he'd have a lot more men protecting his back." At least Rafe hoped his visit would be a surprise. His men were good, so he expected the best results when they were involved. The faster they could take control of the situation, the better for all of his men.

They reached the cattle guard crossing and rolled over it. The ranch house was still not visible. Some working horses were standing under a tree in the scanty shade.

"Another half a mile on this road and we'll see the house. If anyone's watching out the windows or sitting on the porch, sipping a beer, they'll spot us coming and shout a warning," Edward said. "Our men are already in place."

Rafe loved the men on his team. They were team players, and everyone knew the role they needed to play. They would have been there hours ago, set up and ready to take care of business. Rafe might be driving down the road in air-conditioned comfort, but the men in place would be camouflaged against the hot earth, using any cover and concealment they could, and no one would even know they were there until it was too late.

"One of our men said he spotted us. They're moving in now to take control of the situation."

"Any dogs?"

"No."

"Good." They always had orders to tranquilize dogs, not kill them, even if they were trained guard dogs. The dogs couldn't help that they worked for bad guys.

They heard gunfire. Everyone in the car tensed. Rafe figured it would come to that, but he had hoped it wouldn't. Still, he wasn't putting his men at risk by telling them they couldn't use any rounds if they had no other choice.

Edward sped up now on the gravel road, all of them eager to get there and help their comrades.

As soon as they pulled up at the side of the house with no windows, the men all got out, spread out, and were about to charge into the house when Hugh opened the front door and greeted Rafe. "Everyone's accounted for. Mr. Grayton is sitting in his living room waiting to talk to you." Hugh's mouth curved up a hint. "He was swimming in his palatial pool out back, nude. He's not happy. He said this could have been settled with a phone call, whatever the deal is."

"Like hell it could." Rafe knew the type. He was fairly certain the man would attempt to retaliate. Grayton was a top wolf, and this had to be a hell of a blow to his ego. "Hope you gave him a towel."

Hugh nodded, his smile still in place.

The place was decorated as if it were a scene from the Old West: antlers over the mantel, cowhide rugs on the wooden floor, paintings of cowboys roping longhorn steer, and a soulful-looking elk hanging over the mirror above a bar, staring back at him.

Rafe glanced in Todd Grayton's direction next. The way Rafe had checked out his place first showed Grayton the man was unimportant to Rafe in the scheme of things. He was taking his time, not showing the man the kind of respect he was probably used to. They were wolves, and it was important to show the pecking order among them. In Rafe's presence, Grayton was at the bottom of the heap, if he hadn't realized it before this.

"What the hell is going on?" Grayton asked, trying to rise from the leather couch he was seated on. A towel was wrapped around his waist, his chest covered in thick, brown hair that made him look like he had already partly turned into a wolf.

Edward shook his head, his dark look saying he was ready to kill Grayton this instant and ask questions later.

"No one said what was going on. Who the hell are you people? I don't have any quarrel with you." Frowning, Grayton settled back on the seat, his body stiff with tension, like a cornered wolf trying to figure out how to turn this to his advantage—in a hurry.

"We have a mutual acquaintance. Seems he owes you some money," Rafe said, standing in front of Grayton, towering over him in a way that said Rafe was in charge of the discussion.

"All right, now we're getting somewhere. Why don't we talk like civilized men and work something out that benefits both of us. Let me get you a drink."

Rafe motioned to Hugh to stand next to Grayton. "Sit," Hugh growled low under his breath, standing as close as he could without bumping into Grayton.

"All right, all right. So who owes me money, and who the hell are you?" Grayton asked, still putting on the bravado, although his whole body had tensed as soon as Rafe walked into the room.

Rafe waited for Hugh to nod just once, then he said, "Kenneth Ashton." Rafe wanted Hugh to smell Grayton's reaction, as much as Rafe was watching the man's expression. He had to know for certain what Grayton's involvement was in all of this.

Grayton's blue eyes widened.

Rafe had expected that kind of reaction. "So you tell me what kind of a deal the two of you made," he said, his voice low and dark.

"He owes me money." As if Grayton had a death wish, or he was just too cocky for his own good, he added, "You gonna pay his debt?"

"How about I just wipe out his debt by getting rid of the 'creditor' in this situation." The steel behind Rafe's voice proved he had every intention of doing it too. "If Kenneth doesn't have the money, how the hell was he going to get ahold of it? He's still alive, so I'm assuming he promised he'd have it to you by a certain date."

"How the hell do I know? I told him to get it to me by the end of this week or else he was a dead man. Satisfied? What's it to you?" Sweat was beading up on Grayton's brow.

"Why the end of this week? Why not last week or the end of next week? Why this specific weekend?" Rafe suspected it was due to the timing of the charity ball. And Grayton was coming up with answers way too slowly, trying to figure out what he should say to keep from losing his life.

"When was the last time you heard from Ashton?" Rafe asked.

"The prick was supposed to call me today." Grayton's eyes widened, recognition dawning. "Denali..." he said under his breath.

There was only one reason he would know Denali's name in association with Kenneth paying off his debt. He had made a deal with Grayton to wipe out his debt by turning Aidan over to him.

"You see the problem I have now?" Rafe asked. He

hadn't wanted this lowlife to continue to feed off wolves' addictions if they couldn't stop gambling, but the business with his brother made it paramount that Rafe end this for good. Even if Grayton took out Kenneth for failing to pay his debt and Kenneth was no longer a threat to Aidan, Jade, or Toby, Rafe couldn't trust that Grayton wouldn't attempt to grab Aidan at some other time. He most likely had amassed enough wealth that he could hire thugs to do the job.

"I'll cancel his debt." Scowling, Grayton looked like it was killing him to say so, and Rafe didn't trust he'd honor the deal.

"Who else knows about this arrangement you had with Kenneth?"

"No one. I swear it. The deal was too sweet to share with any of my men in case they decided to double-cross me. Hell, it's happened before. I'm no fool. I'll cancel his debt," Grayton said again.

"It's too late for that." The man had sealed his own coffin when he got involved in this scheme to take Rafe's brother hostage.

Grayton grabbed his towel and yanked it aside. Rafe knew he was going to shift, but the change was so fast—he turned into a big, brown, snarling wolf, with teeth bared—that Grayton lunged at Rafe before he could react. Rafe pulled his gun, unable to fight as a wolf when he was fully dressed. He fired on the wolf before it reached him, yet the bullet in the chest didn't stop Grayton, and the wolf took Rafe to the floor. Rafe instantly dropped his gun and grabbed the ruff of the wolf's thick coat to keep from being bitten by its snarling teeth.

Despite the wolf's strength and Rafe being in his
human form, Rafe wouldn't let the wolf get the best of
him. Grayton snarled and snapped his teeth, pissed off
he couldn't end Rafe's life, taking one last act of ven-
geance before the rest of Rafe's men killed him.

Edward shot the wolf, and Hugh fired off a couple
of rounds. Grayton was so hyped up on adrenaline—
and, hell, maybe drugs—that he seemed unstoppable
as Rafe struggled to keep the wolf's teeth from sinking
into his jugular.

Another couple of rounds hit the wolf, and Grayton
jerked a little.

And then Rafe felt the wolf's strength ebbing, saw his
eyes becoming unfocused, his heavy body sagging, until
Grayton collapsed on top of Rafe.

"Damn it." Rafe pushed the wolf off him with
Edward's assistance, and Hugh offered his hand to help
him up. "I'd hoped we could convince him to take his
own life." Standing, he said to Edward, "Check with the
other men and find out if they knew of the arrangement
Kenneth had made with this slimebag of a wolf."

"What now, Boss? If Ashton learns Grayton is
dead…" Hugh said.

"Kenneth is a dead man. He has a gambling addiction. You think he's learned his lesson?" Rafe shook his
head. "He'll be in debt again, owing some other scumbag. How much do you want to bet that he wouldn't
make the same offer? Aidan to pay off his debt? We
can't risk it."

Edward returned to the living room, shaking his head.
"Grayton's men are all dead. They wouldn't give up,
probably figuring that if Grayton lived through this, he'd

kill them for not protecting him better. Our men want to know if they can call in the 'copter, clean up the mess, and make a body drop over the Pacific."

"By all means. We need to get home." Rafe thanked the men working for him. "Until next time." Only he hoped there wouldn't be a next time. But if there was, they would all be ready.

—∿∿—

After Rafe and some of his men looked for records that might say something about the Denalis, they found nothing in that line and headed outside. The helicopter landed, and he called Jade. "It's finished."

"He's dead? Grayton?"

"Yeah. But I can't let Kenneth off scot-free. You know that, don't you?"

"Yeah. I hate to say it. But I don't trust him one bit."

"Okay, well I'll be home in about three hours and take Toby to get his tux."

In any other situation, he would have come home and discussed what had happened with his male friends and had a beer. Life was so different for him now, but he loved it. Loved his new family, and loved the idea of taking Toby to get a tux, especially because it meant marrying Jade. He made a conference call to Aidan and Sebastian to let them know what was up, glad this part of the trial was over.

"So Kenneth's not off the hook," Aidan said.

"No, not by a long shot."

"We'll keep looking for him," Sebastian said. "Glad to hear everyone is safe."

"Same here," Aidan said.

"We'll be getting in soon. See you then." Rafe wished that was the end of it, but he knew it wouldn't be until he took care of Jade's brother, once and for all.

———

When Rafe arrived home, he got a big hug from both Toby and Jade, and he couldn't have been any happier than he felt at that moment. They meant everything to him. He kissed Jade on the cheek and ruffled Toby's hair.

Toby said, "What did you bring us, Daddy?"

Edward handed him the sack. "Your dad said we could all practice with you."

Toby dove into the sack and found the T-ball set. "Just what I wanted forever. Can we play ball?"

"Later," Rafe said. "We need to get you a tux." Then he slipped a small box out of his pocket and handed it to Jade.

She opened it and smiled at the pearl necklace and earrings. "You shouldn't have," she said, her eyes full of tears as she threw her arms around him and gave him a hug.

"They're pearls for the mermaid I caught in the sea."

She kissed him full on the mouth, and he kissed her right back, wanting a bigger thank-you sooner than later. Then he had to leave before the tux store closed. "Be back in a little bit."

"These are lovely, Rafe. Thank you. I'll be waiting."

"Look forward to that," Rafe said and gave her a wink. Then he took Toby, Edward, and Hugh with him to check out children's tuxes.

"Let Rafe spoil Toby a bit," Aidan said to her.

"Toby needs a father, and he's eating up Rafe's interest in him."

She sighed. "I just don't want Toby to think that if I say no, he can ask Rafe and he'll get it for him." She'd tried not to be concerned about it after what Rafe had to do today to keep his brother safe. But she knew that this business of overspending on them had to stop.

"He won't. This is something different. He wants Toby to be as thrilled to take part in the wedding as he is. After that, Rafe will see what you want to do. He did when you were in the store before, right?"

"True."

"Okay then. Not to worry."

When the "boys" got home from their shopping trip, Jade wanted to see Toby's tux, but he folded his arms and said, "You can't see it until the wedding."

She laughed. "All right. I can't wait to see it."

Looking concerned, Edward said to Rafe and Jade, "May I have a word with the two of you? I just got some news."

Aidan said, "Come on. Why don't we take a swim?"

"Yes!" Toby ran off to get his swimsuit.

"Let me help him, and I'll be right back." Jade was worried about what was going on now, but also trying to concentrate on getting a wiggly Toby out of his clothes and into his swim trunks. When he was dressed, he ran to Aidan's door and said, "I'm ready, Uncle Aidan!"

She waited until Aidan opened the door wearing his board shorts and then handed him the sunscreen. "Thanks, Aidan."

"My pleasure." He hurried off with Toby.

Then Jade joined Rafe and Edward in the den. Rafe pulled her to the couch and sat down. "Tell Jade what you learned while we were out shopping."

"I was having my sources check into Toby's father's background to see if there was any dirt on them. But what I discovered wasn't what I expected to find. Toby's father was like Toby is. Stewart's father was a wolf. He was shot and killed in a hunting accident. The hunter swore he killed a timber wolf, but when he came upon the body, it was a naked man. The guy was devastated, but he swore he'd killed a wolf."

"Stewart's father," Jade said under her breath.

"Maybe that's why you were attracted to him," Edward said gently. "Tessa, whose grandfather was a wolf, was attracted to wolves. So was her brother. Even though she didn't know why there was such a draw. Wolves were also drawn to her. So it wasn't so much that Stewart was just…wild that caught your attention. He had genes that were more wolf than Tessa's. Which could very well be why you became pregnant by a human. He was part wolf on his father's side, though unable to shift."

She couldn't believe it. "Then his brother was too."

"Yes."

"That's why he was so close to his family." She knew in her heart that she wouldn't have married him. He still hadn't been a wolf, and he had family who weren't. "Okay, so how does that affect Toby?"

"That's what none of us know," Edward said, frowning. "We know of no other cases like your son's."

"Sounds like good news to me," Rafe said, hugging

Jade. "He's more wolf than we knew, and that can only be a good thing."

She sure hoped Rafe was right.

―――

The next morning, Jade rode with Aidan, Edward, and Hugh to the reception hall where she and Rafe would marry. It had a lovely patio and gardens, perfect for a wolf couple. She'd really just wanted a wedding in his ballroom, but Rafe wanted to make it appear more public, to show the world they were marrying and not hiding the fact.

She was glad she had invited Fiona to be her bridesmaid. The woman couldn't have been any more excited. She was already at the hall and dressed, her hair all piled up in curls on top of her head, barely able to stand still. Even though the woman wasn't a wolf, Fiona had been so nice to Jade for the time she had stayed at the bed-and-breakfast.

Aidan brought Toby to see Jade and gave her a hug, before he remembered she wasn't supposed to observe him in his new tux for the wedding. Or maybe he realized *this* was the wedding, so it was all right.

Wearing a double-breasted white tux and sky-blue cummerbund that matched Fiona's dress, he was so cute. He gripped a ring pillow in his chubby fist, and his arm was wrapped around Buddy, who was dressed in a tux to match the rest of the party. Then Aidan said, "Come on, Toby. You've got a job to do."

Fiona was grinning. "He is just adorable. I'm so glad you and Mr. Denali got back together. This is such a fairy-tale wedding."

Toby waved the pillow at her. "Got to carry the ring for Daddy, 'cept he won't let me hold it yet. Said I might lose it." He grinned at her and ran ahead of Aidan.

Aidan smiled. "I didn't think he could get any more excited about anything. I have to admit he's fun to be around."

She smiled. "Thanks, Aidan. He has his moments."

"We all do. Not to worry." Then Aidan took off after Toby.

Fiona helped Jade get dressed in a separate room furnished with mirrors, a settee, and a dresser while Rafe and Aidan kept Toby occupied somewhere else in the building.

"I was so sorry when you got caught in the rip current," Fiona said to Jade, "thinking your vacation had been ruined. But boy, was there a silver lining. You might not have gotten the nerve up to see Rafe if you hadn't been forced to do so."

"You're right," Jade said, though she had to remind herself of the story from time to time. This was the very first time she was going to marry the hot wolf, and that she wouldn't ever forget.

"I will remember this forever," Fiona said, fastening the back of Jade's gown. "I just can't thank you enough."

"I'm glad you could come, Fiona. Maybe you'll catch someone's eye," Jade said, smiling, but she knew it wouldn't happen. Not when the rest of those attending were wolves—all but Mr. Marks.

"You're perfect for each other, and I absolutely adore your son."

"Thanks, Fiona." Jade agreed.

"You're beautiful," Fiona said, tears in her eyes as she stood back to look at Jade.

Jade thought Fiona looked stunning in a blue gown Rafe had purchased.

Jade gave her a hug. "You are just as beautiful. Thanks for helping me to celebrate this special moment in my life."

Fiona sniffled and dabbed her eyes.

Someone knocked on the door.

"Are you ladies about ready? The groom and ring bearer are getting anxious, afraid you've changed your mind," Sebastian said.

Jade smiled. "We're ready."

Dressed in a tux, Sebastian opened the door for them and whistled. "Hell, if I wasn't giving you away to my boss, I'd just as soon keep you for my own. Don't tell him I said that though."

She laughed. "Thanks, Sebastian."

As the ring bearer for the wedding, Toby was so proud and excited. Aidan was the best man, and Sebastian would walk her down the aisle among the fragrant red-and-pink roses. Even though the event was by invitation only, Jade permitted Marks to take pictures of the wedding as a way to thank him for his lively and interesting posts concerning the fairy-tale, whirlwind romance between the billionaire and the fashion designer.

She was glad he had mentioned she was a designer and not just a poor woman who'd caught a rich man.

Sebastian had gotten hold of Hunter Greymere's wife, Tessa, who photographed wolves and *lupus garous* and was delighted to attend. Hunter, being a SEAL wolf and coleader of the pack, came with her and helped with his mate's photographic equipment.

"Signed, Sealed, Delivered (I'm Yours)" by Stevie Wonder and then "I Got You (I Feel Good)" by James Brown played as everyone gathered. Fiona joined the wedding party up front.

John Legend's "All of Me" began to play and Jade couldn't believe how nervous she was, butterflies fluttering around in her stomach. She was afraid her hands were sweaty.

Rafe looked like he was over the moon when he saw her walking down the aisle. He was holding Toby's hand and leaned down to say something to him.

Toby was grinning, looking like he wanted to run to her, but he was staying put with Rafe. She saw a few more people than she knew, and she figured they were wolves from Hunter and Tessa's pack up north. She saw Tessa photographing the procession and gave her a smile, and then she saw Marks taking just as many pictures and gave him a special smile too.

When she reached Rafe and Toby, her little boy gave her a hug, and she hugged him back. Then he waited with his pillow, the ring nowhere in sight.

"Beautiful," Rafe said. "And all mine, again."

"Mine too. Beautiful, Mommy." Toby began talking nonstop after that, as if Rafe saying anything meant it was okay to talk now. Aidan took him aside and spoke quietly to him, the whole time Toby nodding.

Jade heard "chocolate cake, swimming pool, presents" being mentioned, and she figured Aidan was using his usual cleverness to appease Toby until the ceremony was over.

When the minister asked for any objections, she and Rafe looked back to see if anyone would say anything, not expecting anyone to.

"The boy is mine," a man in the back said as he scuffled with Edward at the entryway.

Stewart Roth. Jade couldn't help seeing him in a different light—a man whose father had been a wolf.

Edward and two other bodyguards hauled him off to a private room to deal with him.

Then Aidan had Toby hold up the velvet pillow to place the ring on it, and Toby brought it over to Rafe.

"Thanks, Toby. Good job." Rafe took the ring and put it on Jade's finger, and they kissed.

She tried not to think about Stewart or the repercussions of him being here. Rafe helped with that as he kissed her deeply, promising her that he would always be her mate, and she would have no more worries while he was in her life.

She kissed him back, wrapping her arms around his neck, loving him, loving the way he had taken Toby in as his own.

"I love you so much," she said.

"And me, Mommy," Toby said.

She laughed and gave him a hug too. "And I love you so much too."

"Love you and Toby," Rafe said, brushing Toby's hair, and then Aidan grabbed the tot as Rafe and Jade walked down the aisle as a married couple.

Then they moved out to a covered patio in the gardens where a dinner and champagne were being served, followed by the most beautiful cake she'd ever seen— topped with a figurine of a mama, a papa, and a baby wolf. She wondered what Marks would think of that, until she heard someone telling him that Toby picked it out because he saw the wolves at the reserve and loved them to pieces.

They danced. Even Tessa took a break from photographing everyone and danced with her mate. Jade ended up dancing with Toby, Rafe, and most of the males except for Edward and the other two bodyguards keeping Stewart at bay. She tried not to think of what was going to happen with Stewart.

Marks was there the whole time, enjoying dinner, champagne, and cake, not bothering to see what was going on with Stewart. She thought she'd really won the photojournalist over when he went for another piece of cake.

Toby was dancing with Fiona at one point and then he wanted to dance with Jade again. When she was dancing with Rafe, Jade wanted to ask about Stewart, but she knew with Marks in the room, it was best to pretend her former lover wasn't intruding on her thoughts.

When they were ready to leave, Edward came out of the room to drive the limousine to the house. Toby rode back with his Uncle Aidan and Sebastian, the long way around, so Jade and Rafe could have some alone time together.

"What about Stewart? I thought someone would make sure he didn't trouble us?" Jade asked Edward.

"He was told you have all the paperwork proving not only that Rafe is Toby's father, but that you married after a whirlwind romance and before Toby was conceived. If Stewart wants to try to claim Toby belongs to him, Rafe and you will file a lawsuit against him for making false statements. But we also dug up some dirt on him—he was abusive to a couple of girlfriends after you left and had court orders against him. So he's not father material anyway. If he persists in pushing this, we'll share what kind of man he is. The other men were going to release him after you, Rafe, and Toby left so there were no more incidents."

Jade sighed in Rafe's arms. "Thank God."

Rafe got a call from Sebastian and put it on speakerphone. "Yeah?"

"Stewart was just released. He's pissed. Wants his gas paid for his troubles. I told him he'd find himself in jail if he hassled either of you any further," Sebastian said.

"Good," Rafe said.

"What about Stewart's brother?" Jade asked.

"Dead. He was killed in a car accident, declared accidental. But the thing of it was, both were in the car to begin with, and then Stewart was dropped off."

"So Kenneth killed Stewart's brother by mistake," Rafe said.

"It appears that way. The car was Stewart's, and Kenneth must have assumed he was driving it when he forced the car off the road. So no worries. We're good."

"Except that we still don't know where Kenneth is," Jade said.

"We've still got men looking for him," Sebastian assured her.

"Thanks," Rafe said. "We'll talk more about it later."

"Agreed. Have a good time. We're going to take Toby for ice cream and a movie, and then head back to your place."

"Thanks, Sebastian," Jade said, then smiled up at Rafe. She was truly his mate, Toby was truly his son, and nothing would ever come between them.

Chapter 18

EDWARD QUICKLY GOT THE LIMOUSINE DOOR FOR JADE AND Rafe. Jade struggled to climb in in her formfitting gown, and Rafe appeared to be salivating. She was the most beautiful bride he'd ever seen. Her blond hair was piled in curls on top of her head, and he couldn't wait to pull out the pins and peel her out of the satin gown that highlighted all her curves. He knew the men who'd gone shopping with her had something to say about the selection. It certainly would have been his choice. He'd been expecting something a lot fuller—princess-like. But this gown perfectly suited the siren he'd rescued from the sea. A wolfish mermaid if he'd ever seen one.

He wasn't waiting to make love to his mate when they arrived home either, not when she smelled so sweet and delectable, she-wolf and woman all in one. Not when she looked so mouthwatering in her white satin, lace, and beads. He wanted her. She wanted him. That's all that mattered.

She sat on the cushioned black velour bench that ran along one side of the roomy limousine behind the driver's seat, the aisle wide for maneuverability and the bench the right size to make love to his mate. He hadn't thought of it initially, figuring he'd carry her across the threshold when they arrived home. But the way she was smiling at him so playfully, the way she'd kissed him and moved so tight against him in the final dance, he wasn't waiting.

Edward closed the door, and as soon as he did, Rafe closed the privacy screen, the tiny white lights in the dark car perfect for the intimate occasion. He sat next to Jade and quickly divested himself of his white tux jacket and laid it on the seat across from them. Edward started the engine, and soft music began to play overhead as the car pulled out.

"Hot," she murmured against Rafe's ear as she ran her hands down his shirt, her gaze settling on his trousers.

"Hell yeah, you sure are."

"Like it?" she asked, sliding her hand under her breast and cupping it, her fingers rubbing the nipple.

Growling, he practically tore off his bow tie. Then he ran his hands over her breasts—firm, luscious, just waiting to be free of the satin and lace.

She slid her fingers up his shirt. "Need some help?"

With her gown? Probably. He wished he'd been better prepared, but he hadn't given any thought to removing her gown in the limousine.

She began unbuttoning his shirt, kissing his mouth as she set his blood on fire. He struggled to unfasten his cummerbund and tossed it aside. Cupping her face, he began kissing her again, slowly and sweetly at first as she matched his pace.

He really couldn't keep going at such a slow speed, wanting in her and all around her at the same time. If they renewed their vows at a later date, they were doing it in a lot fewer clothes.

Yanking his shirt out of his waistband, he kicked off a shoe, then began unfastening his trousers as she parted his shirt and skimmed her warm hands up his bare chest, bringing him to a full stop. Her hands were silky soft, blazing a fiery trail against his skin all the way up to his neck before she licked his lips and kissed him full on the mouth again.

He growled, kicked off the other shoe, and reached behind her to start unfastening her dress. No fasteners? Just ties? What the hell? She was tied into the gown like she would be if she'd been wearing an old-time corset! He groaned.

She smiled against his lips, the vixen. Then she ran her hand over his arousal. He was already agonizingly hard. He began to work on her gown again.

She breathed him in, her pheromones blazing, triggering his own as he leaned against her soft body, still fumbling with the ties to her gown. As tight fitting as the gown was, it wouldn't be easy to hike it up so he could have his wicked way with her without removing it, though he was considering any other options he could think of. She pulled his shirt off his shoulders, and he started to jerk it off when he realized he hadn't unfastened the cuff links. He growled again.

She chuckled and hurried to remove one, then the other. She leaned in to kiss him, her hands caressing his neck, his hands working again on the damnable gown. He couldn't do this without seeing what he was doing.

"Turn around," he said, his voice rough with lust. He struggled with the ties, cursed under his breath, and swore if he had a knife on him, he'd make short work of them.

She laughed and slipped off her heels and then reached back to run her hand over his thigh.

"Ah, hell," Rafe said, but then he felt a tie give a little. Encouraged, he forged on. As soon as he had them untied and felt the bodice of the gown give, he breathed out, "Finally."

He slid his hands inside her gown and wrapped them around her tantalizing breasts, his mouth sweeping across her bare nape. He wanted to claim his bride again and again. He breathed in her delectably sweet scent, loving the sound of her soft moans and the way she melted under his touch.

Unable to wait any longer, he began frantically working at the ties on her gown again until he reached the snaps at the base and pulled them open. He slid the satin garment down her hips until she was free of the dress, and he tossed it over to the other bench. She was braless but wore a white lace garter belt and lace bikini panties.

He licked a trail down her back, making her shiver. He slid the garter belt down, dragging the stockings with it.

Once he'd tossed all the sexy wear onto the other bench, he turned her, and she began to help him out of his trousers. They hit the floor, along with his socks and briefs. He'd meant to be on top, but before he could remove her panties, she was pinning him down on the bench, her knees on either side of his legs, his cock stretched out to her.

She pulled a pin from her hair, and like magic, her blond curls cascaded to her shoulders.

She rubbed against him, teasing him, her hands on his shoulders, pinning him down. Smiling wickedly at him, she leaned down to kiss his mouth. He cupped her warm breasts, his tongue spearing her mouth, her tongue dancing around his.

He slid his hand into her panties, his fingers seeking her nub, and began to stroke. Her breathing growing unsteady, she lifted her mouth from his, her irises darkening to midnight. Her musky feminine scent told him she was ready for him, and he was past ready for her.

Stroking harder and faster, their mouths merged, and he felt her arch against his fingers, heard the swift intake of her breath and then release as she began to sink down on his hand. He took the moment to slide off her damp panties and toss them aside. Then he switched places with her, settling her on her back, and lined himself up between her legs. Her body was open to him, willing, warm, and wet. He planted kisses on her cheeks, then kissed her lips, slowly and deeply. Their bodies rubbed together again before he penetrated her, steadily, slowly, deeply until he was all the way in.

He slipped his hands under her buttocks and thrust inside her again and again, faster and faster. She anchored her heels over the back of his thighs and lifted her pelvis, taking him in even deeper.

The pinnacle was just out of reach, so close, nearly there. And then with a satisfied groan, he released, continuing to thrust until he was totally spent.

"God, how I love you," he said. He resituated her so she was lying against him, wrapped in his arms.

"I love you too, Rafe. You were beautiful standing there with Toby. Both of you." She licked his chest. "*Now* I know why you have this party-mobile," she teased him.

"Never happened. Only with you."

"What do we do now?"

He smiled, wanting to hold her like this forever, but then the car pulled to a stop, and Edward cut the engine.

"I don't think I can get into that gown again," Jade murmured against Rafe's chest.

"Believe me, no way do I want you to put it back on. We'll shift. Edward will get our things."

She groaned. "Somehow I was thinking this would be more private."

Rafe laughed, then helped her up as Edward slammed his door.

"Is he coming to open the door for us?" she asked.

"No. Not until I let him know it's safe to do so."

Both of them shifted, and Rafe howled. Not in a way that said he wanted Edward to open the door for them, but in a way that said he was one damn sexually satisfied wolf.

Jade bit him lightly on the shoulder, and if he had been in his human form, he would have laughed.

He barked at her in joyful glee before Edward opened the car door for them. They bolted out and raced for the wolf door.

"Congratulations!" Edward called out and laughed.

Once inside, they heard Edward pulling the limo into the garage. Rafe and Jade ran down the hall to the master bedroom suite, alternately biting and nipping at each other. Inside the room, Rafe pushed the door shut with his paws, then turned to see Jade lying in wait, ready to tackle him—he thought. Instead, she leaped on the bed. By the time he jumped on top of the mattress, she was on the floor again, waiting for him, lying down, her head and ears perked. Around and around they went until he caught her at last and pinned her with his wolf body. She shifted and laughed. He licked a breast with his wolf's tongue and then shifted too.

With the house quiet and no sign of Aidan and Toby's imminent return, it was time for Rafe to make love to his mate again.

———

Jade hadn't been sure if Rafe had intended to ravish her in the limo, but what a truly wonderful and unique experience it had been, one she wanted to do again in the future. After playing as wolves, their wild sides needing to celebrate the match as much as their human sides, they'd made glorious love again. Now, it was time to get back to reality and make sure her son got off to bed all right. Rafe only smiled and kissed her, saying he would be ready for her when she returned. She'd mated one hot-blooded wolf and loved him for it.

She loved being with Rafe and didn't want to leave him, but she needed to see to Toby when he arrived home. She loved Aidan and the rest of the men who had kept him entertained while she and Rafe had their special time together.

When she reached Toby's room, Aidan smiled and congratulated her again.

"Thanks, Aidan, for everything."

"We had a grand time. Didn't we, Toby?"

"We did," Toby said.

"I'm glad you all had fun."

"Night, Toby, Jade," Aidan said.

"Night," they both replied.

Jade started removing Toby's clothes, letting him

pick his pj's for the night. He chose the stegosaurus ones, but when she went to tug on his shirt, he shook his head.

"Boys don't wear pj tops," he said.

"Who said?"

"Daddy and Uncle Aidan don't. They just wear bottoms."

She sighed. "That's because they don't have really cool shirts for grown-up men. If they had ones as neat as yours, they'd wear them too."

"I can share," Toby said.

She laughed and pulled on his shirt, then hugged him close on the big, red, cushy chair she'd gotten for his room. "They would be way too big for your shirts. But thank you for offering. So, what did Uncle Aidan take you to do today?"

Toby was so sleepy that he snuggled with her like when he was a baby. "Fun, Mommy. Got strawberry ice cream. Uncle Aidan had chocolate mint like you like. Uncle Sebastian had a chocolate milk shake. Then we saw the Turtles. Uncle Aidan and Sebastian said we were going camping. Never been camping. When can we go?"

"At the end of the new moon." She'd been teaching him about the phases of the moon and how they would affect him. "We want you to be able to run as a wolf when we go." She carried him to bed and tucked him in, then brought over the calendar showing the phases of the moon and pointed to the day. Each night, they would talk about the phases, and she handed him his sheet of wolf cub stickers to put on the calendar. One for each day, except during the new moon and the few days before and after it. She, and others like her who had wolf roots for centuries in their ancestry, could shift at any time.

Jade pointed on the calendar to the picture of the new moon. "The waxing crescent has already begun, and you'll see a sliver of a crescent growing bigger every day. We can't be sure when you'll feel like shifting or can shift. Tessa, the lady taking pictures at the wedding, said that she can't turn during the few days before, during, or after the new moon. Which is why we had the wedding during this phase. Do you feel like you need to shift before it happens?"

He nodded, his eyes heavily lidded.

She read him a bedtime story, and then she kissed him good night.

"Can I be a wolf tomorrow?" he asked.

She sighed, figuring he'd missed the point. "If you can shift. You might not be able to for a couple more days." She really hoped he wouldn't be able to so they'd have more time to take him places, safe in the knowledge he couldn't shift by accident. "But yes, you can, if you stay inside. Wolves that aren't shifters like us don't live here," she reminded him. "If people see you running as a wolf, they might shoot you." Not that they would. They'd most likely grab him and put him in a wolf reserve or a zoo because he was a cute little wolf pup.

"I'd scare everyone to pieces," Toby said, nodding, repeating Edward's warning to him.

She smiled, loving the guys because they were all so good about helping to teach Toby. She realized that though they hadn't been one before, everyone who worked for Rafe was now acting like they were part of a pack—and Rafe and she were leading it. She never would have believed it would happen like this, but it was all because of the natural instinct to protect Toby. She found it endearing and comforting. "Yes, you would. We can never let anyone know that we can turn into beautiful wolves. So you have to stay inside whenever you're a wolf. No going out on the patio." Not that anyone could see him, as short as he was when he was a wolf. She still didn't want him outside…just in case.

"Except at night, if there are no lights on, we can run on the beach as wolves."

"Yes."

"I like being a wolf."

She smiled. "I'm glad, Toby. Good night, honey."

"Night, Mommy."

"Love you."

"Love you so much." He yawned and rolled over on his tummy to go to sleep, Buddy and Dino on either side of him.

She kissed him on the head, then left the room, shutting the door behind her.

"Want to watch a movie in bed?" Rafe asked her from the living room, standing up from the couch where he'd been watching the news while he waited for her to return.

She thought he would be sleeping. She appreciated that he had waited up for her. She wrapped her arms around him. "Sure. Do you want some popcorn?"

"Yeah. I'll get us some water."

"Do you know where everyone is?"

"Aidan is taking a shower. He's going to watch something on TV in here so he can keep an eye on things.

He'll switch with Edward after he gets some sleep. The other two bodyguards are spelling each other. One is down on the grounds out front, checking things out. Sebastian retired to his place."

"Okay, good. Butter on your popcorn?"

"Lots of it, and nice and salty."

She smiled, and after a few minutes, they were settled in the bedroom to watch a spy thriller. She had thrown on a pj shorts set, and he was wearing boxers, but she didn't think that would last long when he began slipping his hands under her top to caress her breasts, his mouth nuzzling her ear.

She was about to set the bowl of popcorn on the bedside table so she could turn around and get Rafe back when she thought she heard the patio door open but not shut.

"Aidan *is* watching Toby, right?" she asked, but she was already getting off the bed, setting the bowl of popcorn on the table, and heading for the bedroom door. She knew Toby would be sleeping. He never got up when he was so tired, and he'd sleep soundly through the night. Unless he woke with a bad nightmare.

"Supposed to be. He was just going to take a shower." Rafe hurried after her.

Aidan came out of his bedroom wearing pj shorts and looking puzzled that Jade and Rafe were rushing out of their bedroom as if something was horribly wrong. "Toby's asleep, isn't he?"

"He was, but the back door's wide open." Jade ran for Toby's room and found the door open. His bedcovers were tossed aside. He was gone. "Not here!" she called out, already trying to push back the urge to panic.

She ran toward the back patio, but Rafe had already reached it, turned on the lights, and was looking in the pool. "Not here!"

Then Toby howled from the beach, a frightened pup howl.

"Ohmigod," she said, throwing off her pj's and shifting into her wolf, in protective mother mode. How could he have shifted? Was that why he had asked if it was all right if he turned into his wolf? But he shouldn't be able to shift!

Rafe raced down the stairs and threw open the gate. Aidan was already on his phone, alerting everyone else of the trouble on the beach and to come at once.

Heart pounding, she sprinted down the stairs. When she reached the gate, she heard Rafe growling and saw his and Toby's clothes. She knew Rafe had shifted and that his anger wasn't directed at Toby but someone else.

It was twilight, the pinks and oranges of the setting sun casting a reflection on ribbons of clouds and white-caps. Her kind could see at dusk, but it was still light enough that humans could still see the horizon.

Then she saw the big brown wolf—one of Kenneth's henchmen—snarling at Rafe. Rafe's fur stood on end to make him appear bigger, his lips pulled back, his own fiercely wicked canines on full display as he snarled.

Backed up against the stone wall, Toby was growling ferociously, looking small and unsure of himself. It was one thing for him to fight a man as a small wolf, but another to fight the big, aggressive male wolves. Why had he come out here on his own? Was he afraid she would be angry with him and tried to hide shifting from them by going outside? This was what she worried about—Toby having no control over his shifting and putting himself in danger.

Before Jade could run to him and guide him back in through the gate to safety, she heard a wolf running toward her in the sand, heard his heart beating rapidly, felt the heat of him, right before Kenneth attacked her.

Before she could react, she felt Kenneth's heavy pounce on her back, the weight of a heavier male's bones and muscles pressed against her, smelled his aggression, and knew his teeth would be tearing into her next. With her slighter build, she quickly bolted away from him to avoid being bitten. His teeth clanked as he missed her by inches.

As wild as any wolf could be that was protecting her pup, Jade rounded on her brother and viciously assaulted him back, snarling and growling, jaws snapping. She dodged his brutal attacks and jumped right back in, tearing into him again. All she could think about was that she'd never be safe. Toby would never be safe. She had to end this now.

Rafe was fighting two wolves now, and she saw four others waiting in the wings for a chance to kill them, or maybe serving as bodyguards in case more wolves came and tried to take out their leader. It wouldn't do for them to be embroiled in a fight and not see others attacking Kenneth. At least they wouldn't interfere with Kenneth fighting her. Not when he was their pack leader. And she was just a female.

Then she smelled new wolf scents and saw Aidan running on the beach to her aid, Sebastian and Edward right behind him. She hadn't seen them before in wolf form, but she knew them by scent. She was thrilled, thinking she could rescue her son before he was injured or killed and return him safely to the house.

Smelling the new wolf scents, Kenneth glanced back. As soon as Aidan dashed for her, one of Kenneth's men launched an attack against him. No one would be allowed to aid her. Looking smugly satisfied, Kenneth whipped around and smiled at her with his wicked canines on display, ready for blood. Her blood. When Kenneth attacked Jade again, she dodged away, but Toby raced forward to bite Kenneth, to protect her like Aidan had tried to.

No! Her heart nearly stopped. Kenneth wouldn't hesitate to kill the pup!

Toby got hold of Kenneth's leg and bit down — sharp puppy teeth could hurt and tear skin too — but Kenneth was too busy watching out for Jade's stronger, bigger bite.

She kept after him too, trying to ensure he wouldn't see the ankle biter attached to his hind leg and whip around to kill him. One bite from Kenneth's powerful jaws and Toby would be dead.

She dove in to grab Kenneth's foreleg and break it, but all she managed was a bite that broke the skin. He jumped away before she could really chomp hard, frustrating her. She had to get a good bite in to disable him, or he'd wear her out because of his size and power. He yelped and attacked her so savagely that she had to back out of the path of his canines again. The waves washed over her hind legs and then her forelegs, and she realized the way they'd been fighting, he'd maneuvered her into the water. Again, he snarled and barked, forcing her deeper.

Fearing Toby would drown in the ocean if he tried to follow her, she barked at him to let go. But he was her son, tenaciously hanging on to Kenneth's leg, trying to help her. She loved him, wanting in the worst way for him to back off.

Kenneth lunged at her again, and she turned to avoid him. She nearly fell when the water began to pull out, unbalancing her with its strong tow. Toby must have let go at that point, thank God.

Thinking he was getting the best of her, Kenneth jumped in after her. She was in deeper water, up to her chest now, and he was taller and heavier so he had the advantage. Heart pounding, she couldn't help but worry about Toby and the draw of the deepening water while trying to concentrate on her brother's snapping jaws.

To her horror, she lost sight of Toby just as she realized she'd backed into a rip current and was being sucked out to sea…along with her brother.

She prayed Toby was still on shore in the shallow water, not too deep where he would be pulled in with them. All wolves could swim, but he was so little, and having never been in the ocean, he could easily panic, wear out, and drown.

Then she saw Rafe bounding into the ocean after her, his mouth and fur bloodied, his eyes glistening with menace. He leaped as far as he could with a powerful wolf's jump and was dragged out with them. He was only a few feet from Kenneth, who was trying to catch up to her. She prayed Rafe could reach Kenneth before he tore into her again. Yet, she wished with all her heart that Rafe had stayed on shore to protect Toby.

With a male's powerful paddling strokes, Kenneth

drew nearer, his eyes narrowed on her, his expression one of killing rage.

She thought Kenneth meant to drown her.

Reserving her strength, she let the current carry her out more than half a mile, fighting the panic that Toby could be in the water too. She realized that when Rafe had been with her in the rip current the first time, she'd felt safe, but not now, out here in the dark, a long way from shore. And she knew Kenneth would be bleeding in the water, calling all sharks in the vicinity to come for supper.

Her brother continued to swim toward her, and she prayed Rafe would catch up. She knew she couldn't fight a much bigger wolf in the deep water.

She turned, trying to swim parallel to shore as the rip current's strength began to dwindle. She didn't want to stay out in the ocean any longer than necessary, and she desperately had to make sure Toby was okay. She felt something bump her back and had a panic attack, thinking it was a shark, but it was just as bad. Her brother put his paw on her back, pushing her down, like a drowning swimmer trying to use her as his flotation device. She tried to turn to bite him, but she saw a fin glide by and gulped a mouthful of sea water.

Rafe was close, but the shark and her brother were closer.

Chapter 19

AIDAN QUICKLY KILLED THE WOLF HE HAD BEEN FIGHTING, moving toward the water the whole time, frantic to reach Toby. The cub was in the water, his mom and dad pulled out with Kenneth, and Aidan was afraid the little fellow would be swept out too.

Toby was running in the shallow water, barking, pausing to observe his mother being pulled out with the current, lifting his snout and smelling the air for her, then howling.

His heart thundering, Aidan raced to reach him in time as the pup headed into the deeper water, frantic his parents were leaving him behind.

Aidan barked at him to come into shore, but it was too late. Toby was caught up in the rip current. Aidan couldn't see Jade, Rafe, or her brother in the dark swells. All his focus now remained on his nephew.

At a run, he leaped for him, sailing through the air and landing fifteen feet into the water, only half a foot away from Toby. Aidan swam to him and grabbed the pup by the scruff of the neck, but he couldn't swim to shore against the strong rip current. They were being dragged out like the others had been. Aidan still couldn't see them in the dark waters. He hoped Kenneth had drowned. He prayed Jade and Rafe were still treading water somewhere or swimming toward shore down the beach.

Then he thought he heard a growling way out in the water, but all he could do was try to keep Toby's head above water. The pup never would have made it on his own.

Something bumped against his leg, and Aidan nearly had a heart attack, unable to see what was beside him in the water. Could be a big fish, he told himself. Or a shark.

He tried to turn horizontal to the beach, hoping Jade and Rafe had done the same.

"Jade! Rafe!" Edward and Sebastian yelled from the shore.

Aidan guessed Kenneth's men had assumed he wasn't returning to the shore, and they must have dispersed. With no alpha leader to give the orders, they figured they'd be killed next if they hung around. He couldn't imagine them standing there waiting for all of them to swim back in. Aidan still had a hell of a way to go, and if he was pulled under, he could lose Toby in a heartbeat—for good.

Toby was quiet, like a wolf pup whose parent was taking him somewhere. Normally, he would be a little old to carry in this way, but with the buoyancy of the salt water, Aidan had no trouble holding on to him.

He couldn't understand why Toby had left the house and gone out for a run as a wolf. Then he realized he shouldn't have been able to run as a newly turned wolf during the new moon. Maybe it was because his paternal grandfather was also a wolf.

Aidan had considered shifting so he could carry Toby into shore that way, but he thought he was making progress this way, and he was afraid he'd lose hold of Toby as soon as he shifted.

Another large swell carried them up and down as if they were riding a gentle, wet roller coaster, and then Aidan turned toward the beach and began to paddle as hard as he could.

They were so far out that he began to worry about Jade again. Rafe was strong and trained in water survival from his days as a fighter pilot, but even so, the trek would be tiring for any of them.

And with Aidan trying to keep Toby from being dunked, he was feeling the strain.

Then he saw Jade swimming for the shore as a human. She paused and called out toward the shore, "Toby!"

Aidan's whole outlook brightened. He wanted to tell Toby, "Look, see your mommy," and his heart filled with joy to see her still afloat. But none of them were out of danger yet.

He saw Rafe fighting with Kenneth in the water, and then Rafe bit him hard. Blood. The blood would bring sharks.

―᷈᷈―

Rafe couldn't believe Kenneth's persistence. The bastard was bleeding in the water, and Rafe had seen a shark take a pass already.

Kenneth was still trying to reach Jade, though she'd managed to pull away from him, and Rafe was closing in fast. He was a much better swimmer than her brother. Rafe came up on Kenneth's right hip and bit down hard. Kenneth howled, but got a snout full of water, choking on the salty brine.

Rafe knew Kenneth's blood would make it worse for the two of them. He just hoped Jade was far enough away that she wouldn't be on the shark's menu. But then he saw his brother struggling to keep Toby's head above water as he paddled after Jade.

Hell.

The shark's fin came for another pass, and Rafe shifted. As a human he could swim a lot faster, which is why Jade must have shifted, despite how cold the water was out this far. He swam as far away from Kenneth as he could. His heart was pounding when he saw the great white rise up out of the water, take hold of the wolf, and pull him under.

Rafe hauled ass, swimming as if his life and his family depended on it, which they did.

The wave swelled between him and Jade and he feared it would break over her, afraid she was getting too tired and cold for the swim. He wanted to shout to her that he and Aidan and her son were coming. To yell encouragement to her. To tell her to keep going because they were right behind her.

Then he saw Jade emerge from the foamy water, coughing, trying to catch her breath. Edward was racing down the beach as a human now with two life preservers from the pool slung over his arm, hollering. Sebastian had shifted and had already begun to swim out to her, but Edward yelled, "Here, Sebastian!" and tossed one of the preservers to him.

Edward jumped into the water with the other.

Rafe was damn glad they were going out to her. Twice, she'd disappeared behind a swell, and each time he felt panic and his heart sank with her. Then he'd see her bobbing in the water again and felt guarded relief.

Toby suddenly let out a small woof, perking up.

Until now, he'd been happy to let Aidan take care of him, but now he began to puppy paddle. He had to have seen his mother.

Sebastian finally reached Jade and helped slip the preserver over her head.

When Edward reached the two of them, he was still looking out to sea for Aidan, Toby, and Rafe. "I see them," he said. "I'll get them."

Edward swam toward Aidan and Toby, while Sebastian began swimming toward shore, pulling Jade. She was turned backward in the preserver and called out to them, "Aidan, Rafe, Toby, you can do it!"

Rafe heard the weariness and worry in her voice. He was glad Sebastian was taking her to shore.

Edward had nearly reached Aidan, swimming much faster as a human than Aidan could as a wolf paddling with Toby in his grip.

"I'll take Toby," Edward said, slipping the preserver over his own head, then reaching for Toby.

Aidan released him once he felt Edward take hold of Toby. Then Aidan shifted and held on to the life preserver.

Rafe had nearly reached them, and when he did, he grabbed hold of the preserver, not because he needed to, but because he wanted to stay close to Toby, to reassure him he wasn't going to be far away. He reached up with one hand and petted him. "We'll be in to shore soon, Toby. Good job." Though he wanted to scold the boy for leaving the house, attacking an adult wolf, and putting his life in jeopardy, Rafe couldn't. All he could do was encourage the boy that everything would be all right.

Toby licked Rafe's hand and tried to squirm out of Edward's arm to join him. Rafe smiled at the pup. "Just stay there. Uncle Edward's got you."

They still had to get through the breakers. Rafe looked back to shore and saw that one of his bodyguards had brought down robes from the pool trunk. Jade was already wearing one. Relief filled him that she was safely on shore.

Sebastian was rubbing her arms to warm her. While they were wolves, their coats had protected them from the cold. But swimming in the ocean at night with no sun to warm his body, Rafe was beginning to feel the cold, and Aidan's lips were a little blue.

A wave crashed over them, but they all held on to Toby and the preserver, not about to let go of him.

As soon as they reached the shallower water and were on their feet, they waded in as fast as they could, Rafe carrying Toby in his arms. Toby saw his mom, his tail wagging ninety miles an hour.

On shore, Sebastian handed out robes to Edward, Aidan, and Rafe, while Jade hugged Toby. He squirmed and licked her face all over.

"The other wolves?" Rafe asked, wrapping his arm around Jade and Toby.

"As soon as they were leaderless, they took off," Sebastian said. "Beta wolves. They knew what we'd do to them if they'd hung around."

"Kenneth?" Jade asked.

"Shark bait," Rafe said.

Jade swallowed hard, her eyes filling with tears.

Rafe kissed her and gave her a comforting squeeze.

She scolded Toby then. "No…going…out, Toby,

by yourself as a wolf or as a little boy. Ever. Do you understand?"

He nuzzled his face against her throat, and she hugged him tighter.

Rafe couldn't believe it had all ended well, though he saw Edward limping a little.

"Are you okay?" Rafe asked him.

"Yeah, hell, my back was turned when a second wolf attacked. But I got him back."

"Good. In the morning, I want heightened security so one small wolf can't slip out and give us all heart attacks again," Rafe said.

"Be on it first thing tomorrow," Edward said. "I think I lost years off my life when I saw Aidan being pulled out to sea with Toby, and no sign of Jade or you. The man who was supposed to come to add the alarms on the doors will be here tomorrow."

Rafe couldn't be too angry with Toby, he had to remind himself. He glanced at Aidan, who was smirking at him.

"Brings back memories, eh, Rafe?"

"Don't...mention it."

"Sounds like a story we need to hear," Sebastian said, smiling.

"*Not* in front of Toby," Jade warned.

The men all laughed.

After Jade gave Toby a bath, Aidan watched over him while she and Rafe took turns showering. Then she went to fetch Toby, expecting a wolf and finding her little boy. She said good night to Aidan, and took Toby to her and Rafe's bed. They were worried he'd been too traumatized by what had happened to sleep alone.

"Why did you leave the house and run outside on the beach when we said it wasn't safe to do that, Toby?" Rafe asked as they all curled up in bed. If they knew *why* he had done it, maybe they could ensure he didn't again.

"Mommy said I couldn't shift because of the new moon phase. But she said if I could shift, I was allowed to as long as I stayed in the house."

"Okay, so why didn't you stay in the house?" Rafe asked, still wondering how the hell Toby had shifted. Was it because his grandfather on his father's side was a wolf? Maybe also because he was so young when the change took place.

Toby let out his breath as if he was totally frustrated that Rafe didn't get what he was trying to say. "Mommy said I couldn't shift because it was the new moon. But I felt like shifting."

"So what happened to staying in the house?" Rafe asked again, sure Toby was missing the whole point.

"Mommy was wrong about it being the new moon 'cuz I shifted. I went outside to see if I could find the sliver of the moon and couldn't. So I thought if I went to the beach, I could see it from there. Then I was gonna tell Mommy we got the wrong calendar."

Jade groaned. "It's the right calendar, Toby. I thought you couldn't shift during the phase of the new moon. It doesn't matter when you shift. You still can't go outside unless one of us tells you that you can go, and only if one of us is with you like Rafe or your Uncle Aidan—"

"And Uncle Sebastian and Uncle Edward," Toby said.

"Right. You have to have adult supervision at all times, Toby. You see what happened tonight?" Jade asked.

"Yeah. Uncle Kenneth was being mean to you. I knew he wasn't just playing."

"Neither was I," Jade said.

"Neither was I," Toby parroted. "Maynard grabbed me 'cuz he said Uncle Kenneth wasn't through with me. Said he was gonna fix you 'cuz you ruined everything. Then I howled and Maynard dropped me and threw off his clothes. He turned into a wolf 'cuz he heard Daddy coming."

Rafe wanted to tell Toby that he should have gone back inside the house when the fighting began on the beach. He didn't want Toby in that kind of danger. But that was their heritage, their calling. They learned to play fight for real fights in the future. "Next time a bunch of adult wolves get in a fight, you find a safe place to stay. When you're much bigger, you can help out."

"That's what Uncle Aidan said."

"He was right. Your mommy wanted you to go back to the house where you would have been safe. She was so worried about you."

Toby's brows rose. "I was worried about Mommy. I couldn't see her in the ocean."

"Okay, but if there's another fight where adult wolves are tearing into each other, you just stay out of it."

"Unless Mommy needs my help."

"We both love you and we don't want anyone to hurt you," Rafe said. "You should have gone back inside while all that fighting was going on."

"Someone had to help my mommy," Toby said, his chin up.

Rafe smiled and shook his head. It was an inborn trait and Toby was definitely an alpha.

But the business of attacking full-grown wolves…
Hell, Rafe remembered once when he and his brother had
protected their mother from a male wolf, and they weren't
much older than Toby. They'd made such a ruckus that
their dad had arrived to take care of the rogue wolf.

Rafe and Jade sighed and cuddled Toby between
them. But they had a new worry—him shifting when
they didn't believe he could.

—⁂—

The next morning, Aidan told them the news about a
body washed up on shore while Edward took Toby for
a swim in the pool.

"Some early-morning beach walkers found Kenneth's
body on the shore five miles from us. Naked, chewed on,
no ID. They ran a sketch to see if anyone could identify
him, and it was him. So I'd say that was the end of that,"
Aidan said. "I guess it's okay to release Lizzie and let
her get on with her life?"

"Yeah, go ahead," Jade said, so relieved that Kenneth
was no longer a problem to any of them after she could
have lost her son, Rafe, and Aidan last night.

"What about the honeymoon?" Aidan asked.

"You don't have to go with us, if you don't want,"
Jade said, not wanting him to feel obligated. She'd
assumed he was going because they had been worried
about Kenneth catching up to them.

They were taking Toby to run in the wilderness,
away from humans, so he could enjoy being a pup.
So it was a different sort of honeymoon. They'd have
to take bodyguards in case they ran into trouble, but
Aidan and Sebastian had wanted to go along too. Both

she and Rafe had been surprised because up until now, from what Rafe had told her about his brother, Aidan had been working on his research around the clock.

But once she and Toby had come into their lives, Aidan had seemed to realize there was more to life than his work.

She hadn't just gained a mate and father for Toby, but a pseudo pack of sorts. And she loved them as much as they seemed to enjoy having Toby and her around.

"I haven't been hiking and camping in forever. Besides, you might need a doctor with you. You never know," Aidan said, not to be dissuaded.

Sebastian joined them and asked, "Are we talking about our honeymoon?" He smiled.

"Yes," Rafe said. "Is everyone packed and ready to go?"

"Since you began talking about wanting to do this," Sebastian said, ruffling Toby's hair, "no way do I want to be left behind."

She could tell that not only was Toby excited about the prospect of playing with other kids his age in the Cunningham pack in Montana and going camping, but so was everyone else. She'd never considered having a honeymoon. Few wolves did anything traditionally— not weddings or marriages, and that included honeymoons. Having a newly turned son and a billionaire husband made going to the usual resorts impossible, if they wanted to keep a low profile.

So she was excited to be doing this too. She'd camped when she was growing up, but it still had been some years ago. And with such a fun group, she knew they'd have an unforgettable experience.

Then a man dropped by with the boxes of Jade's and Toby's possessions from her brother's house. When they got back from their trip, she'd unpack the boxes and give Rafe his Daddy's Day card a little late. Right now, they had to pack for their trip and she couldn't have been more thrilled.

Early the next morning, Edward, Hugh, Aidan, and Sebastian flew with them to Montana in the private jet filled with camping gear and nonperishable food. On the first part of the journey, they stayed with the Cunningham wolf pack and Toby was able to shift and play with a number of wolf kids his age and a little older. The adults had a ribs-and-chicken barbecue pack gathering, and everyone told them where the best trails were for their hike, where grizzlies had been spotted, and the perfect spots for camping. The pack even offered a vehicle for the trip.

"Any news on your research?" Paul Cunningham, the SEAL wolf who was the pack leader, asked Aidan.

"Nope, and truly? I don't expect a whole lot any time soon."

Lori Cunningham, Paul's mate and coleader, joined Jade as she watched Toby playing as a wolf with the others. "Your son is so cute. How's he doing with his shifting?"

"It comes and goes. We think he's fine, then suddenly, he's yanking off his clothes to shift."

"It'll get better with time, and his age makes it easier. Our friends Michael and Tessa had a grandparent who was a wolf, so it took them a little longer to get the shifting under control around the full moon. But they're doing fine now. It might be like learning a language for children—the younger they are, the easier to pick it up."

"I sure hope so. But I'm glad, no matter what, that he's one of us. He loves being a wolf and it's like he has always been one. Though, he's needed this too—time to play with children around his age."

Edward was being his usual bodyguard self as he ran interference when bigger wolves tried to tackle Toby in a game of tag.

Lori laughed. "You've got a great pack, Jade. I can tell they mean the world to Toby."

"Me too. They're truly family." Though she didn't correct Lori's assumption that they were a pack.

"If you and Rafe ever want to take a honeymoon just by yourselves, feel free to bring Toby and his nanny here."

"That would be fun." But after just getting Toby back, Jade didn't think she could leave him out of her sight anytime soon.

After two days of visiting with the Cunningham pack and speaking to some women who were interested in relocating to California to help Jade with her designs, they were off in a vehicle the Cunninghams loaned them, ready for their next adventure.

———ᨑᨑᨑ———

Rafe had been trying to envision what taking a honeymoon would be like with Jade, though he'd thought of a more romantic and intimate interlude. Maybe later, when Toby had been around them long enough, they could leave him for a few days with Aidan and the rest

of the gang. Rafe knew they'd have fun, but Toby was
still a little tyke, and he needed his mother too.

They carried all their gear on their hike, stopping
long enough for Toby to strip out of his clothes and run
as a wolf. When he was tired, one of the men carried
him. Five days of hiking into the wilderness, seeing all
kinds of sights, and just enjoying being with Jade in this
way meant the world to Rafe. He'd even grown closer
to the men who worked for him and to his brother, as if
they were kids again. He enjoyed seeing Jade happy as
she witnessed her son having so much fun as a wolf pup,
just as he and Aidan had when they were little.

At their final destination, they set up camp near a
river, and then they all stripped, shifted, and ran as
wolves along the riverbank.

Rafe and Jade suddenly stopped as a grizzly catching a trout upstream came into view. Then they and the
others headed back the way they had come. This was the
perfect way for Toby to learn pack dynamics, though
having siblings would even be better. But he would
learn by seeing what the adults did and imitate them,
just like he imitated them when they were in their human
forms by pretending to be an adult.

When they were around the bend in the river, and far
enough away from the grizzly, Rafe waded in to catch
a fish. He caught one before everyone joined him. He
loved catching fish this way. No waiting for the fish to
take the bait—just a watchful eye and a quick pounce,
and he had dinner. Even Toby managed to catch a fish,
and his tail wagged as he added it to the pile. Then
they carried them to their campsite, shifted, dressed,
and cleaned and cooked the fish; all except Toby who

curled up by the fire as a wolf pup and watched the goings-on.

They ate the fish and then settled in front of the fire to make s'mores. Toby wagged his tail, his tongue hanging out as he waited for Rafe to give him one.

"You have to be human to eat chocolate," Rafe said. "As a wolf, it could make you really sick." At least with dogs it did. No one he knew had tested the theory as a wolf, but chocolate wasn't normally on the wolf menu.

When Toby woofed, then shifted, his hand outstretched for a s'more as he stood naked next to Rafe, everyone laughed. "Not a wolf," he said.

"Can you change back into a wolf?" Jade asked, helping Toby into underpants, then a shirt, his jeans, and a warm hoodie. Then she helped him on with his socks and boots.

"Not now." Toby reached for the s'more again.

Jade washed his hands with a wet wipe. "So you just changed without making yourself change."

"I can't now. I got all my clothes on."

She smiled, crouched down in front of him, and looked him in the eye, his hands in hers. "Toby, if you didn't have your clothes on, could you shift again?"

He looked at Rafe.

"Tell the truth, Son. Can you shift whenever you want?" Rafe asked.

Toby looked at Jade, his mouth turned down and his chin quivering. He nodded.

"Ohmigod, Toby, that's wonderful!" Jade said and hugged him tight.

He chanced a look at Rafe, as if he wasn't sure everyone would be impressed with that.

"That's great, Toby." Rafe gave both Jade and Toby a hug. "That means you can shift when we do, so you can go out and remain as a human when we leave the house."

Maybe still not during the phase of the full moon, but if Toby had any control over when he shifted, that was truly good news.

"So you could have shifted before?" Jade asked, as if she wasn't sure Toby wasn't pretending.

He nodded. "Can I have a s'more now?"

"Why didn't you tell us?" Jade asked, releasing Toby so he could eat one.

"I wanted to be a wolf."

The other guys laughed. Rafe smiled at them. This was such a new experience for all of them—not just a child who was newly turned, but how the mind of a child worked. He couldn't remember ever having a child's logic. It had been too many years ago.

"Okay, being a wolf could be a good thing at times," Jade said. "But sometimes it's dangerous for us, Toby. Remember what I said."

He nodded, scarfing down the s'more and wanting another.

Before they went to sleep that night with the stars twinkling against the black sky, a shooting star left a shimmer of stardust in its wake. A hoot owl "hoo-hoo-hooing," crickets chirping, and a lone wolf howling were like a symphony to the *lupus garous*. The night air was cool, perfect snuggling weather.

"Everybody getting tired?" Aidan asked as Toby curled up on Jade's lap, his eyelids growing heavy.

"Not me," Toby said, which had everyone smiling.

"Who wants to sleep with me in my tent?" Aidan asked. "I've got playing cards, Super Heroes, stories to read, glow sticks, and a lantern."

"Me!" Toby said.

Smiling, Rafe thought that he would be forever in his brother's debt.

Snuggling with Jade in a sleeping bag for two in their own tent, Rafe began to kiss her while Toby and Aidan were talking away across the campsite. "This has been the perfect honeymoon," Rafe said. "All the money in the world couldn't have bought me this much enjoyment."

They had lightweight camping gear, all purchased for the trip because they hadn't gone camping or hiking in years. But otherwise, it was simple and fun, and Rafe couldn't have loved her or Toby or the trip any more than he did now.

"I agree," Jade said, loving him for all that he was and all that he had done for her and Toby. Her son might never have had a father if it wasn't for Rafe. But now Toby had several. She was infinitely glad for the time she could share alone with Rafe, making memories with him, but also spending this time with her son. "I can't remember a time when I got away from it all and had this much fun. I've been wondering about something that you and Aidan said, about getting into trouble when Toby left the house that night."

"Oh, that. Well, there were lots of times we got into trouble, but the one we were thinking of was how we loved to fish in the river that ran near the house. Recent heavy rains had caused it to overflow its banks. And the water was running a lot faster. That made it all the more exciting and adventurous for us. So for three days, Mom wouldn't let us go out and fish. The moon was perfectly full that night, and Aidan and I climbed down from our loft and sneaked out to the river."

"And you nearly drowned yourselves."

"Yeah. We took the boat out and quickly capsized it in the rough water. Somehow, Aidan got hit on the head, and I was struggling to swim him to shore when a very growly Dad rushed into the river in his wolf form and pulled Aidan out. I managed to make it to shore in one piece on my own."

"Was your dad really mad at you?"

"Nah. He said he'd had his own misadventures in his youth. But he told us not to tell Mom. 'Course, first thing she did the next morning after she served us breakfast was ask where the boat had gone. We both looked at Dad. He made up a tall tale about it being washed away with all the flooding, kissed her cheek, and said he was off to find it. 'Coming, boys?' he'd asked. We grabbed our caps and took off after Dad. We learned later Mom had known about it all along. Might have had something to do with our sopping-wet clothes."

Jade smiled, loving Rafe, knowing he was the perfect daddy for Toby.

That was the last thing she thought of as she kissed Rafe back, intending to make love with him as quietly as she could while the sounds of nature and her son and Aidan playing in their tent filled the night air.

"Jade," Rafe said, rubbing her sweet spot, covering her mouth with his, and muffling her sounds of pleasure. "It's just the beginning."

**Can't get enough of those
superhot shapeshifters?**

Read on for a look at:

*Alpha Wolf Need
Not Apply*

SILVER TOWN WOLF SERIES

BY TERRY SPEAR

To Love a Wolf

SWAT (SPECIAL WOLF ALPHA TEAM) SERIES

BY PAIGE TYLER

Alpha Wolf Need Not Apply

PEPPER GRAYLING COULDN'T BELIEVE IT WHEN SHE HEARD two wolves fighting in the woods. She'd caught a glimpse of both male wolves, the snarling, big tan and gray that bit at Waldron Mason, and Waldron himself, a beige wolf with a white front and a smattering of gray hairs. The mystery wolf had snapped at Waldron before he raced off. The way he didn't tuck tail meant he wasn't cowed by the aggressor. And that had intrigued her.

She was furious that Waldron was pulling her away from her own pack to deal with him when she wanted to ensure Susan was properly cared for. As quickly as she was able, she stripped off her clothes, shifted, and ran like the devil to chase Waldron down. Whoever the other wolf had been, he had posed no threat to them. When she ran after the two wolves, she smelled their scents. The mystery wolf was indeed Eric Silver. No way would she want Waldron to hurt Eric after he'd helped Susan!

She was so angry, she could have killed Waldron for his unwarranted actions.

When she spied Waldron still chasing after Eric, she tore into him, growling and snapping to let him know just how angry he'd made her. He whipped around as if to attack, then recognized her and realized that by attacking, he'd lose any chance of courting and mating her—not that he had any—so he backed off. From his narrow-eyed, harsh gaze, she could tell he was irritated to the max with her. If he could have, he would have continued to hunt the other wolf down and finished him off. She worried about Eric—she smelled his blood on Waldron. How badly had Waldron hurt him?

But she knew Eric had been injured even before this because she'd smelled both an antiseptic and blood on him when she first met him.

She listened but didn't hear any sign of Eric. Growling at Waldron again, she turned and ran off. She continued to pay attention to the sounds around her, making sure he wasn't following her back to their campsite. She didn't want to have to say a word to him about any of this when she reached camp. All she wanted to do was see that her cousin Susan was taken care of.

When she didn't hear Waldron following her, she wondered if he had gone back after Eric.

As for Eric, she already had trouble with one alpha male wanting to court her. She sure didn't need a second one bugging her, if Eric had any such notion. Still, she felt bad that Waldron had attacked him, and she really hoped he wasn't hurt too seriously.

⟶⟞⟝⟵

Later that night, after a doctor had x-rayed Susan's leg and found a hairline fracture, Susan and Pepper settled on the couches at Pepper's home in the woods for a late-night glass of wine and chips. Susan had her wrapped leg propped up on Pepper's coffee table to help reduce the swelling.

"You should have played in the creek with us instead running off and starting a rock slide," Pepper said, unable to let go of her annoyance with Waldron. "It would have been safer that way." Had Waldron been watching the women playing in the creek before he attacked Eric? Most likely. She was certain Waldron wouldn't have been spying on the rest of the pack.

She still couldn't believe that Eric Silver had stood up to her about taking Susan to see his own pack's doctor. The challenge in his expression had said he didn't agree with her and that he wanted to do things his way. She didn't know anything about Eric's pack, and she had no intention of relying on a doctor she didn't know. She and her pack might not have a wolf doctor, but they trusted the human ones they saw. Not that their doctors knew anything about the *lupus garous*.

She still could envision Eric finally bowing his head in concession, giving in to her ruling.

"Yeah, but then the most handsome of wolves wouldn't have carried me back to the cabin," Susan replied. "I couldn't believe it when Richard told Eric he couldn't take me to see their doctor. Their pack actually has a doctor! Now how cool is that?"

"Cool." Pepper thought it was great, but she didn't want to get involved with another pack. She was surprised another one lived only four hours south of where she and her people lived. Still, since each pack tended to run in its own territory, Pepper could see how they wouldn't have encountered each other before.

Susan snorted. "You wouldn't know a hot wolf if he knocked you down and licked you all over." She smiled. "Now that gives me some interesting ideas. Let's see." She lifted her phone off the table.

Pepper wondered what she was up to.

"He said his name was Eric Silver, and he's a park

ranger." Susan pulled up an Internet browser. "Yep, here he is. Giving a lecture to a group of senior citizens. With his dark hair and eyes, his height, and that gorgeous smile, he looks like every woman's fantasy." She sighed dreamily. "And," she said in a pointed way, "he's all smiles with the gray-haired women and men, so he wasn't putting on a show just for you."

"He *wasn't* putting on a show for me. He wanted me to do what he said. If he'd wanted to put a show on for me, he wouldn't have suggested taking you to Silver Town."

"He's clearly an alpha wolf, not a beta. And he's a park ranger, so he knows something about taking care of people in the park who are injured." Then Susan frowned. "Ohmigod, you don't think he's the wolf Waldron attacked, do you?"

"Yeah, he was. Though I'm surprised Eric returned to our campsite as a wolf."

"See? He's interested in you. Or, well, maybe he ditched his clothes somewhere nearby and was watching us as a wolf. *Although*"—Susan elongated the word, putting her phone over her heart and looking up at the ceiling—"in *my* fantasy of him, he would be thinking only of me and not of you."

Pepper laughed.

"Did you bite Waldron?" Susan asked. "Richard said you took off after him, and you smelled of blood when you returned. Not your blood. I was in the car by then and missed out on all the action."

"Waldron was chasing him, though I didn't see any sign of Eric. Waldron had bitten him, and I had to do something to get Waldron's attention. He was definitely in hunting mode and determined to catch hold of his prey."

"And kill him?" Susan sounded horrified.

"If he could have gotten hold of him, I'd say that was a good bet." That brought back memories of the alpha who had killed her mate—though her mate had been a beta—and Pepper shuddered.

Susan closed her gaping mouth. Then she set her empty glass on the table. "So, where did you bite Waldron?"

"His tail, the first part of him I reached. I didn't bite too hard, but I still drew some blood."

"Was he pissed off at you?"

"We had a wolf-to-wolf confrontation. Yeah, he was pissed, but I wasn't backing down either, and if he wants me to look at his courting favorably, he has to mind me."

"Oh, wow, I bet that nearly killed him." Susan shook her head, taking another chip from the bowl and biting into it.

"Yeah, he didn't like it. If we'd been mated wolves, I'm certain he would have growled and snapped at me to back off."

"You're not going to, are you? Consider courting him?"

"No way. Look how aggressive he was toward another male wolf who hadn't provoked him in any way. We aren't even courting."

"Agreed. But now, Eric? He's my kind of guy."

Pepper waved a potato chip at her. "You should have given him your number."

"I would have, but I was a wolf. I wish he'd given me his business card."

"He might have. But you were a wolf."

"I should have shifted and given him a big smile and a big thank-you for his help."

Pepper laughed. "You're way too shy to have done that."

"Yeah. I keep telling myself I need to overcome that. I couldn't believe Waldron was watching our pack tonight. Well, and that he tore into the other wolf. He's becoming a real stalker."

Pepper refilled their wineglasses. "He thinks he's protecting his 'property.' But I won't be his mate no matter what."

"Richard said Eric growled and snapped back at Waldron. I've never seen anyone stand up to him. *Besides you.* I wish I'd been there." Susan sighed.

"Eric is a real alpha wolf. I was surprised he didn't stay and fight Waldron to the end." But Pepper was glad for it. She wouldn't have wanted to see Eric hurt further since he'd already been wounded. Even now, she wondered if he was okay.

She didn't want to call and check on him though. She let out her breath on a frustrated sigh.

She hadn't expected to have any trouble on their camping trip into the national forest. She was a forester and used to working with groups on forest management. Many of her pack members worked in some forestry job or another, with Susan supervising their own forest nursery and Christmas tree farm. Some of the pack members worked there or on other tree farms, and some worked on other forestry projects, such as tree removal. But they hadn't had a chance to visit this forest together as a pack in five years or so. It had been a vacation, and before Susan injured herself, they'd been having a blast.

Pepper had a lovely log home for pack meetings, with 250 acres of woods and a covered stone patio for outdoor gatherings. Most of her pack members had log homes of their own situated all over the territory to give them privacy, but close enough together that they could gather as a pack whenever they needed to.

"What if Eric could chase away Waldron permanently?" Susan asked.

"Then what? What if he expected something in return for his help? Our pack? Our land?"

"You? If I were the pack leader, I'd seriously consider it."

"Yeah, well, I'm not interested. We'll continue to deal with Waldron like we have since he moved into the area with his pack two weeks ago."

"I don't think Waldron will get the message without someone taking him to task physically. As alpha as you are, you couldn't beat him as a wolf. Not one-on-one. Not like you took that other wolf down." Susan moved her leg off the table and winced. "I'm going to call it a night. When do you see the Boy Scout troop tomorrow to talk about being a forester?"

"First thing in the morning, and another after that. And I have two sessions after lunch, so I'll be hanging around the area. I'll have someone stop in to feed you while I'm gone." Because Susan was using crutches, she was staying with Pepper for a couple of days. Longer, if she needed to.

"Thanks for putting me up for a couple of nights."

"No problem, Susan. You know I always enjoy your company. If you think of it tomorrow, you could give Eric Silver a call and tell him that you're all right. I'm certain he'd like to know that. While you're at it, you can thank him for the rescue and, if it comes up in the conversation, ask him if he's okay."

Susan smiled broadly at her. "You *are* interested

in him! But I doubt he'd want you to know if he was injured. Macho wolf syndrome, you know."

"Possibly. Unless he wanted to get our sympathy. The doctor said it should take about four weeks for your leg to mend, which means half or less time for us. Just don't put any stress on the leg for now. You don't want to increase the fracture."

"No, that's for sure. It already hurts enough. I hope Pauline can run things until I return to work."

"Pauline will be fine, but I'll run over there to check things out. You don't have to worry about anything. Just rest." Then Pepper raised her brows. "You didn't do this on purpose to get some time off, did you? You know I'd spell you for a while if you needed vacation days."

Susan laughed and hobbled off to bed, saying good night.

Pepper retired to her bedroom, hoping she could figure out how to keep Waldron away from her pack and her lands without having to take more drastic measures. He'd been scent-marking all over her territory and so had some of the males of his pack. She'd taken him to task for it, but what else could she do? They outnumbered her more than two to one, from what he'd said. And she couldn't complain to human law enforcement about Waldron and his men peeing all over her property. She still wouldn't give in to him no matter what. But his actions could be a real problem for the wolf pack if they ignored them.

She tucked herself into bed, thinking about Waldron attacking Eric and drawing blood. She should have told Susan to call her when she learned how Eric was, *if* he was willing to tell her the truth.

His injuries throbbing, Eric answered Sarandon's call while he got on the road to return to Silver Town. "Hey, what's up?" Like Eric, his brother loved the outdoors. He was a guide for anyone who needed one — photographers, nature lovers, hikers, and rock climbers. He loved doing it all.

"Just a heads-up. I might be a little late to the forestry careers talk tomorrow," Sarandon said. "I've got a Lepidopterist Society meeting first thing in the morning so the members can count butterflies and identify different varieties. If we have a big showing, we'll be there a while. So I might have to talk after you do."

"I'll let the Scout leaders know," Eric replied. "I have something to do after I speak, so if I'm not there, just give your lecture and I'll meet you after lunch at the next Boy Scout campground. They'll love hearing what you do."

"I thought you said you had the whole day scheduled to talk to troops."

"I do. We have two other Scout troops to meet in the afternoon, but when everyone's busy with lunch, I have other business to take care of."

"I thought we could get lunch together. We don't often see each other during the duty day."

Eric suspected his brother sensed something was up. He couldn't get anything past Sarandon. His younger brothers, sometimes yes, but not Sarandon. Even though the quadruplet brothers were born only minutes apart, he and Sarandon were the closest to each other, just like Brett and CJ were close.

"Okay, so what are you going to do that's so important?" Sarandon asked.

"Nothing. Just checking out an area on the nearby creek." He wanted to learn more about the pack that had rented the cabin, like where the wolves lived. Which meant checking their reservations. Since he worked for the park, that would be easy to do. He needed to know if they were involved in the illegal cultivation of cannabis.

"For…what?"

Eric couldn't lie to his brother. After the way their father had lied to Eric and his brothers, Eric wouldn't do that to them. But he wasn't about to tell Sarandon he'd seen a fantasy in the forest that he wanted to know more about, and that he wanted to prove to himself in the worst way that Pepper was innocent of any wrongdoing. Pepper was the only name he had to go by. And she was just as hot and spicy as her name. "Just checking it out."

"Okay, well, let me know if you discover anything interesting."

"Will do."

"I bet," Sarandon said, sounding skeptical.

Eric knew he had to get his injuries looked at, and better that Sarandon hear about the fight from him rather than through pack gossip. "A couple of wolves bit me."

"Is it bad? It has to be, or you wouldn't have told me. Do you need me to come get you?"

Sarandon knew not to make a big deal of it.

"Not a problem. And I wouldn't have mentioned it if I hadn't wanted Doc to look at it."

"Hell. It is bad or you wouldn't be seeing Doc."

"Just to be on the safe side."

From Paige Tyler's

To Love a Wolf

Dallas, Present Day

IT MUST BE PAYDAY. EITHER THAT, OR GOD HATED HIM. As Cooper strode across the bank's lobby and got in line behind the twenty people already there, he wasn't sure which.

He'd been so exhausted after work he hadn't even bothered to shower and change into civvies at the SWAT compound like he usually did. Instead, he'd come straight to the bank in his combat boots, dark blue military cargo pants, and a matching T-shirt with the Dallas PD emblem and the word "SWAT" on the left side of the chest. He'd cleaned off the worst of the day's dirt, but he still felt grimy as hell. He couldn't wait to get home and throw everything in the wash so he could grab something to eat and fall into bed.

He bit back a growl as the man at the front of the line plunked down a cardboard box full of rolled coins on the counter and started lining the different denominations in front of the teller.

"You've got to be kidding me," Cooper muttered.

A tall, slender woman with long, golden-brown hair gave him a quick, understanding smile over her shoulder. He smiled back, but she'd already turned around. He waited, hoping she'd glance his way again, but she didn't.

Giving it up, Cooper glanced at the other line, wondering if he should jump over there. Definitely not. It was even longer.

He hated going to the bank, but his SWAT teammate Jayden Brooks had finally paid off the bet they'd made months ago about whether his squad leader and the newest member of the team would end up a couple. Instead of giving Cooper the hundred bucks in cash like a normal person, Brooks had given him a frigging check. At least he hadn't paid Cooper in pennies, or he would have been the one lining up rolls of change for the teller to count. But it wasn't Cooper's fault that he was more observant than most of the other werewolves in the Pack. Brooks had suggested the stupid bet. Cooper had simply agreed to it.

When Officer Khaki Blake had walked into the training room for the first time, every pair of eyes in the room immediately locked on her—except for Cooper's. Oh, he'd noticed she was attractive, make no mistake about that. But he'd been more interested in seeing how the rest of the SWAT team reacted to the first female alpha any of them had ever seen. While most of the guys had checked her out with open curiosity, none of their hearts had pounded as hard as his squad leader's—Corporal Xander Riggs. Cooper had immediately pegged Khaki as *The One* for Xander, and vice versa.

Other members of the SWAT team were still on the fence about whether they believed in *The One*, the mythical one-in-a-billion soul mate supposedly out there for every werewolf. But the way Cooper saw it, denying the truth was stupid. In the past ten months, three of the Pack's members had stumbled across their mates in the most bizarre and unbelievable ways. A werewolf would have to be an idiot not to see the women the guys had fallen in love with were their soul mates. It was obvious the moment you saw them together.

But just because Cooper accepted the concept of a werewolf soul mate didn't mean he automatically bought into the idea there were women in the world for him and the remaining thirteen single members of the Pack. Cooper wasn't jaded when it came to love, but he wasn't naive either. He'd been around the world enough times to know that not all stories had happy endings.

The jerk cashing in his lifetime supply of pocket change finally walked away from the counter, grumbling under his breath about the teller miscounting his nickels and dimes. Cooper leaned out and counted the number of people ahead of him and reconsidered whether it was worth his time to wait. Maybe he'd deposit the check on the way to work tomorrow. But that would mean getting up at least an hour earlier. He groaned at the thought. No way in hell was he getting up at four thirty, not after the day he'd had.

He and Brooks, along with their teammates, Carter Nelson, Remy Boudreaux, and Alex Trevino had been working with explosive investigative teams from the ATF and FBI since before the sun had come up. Some nut job had planted an IED in one of the parking garages of the Grand Prairie industrial area last night and killed a young Dallas PD officer moonlighting as a security guard. None of the investigators believed Officer Pete Swanson had been the target. He'd just been unlucky enough to be doing a security sweep of the garage when the bomb had gone off.

Instead, the feds thought the real target had been someone who worked for a company based out of the industrial complex. There were several defense firms that used the garage, as well as a biomedical research company and a consulting group that specialized in job outsourcing solutions. In other words, lots of people someone might want to blow up. Then again, it was also possible the bomber had picked that particular location purely by chance with no specific target in mind. Now that was a thought to keep any cop up at night.

But Cooper and the SWAT team hadn't been invited to the party to catch the guy. They'd been brought in to help with the long, painful process of combing the crime scene for every shred of evidence they could find to help the FBI track down the bomber.

They'd spent the entire day on their hands and knees searching the parking garage and surrounding area, as well as nearby rooftops, storm drains, and trees for pieces of the device. The FBI agent in charge was a friend of Cooper's and promised to call once they got all the pieces laid out so he could help put the IED back together. The SWAT team and the Dallas FBI field office weren't on the best of terms these days, and the feds would have a cow if they knew he was involved in the forensic part of the case. Between Xander and Khaki apprehending bank robbers the FBI had been chasing, and his teammate Eric Becker unofficially going undercover to save the woman he loved and taking down a group of Albanian mobsters, the feds weren't too happy with them. But what the FBI didn't know wouldn't hurt them.

The two people ahead of Cooper got fed up with

waiting and walked away. He quickly stepped forward
to fill in the gap and found himself behind the attractive
woman who'd flashed him a smile earlier. He couldn't
help noticing that she looked exceptionally good in a
pair of jeans. Or that her long, silky hair had the most
intriguing gold highlights when the sun coming through
the window caught them just right. She smelled so deli-
cious he had to fight the urge to bend his neck and bury
his nose against her skin. Damn, he must be more tired
than he thought. If he wasn't careful, he'd be humping
her leg next.

He opened his mouth to say something charming, but
all that came out was a yawn big enough to make his
jaw crack. The woman in front of him must have heard
it too, because she turned around.

"And I thought I've been waiting in line a long time,"
she said, giving him a smile so breathtaking it damn near
made his heart stop. "You look like you're ready to fall
asleep on your feet."

Cooper knew he should reply, but he was so mesmerized by her perfect skin, clear green eyes, and soft
lips that he couldn't do anything but stare. He felt like a
teenager in high school again.

"Um, yeah. Long day," he finally managed.

What the hell was wrong with him? He'd never had
a problem talking to a beautiful woman before. But
in his defense, he'd never been in the presence of one
this gorgeous.

He gave himself a mental shake. *Get your head in
the game before she thinks you're a loser and turns
around again.*

"Catching bad guys, huh?" she asked.

"Something like that." He gave her his best charming smile. "Luckily, I'm off duty for the night."

She laughed, and the sound was so beautiful it almost brought him to his knees. Crap, he actually felt a little light-headed. He chalked it up to being out in the hot Texas sun all day. That could be hard on anyone, even a werewolf.

She tilted her head to the side, regarding him with an amused look. "Is that your way of saying you're free for dinner?"

Could she read his mind? "Depends. Would you say yes if I asked you out?"

Her lips curved. "I might. Although most guys tell me their names before asking me out on a date."

Cooper chuckled. He'd been attracted to her from the moment he saw her, but after talking to her, he was even more mesmerized. He'd always appreciated a woman who was confident enough to hold up her end of a verbal sparring match, and she seemed more than capable.

He held out his hand. "Landry Cooper at your service. Now that you know my name, how about dinner?"

He might have imagined it, but when she slipped her smaller hand into his much larger one, he could have sworn he felt a tingle pass between them—and it wasn't because of static electricity.

"I'm Everly Danu," she said. "And dinner sounds great."

Everly. Even her name was beautiful.

Cooper opened his mouth to ask Everly if she wanted to grab something that night—the hell with going home and falling into bed—when voices nearby caught his attention. Thanks to his keen werewolf hearing, he picked up every word.

"Are we still robbing the place with the cop here?" a male voice whispered.

"We're in too deep to back out now," another deep voice said softly. *"We were going to kill the guard anyway. Just make sure to take out the cop fast."*

Cooper snapped his head around, trying to figure out who'd said that. He scanned the crowded bank, looking for anyone who stood out, and immediately, zeroed in on a man over by the entrance. Average height with light brown hair, the guy was wearing mirrored sunglasses and a black windbreaker. On his own, the man wasn't that remarkable, but the small radio receiver in his ear sure as hell was. It wasn't hard to miss the telltale bulge under the man's left arm or the way he kept glancing at Cooper while keeping an eye on the door.

Cooper swept the bank lobby with his gaze, looking for the man's accomplice. He found him sitting by the manager's desk, pretending to wait for the woman to come back. Thanks to the identical sunglasses and the same black windbreaker the guy was wearing, he was easy to spot.

Cooper quickly ID'd two other men—one positioned a few feet away from the bank's security guard, the other near the big row of windows that looked out onto the main road. This one had a soft-sided computer bag big enough to hold several pistols—or a small submachine gun— hanging from his shoulder. Both were wearing sunglasses and windbreakers.

The guy by the door checked his watch, then nodded at his friend by the security guard. Cooper tensed. Shit, these assholes were really going to hit the bank with an armed cop standing right in the middle. Were they suicidal or just plain stupid?

Acknowledgments

Thanks to Doni Miller, Diane Wylie, Betty Johnson, Seanna Yeager, Barbi Davis, Fern Martin, Tiffany Upperman, Torie Inman, Jennifer French, Heather Doyle, Tanya Guthrie, Melissa Pascoe, Cristina Ortiz, Charles Cannaday Jr., and Sara Bowman for some great tips on three-year-olds and sharing some of their cute snippets of life for the story! Thanks to Donna Fournier who always helps me so much in brainstorming, catching name errors, and making sure I don't forget things in the stories, like Toby's blue rainbow teddy bear. Big hugs! And thanks to Deb Werksman, my editor; the cover artists; Amelia Narigon, who helps with promotion; and Sara Hartman-Seeskin, who is helping to bring the books to life in audiobook form.

About the Author

Bestselling and award-winning author Terry Spear has written over sixty paranormal romance novels and several medieval Highland historical romances. Her first werewolf romance, *Heart of the Wolf*, was named a 2008 *Publishers Weekly*'s Best Book of the Year, and her subsequent titles have garnered high praise and hit the *USA Today* bestseller list. A retired officer of the U.S. Army Reserves, Terry lives in Crawford, Texas, where she is working on her next werewolf romance, continuing her new series about shape-shifting jaguars, cougar shifters, and a new bear shifter, having fun with her young adult novels, and playing with her two Havanese puppies, Max and Tanner. For more information, please visit www.terry spear.com, or follow her on Twitter, @TerrySpear. She is also on Facebook at www.facebook.com/terry .spear. And on Wordpress at:

Terry Spear's Shifters

http://terryspear.wordpress.com/